Bob Blake would not look back on the year ⸺ been a bloody awful year. If anything coulc sign that it was going to be a year to forget came in rebruary. ⸺ redundant from his job at the brewery. He had been transport manager for over six years working his way up from a delivery assistant when he started in 1985. In 2004 the brewery in Mansfield had been taken over by a larger brewery based in Dudley. In the early days he thought that his job would be safe. He had an excellent working relationship with his manager in Dudley and business at the brewery was good. His role gradually changed and latterly he was mainly involved with the soft drinks side of the business. As the recession started to bite people started to socialise less and as a result beer consumption dropped rapidly. Beers and soft drinks sales fell by 40% in 2007 and in February he lost his job along with all of the staff in the Mansfield operation. The soft drinks side of the business was transferred to other parts of the country He received eleven weeks pay in a redundancy package, one week's pay for every full two years that he had worked at the brewery. The banking crisis was taking hold and jobs were scarce. He had applied for over sixty jobs but only once made it to an interview. That was for a driver with Asda delivering on line orders but he didn't get the job. For most of his applications he never even got a reply. He hadn't worked since February a fact that was replicated in large numbers all across the country. This contributed to troubles at home.

Things had deteriorated even more with Debbie, his wife of 20 years, since his redundancy. Money had been tight even before he lost his job. The children, Ellie who had just turned 20 and Wayne who is 17, still lived at home, which was a three bedroom semi detached house. Ellie, who is very bright, had started work at a local firm of accountants and had her mind set on qualifying as an Accountant. Wayne was still at school studying for A levels, Debbie worked part time at Cameron Estate Agents working Fridays and Saturdays doing viewings, follow ups etc. Occasionally she would do the odd extra day which helped with the family budget. House sales slowed down dramatically throughout 2007 and he was surprised that she had been kept on. In March he found out why. She was shagging Derrick Cameron who owned the agency. Cameron was 44 year old, divorced without children. He was a good looking bloke. He probably stood six foot three, had fashionably styled blond hair, a permanent tan and had the gift of the gab. He still played rugby for the veterans at Mansfield rugby club and as a result was in good shape physically. He played as a lock forward and gave the impression that he could look after himself both on and off the field as he was a big unit. Business had been very good to him and his affluence showed as he lived in a very large detached house in Clipstone Village, drove a top of the range Lexus and took regular holidays in the villa that he owned in Portugal on the Algarve. Blake had met him a couple of times and thought he was a smug bastard. Blake didn't like him and made no secret of the fact. He liked him even less when he found out what was going on between Debbie and Cameron.

One evening Blake had a massive row with Debbie. It started because he hadn't put away some cups and plates that were drying on the draining board from breakfast. He hadn't cleared up cups and plate from lunch either. The row had been simmering for weeks and the atmosphere between them had been tetchy at best. Out of the blue she told him that she wanted a divorce. She confessed that she had been having an affair with Cameron for over a year. He hadn't suspected this and was shocked. She gave him a right coating. `I knew you wouldn't have noticed. All you care about is your fucking allotment and that bloody football team, meaning Mansfield Town. Just look at the state of you. You are 42 years old but look years older. You take no pride in your appearance. That fucking beard is a mess, you have had the same hairstyle since we first met, you have a beer belly, you live in sweat shirts and jeans .You haven't done anything around the house since you lost your job. How often have I asked you to paint the walls in the hall? All I do is work, cook and clean. Our social life consists of Saturday nights at the working men's club and as for our sex life.....'
He had replied by saying that he been trying to find another job and spent hours on the internet combing the country trying to find something but it wasn't easy. There were millions out of work. The allotment kept him busy and was a release from the depressing task of trying to find a job. He said that he didn't hear her complaining about the allotment when it was bringing in plenty of fresh fruit and vegetables which helped with the budget for feeding the family. He argued that he only went to home games since he lost his job and that cost little as he had already got his season ticket. He thought that she liked going to the working men's club. She got on well with Jack, Pete Jan and Mary.
`They bore me to tears' Debbie had replied. `All they want to talk about is their holidays in Majorca and how well their kids are doing. Life with you is a drudge. Did you know that everybody calls you boring Bob behind your back? I want to start enjoying my life again and Derrick can give me what you can't and I mean everything. I want a divorce and nothing will change my mind. It's over between us because I don't love you anymore. Derrick wants me to move in

with him. He has been trying to persuade me to leave you since before Christmas .He said that he has plenty of space for Ellie and Wayne to come with me if they want to. He has a two bedroom annexe that his mother lived in before she went into a care home. He said the kids could live in there and give themselves some independence. He says that we could probably get £95,000 for this house so I want to put it on the market by next weekend. If you don't make it difficult I will be reasonable about the divorce and split everything down the middle with you. With what we will have left over from the house sale and what is left from your redundancy money we will have about £20,000 between us'

It was a real outburst. All the vent up feelings were released

He responded to this outburst by asking her what he was supposed to do. He had no job and no house because £10k would not get very far. What had Ellie and Wayne said about it? Disruption like this is going to do them no favours with their studies.

She said they were both fine with it. They liked the idea of having their own space. Wayne said that you were always having a go at him and Ellie had never forgiven him for being so rude to her boyfriend last summer. She had spoken with them about it at the weekend. They had both met Derrick when they had called into the office to see her when they had been in town. He had said that they can all go to his villa in the summer and they were both excited by this. She suggested that he went back to his Mum until he sorted things out as she had plenty of room for him

That's what he ended up doing. He felt betrayed by Debbie and it hurt to think that she had been cavorting with Cameron behind his back. He wasn't going to fight her as they had definitely drifted apart. He had to accept some responsibility for this but she could be a moody cow. They had never had much money so they couldn't afford to go out for meals except on special occasions and holidays were out of the question on their budget. Every time they put a few quid away something in the house went wrong or the cars needed money spent on them. Debbie drove an old Fiesta and he drove and even older Cavalier which always needed repairs done to them.

The house went on the market and to his surprise sold within ten days to a couple with two young children who were in rented property. There wasn't much else selling so it was a turn up for the books that the house had sold so quickly. He wondered whether Cameron had valued it at a lower price for a quick sale and he was very keen for them to accept the offer of £91,000. There were not many houses like theirs on the market at that time so he didn't have too much to compare it with. The house was a 1950's semi detached house with a garage. The large garden was a big selling point as it backed onto a park and would appeal to a couple with young children. Blake had lived in the house for eighteen years. After they got married they purchased a one bedroom flat before they bought the house. The flat served as a stop gap. It got them on the property ladder and was fine while Ellie was a baby in a cot which they kept in their bedroom but they needed something larger that would serve as a family home for the foreseeable future. Having remortgaged a couple of times they had a £68,000 interest only mortgage on the house so at least there would be a reasonable amount of equity left to split between them.

2

Blake went back to living with his mother. It was supposed to have been a temporary measure until he was able to find somewhere which he could call home. He was effectively homeless and until the divorce went through the only money that he had was his half of what left from their bank account which amounted to £900. They had agreed to split everything 50/50. The last of his redundancy money was included in this amount. His dole money amounted to £62 a week. He never even had a bank account in his own name so he had to go through the hassle of opening a new bank account using his mother's address as a temporary address. Mum lived alone. His father, Bert, had died nine years ago. He had been a miner until the 1980's when the mining industry went into an irreversible decline. He worked at Sutton Colliery which finally closed in 1989. He had worked there since he joined as a 15 year old boy and had survived the disaster at the mine in 1957 when five men were killed after an explosion at the coalface. He spent the last ten years of his working life at the brewery where he worked as a delivery driver. It was his father who first got him a job at the brewery. Bert was very much a working class man. He voted Labour all of his life. He was a staunch union man and despised Margaret Thatcher for what he says was her role in the demise of the coal industry. It was the subject of much friction between Blake and his father. Blake had voted Conservative as he liked some of the things that they had done under Thatcher must to his father's disgust. Bert never set foot in the kitchen or did anything towards housework but the house was always well decorated, the garden was always tidy and Mum always had her housekeeping on a Friday when he got paid. He liked a pint and was a heavy smoker which combined with his days as a miner didn't do his health much good. His father suffered with Emphysema and died at the early age of 67. His mother never considered re marrying even though she was still relatively young at just 61 when his father died. His parents had inherited money from his grandparents on his mother's side. His grandmother had left them a sum of money in her will. It was enough to buy the three bedroom semi that he grew up in and that his mother still lived in. He vaguely remembered Granny Hall who died when he was four. Grandpa Hall died a few months after he was born so he never knew him. He was very well known in Mansfield. Everybody knew of Jack Hall. He also worked in the mines and was the local union rep. He was a big man standing at over six feet and had the reputation for being a tough brawler so very few people crossed him. He was a big gambler with the horses being his speciality. His father often told stories of Grandpa Hall's large wins. He once won over a thousand pounds when a ten bob treble including two big outsiders came up. That was a big win in the 60s. He knew a few people who worked in the stables of some of the local trainers and often got wind of a horse that had been readied for a particular race. There were rumours that he had also won a few thousand pounds on the football pools which would perhaps explain why there was a decent amount in the will.

Mum was quite pleased to have Blake back home. She had a few friends that she saw at the Bingo on a Thursday afternoon but she was never one for going out much. She was quite happy keeping the house clean, cooking and watching TV. She loved old black and white films. She also liked to watch cricket, tennis and football which were probably the influence of his father who was a keen sports fan  The TV was never switched off when Wimbledon fortnight was on and test matches, until they were lost to Sky TV, were on for the duration of play. She only lived a few streets away from Blake's home but rarely came to the house. Debbie didn't invite her over very often. She was never that close to Debbie and they never got on. Mum confessed to him that she wasn't that keen on Debbie right from the start. She worked as a barmaid at the social club that Blake was still using today when he first met her. He used to go there with his father when they both worked at the brewery. Mum occasionally came with them. Debbie was and still is slim and quite busty which she made obvious as she wore low cut tops. She had red shoulder length hair and was very popular with the customers at the club, especially the men. Mum thought that Debbie dressed a bit "tarty" and used to say that she looked like the barmaid in Coronation Street. Blake never watched it so he hadn't a clue who she was talking about. Debbie was a year older than him and seemed a lot more experienced in life. He was only 19 when he first met her.
The job at the brewery was only his second job. He had left school with six O'levels and had worked for a firm of solicitors. The firm seemed very old fashioned. He had to call everyone Mister or Sir. The work was very dull and he was soon bored with filing, which is all that he seemed to do. He left after less than a year and joined he brewery. He hadn't had many girlfriends by the time he met Debbie. There had been a couple of girlfriends at school and one or two since. He was in good shape from playing sport and humping barrels of beer around so he didn't have too much trouble in attracting girls but there was nothing serious. Most of his free time though was spent on following Mansfield Town around the country and playing Sunday morning football for the Mansfield Supporters Club so girls were on the back burner. Debbie was his first serious girlfriend and they married in 1987 after a two year relationship which was often feisty. They broke up a couple of times but always

made up again. Debbie was pregnant with Ellie when they got married at Mansfield registry office. Mum was ashamed that they "had to get married" and blamed Debbie. Debbie's parents blamed him of course. They moved to Northampton soon after the marriage and much to Blake's relief he didn't see much of his in laws. Debbie's mum, Joyce, was not a pleasant woman. She could nag for England. Debbie's father Alf was hen pecked and obeyed whatever he was told to do just for a quiet life.

May bought a double whammy for Blake. For some it wouldn't have been a big deal but for Blake it was lamentable. He received a letter from the allotment society saying that the Council were not renewing the leases for 2009 as they had sold the land to a developer. The allotment holders were told to vacate the sites in November. They were told that they could, if they wished, be put on the waiting list at other sites around the town. Blake had worked the plot for fifteen years taking over from his father who struggled to keep on top of it as his health got worse.  He was really fond of the plot and it was big loss when he had to give it up. He would sorely miss the other allotment holders many of whom were much older than him. There was always a bit of banter about who was growing the best vegetables.

Just to put the icing on the cake his beloved Mansfield Town were relegated from the Football League ending their 77 year stay as a football league club. It had been a very poor season in which they were always threatened with the drop. He thought that they would escape after winning a couple of games towards the end of the season and with two games left they were only three points behind Chester. They needed to win both to have a chance but managed to lose one nil to Rotherham who scored a lucky goal after Mansfield had all the play.  Chester got a point in a home draw so Mansfield got relegated.

Life was tough for him. He was getting the bare minimum sixty two quid a week on the dole. He gave his Mum twenty quid of this to pay for the extra cost of having him living with her. She was only had her state pension plus a bit from his father's miners pension scheme so she didn't have a lot of money  His parents house was built in the 1920's. It was on a corner plot. They installed gas central heating in the 1960's but it was never the warmest of houses. The rooms were large and even his room, which was the smallest, had just enough room for a double bed, a wardrobe, chest of drawers and a desk. It was expensive to run and although he did a bit of decorating for his mum after his father died money needed to be spent on it to bring it up to date. The house still had sash windows and wasn't double glazed. There was no wall insulation so it cost a fortune to heat it. The kitchen and bathrooms were tidy enough but were over twenty years old so needed updating. It was the sort of place that if money was spent on it the house could be something special. There was room to extend it to both the side and back and the garden was eighty foot long with an apple and pear tree in it. It was mainly laid to lawn with flower borders which had become overgrown. There was even an old small vegetable plot that his father had made when he was forced to admit defeat on his allotment. This too had become very overgrown. Blake spent many an hour trying to get it tidy while living at his Mum's. He had planned to grow a few runner beans and some salad stuff next year but it was too small for much else. The garage was in a state of disrepair. It was made of concrete slabs with a corrugated roof and had old wooden doors which were starting to rot. Blake did some repairs on the doors. He dug out the worst of the rotting wood and replaced the gaps with some filler. They looked a bit better after a coat of paint but it didn't improve the overall look. He could imagine that a builder or property developer would transform the place because it was on a large plot. There was probably enough land to squeeze in another detached house on the side of the house if the garage was removed.

His days were spent searching for jobs and gleaning the most that he could get from the allotment in the few months that he still had it for. He checked the agencies on line every morning to see if anything new had come in. He had to sign on every couple of weeks and show that he was making an effort to find something new in order for him to continue receiving dole money. He got the impression that the staff at the job centre were just going through the motions. They knew that there weren't many jobs around and that there were too many applicants for any that did come up. The only jobs that they seemed to have were warehouse packers and kitchen assistants at hotels around the area. Both paid poor money and involved shift work. He wasn't prepared to work nights so he never applied for these jobs. Most of the industrial jobs in Mansfield area had gradually disappeared. New jobs in the area were now, like a lot of other towns in the country, in the service or retail area. He started to look further away from Mansfield and the twelve mile radius around it. He contacted agencies in Sheffield, Stoke, Derby as well as Newark and Lincoln. He had already registered with agencies in Nottingham and Chesterfield but still found nothing. He was spending most of his spare cash on petrol driving to these towns and cities to register. He would take a pile of his CV's and just call in on any agency he found.

June and July came and went without any luck on the job front. The sale of the house had gone through on May 22$^{nd}$ but he and Debbie had agreed that a final settlement would only be made once the divorce was finalised so he hadn't received anything. It was all sat in a solicitors Escrow account and they didn't appear to be in any hurry to expedite the divorce settlement. His money from his share of the redundancy was slowly dwindling away and he was beginning to get really concerned. On August 1st he decided to drive down to Leicester. It was over forty miles away and an hour's drive on the M1 if traffic was moving but he had to do something. He spent most of the day in Leicester before setting off for home at around 4pm. When he finally arrived home ninety minutes later after sitting in a jam on the M1 Mum was asleep in her armchair and nothing appeared to be in the oven for tea. He called out to her but got no response so he went over to give her a gentle shake. She just slumped to one side. He panicked and tried to wake her up by shaking her even more. It suddenly dawned on him that she wasn't going to wake up. Not knowing what to do, he phoned for an ambulance which arrived thirty minutes later. They confirmed what he already knew. She was dead. He found out later that she had a massive stroke and had died almost instantly. He was numb. When was this awful run going to end? He rang Debbie to let her know what had happened. She said that she was sorry but he knew that she wasn't that bothered as there was no love lost between them. Ellie used to call on her Gran regularly and was very upset. Wayne just seemed to accept it without any fuss. The funeral was poorly attended with other than family only a dozen or so people turning up. He managed to get some money released from his mother's building society to pay for most of the funeral cost but he spent some of my own money on the small wake further reducing the small amount of money that he had left. Fortunately the divorce was finalised the following week. After legal fees for both the house sale and the divorce he walked away from his marriage with six thousand seven hundred pound.

His Mum never had a will so everything had to go to probate. He was an only child so the solicitor said that everything would go to him. He decided to put the house up for sale shortly after speaking with the solicitor. Cameron was keen to market it and used Debbie to try to convince him to sell it via his agency. They were probably the leading agency in the area at that time with regards to volume of sales but there was no way that arrogant fucker was getting his business. He put the house up for sale with Brownlees who were Cameron's biggest rivals. He eventually managed to sell the house in mid October after accepting an offer of £109,000 from a builder which was £10,000 lower than the asking price. The builder had a place to sell but had an offer from a first time buyer. Even though it was a very short chain it dragged on for ages. They seemed to be waiting forever for mortgage applications and survey reports in the chain until the sale finally completed on January 5th 2009. The delay made a big hole in his finances. He still had to pay council tax and utility bills for the house while he was waiting for the sale to be completed. When the sale completed he moved in with a Tony Martin an old mate from the supporters club at Mansfield Town. He was a Stags fanatic. Tony had a two bedroom ground floor flat close to the town centre and he let Blake rent a room for twenty quid a week. He had got rid of most of his mother's furniture with a house clearance company just keeping a bed, a chest and a small wardrobe that had been in his bedroom plus a small desk for his laptop. After the sale proceeds from the house less fees and five hundred pounds that his mother had left in her building society account he estimated that he would get £103,000 after the solicitor's fees but it was going to be a few more weeks before probate was sorted and he could get his hands on it. The probate money would keep him going but he was desperate to get a new job and start a new life. He didn't want to stay with Tony for any length of time. Tony liked a beer and if he wasn't careful his money wouldn't last long if he kept spending it on beer and takeaways. He wanted to buy his own home. He fancied a modern property, preferably one with a bit of a garden so that he could grow a few vegetables. During the last few months of 2008 he had decided to lose some weight. His old Cavalier finally gave up the ghost. It failed the MOT. It needed new tyres, brake discs, an exhaust and rear wheel callipers. That was going to cost him six hundred quid and the old car just wasn't worth it. He wasn't driving to agencies around the area any more. He had registered with most of them in the towns and cities that he had visited by now. He kept in contact by phone and email. He had a couple of tentative responses but nothing came of them. He found an old rusting push bike in his mother's garage. It was his father's and had been in the garage untouched for years. It needed some new tyres but it was still usable so he started cycling. He lost a few pounds after a couple of weeks from the cycling and not eating as much food. Mum used to fill the plate up and he always tucked it away. He set himself a target of dropping a stone before Christmas but managed to lose almost two stone. Blake was six feet tall and at sixteen stone was overweight. The lads at the supporters club used to joke that he wasn't fat but that he was just short for his weight! Although he had not renewed his season ticket he started going to the occasional game as the lure of Field Mill was too strong to ignore. He went to three games and Mansfield lost the lot. The last game was against Burton and even though it was on Boxing Day the crowd was very low. Mansfield got stuffed two nil. Most of the players who were relegated had gone. It was a new team. They were in the lower half of the Conference and the football was shit. Blake didn't have a lot of money and decided that this would be his last game until he got a job. As it turned out it was his last game for over two years.

A few days after the sale of his mother's house completed he took a call from the Newark branch of Manpower. Collins Transport of Flixham in Norfolk had seen his CV and would like him to attend an interview for the role of Transport Manager on Monday of next week. Manpower told him that Collins Transport imported flowers fruit and vegetables from Holland and distributed vegetables from local growers to small supermarkets and village stores in East Anglia. The salary on offer was £19K which close to what he was getting at the brewery. After almost a year out of work he was going to an interview for a job that he thought that he stood a chance of getting. It was just as well as his money was down to just over a thousand pounds which was all the money that he had left until probate was sorted out.

3

Detective Sergeant Dave Daley was in bed when his mobile phone rang at 1145. He had been in bed for less than an hour and both he and his wife Bev had been sound asleep. It was PC Graham "Polly" Perkins and Daley wasn't best pleased. He didn't like taking calls at this hour especially as they tended to be for minor matters that could have easily waited until the morning. Flixham was a small market town with a population of just over nine thousand. Crime was relatively low and what crime there was tended to be of a less serious matter. Car thefts, burglaries, fighting after chucking out time in the pubs were the norm. It was a tired town which was feeling the effects of the recession. Several shops had closed down and it was looking a bit scruffy as a result. Perkins was a young PC at just 22, who had only been on the job three months. He was on duty that night with Steve Brooks who was both several years older and a couple of years more experienced. Brooks was a lazy bastard who, if he could, would avoid responsibility. Brooks and Perkins were working the late shift and this being a Thursday night the shift would end at midnight. The pubs would have shut and the late night kebab shop would have served their last customers by this time so the small town centre would be dead. Daley suspected a fight in one of the pubs and Brooks wouldn't want to do anything at this late stage of his shift if he could pass responsibility upwards. He took the call downstairs so not to keep Bev awake.

`What is it Perkins? It had better be something urgent to wake me up at this time of night'.

`Sorry Gov but there has been a shooting in Barham Road. An ambulance is at the scene tending the victim who is in a bad way. The victim has been identified as Ilie Radu a 38 year old of 47 Barham Road. He shares a flat with Ion Rosescu. It was Rosescu who called the police and for an ambulance'

`OK Perkins I will be there in ten minutes. Make sure that Brooks clears the area so that forensics can do their work. Have you phoned this into Kings Lynn yet?'

Neither Perkins nor Brooks had contacted Kings Lynn. Brooks had just told Perkins to phone Daley and as it was the end of their shift he would be looking to clear off early. He was out of luck and he would be pulling a late one on this.

Alarm bells started ringing in Daley's head. Ion Rosescu had ended up in hospital a few weeks earlier. Somebody had given him a hiding outside of his flat and he had ended up in the Queen Elizabeth in Kings Lynn with head injuries and some busted ribs. He was unconscious when he was found by the same Ilie Radu. When Daley eventually got to speak to Rosescu he couldn't or more likely wouldn't give any description of the person or persons responsible claiming he had been jumped from behind as he was about to enter his block of flats. The two Romanians were small time drug dealers and had been arrested at least once each in the past. They were a nasty pair and had been involved in several altercations in town recently. Both had received suspended prison sentences in the past couple of months for possession with the intent to supply. The amounts involved were small, and usually involved Ecstasy tablets, Amphetamines and some weed. Daley was disappointed that the judge had been lenient and had given them suspended sentences. He wanted them off the streets. Daley was retiring in six months after 35 years in the force. He was 54 and was hoping for a nice quiet stretch before retirement. He had never been ambitious during his time with the force and had only been promoted to DS four years earlier. He had spent 20 years as a PC before passing his detective exams and spending eleven years as a DC in Kings Lynn.  Most of his time with the police had been spent in Kings Lynn but he was moved to cover Flixham when the new DCI arrived at Kings Lynn two years ago. Flixham was a quiet place and it suited Daley. He and Bev, his wife, had lived here for 15 years.  He suspected that he had been "put out to grass" here by his new boss in Kings Lynn. The town had a small police station which closed at 6pm each night. The town's police force consisted of him, six police constables and a desk sergeant. The team was augmented by four PCSO's. Daley was senior officer and reported in to King's Lynn. His team covered the area in and around the town to the west and southwards. Major crimes, not that there had been many, were handed over to Kings Lynn as were any out of hour's incidents. His boss was DCI Shirley Booth. She was a high flier and suited the current profile for advancement in today's police force. She was young at 34, female, single and of mixed race. Definitely a career copper and was well on her way to a Superintendant's position at sometime in the not too distant future. She knew how to work the system by ticking all the right boxes. Her rise to DCI had been unprecedented in terms of length of service. She just about tolerated Daley but he suspected that it was only as he was seen as no threat to her progression and that he was due to retire shortly. She had approved his early retirement application. She had no time for old coppers like him who worked in the old ways that were alien to hers. She was known, behind her back of course as "Surly Shirley" and wasn't popular with her team. She demeaned the team on every possible occasion. Overtime was a thing of the past on her watch as she always claimed that there was no budget for it. She took credit for anything that she could and as a result no credit was ever passed down to her team. Backstabbing was a necessary tool for her in her relentless climb to the top of the force.

Daley arrived at the scene fifteen minutes after the call. Brooks and Perkins had cordoned off the area to give the paramedics space to do their jobs. Steve Brooks had a face like a smacked arse. Working beyond his shift was against his principals and this was plain to see. Barham Road was part of an estate that had been built in the seventies. The estate consisted of around four hundred properties which were a mixture of two and three bedroom houses and flats. When the estate was eventually finished it was considered to be the place to live in Flixham for young professional families but it was now showing signs of age. Many of the properties, especially the flats had been purchased as buy to let investment properties which resulted in some unsavoury characters moving into the area.

Daley interviewed the neighbours that were milling around outside. Nobody had seen the incident or had recognised the sound of gunshots. Before they left the scene Daley asked the medics how the patient was and was told that he was in a serious condition with two gunshot wounds, one to the stomach and one to the chest. He had lost a lot of blood and they said it was touch and go if he would survive as they didn't know if any vital organs had been damaged by the bullet to the stomach.

Daley decided that he best let Booth know so he phoned her mobile to give her an update. Like him she wasn't pleased to be woken up in the early hours

`What is it Arthur'? She growled in a bad tempered voice. Daley had been known by the nickname Arthur after the George Cole character in the TV series Minder since his days as a PC. Even the young detectives who had probably never watched the show called him by this nickname.

`There has been a shooting in Flixham Ma'am. The victim is Ilie Radu a Romanian known to the police for minor drug dealing. He was shot outside his flat in Barham Road. He has gunshot wounds to the stomach and chest. The medics say that his condition is serious and he has been taken to the Queen Liz for surgery. Our initial enquiries have thrown up no reliable witnesses. Somebody heard a car driving away at speed at the time of the shooting so it could be a drive by. The incident was reported to us by Radu's flat mate Ion Rodescu who is also known to the police. He is also a small time drug dealer with a history of violence. He himself was the victim of a beating a couple of weeks back which also resulted in him ending up in the Queen Liz. My initial thoughts are that this could be a drug related crime with somebody moving in on their little patch'

`OK, Kings Lynn will take it from here. I want you to organise door to door enquiries first thing in the morning to see if anybody knows or saw anything. Get the PSCO's on it as well. I want Rodescu in for questioning. I want to interview him to see if he knows any reason why Radu was shot. Bring him over to Kings Lynn for 0930 and tell him that he will be needed to assist with our enquiries. Make sure that you keep me updated about Radu's condition. If he dies we have a murder case on our hands and I want to be on top of things from day one. I want no cock ups on this'

`OK ma'am I will see you at nine thirty'

This was going to be a long day he thought to himself. It was 0100 now and by the time he sorted things out at the scene as officer in charge until Booth's team took over he wasn't going to get much sleep. Saturday would probably be spoilt too because Booth was bound to have him running around. He had planned to take Bev into Norwich as she wanted some new curtains for the lounge. That wasn't going to happen. He would be working most of the day. It would be just like Booth to hope that Radu didn't make it as a nice murder case would look good on her record especially if it was solved quickly. To make his mood even worse it started to rain. It was one of those typical Norfolk November rains. A heavy drizzle that soaked you through before you noticed it and it was bloody cold too.

4

As he was instructed by Booth Daley arranged for Rodescu to be taken to Kings Lynn station for questioning at 0930 the following morning where he was interviewed by Booth. DC Butler, a new young up and coming detective sat in on the interview which was recorded. Rodescu protested about being brought to Kings Lynn so early in the morning after being up half the night. He told them that he thought that Radu was shot as he walked towards the entrance from his flat. He managed to stagger to the entry door where he collapsed after attempting to ring his own flat number. It would seem that he rang the wrong number. Instead of ringing his own flat he rang a neighbour who said that she could hear him calling for help. She went downstairs to see what was happening, saw Radu and panicked. She went back upstairs and banged on Rodescu's door. He went downstairs and found Radu collapsed in the doorway. He saw that Radu had lost a lot of blood and thought that he may have been near to death so he immediately phoned the police and an ambulance. He said that he had no idea who was responsible and claimed that it may have been a case of mistaken identity. Daley had already spoken to the neighbour, Mrs Elaine Woodman, who confirmed Rodescu's story. She said that her husband had apparently slept right through the incident. Booth had another attempt to get Rodescu to say who he thought was responsible. She reminded him that he had been beaten up less than three weeks ago and that she thought the two incidents were related but Rodescu stuck to his original statement. He was released after two hours of questioning.

After the interview she called Daley into her office. DC Butler was present too.

`I don't believe a bloody word of what he told us. There has got to be some connection between the two incidents. Are you aware of any new activity in the drugs market on your patch Arthur? Have these two pissed somebody off?'

`It's been quiet for weeks Ma'am. Since Rodescu got beaten up Radu has kept a low profile. PC's Fowler and May are speaking to the landlords of all the local pubs as we speak to see if there has been anybody else on the scene. I will

check with them and get back to you if there is any news. Have you heard anything from the hospital yet about Radu?'
`They have operated and removed his spleen. They say he is in a stable condition but he won't be allowed to speak to anybody for at least 24 hours' She didn't seem happy about this news.

Ion Rodescu knew exactly who had been responsible for shooting his friend. For the past eighteen months they had been on a nice earner acting as a courier for Danny Collins who was the owner of Collins Transport. The company made trips to Rotterdam on a regular basis transporting food stuff and flowers both into and out of the UK. Collins had been approached by a big time Rotterdam drug dealer to bringing in quantities of Cocaine, Ecstasy pills and a variety of other pills into the country hidden amongst the cargo. Most of these came via Harwich and Felixstowe. Collins was a scheming individual who kept everything at arm's length. He arranged for the drugs to be moved on to a Peterborough drug lord named Bogdan Stancvic using couriers. Rodescu and Radu had been the couriers. They were paid £1000 by Collins to meet up with Stancvic's representatives in a picnic area ten miles out of town. This area was deserted late at night so they were never disturbed. The drugs were handed over to Stancvic's representatives in exchange for a locked bag which Rodescu knew contained a large sum of money as it was shown to him before being locked. Rodescu handed the bag to Collins in the car park of the Star Tavern which was on the outskirts of town. He collected an envelope which contained £1000 in fifty and twenty pound notes at the handover. Unknown to Rodescu, although he knew that it was a fair chunk of money, the bag usually contained between £200,000 and £300,000 in used notes. Collins arranged for the bag containing this money less £25,000, which was his cut for moving the drugs, to be sent to Rotterdam on one of his trucks. It was often hidden in grab bags full of Swedes and Turnips. How Ivan Petrescu, the Rotterdam drugs lord, recovered the money was not of interest to Collins. He acted as the middle man. By using couriers he wasn't directly involved with the movement of the drugs. He always used the same two drivers to ship both the drugs into the country and the money going back the other way. The drivers, both Romanian were paid £2000 in used notes by Collins for each round trip. If the drugs or the money were found at customs Collins could claim that he had no knowledge and blame the driver. Similarly if the couriers got stopped he couldn't be implicated. He could deny all knowledge. He would just say that the Romanians were acting amongst themselves and that he was the innocent party. He would argue that he wasn't to blame if one of the self employed drivers that he was using was doing something illegal that he had no knowledge of. He was picking up £22,000 each time the drugs were brought in and it was particularly handy as business had suffered in the recession. It still made a profit but not enough for the lifestyle he had. He liked to have two or three holidays in Portugal or the Canary Islands each year with his wife Paula and his daughter Charlotte. He rented nice villas which had their own pool and while on holiday they ate out every day. He was also a heavy drinker as was Paula who despite her petite frame could almost match him drink for drink. The money from his little sideline was squirreled away in offshore bank accounts. Collins didn't want to work for many more years. By the time he was in his mid fifties he would have enough money tucked away to be able to move to a warm climate overseas. He'd had enough of bloody Norfolk with its freezing winter winds blowing in off the North Sea.

Radu and Rodescu had been selling weed in the area for over a year but they had gotten greedy. They had started lifting a bag or two of Ecstasy pills from each shipment and were selling these in the pubs in and around Flixham. Radu had managed to pick the locks on the holdalls that they collected from Collins. Somehow Stancvic found out that they had been stealing his drugs. Rodescu was beaten up and was told to pay Stancvic five thousand pounds within two weeks. Rodescu and Radu didn't have the money and asked for an extra two weeks to give them time to raise it. They tried to raise the money by selling the last of the pills that remained from the last bags that they stole. They had branched out to Kings Lynn but were still short of the five thousand despite selling all of the pills. They only raised three thousand which was handed over at the usual picnic site. Radu was shot the next day as a further warning to Rodescu who was seen as the senior partner in their partnership. Rodescu decided that it was time for him to do a runner. Stancvic was a vicious bastard and he had a reputation to keep up. If word got out that somebody had been tucking him up it would damage this reputation. Rodescu phoned Collins after he got back from the police station to tell him that he wasn't going to do any more courier runs and was moving on. Collins had heard about the shooting and had tried to persuade Rodescu to do a drop on his own saying that he had a shipment due in the next week but Rodescu was adamant that he had done his last drop. He confessed that they had been stealing a few pills and Stancvic had wanted retribution. He had received a beating, his mate was in hospital and Stancvic was still owed money. He now wanted three thousand pounds claiming a further thousand pounds as interest on the original five thousand. Rodescu thought that it was one of the two Romanian drivers that Collins used who had been responsible for alerting Stancvic about Rodescu and Radu selling pills in the area. He needed to put distance between himself and Stancvic. He decided that he would head to Eastbourne where some of his cousins lived.

After Rodescu took off the police trail went cold. Radu, when he was eventually considered well enough to speak to the police, was unable or unwilling to help the police find out who shot him. He stayed in hospital for three weeks before being released just before Christmas and he too left Flixham for an unknown destination shortly after. The CCTV cameras didn't help as that part of the town wasn't covered. There were some cars that showed up on the cameras that covered Main Street and other streets in the town centre but nothing conclusive was discovered.

DCI Booth was pissed off that none of her team had been able to resolve the case. She made everyone aware that she wasn't happy about it and they all were given a hard time by her. Daley seemed to bear the brunt of her disappointment. She told him that she couldn't believe that an incident like this in such a small town didn't give any concrete leads and criticized him for not being more proactive. For Daley this just made the prospect of an early retirement more appetizing. He just wanted to pack it all in and as far as he was concerned May 2009 couldn't come soon enough. He didn't need shootings in his area because it meant involvement by Kings Lynn. As far as he was concerned the less contact that he had with Booth the better. He hoped that the remaining months of his working life would be as quiet as the previous years had been.

Danny Collins was in a quandary. He was annoyed that his couriers had been ripping off Stancvic and had a go at Rodescu for being both stupid and greedy. Collins was well aware of Stancvic's reputation and wondered if he would come after Collins for the money that he claimed he was due from the two couriers. He phoned Stancvic and told him that he was disgusted with what the two Romanians had been doing and that he wouldn't use them again. Stancvic said that he would take the three thousand pounds that he was owed from the next drop which would come out of Collins cut. He told Collins that his couriers had been stealing several bags from each shipment not just a few bags. Collins decided that he wouldn't argue. Without the two Romanians doing the drop it looked like he was going to have to do the next one by himself. He had wanted to stay as an anonymous link in the chain but needs must unless of course he could find somebody else. Ideally he wanted to use couriers that were not known to any of his large circle of friends in Flixham which was why the Romanians had been the perfect choice. Much to his surprise he found a couple of suitable candidates at a football match.

Collins Transport sponsored Flixham Rangers FC. His brother in law Roy Gayle managed the team who played in the North West Norfolk League Division One. Collins Transport sponsored the team shirts. The company's name appeared in black letters across the front of the gold shirts that they wore. The team were a mid table team and played home games at Flixham sports ground. The sports ground was the beneficiary of a lottery grant and now had a smart pavilion with modern changing rooms, showers and lockers. There were tennis and netball courts, a bowls green as well as two adult football pitches and a junior football pitch. Flixham Rangers played on the pitch nearest to the pavilion. The other slightly smaller rougher pitch was used by the social club who played in the Kings Lynn Sunday league. It also had a club room with a bar which often held events to raise money. They had weekly bingo nights, a monthly quiz, dances, discos and jive classes. During the day mothers and toddlers groups met a couple of mornings a week and there were a couple of keep fit classes for the ladies. The club was doing well even in the current tough conditions. Collins often watched the football team play on a Saturday afternoon and today was no exception. He arrived at the game a few minutes after the two o'clock kick off but the game was goalless. He approached Roy who was shouting instructions to the team who were on the defensive.

'Who are the two spades?' he asked Roy referring to two black players that he hadn't seen before.

'They turned up to training two weeks ago. Apparently they are staying at a holiday home owned by the tall one's father. The tall one at the back is a bloody useful player. He played at a decent level when he was a youngster. He has improved the defence no end. You can hear him talking to and organising the other defenders all the time. We kept a clean sheet for the first time this season last week and he isn't match fit yet either. The other one is built like Cyril Regis but that's where the similarity ends. He isn't much of a player. He is very strong but is far too aggressive. He is always giving away fouls and is always looking to pick a fight with somebody. He came on as sub last week and got booked within five minutes. He is only playing because we are a couple short this week. '

As they spoke he outmuscled two defenders and hammered a shot into the top corner from close range.

'Bloody heck,' Roy said with a smile on his face 'that's the first thing he has done since he joined'

'What are their names?' Collins asked

'The tall one at the back is Dennard Hoyte. The one who just scored is called Lynton Andrews. I think they are both Jamaican. Hoyte seems a decent bloke but Andrews seems to be a moody sod with a short fuse. He is an ugly bastard and his looks seem to suit his personality. The rest of the team joke that Hoyte is hung like a horse and Andrews looks like one. They say it well out of the two's earshot though'

Collins watched the remainder of the game. Flixham won two nil. Just as Roy had said Andrews was aggressive. He clattered the opposing goalie on a couple of occasions and went in hard and late several times. One particularly late tackle resulted in an injury and substitution for the opposition's centre back and when he flattened the replacement defender jumping for a ball in the air he got booked. How he had avoided being booked for so long bemused Collins. He thought that the referee must have been intimidated. The tall guy got the second goal when he headed home after a corner.

After the game the team went for a drink in the bar. Collins approached the two Jamaicans who were stood by themselves.

'I'm Danny Collins of Collins Transport, the team's sponsor '. He announced 'You scored a couple of nice goals there lads. Roy is my brother in law. He says that you are new in town. What are you doing work wise?'

`We are having a career break.' Hoyte said gaining a rare smile from Andrews. Collins offered them a drink. Andrews had a lager. Hoyte said that he didn't drink alcohol and asked for a coke. Hoyte seemed happy to chat with him, Andrews was less so. Collins chatted to Hoyte for twenty minutes or so. He discovered that Hoyte had lived in Edmonton in London until he was 26 when he moved to Bristol where he met Andrews. Hoyte was a good looking lad. He was tall with an athletic build and was quite light skinned. Collins suspected that he was of mixed race. He told Collins that his mother had died suddenly from cancer of the pancreas just over a year ago. His father worked as a mechanic and was a keen fisherman. His mother decided to take up fishing as well coining the phrase "if you can't beat them join them", after being left at home too often for her liking. His parents had purchased a two bedroom park home five years ago on the outskirts of Flixham as it was fairly close to the Great Ouse. The Great Ouse was considered to be a fine fishing river. It was the only property that they had ever owned as they had lived in the same council flat since they were married thirty years ago. They had purchased the park home at a bargain price as it had needed a lot of work done to it. It was now in good order thanks to the work Hoyte's father had done on it. It was their pride and joy and both his parents had spent many happy days fishing on the Great Ouse but since his mother's death it had remained empty. Hoyte told Collins that they were both living in it until they decided what to do next. There was a clause in the lease which meant that the property could only be occupied for forty eight weeks a year so they had plenty of time to consider their options. Hoyte's father had recently returned to Jamaica after he lost his job during the recession. He was planning to sell the park home but not until he had decided whether to stay in Jamaica or to return to England. He had given up his council flat and moved his possessions, of which were not many, to the park home. Hoyte had a key to it and promised his father that he would check on it every couple of months. Despite his promise this was the first time he had been to the place. Hoyte had a younger sister who was a sales assistant selling perfume at Debenhams in Watford where she lived with her husband. A park home in the wilds of East Anglia held no interest to her and she had no plans to use it.

Hoyte told Collins that he had worked as a tyre fitter at Kwik Fit in Edmonton. He had played football at a decent level. He signed on schoolboy terms with Leyton Orient but got released at 17 after being told that he lacked the discipline to become a professional footballer. He then played a few games for Fisher FC who played in the Southern League. He had joined them after signing a one year part time contract. Hoyte admitted that he didn't like the travelling to training and with his fondness for the ladies he wasn't as focused as he should have been so eventually, after missing too many evening training sessions, he was released by Fisher before the end of his contract. He played for a few other local teams but found it difficult to get time off work so his football was restricted to five a side games and Sunday mornings. He had moved to Bristol and had lived with a woman there for two years before they split up after she found out about yet another one of his many affairs. He had met Andrews playing football for a local league side. Andrews got him some part time work on the door at a club in the city centre. They had shared a flat together after Hoyte split with his girlfriend and had become good mates. Andrews was the opposite of Hoyte. He wasn't quite as keen to tell Collins too much about himself. He was stocky and looked as though he had spent many hours in the gym. He was an ugly bastard with a shaved head. His teeth were very prominent and gave him a bit of a goofy look. He said that he came to England from Jamaica with his parents in 1979 and had lived in Bristol all of his life until he decided to leave with Hoyte and spend a few months in the quiet of Norfolk. He admitted that he had spent time in prison but didn't go into any details of the reasons.

Collins decided to sound them out to see if they would be interested in some work. They were both big lads who looked like they could handle themselves. He told them that he may have a couple of cash jobs coming up that may be of interest to them. He asked them to give him a call on Sunday morning where he would go into details. He didn't want to discuss the jobs in public. He gave Hoyte the telephone number of a pay as you go phone which was what he used for the drugs business.

7

Hoyte and Andrews hadn't given any clues to anybody why they had moved to Flixham from Bristol and were certainly not prepared to give Collins any details. Andrews had been a career criminal. He had taken part in a couple of armed robberies at sub post offices in and around Bristol and had managed to get away with them. Breaking and entering into shops and factories was another of his specialities but he wasn't quite as successful with getting away with it as he had been with the armed robberies. Andrews, who was two years older than Hoyte, had taken him under his wing and recruited him on some of his jobs. Both had also dabbled with drug dealing in Bristol but Andrews had crossed the wrong person. He got involved in fight when he was dealing on somebody else's patch. He had badly beaten up the dealer who was connected to a big Bristol gang. Three of this gang had confronted Andrews but they had under estimated how tough he was and he had kicked the crap out of all three of them. It was going to prove to be a mistake.

He had spent many years in prison in his short life. He had done time in a young offender prison in Aylesbury when he was 18 and another term for breaking and entering when he was 21. His last prison term was for four years prison. It was for actual bodily harm when he had set about somebody in a fight in a nightclub. He had broken the man's jaw and ruptured his spleen. He would most likely have killed the man if the four bouncers that it took to stop him hadn't been there. He was 28 when he was released from prison where he had spent seven of his past ten years. He had always lived with his mother who had a council flat in the St Pauls area of the city. His father had left his mother when he was eight and nothing had been seen or heard from him since. His father had been a petty thief and a womaniser. He was also handy with his fists especially at home where he often hit his wife and frequently beat his young son. After Andrews finished his latest prison term he returned home to his mother who had met somebody else. Andrews found it difficult sharing a home with a man he hardly knew so after securing some door work he rented a rundown flat from one of his old mates in Bristol at a very reasonable rent. Hoyte moved in with him shortly after he had first got the flat. That was three years ago and during this time they eked a living from petty crime, dealing and door work which was their only regular work. They were on the nightclub company's books and even paid tax and national insurance. Everyone in Bristol knew of Andrews' reputation as a hard man so only the very brave or foolish tangled with him. Andrews relished these occasions. He enjoyed fighting especially when it gave him a chance to hurt somebody. He was basically a bully. At the same time as Andrews run in with the Bristol gang Hoyte had been caught screwing one of this gang's women. The word on the street was that retribution was going to be taken on both of them. The gang were violent criminals who had settled in Bristol after leaving South London. Most were Jamaican and some were rumoured to be Yardies. Andrews was a hard case but he wasn't too hard not to stop a bullet. Hoyte was scared shitless. He could handle himself but wasn't in Andrew's league. He had suggested the park home to Andrews as a hiding place until things in Bristol had quietened down which he had agreed with. Hoyte sold his BMW 315 Series to a cash buyer for five grand and purchased an older Ford Mondeo for two grand so he had a bit of cash to last a few months. Andrews only had a few hundred quid to his name. He had never learned to drive so apart from a sound system and a TV he had no other assets. Their money wouldn't last too long. All of their belongings were squeezed into the boot and back seat of the Mondeo and they set off for Norfolk early on a Sunday morning. They both possessed hand guns. Andrews had obtained a couple of old Taurus 9mm pistols from one of his many underworld contacts. The models were old but were reliable and they came at a reasonable price as they were not fashionable.

They had moved in to the park home four weeks ago. It was on a small holiday park about three quarters of a mile outside on Flixham. The weather was damp and cold so they were going through the gas bottles like they were going out of fashion. The landscape around the park home site was as flat as a witch's tit. There was nothing to shelter the site from the wind which seemed to come straight off the North Sea. None of the other park homes seemed to be occupied. The owners probably had more sense.
Hoyte had never been to the place before and it took them a while to find it. When they did find it they were underwhelmed. It was small. It had two bedrooms. One was a double with a double bed in it. The other was smaller with just a single bed in it. He remembered his mother saying that it was ideal because she could sleep in it when his father had one of his regular snoring bouts. There was a small lounge with a two seat sofa and an armchair and a very small kitchen which contained an electric cooker and hob a fridge and some limited cupboard space. Outside there was a padlocked plastic box which contained his parents fishing equipment. There wasn't a TV or radio so it was fortunate that they had Lynton's TV. Hoyte had commandeered the double

bed arguing that it was his parents place and with him being so tall he wouldn't fit in the single bed. This meant that Andrews had the small room with the single bed which made his mood even worse

Hoyte or Andrews didn't cook so they ordered takeaways most nights or purchased readymade dinners. They had only ventured into town at night two or three times. Hoyte always took the car as he didn't drink and it was a bit too far to walk especially in the dark. There wasn't a footpath for the last part of the journey and it was dangerous to walk along especially with the speed that some of the cars drove along it at... He was always comfortable in new places as he had always had the ability to chat to anyone. As a good looking bloke with an easy manner in a small town like Flixham he attracted women like flies around cow pats. He could have easily pulled plenty of the women that he had been chatting up but felt restricted by the presence of Andrews who had been particularly moody on the nights out in town. On their second night in town he had threatened a young lad who Andrews had claimed was starting at him. The young lad crapped himself when Andrews grabbed him by the shirt and if Hoyte hadn't calmed him down its likely he would have thumped the young lad. Often in the past when Hoyte had pulled Andrews would end up with Hoyte's girl's mate. The trouble with Flixham was that everywhere was so quiet. There was one decent sized pub, The Red Lion, that would occasionally have a band playing on a Saturday night but the music they played was not the type that appealed to the two Jamaicans. Andrews had laid somebody out in there on their last visit.

 A young lad of about eighteen had accidentally knocked into Andrews' arm on the way to the toilet giving Andrews an excuse to start a fight not that it was much of a fight. Andrews grabbed him by the shirt and punched the lad four or five times before he let him drop to the floor with blood pouring from his nose and mouth. They had avoided the place lately as they were trying to keep a low profile. Since then they had stayed indoors playing Nintendo computer games on the TV. The football team had been their release. They trained on a Tuesday night and had a drink in the bar after.

`What do you think of that Collins bloke then Denny?' Andrews asked

`He seems a bit dodgy to me. What was with the "I don't want to talk about the cash job in here". What's that all about? We could do with some money though. Between the fucking gas bottles, petrol and the takeaways we are going to be running out of money in a few weeks. I reckon we should give him a bell in the morning to see what he is offering'

`Yeah we should. We need to get out of this shit hole as soon as possible. I have never known anywhere so bleeding cold'

The next morning Hoyte called Collins. Collins told him about the courier drop and that they would get five hundred quid each for every drop they did.

`Why are you prepared to trust two blokes that you hardly know with whatever you are delivering and that we will bring the other bag back to you?. What is in the bags? Is it drugs? What's to stop us clearing off with whatever we are handing over?'

`You don't need to know the bags contents which will be going to nasty pieces of work that you don't want to cross. They will find you and deal with you. Did you hear about the shooting on Thursday night?'

Neither of them had

`Well I can promise you that it was down to one of these men's gang. The man they shot had only nicked a few pills. What do you think that they would do if somebody tried to steal their bags?'

`Why don't you do the drop by yourself?'

`It is because I want to stay out of the chain as much as possible. I am an invisible cog in the chain and I want to stay that way. I will meet you in the Star Tavern to hand over the goods and stay there until you return an hour or so later to collect the bag from the swap. You get your cash when you give me the bag. The Star is close to my home so I often call in for a beer on the way home from work. You just have to call me when you get back to the Star and I will just come outside so it looks like the call is about work and I have to take it outside'.

`What you are saying is that if we get caught we are in the shit not you'

`That's what you are getting paid for. Is the risk worth a grand? Talk it over with your mate and decide if you are in. If you are in let me know by six tonight. I need a drop to be done on Tuesday night. You would have to meet me in the Star at 8pm and meet up with my contacts at 830pm at a picnic site about twenty minutes out of town on the A1101. It will be deserted at that time of night. You just do the swap and bring the bag that you collect back to me '

Hoyte told Andrews what Collins had said about the drop.


`It sounds easy enough but we don't know what the people we are meeting are like. Will they try to rip us off?'

`Collins told me that there are some pretty heavy people involved. These blokes appear to be big time and the people we are meeting up with shot the previous courier for nicking a few pills.'

`We should go tooled up' Andrews said `I don't like going in blind. We don't know these people and I don't want to take any chances'.

Apart from when they fired off a few rounds in an old warehouse when they purchased the guns illegally in Bristol neither of them had ever used the guns in the anger They were simply used as a deterrent and were for show as was the case with most of the gangs in Bristol.

Hoyte phoned Collins later that evening to tell him that "they were in". Collins gave them the directions to both the Star and picnic the site. He suggested that they drive out there before Tuesday night so that they know where they are going on the night.

The next day Hoyte and Andrews did drive out to the picnic site which was near a village called Welney. It was a bleak looking place but there were a few trees and bushes separating the lay by from the road so any cars wouldn't be visible from the road. It wasn't much of a picnic site. There were just four picnic tables and a couple of waste paper bins. There was some evidence of throw away barbecues in the bins and some areas where the grass had been burned presumably by the barbecues. The few bushes that were growing were bare of leaves but there was still a distinct smell of piss around them. There were also piles of what looked like human shit under the bushes. Hoyte suspected that the area was used as a toilet by lorry drivers.

8

Collins arrived at the Star at 730pm on Tuesday night, ordered a pint of lager and struck up a conversation with a couple of regulars at the bar. He had his pay as you go phone with him. He used this phone solely for contacts with Petrescu in Rotterdam, Stancvic and his couriers. Petrescu had phoned him on Sunday evening. The call was a very brief call. He just said that the package was ready for transportation. Collins phoned Stancvic straight after to tell him that he had two new couriers who were both black and would be driving a white Mondeo. Hoyte phoned Collins at 8pm on the dot. Collins went outside pretending to continue the telephone conversation. His white Range Rover was parked on the far side of the small car park which would probably hold no more than a dozen cars. The only light was a small security light on the pub wall which covered the back entrance to the pub. The white Mondeo was parked next to the Range Rover. Collins opened the boot of his car and took out a combination locked black holdall. He passed this through the window of the Mondeo.

`Don't fuck this up. Bring the holdall they give you back here. If the contact is on time and they usually are you should be back here by 9pm`
He gave them a cheap pay as you go phone.
`Use this for any future phone calls between us. My number is the only number that is on it. Keep it that way. Call me when you get back and I will come out and collect the holdall from you.'
He showed them a brown envelope which was in his jacket pocket.
`There is a grand in here for you when you get back. If you do this well you can do another drop in two weeks time. There is a demand for the product leading up to Christmas'

Hoyte and Andrews didn't fuck it up. They were nervous but the drop went without a hitch and they were back at the Star before 9pm. They collected the promised fee and told Collins that they would happily do as many drops as he wanted. Stancvic's men were wary of dealing with new people. Two had turned up at the drop driving a dark coloured Mercedes. Both were big thickset bastards who looked like they would enjoy a fight. They didn't say too much to the Jamaicans only asking where the product was. They inspected it and once satisfied handed over a black holdall which was locked after they showed its contents. It contained a large amount of bank notes. They later discovered that only Collins knew the combination. They also wondered how the previous couriers managed to steal a few pills if the bags were locked.

The two of them did another two drops for Collins and both went without a hitch. The first was two weeks after the first drop that they made and the second was a couple of days before Christmas. Things improved for them socially as well. Hoyte had hooked up with Val, a married woman who he met at a pre Christmas celebration night in the Red Lion. The Red Lion was by far the busiest pub in town and the two of them had started to use it again. They had a DJ occasionally playing on Friday nights and it was packed on the Friday before Christmas. He ended the evening with his tongue down Val's throat. Her husband was a rep for a food company in Norwich. He covered an area from the Wash down to the South Coast as far as Bournemouth and was away at least two nights a week. Val was 32 blond tall and slim and she wore black rimmed spectacles. Hoyte could tell that she was definitely up for it. Her mate Lesley seemed reasonably keen on Andrews as well so Hoyte thought that would be both getting a leg over in the not too distant future. With a bit of money in their pockets they were feeling a bit happier in their temporary home.  The fly in the ointment as far as Hoyte was concerned was that Andrews was drawing attention to himself by getting into scrapes for no apparent reason. He just seemed to like hitting people. He even got himself sent off for violent conduct in a recent game for Flixham. Hoyte was wary of saying too much to his friend because Andrews was so volatile and with a few beers inside him he was likely to have a go at Hoyte as well. He was definitely a loose cannon and he seemed to be getting even more aggressive as he got older. Hoyte was concerned that Andrews would get arrested and charged which could lead to them being found by the gang in Bristol that they were trying to avoid. The Bristol gang had a one or two friendly coppers who might pass on info about them. Danny Collins had told them that he wasn't expecting another drop until late January so the money that they had earned was going to have to tide them over until then. It was fucking freezing in Norfolk at that time of the year. Everywhere would be quiet after the New Year celebrations so Hoyte planned to spend as much time with Val as he could. He hoped that Lynton would go with Lesley. She wasn't Hoyte's type. She was short and a bit overweight. But she had a big arse and a pair of big tits which was Andrew's type so here's hoping Hoyte thought.

Hoyte decided that they would make up a foursome and invited the girls out for a meal in Kings Lynn. There was an Indian restaurant that the lads at the football club had said was decent. Val's husband was working away. Lesley had split up with a long term boyfriend six months ago. She lived with her two boys in Bruce Road which was just around the corner from Val's flat in Rosario Close. Val and Lesley had been mates at school in Kings Lynn. Lesley had got married at twenty three to Simeon Farmer. Val was never keen on him and could never understand what her friend had seen in him. They had children soon after they got married and had two boys Oliver and Harry. Simeon left Lesley when the boys were five and three. He moved in with an older woman who worked in the same office in planning at the North Norfolk Council. That was over two years ago He was paying maintenance and had alternate weeks with the boys who were both now at school. He was living with his new woman in a three bedroom house on a small new estate in Flixham. This meant that he could see the boys regularly who stayed with a child minder after school.

Val had married Pete Davey when she was 25. They had dated for six years before tying the knot. The area that Pete was asked to cover increased massively two years ago and it required him to stay away from home two or three nights each week. Val became bored with sitting at home by herself for most of the week so on Simeon's week with the kids she started to go out with Lesley. They would go for a drink in the Red Lion. Lesley had put on a couple of stone in weight since the boys were born. She had always had big boobs but they seemed massive now and she liked to show them off when she went out. This invariably attracted the attention of men and on one night two builders who were working locally started to chat to them. Val got quite drunk and ended up sleeping with one of the builders, Colin, after she invited him in for a coffee. Until that night the only man she had ever slept with was Pete. She thought that their sex life was good but she had never had anyone to compare Pete with. Colin showed her what she was missing. She didn't enjoy cheating on Pete but she felt that things were going stale with their marriage. She wanted children. Pete didn't saying that they couldn't afford them yet. They had a forty five thousand pound mortgage on their flat and were only paying off the interest as the mortgage was interest only. It was costing them almost three hundred pound a month. Pete was finding it hard to hit sales targets during the recession and as a result his commission was lower than he had been making two years earlier. His basic was only thirteen thousand. In a good year he was making twenty thousand but this year he was struggling to bring home a nine hundred pounds each month. He was being hammered for his company car which increased his tax liability. With such a large area to cover it often resulted in him having to stay in a cheap hotel on Friday nights which meant he didn't get home until Saturday. His company agreed to foot the bill as it was sometimes more economical to stay in a hotel. Val's job at the builder's merchant was poorly paid and she brought home less than four hundred pounds each month. She argued that with maternity pay they wouldn't be that much worse off but Pete was adamant that they should wait until the economy picked up again. They had an argument on Monday night and they hadn't spoken when Pete left for a long trip down to Kent. He was staying down there for three nights and wasn't coming home until Friday morning. Val had given Denny her phone number when they had met in the Red Lion and she was hoping that he would call her to meet up. When he phoned her on Tuesday afternoon she was at work. When he asked her if she and Lesley wanted to make up a four and go out for a meal in Kings Lynn on Wednesday night it cheered her up no end.

When Val called Lesley to say that Denny and Lynton wanted to take them out she wasn't overly keen.

`I will go if you want to go. I know that you fancy Denny. He is fit but that Lynton isn't much to look at but I will give him his due though he is ripped. He must spend hours in the gym.' She went quiet for a minute before continuing. `He does have a good strong body on him so he will probably have loads of stamina and I am in desperate need of a good fuck.'

`Denny is fit isn't he? I wouldn't mind a piece of him. I need some fun. I had a row with Pete this morning about starting a family.'

`Have you ever been with a black man? I haven't but they are supposed to be good as well as being well endowed'

`I haven't' Val giggled `but if I'm lucky I might tonight'


Hoyte decided to have a word with his mate before they went out.

`Lynton try to chill tonight mate. Don't get involved with any aggro yeah. Let's have a nice night with the girls and hopefully we will end up fucking their brains out'

`I don't take shit from anybody. If anybody pisses me off I will sort them out. OK' came the angry response. `I'm not that fussed about taking them out anyway. Yours is nice looking but her mate is a bit hefty. She looks like she could eat through the fucking menu so it could cost us big time'.

`She isn't that big and she has a set of lungs on her. I thought you were a boob man? Try to take it easy mate. Don't go looking for trouble. We don't know Kings Lynn so let's keep a low profile'.


Hoyte's words seem to have had an effect on his mate because the night went well. They had picked the girls up from Val's flat. They had a couple of drinks first in a Wetherspoons bar in Kings Lynn and then went to the restaurant. The food was good. Val looked horny in a tight fitting light blue dress. She was tall, very slim and looked as though she had worked out. Her stomach was flat and she had a nice arse. Lesley was wearing an ill fitting low cut red dress which exposed her lumps. It wasn't the doing her any favours but Andrews hardly took his eyes off her tits all night. As Andrews had warned she did like her food and devoured her dish and most of Val's too. They ordered wine with the meal for the girls and the pair of them got through the best part of two bottles so they were half cut by the time they left the restaurant. As they had hoped the both spent the night with their girls. Hoyte gave Val the shag of her life. She was mad for it. Happy days he thought.

9

Bob Blake set off for the small town of Flixham at seven in the morning. He expected to be there by nine o'clock well in time for his eleven thirty interview. He wanted to have a good look around the town just in case he got the job. He didn't know that part of the country. He had spent £250 on a ten year old Astra diesel car. It was a bit tatty but it had a new MOT and hadn't done too many miles but it had left him with about £800 left in his bank account and all that he had to survive on was that and dole money until the probate money was sorted. He made good time and after stopping for a bacon roll and a coffee at a roadside food truck he arrived in Flixham at nine fifteen. After locating the Collins Transport depot he parked in a parking space that gave him an hour's free parking and had a look around the small town. The town looked tired but the weather did not help. It was a grey cold overcast day. He had driven past a Morrison's supermarket on the way into the town centre and that appeared to be the only well known large supermarket in town. What looked like the main shopping street was run down. There was a small Budgens grocery store, a scruffy looking shoe shop, a hardware store , chemist, a Ladbroke betting shop, a ladies hairdressers, barber shop, a couple of charity shops, a butchers , a small travel agent, half a dozen pubs and a newsagents. There were several empty shops which were probably as a result of the recession.  The only bank that he could see was a NatWest branch which would be handy if he got the job as he banked with them in Mansfield.  Just off the main street was another small road which contained an off license, two estate agents, a Value Shoppers supermarket, a fish and chip shop, a Chinese and Indian takeaway, a pizza shop and another two charity shops. There was also a bakery which sold coffee so he bought a cup and wandered down to the estate agents offices to see what there was in the way of rental property should he be successful at the interview which was still over an hour and half away. It began to drizzle heavily and there was a chill in the air so he pulled up the collar of his coat and studied the window of the two agent's offices that were close to each other. He discovered that there were one bedroom flats that could be rented for £300 a month and one and two bedroom house would cost between £350 and £425 each month. There didn't appear to be much of a selection of properties to rent. One of the houses looked appealing. It was a one bedroom end terrace modern house with allocated parking. The rent was £385 a month. He daydreamed about living in the house. The rain was coming down heavier now. He had bought a new suit shirt and tie for the interview so he didn't want to get soaked. He wandered back down the depressingly scruffy main street and went back to his car where he sat drinking his coffee watching the world go by.

There were few people around. He saw a couple of young men enter the betting office. He watched a bored looking man in his forties wandering up the road with an old mongrel dog which was sniffing at every post. It stopped and crouched for a crap which the owner couldn't be bothered to clean up. It earned him a filthy look from an old girl walking a poodle in the opposite direction. There were no signs of a traffic warden so Blake waited in his car until it was time for the interview. He was feeling extremely nervous. He desperately needed this job so he used his mobile to go over all the information that he had managed to find about the company as well as Value Shoppers who it seemed were quite a big company in East Anglia. They had small stores dotted around in East Anglia. They were the only shop in some of the larger villages. They ran many of their own brand products. Their shops were franchised and the whole operation was successful. The central warehouse was based in Thetford where they employed over two hundred staff. The rain had eased off and it was still over half an hour until his interview so he got out of the car to have a look in the Value Shopper which was near to one of the estate agents office. There was still no sign of a traffic warden. He went in and had a good look around. The store was only about 1500 square feet but was well stocked. He estimated that over half of the stock in the store was own brand. Value Shopper had everything from toilet rolls to cans of soft drinks. He purchased a bottle of still water and a packet of Polo Mints. The water cost 35 pence so it was good value. A similar sized bottle in a big name supermarket would have cost at least 50 pence. He spoke to who he assumed was the owner, an Asian man in his fifties, when he paid for his items. The man told him that business was good and that the company looked after their franchisees. Blake was pleased that he had gone into the shop. It gave him confidence that Collin's biggest customer appeared to be doing well.

10

Danny Collins had a busy morning. He had arrived at the office just after eight and was immediately put on the back foot by some unexpected news. He was interviewing for a new transport manager because Keith Barnes who had been performing that role at for fifteen years was retiring on his sixty fifth birthday which was in three months time. Collins had planned to hire somebody to give Barnes sufficient time to show them how things were done at the company. Barnes was suffering with a heart condition which was going to need an operation. He was feeling unwell at the moment and had been to see his doctor who in turn had sent him for tests at the hospital. Barnes had received a call from his doctor on Friday evening who told him that he needed urgent heart surgery. There was an unexpected space for this to be done at the famous Papworth hospital in twelve days time on Wednesday of next week. Barnes told Collins that this would result in him not being able to return to work before he was due to retire. He was very apologetic and was tearful but he said he needed this operation as the tests had shown up something which needed very urgent attention. This of course threw Collins' plans for somebody working with Barnes out of the window. He had three interviews lined up that morning but even if somebody started the following week Barnes wasn't going to be around to show them the ropes so they would be on their own in the job with just Collins to aid them. There had been five interviews lined up for the day but two had cancelled at short notice saying that they were no longer looking for a job. He didn't like the first candidate that he interviewed. He was a 31 year old from Norwich who had less experience than he had made out in his CV and his interview with the agency. He was full of bullshit and Collins swiftly discovered this. The courier firm that he worked for consisted of a few vans and not the many that he had claimed in his CV.

The second interviewee was a possible but he was in his early fifties and seemed a bit of a plodder. He lacked the energy that Collins was looking for. He had been working for North Norfolk Council in their distribution team based in Kings Lynn but had been made redundant just before Christmas. At best Collins thought that he could offer him a short term contract as he needed somebody soon as a result of the news he had been given earlier. He was disappointed with the results of his search. It seemed nobody wanted to work in this part of the country and those that did wanted far more money than Collins wanted to pay. On paper the last interviewee looked the promising but he had thought that about the first one.

Blake turned up at the Collins depot five minutes before the interview was due to start. The depot was large. There was a low loader being worked on in what looked like a workshop. There was also a flat bed parked on the far side of yard. He walked into the reception area where he was met by a blond woman who was probably in her late thirties. She asked him if he wanted a coffee which he declined.

` Mr Collins will see you shortly'

Blake waited for five minutes before Collins came out of his office and introduced himself. Blake's first impression was that Collins was probably a bit older than himself. He was average height, had short dark brown hair which was receding. He was red faced which made Blake think that he was a heavy drinker. He wore a white checked shirt which was struggling to contain his ample stomach. He wasn't wearing a tie or a jacket. What struck Blake the most was Collins dark eyes. They seemed to be very alert and his stare was intense, even a little intimidating
They shook hands and went into Collins office which was sparsely furnished but was bright, clean and modern. Blake went into details about what his duties had been at the brewery .The brewery had a fleet of 20 trucks mostly flat beds and curtain sides which were used for delivery barrels of beers and crates of soft drinks to pubs and clubs around the Mansfield area. He worked out the most economical routes. He had to make sure that the vehicles were all serviced on a regular basis; their MOT's and tax were up to date. He also had to monitor the driver's tachometers. He said that he hadn't much experience of deliveries to and from the continent but said that he had read plenty on the subject.

Collins liked what he had heard so far from the latest candidate. He thought that Blake had made an effort to look the part for the interview. He suspected that the dark grey suit that he was wearing was new and that he had also purchased a new shirt and tie for the interview. He looked to be in good shape standing around six feet tall. His light brown hair was cut short. Collins explained that the day to day business revolved around deliveries to the 120 or so Value Shopper supermarkets that were dotted around East Anglia. Collins had the contract for their deliveries. Each day at just after twelve the Value Shoppers central warehouse would send details of the drops that were required for the following day. It was the responsibility of the transport manager to arrange for the deliveries to be done in the most economical way for the company. They also collected from some of the large fruit and vegetable farms in the area. Some of this product was for the export market so ferry bookings needed to be made out of Harwich, Feixstowe and Kings Lynn. Flowers were brought in via Kings Lynn. Meat products, salad stuff and fruit and vegetables were also brought in via Harwich and Felixstowe. All in all Collins had a fleet of fourteen vehicles which was consisted of flatbeds, low loaders, beaver tails, curtain sides , fridge boxes and some large transit vans. They also sub contracted vans from small local firms in Fakenham and the surrounding areas and on most days they had between 20 and 25 trucks out on deliveries and collections. He would also be responsible for organising servicing of the firm's own trucks which was mostly done in house, MOT's, Tax, Insurance and the driver's tachometer readings. He would be required to work on a Saturday morning.

Collins gave Blake details of the package on offer. He explained the situation with regards to the current transport manager and asked Blake if he was successful when he would be able to start.
`I can start as soon as required but I would need to find some accommodation. I had been living in my mother's house but when she died I sold it so I'm staying with a mate in Mansfield. It's too far to commute on a daily basis'
`If you leave me your mobile number I will call you this afternoon and let you know one way or the other. What network are you with because the reception is poor in many areas around here?'
`Orange'
`They're not too bad in some parts of the town but not in others. They are not great two miles out of town. I'm with O2 and they are much the same'
Blake said that he was going to have a look around Kings Lynn. He didn't know the area and wanted to see the docks to see what was coming in. He knew that it wasn't a large dock and was mainly used for chemicals and agricultural products.

As soon as the interview was over Collins decided that Blake was his man. He contacted the HR department at Dudley Breweries who Blake had previously worked for. He explained his current predicament to the HR manager that he was put through to and asked if they could supply a reference by email. The HR manager knew of Blake and said that he had been a good employee and that it was only due to the recession that he had been made redundant. He asked Collins to send him the reference request and said that he would reply quickly. Collins hadn't expected a prompt reply based on his past experience of HR staff. They were usually hopeless but the HR manager kept his promise and by 230pm, much to his surprise Collins had received a good reference from Dudley Breweries. He phoned Blake at 3pm.

'Hi Bob. It's Danny Collins here. I am pleased to say that I would like to offer you the position of Transport Manager at Collins Transport... that is of course if you want the job'

'I would be delighted to accept the position. Thanks Mr Collins '

'Drop the Mr Collins crap Bob, call me Danny. When is the earliest that you would be able to start'

'That depends on how fast I can find somewhere to live. As I said earlier it's too far to commute from Mansfield on a daily basis'

'I am prepared to cover the cost of a guest house for a couple of weeks until you find somewhere if that helps. I presume that you will be looking to rent somewhere. I can probably help you there as I know the owners of the two agents in town. They are mates of mine so I can get them to speed up the process if you find anywhere'

'That would be very helpful. I can start next Monday but there is no reason why I couldn't start on Wednesday if you would prefer that'

'Excellent. Welcome to Collins Transport. I will email a confirmation letter now and I will see you sometime on Wednesday morning. Don't bust a gut trying to get here first thing. Aim to get here by late morning. We can sort out a guest house in the town centre for you'.

Blake felt good on the drive back to Mansfield. He'd had a good feeling about the interview so he had hung around in Kings Lynn before the drive home. He had stopped at a lay by cafe and was drinking a cup of tea when Collins had phoned him. The second half of the drive saw him floating on air as a new start and a new life in a new part of the country was beckoning. His favourite Elbow song, Powder Blue was playing on the Steve Wright show on the radio. That must be an omen he thought to himself while singing along to Guy Garvey's mournful lyrics.

Now that he had got the job his first thought was to find somewhere to live. He didn't fancy living in a guest house for any longer than he could. He was desperate to bring some semblance of normality back into his life. He remembered the name of the two agents whose windows he looked through this morning so that evening he went on to RightMove the property website to look at the details of some of the houses that he had noted. Three stood out to him. All were one bedroom terraced houses with rents ranging between £375 and £395 a month. He decided that he would go back to Flixham in the morning after calling the agents and trying to arrange viewings of the three houses that he had picked out. By the time Blake had arrived home Collins had sent the letter confirming his offer of employment and included details of the package attached to an email.

He went out with Tony for a few beers to celebrate the job and slept like a log. He woke up early and beat Tony to the bathroom. After a quick shit, shave and a shower he packed some clothes into a holdall. He had purchased his new suit from Marks and Spencer and it had come with a cheap suit holder which he used to store his suit. He decided that he would treat himself to some new shirts, sweaters, trousers and shoes at the BHS store on the retail park on the edge of town. He was heading in that direction anyway for the drive to Flixham. It would have to be on his credit card though. He made appointments to see the three houses between 2pm and 3 pm so he had plenty of time to get to Flixham. He had brought all four of his Elbow Cd's with him for the journey. They were his favourite band. He loved the new album "The seldom seen kid" and that got first play. Traffic was light when he left Mansfield at 1045. There had been a sale on in BHS. The store had a buy two get the third free of charge offer so he ended up buying nine shirts as he was going to need plenty while he was in the guest house. Six were plain colours, a mix of blues, white, grey and a pale green with the other three white or blue with stripes He also bought three pairs of trousers which included a pair of blue chinos and three sweaters, a V neck and two round necks. That would last him for a week he thought. It took him just under two hours to get to Flixham. His first task was to find somewhere to stay for the night. He noticed several guest houses with vacancies. One was called for Belway Guest House. It had a sign for vacancies in the window. It looked very clean from the outside with fresh looking net curtains in the windows. He would return later and hopefully get a room. He was due to see the first house at 2pm. He was hungry and needed to find somewhere to eat. The Belway guest house was within five minutes walk to The Red Lion pub. The pub was large and did food every night. Looking at the menu outside it was your typical pub chain grub but was reasonably priced. He popped in for a quick drink. He had a very pleasant pint of Bateman's bitter and a ham and cheese French stick which cost him just over four quid. The pub was only a few minutes from the agent who was showing him two properties. First though he called into the Nat West Bank and arranged for his account to be transferred from Mansfield to the Flixham branch. It would be handy having a bank so close to where he worked even if he eventually decided to live outside of Flixham. Even though the bank was empty when he went in it still took the best part of twenty minutes to arrange the transfer so he was running a few minutes late by the time he got to the estate agent. He was met by Steve Kenyon who appeared to be the senior person at the agency. He was a small man in his late thirties with red hair. Blake explained that he had been offered a job with Collins Transport. Kenyon told him that he was a mate of Danny Collins. He said they played tennis together with their wives. The first house that Kenyon showed him was disappointing. It was much smaller than the images on RightMove had indicated. The kitchen was tiny and the white goods looked dated. It was the cheapest of the houses that he was looking at and he could see why. The next house was the one which had caught Baker's attention in the window of the agency yesterday. Kenyon took him in and asked him to put on shoe covers as the owner had just fitted new carpets. The carpet which was a charcoal grey seemed to be of a good quality. The lounge was thirteen foot by ten with a radiator under the window. Blake had noticed that there was a sky dish on the wall and there was a sky box on the window sill. The room had curtains which were silver and dark grey stripes. He liked the room which had a homely feel about it. The kitchen was compact but bigger than the last place. It had a fridge/freezer, washing machine and an electric oven and hob. All of the white goods looked fairly new and were in good condition. There wasn't too much in the way of cupboard space. The kitchen looked out onto the back garden which was small and was laid to lawn with a flower border. Most of the plants in the border had died down over winter.

There were houses beyond the garden but their gardens backed onto that of this house. Upstairs there was a bedroom which was at the front of the house and was just a bit smaller than the lounge. It had a mirrored built in wardrobe with a hanging rail and shelving area. The wardrobe ran the length of the room up to the door. There was plenty of room for his double bed. The carpets were the same throughout the house. The bedroom also had curtains which were in a black and grey pattern. The final room was the bathroom. It wasn't very big but it had a bath with an electric shower over it, a basin and a WC. All were white and there was a glass shower screen. Outside there was a small back garden which Blake had seen from the kitchen window and two allocated parking spaces outside the front door. Blake asked Kenyon how early the house could be occupied as the advert on RightMove had said available in February.

`It's available now' Kenyon told him. `You would need to pay a month's rent up front plus a further month's rent as a deposit. We would need to take up references with your bank and previous landlords if you had them but we could push it through by the weekend after next'.

`I have another house to look at with another agent straight after but I do like it so I will definitely let you know as soon as I have seen the other house'

`OK, but don't dwell on a decision as there has been a lot of interest in this property' Kenyon told him. He was obviously keen to get a tenant into it.

He went straight to the other agent who took him to the next house which was just around the corner from the previous house. The third house was another good property. It was a little bigger than the second house and at £395 per month it was the most expensive but it didn't appeal to him as much as the second house. He told the agent that he had preferred the second house and thanked him for showing him around. The second house was the one that he wanted. It was on what appeared to be a quiet estate and was less than a ten minute walk from the main street in town. He could walk to and from work in good weather. Blake went back to the first agency and told Steve Kenyon that he wanted to rent the property. He completed paperwork which gave him a six month rental term subject to references. As Blake had lived in houses that he mortgaged he had no references for rentals. He gave Tony Martin as a personal reference and Dudley Breweries for a character reference. He hoped his bank would respond quickly. He had a good record at the bank and had never exceeded his small overdraft. The deposit and the first month's rent in advance left would leave him dangerously short of money so he was praying that the probate would get done quickly. He was always very careful with using his credit card and he was wary about running up too much on it. He had forty quid's worth of petrol on it plus the money he had spent on clothes that morning. Thankfully it was almost six weeks until he had to pay the bill.

It was nearly four thirty be the time he had finished at the estate agents so he went straight to the Belway guest house. It still had the vacancies sign in the window so he went in and checked it. The guest house was run by Gary and Lorna Lindsall who looked like they were both in their late fifties. Fortunately they took credit cards. The room Blake was shown was very clean and bright. It had a small en-suite shower room with a basin and WC. It also had tea and coffee making facilities and a small colour TV.

`Breakfast is between 0715 and 0830' Lorna told him `but we are quiet at the moment so if you want breakfast outside of those times we can accommodate'
`I may want to book a room for the rest of the week and probably next week too. I am starting work at Collins Transport tomorrow. My boss told me that he would pay for a guest house until I found somewhere permanent to live. I don't know if he has an arrangement with somebody in the area. He doesn't know that I have come to Flixham a day early as he was happy for me to drive down from Mansfield in the morning and start later. I will let you know as soon as I know'
`We have occasionally had people staying here from the transport company. I hope you can get something sorted' she said as she left the room.

They are probably in need of business Blake thought to himself. He was tired from the excitement of the day so he had a quick kip. He woke up an hour later, made himself a cup of tea and watched the news on BBC. The weather forecast followed and it promised a cold snap with the possibility of snow showers down the East of the country. Blake had noticed that the temperature had dropped after he left the estate agents. He changed into a pair of the new trousers that he had bought earlier, slipped on one of his new sweaters and put on his thick coat before setting off for a walk into town. He thought that he would eat in the Red Lion which looked as though it was a chain pub and have a couple of pints  before trying to get a good night's kip before starting his new job

He arrived at the Red Lion about 7pm. It was quiet in the place. There was an old man shovelling coins into a fruit machine and two old couples eating at tables by the TV. Blake walked up to the bar where an attractive mature blond was serving.

`Is it always this quiet in here'? He asked the blond
`It gets a bit busier later on but Tuesday's are generally quiet. It's even worse in January because nobody seems to have any money after Christmas. The

landlord is introducing a new "pie and a pint" deal next week to try to drum up some trade for February.'

He ordered a pint of Bateman's and a lasagne and chips.

'What brings to Flixham? It's hardly a tourist trap'

She seemed keen to talk, He thought that's because she was probably bored stiff and was glad of someone to talk to.

'I'm actually coming to live here' he told her 'I'm starting a new job in town tomorrow and I have just found a place to live.'

'Where are you going to be working?'

'Collins Transport, I'm their new transport manager'

'I know Danny Collins and his wife Paula. Danny comes in occasionally for a drink after work. Where are you going to be living?'

'Turnberry Close. Do you know it?'

'I should think so. I live there too at number 15. What number are you going to be living in?'

'Number78. It's at the top end'

'We will be sort of neighbours then' she said with a smile

Two younger men came into the bar and the barmaid went to serve them. She was just as chatty with them and just seemed pleased that there were actually people in the bar.

He took a seat in a raised area which served as the restaurant area. The food arrived within 15 minutes. The lasagne was piping hot so it was obviously straight from the microwave. There were plenty of chunky chips with it which was just as well because he was hungry.

After finishing his meal and having his table cleared by the barmaid he downed the remainder of his pint and ordered another at the bar.

'The landlord is going to try out a quiz night on Thursday if you are at a loose end' the barmaid said to him 'I think that any entrance fees will be paid out in prize money'

'I may come along .What time does it start?'

'830pm so get here twenty minutes before' She was drumming up customers. Blake finished his second pint bade farewell to the barmaid who said she was called Helen and made his way back to Belway guest house. It was even colder than it was earlier and a frost was starting to appear on the grass in the gardens that he walked past. He was looking forward to starting work the next day. He made a point of looking out for the barmaid's house. It looked very similar to his and there wasn't a car in either of the parking spaces outside her house.

12

After a good night's sleep and a hearty breakfast Blake checked out of the Belway and set off for his new job just after nine thirty. It took him less than five minutes to drive to the depot. Collins was surprised to see him so early in the day

`You are keen. I wasn't expecting you until eleven at the earliest. What time did you leave Mansfield?'

Blake explained that he had come down the day before and that he had sorted out somewhere to live saying that he hoped to move in by the weekend after next. Collins told him that he knew the senior partner and that he would try to speed things up.

`Have you got much to move down from Mansfield?'

`I have a bed, a wardrobe, a chest of drawers, a music centre, a TV and a few pots and pans, some crockery and clothes. I will get hold of a sofa, a table and some chairs when I move in. I will go to Kings Lynn on Saturday afternoon to see if any of the charity shops have anything half decent. If I can get the keys before next weekend I will move everything on the Sunday'

`Feel free to use our own smaller vans if you want. It will save you hiring something'

`Thanks. I might take you up on that'

Collins took Blake into the offices where he met Keith Barnes, Susan Rudd, a young girl with bad skin who looked after invoicing, enquiries and anything else required by the Transport manager. The receptionist was called June Eason and worked part time between 9.15 and 2.30

He was then introduced to Ray Nash who looked after the trucks with an assistant, Bob Parsons. Nash looked to be in his late 40's. He was short with a head of thinning dark hair. Parsons was a good looking guy, probably in his 20s, tall with short brown hair. Both seemed friendly enough

Next was the accounts department. This is was run by a large lady called Ruth Cross. Ruth looked like she was in her late fifties.

`This is Bob Blake our new Transport Manager' said Collins doing the introductions

Blake said hello to her and she did the same.

`Bob is going to be staying in a guest house until he finds somewhere to live so I have agreed that we will pay for a guest house for him until then. Where did you stay last night?'

`A place called Belway. It was £30 a night and it was comfortable with a decent breakfast. It's a fifteen minute walk from here or five minutes in the car'
`It's not one that we have used in the past but if you like it book in for the next week or so. Get them to give you an invoice every week and Ruth will refund the cost to you together with any expenses that you have. I will talk to you about expenses later'
There was a lad of about twenty called Ray Pearce working with Ruth. When Collins introduced him he grunted hello and continued with whatever he was doing on the computer.
`That is all of the office staff' Collins said as they left the accounts department. `My wife Paula comes in for a few hours every day to do some admin. We run a tight ship and keep them all busy.  All of the drivers that we use are on self employed contracts. That way we are not liable for national insurance, sick pay or holidays. They invoice us every week. Paula looks after the payments and also our payroll. I will introduce you when she gets in. She will need your bank details so that we can pay you. I will leave you with Keith now and he can show you how we do things'.

The first day flew by. Keith went through the processes used by the company. Blake didn't think that he would find it too difficult to adapt to a new way of doing things. He also thought that there were areas that were open to improvement. He grilled Barnes on the overseas shipments which were something quite new to him. It sounded reasonably straight forward. Before he knew it the week had gone.  He only had to work for a few hours with Keith on Saturday morning which was part of his contract but he had planned the routes for Monday and also the few that had to be made on Sunday. He took a phone call from the agents to say that he could pick up the keys for his house that afternoon. The agent had said that with Collins recommendation that they had been able to progress matters quicker than usual. He just had to pay the deposit and the first month's rent in advance. He phoned Collins to ask him he if he could have the use of a Luton Box Van that was going to be idle until Monday and by 5pm that evening he was on the way back to Mansfield to collect his meagre possessions from Tony's flat. He took Tony out for a curry and a few beers on Saturday night as a thank you for letting him stay at his place over the last few weeks   He offered the small wardrobe to Tony as he didn't need it. Tony gladly accepted it as there was no wardrobe in his spare room. He hadn't seen much of Wayne and Ellie since he had split with Debbie so he rang them. He told them that he had got a new job and was moving to Norfolk and asked them if he could take them out for lunch on Sunday as he wouldn't be back in Mansfield that often. Wayne didn't want to go as he was playing football on Sunday morning. Ellie was reluctant but eventually agreed. Blake explained that his car was back in Flixham and that he had a van with him to take his furniture back with him , Ellie said that she would meet him at 130pm at The Fox and Hounds which was a Chef and Brewer chain pub which did a decent Sunday lunch. Wayne texted Blake later and said that he would come too as his match had been cancelled because of a frozen pitch.

Nursing a slight hangover after one too many beers with Tony the night before Blake with Tony's help loaded everything into the van. He gave Tony his new address and said that he was welcome to come to see him if he fancied a break out in the sticks. He managed to buy a small two seat sofa for £20 in a charity shop in the town centre so at least he had something to sit on. Tony had come with him as he had wanted a lift into the town centre and had helped him load it.

`Thanks again mate for putting me up.' He shook hands with Tony and left for the Fox and Hounds

Ellie and Wayne arrived together in Ellie's little Citroen.

`Hi Dad' she said `You look well. You look as though you have lost loads of weight and I like the new haircut. I am pleased that you have got rid of that scruffy old beard too'

`I have lost two and a half stone. I did a lot of cycling when my car packed up. I stopped drinking and started to eat a bit more healthily.'

`When did you get the van' Wayne asked

`It's not mine. My new boss let me use it for the weekend to bring my things back. I have an old green Astra. It's not much to look at as it's a bit tatty but it has been reliable and gets me from A to B'

Ellie was interested in hearing about her father's new job and his apparent new life in Norfolk.

`Have you had any new girlfriends since you and mum split up?'

`No, I haven't had time. I have been really busy what with Gran's funeral and the sale of her house. I was spending a lot of time looking for a new job and too be honest I wasn't exactly flush with money so a new girlfriend was low on my priorities'

`I bet you have got plenty of money now. Mum said that you will get everything from the sale of Gran's house. She was hoping that you would give her some' said Wayne with a trace of bitterness in his voice.

`I haven't got anything yet. Gran never left a will so everything has to go to probate before I, as her next of kin, received anything. It should all be done in a few weeks. I will give some to you and Ellie because I am sure Gran would have wanted that but you can tell Mum that she won't be getting anything from me. She must be well off now living with Cameron.'

`How much are you going give us?' Wayne asked greedily

`That depends on how much I get, how my new job goes and whether or not I decide to buy a house in Norfolk. I haven't worked for nearly a year and after paying for Gran's funeral, the deposit on the house that I will be renting and all my expenses since I split up with mum I don't have much left from the settlement with Mum and that has to last me until I get paid at the end of February'

`I thought that you might be giving us some today.' Wayne said.

`Well you thought wrong'. Blake replied.

He wondered if this was why the two of them agreed to meet with him. The rest of the lunch went quietly. The kids didn't say too much about Debbie and Cameron. They did say that they were going to the villa at the end of June'
Wayne told Blake that he had been accepted for engineering apprenticeship and that he would be going to a training centre in September.

`I have my driving test in three weeks time as I will need a car to get to the training centre' Wayne said.

Blake took this as being a hint. He was hoping that Blake would give him money to get a car

After the meal they said their goodbyes. He wished Wayne good luck with his driving test. Blake promised to phone them and they both said that they would phone him too. He drove back to Flixham on Sunday afternoon and later that evening he was sat watching TV in his new house. The Sky box enabled him to watch most of the free view channels. This included Sky sports news which was a bonus. He couldn't believe how fast things had turned around for him. All he needed to find now was a new circle of friends. He thought that he would start with Helen the barmaid at The Red Lion. She seemed a bit too friendly and he thought that he had a chance with her. She wasn't wearing a ring and certainly hadn't mentioned a boyfriend.

13

By midweek it had turned bitterly cold with the temperature dropping to minus six overnight and not getting much above freezing during the day. A strong North Easterly wind was blowing and the wind chill factor made it feel a lot colder. Hoyte and Andrews were not in the best of moods. The park home was freezing cold. The only heating in the place was gas heater. The gas in the small bottle was lasting less than a week and they were firing 50p coins into the electric meter like they were going out of fashion.

Andrews was particularly grumpy.

`It's fucking freezing mate. We need to get out of this shit hole before we freeze our bollocks off. I reckon things will have quietened down in Bristol. Do you want to chance it and go back?'

`Not yet. Basil Smith is a head case. He thinks that we took liberties and he will be after revenge to protect his reputation'

`Well I'm not staying here for much longer. We're not earning apart from the occasional job for Collins and this fucking place is an ice box. I reckon we should take off after the drop next week'

`A grand won't last long and we don't have anywhere to go'

`I know a bloke in Liverpool that I was in the nick with. I acted as his minder in prison so he owes me. I am going to call him when we go into town to see if he can fix us up with anything in Liverpool. I can't even get a signal on the phone here otherwise I would do it now' Andrews moaned

Hoyte's had an idea.

`Do you reckon we could mug off those two Romanian's at the drop next week? If we nicked the drugs and the cash we could shoot off to Liverpool with enough cash in our pockets to keep us going for a couple of years. We could flog the drugs as well'

`I reckon it would be a piece of piss' Andrews replied suddenly getting very interested at the plan. `It is something that had crossed my mind too'

They spent the afternoon hatching a plan to rob the money and the drugs. They planned to pile all of their possessions that would fit into the boot of the car and take off after they had turned over the Romanians. They thought that they might need their guns to force the Romanians hand.

`Do you think that you could use it if you had to Denny? I wouldn't have any problems with it but I'm not sure if you would'

`Do you think I don't have the bottle? I know I'm not as hard as you but I am not a chicken'

`I'm not saying you are but I just wanted to hear you say it'

They decided to go to Morrison's to get some food as they had nothing much in the fridge. Neither of them had much idea of cooking so they always bought readymade meals and plenty of beer and vodka for Andrews and coke for Hoyte. Andrews seemed to brighten up after they had made their plan and had a smile on his face when they got to the shop. He told Hoyte that he was going to give his mother a quick ring and that he would catch up with him in the shop. He hadn't spoken with his mother since they had left Bristol save for a quick call on Christmas Day which he had only done because he was bored sat indoors with Hoyte. It was even colder than it had been earlier in the week so it was only a brief call. He told his mother that they were staying in Norfolk at a place Denny's father owned and that he hoped to be back home soon. He soon found Denny in the frozen food sector looking at pies and pizzas.

Morrisons had plenty of family sized meals that only required bunging in the oven for a half hour or so or in the microwave for a few minutes. They soon filled the trolley with food and drink. They returned to the car laden with shopping bags. Hoyte went arse over tip on a slippery patch of ice. The shopping went everywhere and he landed in a heap on his arse. Andrews was pissing himself with laughter. He was doubled up.

Hoyte had the hump

`I could have broke my fucking arm 'he complained 'you wouldn't be laughing if I can't drive and you had to fucking walk everywhere'

`You looked like Bambi. Your legs and arms were going in all direction. The shopping was scattering everywhere, I just wish I had caught it on the phone's camera' Andrews almost crying with laughter. `I haven't seen anything so funny for ages. I could have sent it to that TV show with Beadle and got £250'

He kept chuckling all the way back to the park home much to Hoyte's annoyance. His arse was sore from the fall not to mention his pride.

Winston Chinn had heard his woman talking to her son on the phone. When she was out of sight he rang 1471 and took note of the number that had just called. He asked her where Lynton had called from so she told him. Five minutes later he made an excuse to go out and rang one of Basil Smith's gang. Smith had wanted to know where Andrews had run to and had sent some of his heavies to see Chinn to threaten him into giving anything that would enable them to track down Hoyte and Andrews. Smith ran the drugs market in Bristol. He was a violent thug who was not to be messed with. Chinn had no time for Andrews who was he thought a bully and a waster. He had made his mother's life a misery so Chinn felt no loyalty to him. He couldn't give a toss if Smith caught up with him and it would get him off the hook with Smith. Smith might give him a few quid for the info too.

14

On Thursday night Blake decided to go to the quiz which was being trialled in the Red Lion. Helen suggested that she joined him to make up a bar team. There were about twenty customers in the bar who made up five teams in all. During a break in the rounds Blake noticed two black guys come into the pub. He noticed that one was tall and good looking and the other was a squat ugly bastard. They were wearing thick woolly hats and gloves as well as scarves. The ugly one ordered drinks. Helen served them and when she handed the change the ugly one started shouting at her saying that she had short changed him.
`I haven't 'She protested `your drinks came to £5.20 and I gave you £4.80 change'
`How comes it cost me £3.80 for the same drinks in here last Friday then?' the ugly one complained
`Did you come in between 5pm and 7pm because that's our happy hour? The prices are cheaper between those times'
Blake was listening to the argument when the guy suddenly turned and stepped towards him
`What are you gawping at mate' said and he pushed Blake in the chest with both hands
Blake remembered his dad saying to him "always get in the first blow" so he did and caught the guy on the chin with a solid right hand punch. He may as well have hit him with a pillow because the guy never even flinched. Blake saw a big black fist coming at him and the next thing he remembered he was flat on his back with the black guy towering over him. Helen was shouting that she was going to call the police. The tall guy was pulling him away
`Leave him Lynton. We don't need the police getting involved'
Fortunately for Blake he took his mate's advice and they both sat down near a TV showing basketball
`Are you OK Bob?' Helen asked
Blake was embarrassed having been decked by one punch.
`Yes I think so. Who is that bloke? I hit him full on the chin and he never even felt it'
`They started coming in here a few weeks back. The tall one thinks he is god's gift to women and is always trying it on with the ladies. He is friendly enough though. His mate though is always looking for trouble. He has been in a couple of fights already. I have asked the manager to ban him but I think that he is too scared to do it in case the bloke goes for him'
Blake's jaw started to stiffen up as the night went on and he could feel that the side of his face was swollen. The quiz finished with Blake and Helen finishing

third out of five teams. Helen asked him if he would like to make up a team next week. She said that there was another regular who could probably join them and give them a better chance as the winning team had six players. Blake was convinced that she had been flirting with him all evening and was more than happy to join up with her again

The weather worsened over the weekend. The temperature dropped to minus 11 at night and it snowed resulting in a light dusting. This quickly froze and the roads and pavements turned into an ice rink. It was forecasted to stay this way for a week. Collins phoned Hoyte to confirm that the drop was still on for Tuesday but they had decided to bring it forward to 8pm. They agreed to meet at 730pm in the usual place in the Star car park. Hoyte had arranged to go round to Val's that afternoon. Her husband was going to be away that night and with the bad weather forecast to get even worse with the threat of heavy snow she said that it might be their last chance to get together for a while. She told work she had a dentist appointment so she could leave work at 3.30pm. Hoyte had seen her the previous week and thought that he would give her one for the last time as he and Andrews had planned to make a run for it later that evening. Andrews had made contact with his mate in Liverpool who had said that they could crash at his place for a few days so everything was set. Andrews had lost interest in Lesley so he was at a loose end on the Tuesday afternoon. He decided that he wanted to go into town for a couple of beers and to get something to eat. It was too far to walk into town from the park home especially as it was freezing cold so Hoyte dropped him off in town at 3.30pm.He arranged to meet up with Hoyte in the Red Lion later before going to meet Collins in the Star car park.
`Try not to get pissed'. He said aware that Lynton was going to be drinking for over three hours
`I will only have three or four pints. At least it is warm in the pubs. It's doing my head in staying in our place. I will be in the Red Lion by 6pm. They will have the football on. I think there is a Champion's league game on a six. Chelsea will be playing some Russian team so I will watch that. I'm going to start in the Three Feathers. They do a nice curry in there. That will warm me up a bit'
`Terrific 'Hoyte moaned `beer and curry! Your arse is going to be lively on the drive up to Liverpool. I will meet you in the Red Lion at 7pm'

Blake had almost finished planning the routes for the next day when Collins came into his office. It was just past 4pm.
'Can you leave Dimi on the Rotterdam runs in the future? He knows the people at the other end and he often negotiates to get some additional cargo if

he isn't full. Some of the small local butchers are open to some cheap bacon and if there is any going spare the depot in Rotterdam will just adjust our bills for it.'

Blake thought that was a bit odd but agreed to leave Dimi on the Rotterdam runs. He had noticed that Collins had been in deep conversation with Dimi when he had returned from Holland that morning and was unloading. He thought that Collins had seemed a bit nervous. He kept checking his phone and his watch.

`You will have to come to ours on Sunday for lunch. My brother in law Roy is coming over with his missus and daughters. They have two girls about the same age as my Charlotte who is 15 so they entertain themselves while we get stuck into the wine. If you are not busy come round for 2pm. Paula does a lovely roast dinner'

`Thanks Danny I may well take you up on that'

Collins left the office and Blake carried on with the logistics for the next day. When he had finished the rota's he went down to speak to Ray Nash to see if there were any issues with the trucks that needed dealing with. A police car pulled into the depot while he was chatting to Ray.  A burly policeman got out of the car and walked towards them.

`Hi Ray' he said ignoring Blake `Is Danny about?'

`Hello Graham.  He is in his office. You know the way so go on up'.

The policeman went into the offices.  Danny was talking to Ruth Cross

`Can I have a word in private please Danny? '

Collins went white. He immediately thought that he was going to be questioned about the bag of drugs that were in the boot of his car.

`Come on through to my office. Ruth can you get PC May a cup of tea' May declined the tea and followed Collins into his office

`I'm afraid that I have some bad news Danny. Your wife and daughter were involved in an accident this afternoon. It seems that they come off the road near Kings Lynn and ended up in a ditch. They were taken to the Queen Liz. I don't know many details but they had to cut your daughter out of the car.'

Collins was stunned. `Are they alive?'

`Yes but I don't know their condition'

`I will go straight to the hospital now. Thanks for coming in to tell me personally, Graham'

`I thought that it would be better than getting a phone call. Drive carefully though Danny the roads are lethal'

He left Collins sat at his desk white faced.

Collins was panicking. He had to deliver the drugs to his couriers and collect the money later. He had no idea how long he was going to be at the hospital.

He rang Stancvic but the call went to voicemail. He didn't leave a message. He then rang Hoyte but got an unable to take your call message. It was a poor signal in most parts of the town. He rang Andrews and to his relief Andrews answered

`Where are you'? Collins demanded

`I'm having a beer in the Red Lion. Why, we are not due to meet until 7.30pm'

`I need you to meet me in the Red Lion car park in five minutes. There has been a change of plan. My wife and daughter have been in a car crash and are in hospital in Kings Lynn. I will hand you the goods in the car park. Keep them with you until you do the drop. Don't let them out of your fucking sight. I will meet you back at the Star at 8.30pm unless I need to stay at the hospital. If I don't get back in time keep hold of the goods until I contact you'

`Keep your hair on. Do you think we are fucking stupid? I'm capable of holding a bag for a couple of hours. See you in the car park in five minutes'

Danny left the depot after telling Ruth what had happened. He drove to the Red Lion. He was nervous as it was still light. The days were getting longer and he hoped that nobody noticed him handing the holdall to Andrews who thankfully was stood in the quietest corner of the car park.

`Where's Denny?' he asked noticing that Hoyte's car wasn't in the car park

`He is off shagging with some woman. I'm meeting him here at 7pm'Andrews took the bag.

`I hope your wife and daughter are OK. Don't worry about the drop. Denny and me can handle everything' Andrews said.

With a bit of luck Collins will still be at the hospital so Denny and him will be well away before he realises what has happened. Their plan would be made easier he thought to himself.

He rang Hoyte to tell him about the change of plan but there was no signal. It wasn't a problem because he was meeting Hoyte at 7pm in the Red Lion anyway.

15

Hoyte had dozed off. He had been shagging Val for over two and a half hours. The woman was insatiable and after the third time they had both fallen to sleep. He checked his watch and saw that it was 725pm.

`Fuck... I need to be out of here. I was supposed to meet Lynton at 7pm' he said quickly pulling on his pants and trousers.

`Don't go' Val said patting the bed `It's nice and warm in here so why don't you stay here. Lynton is a big boy. He won't miss you' She put her arms around him.

`We are working tonight' he said pushing her away `and we need the money' He was out of the house less than two minutes after waking up. At Val's request he had parked around the corner. It was freezing with heavy snow falling. When he got to his car he found that the window screen was frozen. He started the car and put the heaters on full blast. He found a window scraper in the glove box and started scraping ice off the windows of the car. He made a hole just about big enough to see through and drove off at some speed. He had only gone two hundred yards when an old man out walking his dog suddenly appeared in the road in front of him. He hit the brakes, skidded, bounced off a parked car and went through a brick wall into someone's garden. His airbags went off and he banged his head heavily on the side window. Groggily he got out of the car. The front was buckled and he doubted if it would be able to drive it. The home owner and several neighbours came out to see what had caused the big bang they had heard.

`Look at the state of my bloody wall. How fast were you going?' the middle aged man who Hoyte assumed was the owner said

`I hit the brakes when that silly old bugger over there with the dog stepped out in front of me without looking. I skidded and lost control of the car. It was an accident'

`Can somebody call the police?' another neighbour said.

The man with the dog protested his innocence

'He was driving too fast for these conditions. I never even saw him coming' Hoyte's phone rang. It was Andrews.

`Where the hell have you been? I have been phoning you for ages 'Andrews screamed down the phone.

`I have had a car crash. Somebody has phoned the police so I can't leave the scene' He said quietly

`Collins dropped the goods off to me early. His wife and daughter had an accident and are in hospital. I've phoned you loads of times'

`There is no reception at Val's place. I've only got two bars here so you were lucky to get through. Call Collins and tell him the drop is off tonight and we will try to sort something for tomorrow Hoyte whispered into the phone'

`Can't you nick a car and we can go later tonight?'

`I've got to go. The police are here now'. He rang off

Andrews was in the car park of the Red Lion. It was already a quarter to eight so there was no way he would get to the meet on time. He swore loudly and was pissed off that Hoyte had been with Val all afternoon while he was on his own. It had started to snow very heavily and it was already starting to settle on the ground. The wind was blowing the snow into Andrews' face. A car pulled into the car park and a man got out. It was the bloke that Andrews had chinned last week. Andrews suddenly had an idea which could save the situation. He pulled out his gun and walked up to the bloke as he was putting a plastic screen on the window of his car. Andrews jabbed the gun in the back of the man's ribs.

`Get back in and don't make a noise or I will blow your fucking brains out'

Blake got back in the car. He recognised the man with the gun as the one who had decked him last week and thought that the man felt that he had unfinished business.

`I'm sorry about hitting you last week. Can you let me buy you a drink as an apology?'

`Shut the fuck up and drive. Take the road out of town and head towards Wisbech. I will tell you when to stop'

Blake protested that it would be dangerous to drive in these blizzard conditions. He was now regretting his decision to drive to the pub just to try to chat up Helen. He wished that he had walked down instead. Andrews ignored his protests and just said "drive."

Andrews was planning as he went. He thought that he would be able to handle the two Romanians by himself but he would probably need to use his gun. He would get the driver to take him back to their place and nick his car for the drive up to Liverpool. The only problem he had yet to resolve was what to do with the driver but he would worry about that later. He sent a text to Denny *'Problem sorted. I got a lift. I will Xplain later u at our place at 9.'*

Blake drove for nine or ten miles before the Jamaican told him to pull into a picnic area. Blake thought that he was going to be shot and was shitting himself. He had driven very slowly which had earned him some abuse from Andrews. He thought that the picnic site would be where he met his end until he saw that another car was parked in the picnic area.

`Stop the car and give me your keys' the Jamaican told him.
Blake noticed that two men were sat in the other car which was a dark
coloured Mercedes. Andrews pocketed the keys and got out of the car carrying
the black holdall. As he got out two large men got out of the Mercedes. One
was carrying a dark coloured holdall
`You're late' the smaller of the two men said ` Where is your mate? Who is the
bloke with you?'
`My mate crashed his car so this geezer gave me a lift. He isn't anything you
need to worry about. I will deal with him later. Let's get this over with. It's too
cold to stand here yakking'
It was still snowing heavily and the snow had settled. It was already over an
inch deep and their footprints showed. Andrews moved towards the two
Romanians and dropped the bag at their feet. The smaller man opened it and
checked through the contents to make sure that it hadn't been tampered with.
The bag contained cocaine and it was a large amount.  The larger of the two
Romanians opened the combination lock on the holdall that he was carrying
and dropped it at Andrew's feet. Andrews looked in the bag. There was a lot of
cash in used notes in the bag.
 `All good' he said
The larger of the two men bent down to pick it up the bag to re-lock it.
`Leave the bags and keep walking back to your car' Andrews shouted at them
pointing his gun at them.
The two Romanians reacted in unison. The smaller one's hand went into his
jacket and he pulled out a gun but before he got the chance to use it Andrews
shot him in the face. The other man rushed at Andrews at a speed that belied
his size. He jumped on Andrews and slashed at him with a knife trying to get
Andrews to drop his gun. Andrews' strength was put to the test as they
grappled with each other both trying to use the weapons that they held while
stopping the other using his. Andrews lost his footing on the snow covered
ground and he fell to the ground pulling the Romanian down with him as they
struggled to gain the upper hand. The Romanian's hand got free and he
stabbed at Andrews' neck and shoulder. He had fallen on top of Andrews who
at the same time managed to manoeuvre his gun into a position that enabled
him to fire a shot into the chest of the Romanian as he was stabbing at him
with his knife. He slumped forwards pinning Andrews to the ground by his
dead weight. Blood was pumping out of Andrews neck wounds. He managed to
push the dead Romanian off him but the strength was draining out of him. He
staggered to his feet and went to pick up the two bags. He turned around
shuffling towards Blake's car before falling to the ground holding both bags. He
tried to regain his feet but suddenly fell forwards. His face thudded into the

ground where he remained motionless. Blake had watched this unfold in horror. He was certain that if the two Romanians had got the upper hand he would be dead by now. He sat frozen with shock for five minutes. Andrews hadn't moved. Blake had to get away from the scene. He tried to call the police on his mobile but had no signal. Blake thought about his options. Common sense told him to alert the police and tell them what had happened but he just wanted to get away from the scene which was like something out of a film with three bodies lying around. Blake didn't know if any of the men were alive but he wasn't going to hang around to find out. He had to get his keys back from Andrews' pocket. He thought that the Jamaican had put them in his right hand coat pocket. Blake walked over to where Andrews was laying. There was blood everywhere and he looked as though he was dead. Blake was concerned that the police may think he was involved. If the men were dead he would have loads of questions to answer and no doubt have to spend hours answering them. He walked over to Andrews' body. He bent down and felt for a pulse on Andrews' wrist. He couldn't feel a pulse. Blake had done some basic first aid training many years ago but he wasn't a medical expert. He turned Andrews on to his left side and retrieved the keys. As he got up to go back to the car he noticed that the bag closest to Andrews contained money. It was a large amount of money. He then checked the other bag. It contained what looked like drugs. He had never used drugs and hadn't ever seen any but he had seen plenty of films which showed white drugs in plastic packaging. Blake looked at the scene again. Nobody else was here. Nobody had seen him drive here and if any police cameras had been working on his route to the picnic area surely the snow would have reduced visibility as it had turned into a blizzard since they had left Flixham. There was a large bag of money laying here in the open. 'If I was to take it who would know' he said talking to himself. He had never been in trouble with the police as he had been a law abiding citizen for all of his life. Where had it got him though? He was 43 years old with a broken marriage and renting a small house in a small town in the middle of nowhere. Suppose he took the money and the drugs with him? He thought about it and then changed his mind. What would he do with a bag full of drugs? He changed his mind again. He would just take the money and leave the drugs behind. The snow was heavy and would soon cover his tracks. Before he left he felt for a pulse on the other two bodies. The smaller man's head was a mess and Blake retched at the sight of it. He felt sick but just about managed to avoid throwing up. He was convinced that they were all dead. Temptation had overcome him and for the first time in his life he took something that didn't belong to him. It was a decision that didn't sit easy with him. Twice on the journey back to Flixham he had almost turned around to go back to the picnic site and dump the bag. He was going to give Susan a bollocking in the morning. She had sneaked out while he was talking to Ray Nash but not before she had put a fax on his desk that had been sent earlier in the afternoon. Blake had to spend time re-arranging his schedules to fit in the delivery requests. He didn't leave the office until 6.50 pm .He had to go to Morrison's for food shopping after work and as usual he picked the slowest checkout queue where an old girl in front had vouchers and took ages to pack away so he was running late. He drove straight to The Red Lion from Morrisons. He had wanted to see Helen and was considering asking her out and as he was late he planned to eat there as well. If Susan hadn't sat on the fax he would have been home much earlier and he probably wouldn't have taken the car so he wouldn't be in his current situation. The snow was easing ever so slightly as he arrived back in Flixham. It was 8.50pm when he finally got home. He was starving so he put some fish and chips in the oven and opened a beer.  He opened the holdall and counted the money that it contained. It was rolled up in elastic bands. It totalled £250,000 in £50 and £20 notes. Blake noticed that there was blood on the holdall. He would have to get rid of it. Luckily for him the dustmen were due on Thursday so he could dump it in his green bin. It was almost empty so if he chucked a few bits on top nobody would notice. He carefully checked his clothes to make sure that there were no traces of blood on them. There wasn't but he put the clothes that he had been wearing in the washing machine just to be safe. Fortunately he had been wearing gloves so there would be no trace of his fingerprints on the other holdall which he had briefly touched.

16

It was over half an hour before Hoyte left the scene of his accident. The copper wanted Hoyte's details. He seemed to accept that it was just an accident caused by the conditions. The owner of the car he had hit wanted his insurance details as did the house owner. Hoyte told them both that he had the details at home and that he would return in the morning with them. He would also get the car towed away and asked them if they knew of any garage locally that would do it. He had acted as though he was being genuine but he knew it was bullshit. He would be long gone by morning. His problem for the moment was getting back to his place. He was wearing trainers and a leather jacket. It was snowing heavily but he had no choice but to walk back to his place. He thought about going back to Val. She had little blue Micra. Perhaps she would give him a lift back or lend him the car. He decided against it and set off on the walk home. He was going to have to nick a car when Lynton got back. He wondered who Lynton had persuaded to give him a lift to the trade.

Danny Collins arrived at the hospital just after 615pm. The drive took an age because of the worsening weather. Although conditions were difficult some motorists were over cautious and were driving at ten to fifteen miles per hour. He went straight to the A&E department and told the nurse on reception that his wife and daughter had been brought in earlier after a car accident. The nurse made a phone call and told Collins that a doctor would be out to see him shortly and asked him to wait in the waiting room which was three quarters full. After thirty minutes of what seemed a longer wait the nurse called him to her desk and asked him to follow another nurse who took him into a ground floor ward which seemed to be some sort of extension to A&E where a thin Asian doctor was waiting for him
`Hello Mr Collins I'm Doctor Dawhani. Your wife and daughter were quite fortunate in that they have avoided serious injuries. We suspect that your wife has broken her left wrist and she has had some stitches in a cut to her head. Your daughter was very lucky as I believe that the fire brigade had to cut her out of the vehicle. She has had fourteen stitches applied to a nasty cut on her head and has some sore ribs. She has some bruising to her legs and one of her knees is swollen quite badly but there are no broken bones. We think that it would be advisable if we kept them both in hospital overnight for observation. They both lost conscious after the accident and we want to be on the safe side. You can see your daughter who is in the last cubicle on the left. Your wife is in

the x ray department having her wrist checked. She may be a while as we have many patients to see as there have been several falls on the ice today.'
`Thanks Doctor 'he said relieved that they were both OK. He found Charlotte in a bed looking poorly. Her head had been shaved so that the stitches could be applied. She looked so small and frail laying there. He gave her a kiss and a hug
`Where is mum. Is she OK? I haven't seen her since we came in' Charlotte said tearfully
`She is OK. I haven't seen her yet. She has a few cuts and bruises and they think she may have broken her wrist. She is in the x ray department getting checked out but they say she may be while as it's like a skating rink outside and everyone is slipping over on the ice'
Collins sat with his daughter for about an hour. A nurse then appeared to tell him that his wife was back from X-ray and that he could see her now. He found her in a wheelchair in the waiting room. She had a swollen face and bruising was appearing around both eyes. She also had some small cuts of her forehead which had needed a couple of stitches. She burst into tears when she saw Collins
`Where is Charlotte? They told me she is OK. I thought she had been killed because they had to cut her out. I wouldn't have been able to forgive myself if anything had happened to her. I wasn't driving fast but I lost control of the car'
`She is fine love. She has a nasty cut on her head and some bruises but it seems you both had a lucky escape. Don't blame yourself. It's like a skating rink out there. I saw two cars in the ditch as I drove here. They are going to keep both of you in tonight for observation so I will take you home in the morning.'
`We were very lucky to walk away with just cuts and bruises. My arm isn't broken. It's just badly bruised. I will have to wear a sling for a couple of days'
He sat with his wife for a while. He checked his watch. It was 8.25pm.
`I'm going to have to go. I need to meet somebody' He said winking to his wife.
She was aware of the arrangement that Collins had with the Romanians
`I had forgotten all about that'
`I had to make some last minute changes but it should have worked out' he said in a hushed voice
He asked a nurse if he could take his wife down to see her daughter. She agreed and he left them in tears hugging each other.
Collins went to his car and was relieved to find that the snow was beginning to ease. It was now 8.45pm and he thought that if he drove sensibly he could be back at the Star by 915pm. He phoned both Andrews and Hoyte to check if things had gone smoothly. Neither of them answered their phones. There was usually some signal at the Star but he thought that they may have been

delayed because of the weather. When he eventually arrived at The Star there was no sign of them. He went in and ordered a beer. The place was empty.

`Nobody wants to come out in this weather' Bill the landlord said as he was pulling the pint `I'm surprised to see you so late as well. I was about to close up'

`Paula and Charlotte had an accident on the King's Lynn road and ended up in hospital. Thankfully they have escaped with cuts and bruises. I have just come from there and needed a pint'

Bill expressed his concerns and asked Collins if he had heard the weather forecast.

`Will it mess up your deliveries?' He asked

`The forecast I heard on the local radio said that it would clear through later tonight and then start to warm up tomorrow. With a bit of luck the snow will be gone by tomorrow night'

Twenty minutes had ticked by and there was still no sign of them. He was getting concerned now. He went for a piss and phoned both of them. There was no answer. He phoned Stancvic as a last resort to see if his guys were back yet or if he had heard from them. Stancvic wasn't happy. He said his men were not answering their phones and said that the weather may be causing problems. It was still early enough for them to get back because the conditions would make the journey slower. Collins suggested that his guys may have had an accident which would explain why they were late back to the drop. Stancvic told him that he would call in the morning.

Collins had another pint and left the pub at 1010. They would be back by now he thought to himself. He was starting to panic. What if they had all been arrested at the picnic site? Could they have had an accident or an even worse he thought...had they legged it with the money. He decided that he would drive out to Hoyte's place. Perhaps they had got back on time and saw that Collins wasn't in the pub and presumed that he was still at the hospital so had gone home with the money. Collins convinced himself that this is probably what had happened and felt a bit happier.

By the time Hoyte had walked home he was cold and wet. He turned the gas heater up to full blast. His trainers were wet through and his feet were freezing. He took off his wet socks made a coffee and waited for Lynton to return. When it got to 10pm and he still hadn't showed up he began to get worried. Had things gone wrong at the drop? Had he been caught by the police? Who was the mystery driver? Had Lynton stitched him up and fucked off with the drugs and the money?

It took Collins less than ten minutes to get to Hoyte's place. His Mondeo wasn't there so Collins immediately feared the worse. Hoyte heard the car pull up so he opened the door fully expecting to see Lynton. He hadn't expected it to be Collins.

`Where the fuck is the money' Collins shouted angrily

`Calm down and come inside. I couldn't make the drop. I crashed my fucking car ending up in someone's garden. Lynton text me to say that he had got somebody to drive him to the drop'

`Who was it?' Collins demanded

"Fuck knows. I couldn't get a signal on my mobile. All I got was this text message'

He showed the message to Collins

`I have tried to phone him but there is no reception here and he didn't answer when I phoned him from town after I was finished with the police. I don't know where the fuck he is or who is he is with'

`Why is he involving strangers? You know how this thing works. The less people who know about it the better'

`He probably thinks he made the best out of a bad situation. I got hold of him to tell him that my car was wrecked. I said that we should call you and call it off for tonight. He suggested nicking a car but the police arrived so I had to deal with them. I hit another car and demolished a wall in somebody's front garden. They were not happy'

`Why were you two not together? You knew you had a job to do yet you were off shagging'

Hoyte guessed that Lynton had told Collins where he was when he handed the goods to him.

`A man has got needs' he said `and it isn't as though I have been getting much since I came here'

`What a fucking mess. The Romanians haven't showed up at their bosses place either. They must have all been nicked. That head case in Rotterdam will be after blood if they have'

By midnight Collins, Hoyte and Stancvic had realised that something had gone wrong. Nobody could get an answer from anyone involved in the drop.

Stancvic phoned Collins to say that his men hadn't shown up and Collins told him that his men hadn't either not letting on that only one of them had made the drop. Hopefully they would all get answers in the morning.

17

John Beattie had left the Toyota dealership in Cheshunt early. He wanted to make delivery of the new Toyota Avensis that was needed at another Toyota dealership in Wisbech by 10 o'clock. He had looked at the route and decided that he would stick to the A10 which was very quiet and then take the A1101 up to Wisbech just outside of Ely. Allowing for the conditions he would arrive on time. The snow had stopped and most of the main roads were passable. The A10 wasn't a bad road to get lifts on when he displayed trade plates so he would hopefully get back by lunchtime and do another trip that afternoon. He was self employed and got paid per trip. If he could hitchhike he could save on fares. He had made good time and was on the A1101 by 9.00. He desperately needed a slash so when he saw the sign for a picnic site he pulled into it. There was an area surrounded by trees which was like an oasis in the flat landscape so he drove towards it. He noticed that there was another car parked there and then saw what appeared to be bodies on the ground. Feeling apprehensive he stopped his car and got out. There was a black guy covered in blood laying face down in the snow. Two other men were also on the ground. Beattie went over to the other two and saw one of the men had half of his head blown off. He threw up and ran back to his car to phone the police. He couldn't get a signal. He drove off in the direction of Wisbech until he eventually got two bars on his phone. He dialled 999 and said that he had stopped in a picnic area off the A1101 and had found three bodies in the car park. He was told to go back to the scene and to give a statement to the police when they arrived. He did as he was told and within 15 minutes the picnic site was crawling with police. Daley was on his way to take details of a break in the village of Lakewell when he got the call. He was the first detective to arrive at the scene. Brooks and Perkins arrived in their Panda car soon afterwards. They were told to secure the area by Daley. Everyone put on gloves and shoe covers. Daley pulled on his white paper overalls. He took a statement from Beattie who told him that he had stopped for a piss and found the bodies. He said that he had been sick near the body of the man with his face shot off. Beattie was as white as a sheet. He said that he was on his way to deliver a car to the Toyota dealership in Wisbech when he had stopped for a slash. He hadn't seen any other vehicles near the area other than the dark blue Mercedes that was parked by the trees. Daley looked around the scene. There was a holdall which contained what looked like cocaine left at the scene which immediately struck Daley as being rather odd. There was only one car in the car park which was also odd. He wondered how the three of them had got to the car park The black man looked to have stab wounds to his neck and Daley suspected that his Jugular artery may have been stabbed when he saw the amount of blood around the body. One man had been shot in the head and the other appeared to have several gunshot wounds to the body. DS Linda James from Wisbech was the next to arrive at the scene followed by DCI Booth who assumed charge

` What's the story Arthur?' she barked at Daley getting out of her red Audi.

`It looks like some sort of confrontation between rival gangs. There are three bodies, two with gunshot wounds and one with stab wounds. What is odd is that there is a holdall full of drugs left behind'

`Do you have any idea who they are?'

`The one with half his head missing appears to be Stanislav Petrov. He had a credit card in his wallet and he is the registered owner of the Mercedes. PC Brooks got the details from DVLC. The biggest man has no identification on him but I think the third man is local. I believe that he is somebody that I have seen around Flixham recently. The chief medical examiner had arrived at the scene and said that all three were dead. He suspected that two had died from gunshot wounds and one had died from a loss of blood following a wound to the Jugular artery. His early estimation was that the time of death was between 6pm and 11pm the previous night but he would confirm everything later'.

Booth instructed Daley to confirm that the black man was the same person that he had seen in Flixham and to get a name. He left for Flixham and was happy to do so. Booth would in her element handling a triple murder enquiry. He was best out of it.

18

Danny Collins arrived at the depot just after eight. Blake had arrived a few minutes earlier.

`How are your wife and daughter' Blake asked

`They are OK but Sunday lunch is cancelled' he said without adding anything else as he went into his office closing the door behind him.

Blake thought that Danny had looked awful. He had dark rings under his eyes and looked as though he hadn't slept the night before.

Collins decided to make the call to Petrescu. He told him that he didn't know where the money and the drugs were. Stancvic's men still hadn't shown up and nor had his team.

Petrescu didn't say anything at first as it seemed as though he was thinking about his response to the news.

`I am owed £250,000 for my goods. They were handed to you so you were responsible for them and you have lost them so unless they turn up you owe me for the money that I should have received today and £250,000 to Stancvic for goods that were lost. Stancvic has already been in touch to tell me that he hasn't received his goods'

Collins felt sick.

`How do you know that it isn't Stancvic's men that have the money and the drugs? They haven't shown up anywhere. Why is the blame being put at my door?'

`Stancvic's men have been with him for years and he trusts them like they are his own family. You brought two schwartzers into the set up a few weeks back and all of a sudden the goods have gone missing. That is why the blame is on you. I want my money by the end of the week'

He ended the call leaving Collins white with fear. How the fuck was he going to find money for the two Romanians? He felt angry because it wasn't his fault but he was being blamed.

Hoyte hadn't slept well and had finally got some sleep in the early hours. He woke up at 1000, showered and made himself some coffee. Shortly before 1130 he decided that he would go into town and try to get through to Lynton. The snow had frozen overnight but with the sun out it was starting to melt. It was still slippery and he nearly went over on a couple of occasions. There was an area in Flixham near Goss Road where the signal was strong enough to make calls. Once he had reached this area he was going to phone Lynton to see what the fuck was going on but when he got there he realised that his phone wasn't in his jacket pocket. He cursed because he would have to walk back to his place to get it. He decided to have a coffee and a bacon roll at the bakery that served take away food as well. He sat on a bench in the town centre and was eating his roll when a car pulled up. An old guy in his fifties wearing a grey overcoat and a flat cap got out of the car.

`I'm Detective Sergeant Daley. I need to ask you a couple of questions' he said showing his badge to Hoyte

`What about?' replied Hoyte defensively.

`It's about a man who I think that I have seen you with around the town recently. He is West Indian about five ten and his well built. He has rather large prominent front teeth and a shaved head. Does that sound like anybody you know?'

`Not really 'Hoyte lied, wondering where this is going `Why do you think that I would know him?'

`It's just that he resembles somebody that I have seen you with in Morrison's recently. There are not too many West Indians in town and with you being so tall you tend to stand out a bit. Can I ask you where you were between 6pm and 11pm last night?'

`I was at my girlfriends until 7.30pm and then I crashed my car on the way into town. One of you lot interviewed me at the scene. I think he was called PC May. I was there until 830ish and then I had to walk back to my dad's park home just outside of town. I didn't go out after that because it was snowing and I didn't have a car as mine is stuck in someone's garden in Deehan Road. What has this bloke who you think I know done?'

`I am afraid that he was found dead this morning'

The look of shock on Hoyte's face convinced that he was the same man that he had seen with Hoyte in Morrisons.

`Am I right in thinking that it is your mate?'

Hoyte nodded.

`Can you give me his name and address?'

`His name is Lynton Andrews. We used to share a flat together in Bristol but we moved here in November from there and we have been living at my father's park home.'

`Do you know anybody who might have wanted to cause him any harm'

Hoyte immediately thought of the two Romanians but if he told the copper this he would implicate himself.

`I do' he said. `I think that it may have been a gang leader from Bristol named Basil Smith. We got on the wrong side of him which is the reason we left Bristol and came here. I expect that he has been looking for us'

`Will you come with me down to the police station and give a statement.'
Hoyte agreed.

At the Flixham station Hoyte gave a full statement. He told Daley that Andrews had got into a fight with some of Smith's gang and had beaten them up. Smith was after revenge. He also told Daley that he had been fucking the girlfriend of Smith's second in command. His name was Walter Burnett. Burnett had found out about it and was going to cut Hoyte's balls off if he caught up with him. They decided to get away from Bristol and lay low for a couple of months. Hoyte said that he had traded his car and bought a cheaper model. He said that Andrews had money tucked away so they had moved into Hoyte's father's park home as it was a cheap place to stay. He said that he had been to see his girlfriend that afternoon and had arranged to meet Andrews in the Red Lion where they were going to watch the Chelsea game on TV.  Hoyte said that he didn't drink and was on the way to the pub when he crashed his car. He signed the statement. Daley felt that he was telling the truth.

Hoyte asked him if he was free to go. He said that he would probably leave town and go to stay with his sister and that he needed to get his car sorted out because it was still in the garden that he had crashed it into.

`When are you planning to leave the area'? Daley asked.

`Probably at the weekend' he lied.

 He was out of here as soon as he could steal a car. There were several VW's on the estate where Val lived and they were easy to nick.

`Where was Lynton found' He asked

`He was found in a picnic area outside of town. Do you have any idea what he was doing there? '

`I would guess that Smith took him somewhere quiet before he killed him'

 Hopefully Smith would get lifted by the police and be made aware that Lynton was dead. He hoped that this would result in Smith's gang calling off the search for him. He was released from the station and made his way back to the park home. He didn't know where he was going to go. He thought about going to his sister's place in Watford but considered this to be somewhere that Smith would be watching. Perhaps he could go back to Edmonton and crash at one of his old mates places. He was going to have to nick a car as soon as it got dark so he had a while to think about his next move.


It was almost one thirty by the time he had finished giving his statement. He couldn't face going back to the park home just yet so he called into the Red Lion and ordered pie and chips. The pub was unusually busy for a Wednesday lunch hour so he had to wait for twenty five minutes before his meal arrived. There was a lot of chatter in the pub about the incident at the picnic site. He overheard some ridiculous versions of what was supposed to happen. He just sat quietly drinking his coke. Although he could be an awkward bastard Lynton was a good mate to him. He would miss him. He felt very lonely in a place with no friends. He called Val on her mobile but her phone went straight to voicemail. He didn't leave a message. He left the Red Lion at two thirty and started the walk back to the park home. It had become very overcast and Hoyte wondered if it was going to snow again. It was dark for the time of day and he had to be careful when walking along the road for the last half mile to the site. There were no footpaths on this section of the road. When he got home he saw a black Range Rover with dark windows parked in the far end of the car park. The park home site, which housed a dozen homes, had been empty for the whole time that he had been staying there. He thought that an owner may have come to check out a home because of the snow. He didn't give it a second thought. It was getting quite dark now even though it was just after three. He still felt hungry so he popped the last pizza that was in the freezer into the oven and made a cup of tea. He was just about to drink it when there was a knock on the door. He immediately thought that it was the police but when he opened it he got the shock of his life. Before he could turn to run he was grabbed by a man who he recognised at Walter Burnett. Burnett punched him in the stomach and then in the face and dragged him into the living room. Another two men got out of the Range Rover and entered the park home. One was huge and stood about six foot seven in height. It was Basil Smith.

'Did you think that you could hide from us in this shit hole? Where is Andrews?' Smith asked

'He is dead. Somebody killed him last night at a picnic site about ten miles from here. I have just been taken down to the police station for questioning. They said that they will want to ask me more questions later. I thought it was them when you knocked on the door. They may be watching this place for all I know'

It wasn't the answer Smith was expecting

'You had better be telling the truth Lover Boy' Smith replied menacingly. 'Do you know who did it?'

'No I haven't got a clue' he lied not wanting to let on what Andrews and himself had been doing while in Norfolk 'I didn't want to leave Bristol but Lynton forced me to. You know what a head case he can be. He has been in several fights here already. Perhaps he pissed off somebody else. He said he would beat the shit out of me if I didn't drive him out here. I'm sorry about screwing your bird Walter but she told me that you had dumped her. I wouldn't take liberties with you ...Honest.'

One of Smith's men spoke and mentioned that he thought he had heard something about a triple murder near here on the radio a bit earlier.

`Where is your car?' Smith asked ` I noticed that you walked here'

`In someone's front garden in Flixham. I slid off the road last night and wrecked a wall. The police want to talk to me about that as well. I half expected it to be them when I opened the door to you' he said repeating the warning that the police may be turning up at any minute. `I was supposed to meet Lynton and drive him out to the picnic site where he had set up some deal.'

`What was the deal that Lynton was doing?'

`He was delivering a package for some dodgy businessman. I didn't trust the guy but Lynton was happy to earn some money from it. We were both potless so he was keen to earn. I was just the driver so other than that I don't know any more'.

`What's the name of this businessman?'

`I'm not sure, I think he was called Danny something or other. I never got to speak to him '

Smith nodded to Burnett and left the room with his other men. Burnett was about six foot tall and around seventeen stone of solid muscle. Hoyte realised what was about to happen and it wasn't going to end well for him

Burnett said `I'm going to teach you to leave your cock in your pants

Suddenly he kicked Hoyte in the balls and then continued to beat the shit out of him. He left him unconscious in a heap on the floor covered in blood. Another member of the gang searched the park home but found nothing worth taking. He did however take Hoyte's untouched pizza which was just about ready. He was hungry and hadn't eaten all day. Smith and his gang left and started back on the long drive to Bristol.

19

The incident room at Kings Lynn station was buzzing. Booth had called the meeting for 0800 on Thursday which required the presence of her team and some help from Wisbech CID.

'As you know we have a murder enquiry on our hands. Three males, two white Caucasians and an Afro Caribbean were found dead at a picnic site on the A1101 yesterday morning. The men have been identified as Stanislav Petrov aged 39 of 141 Nene Road Peterborough, Adrian Dumetrescu aged 34 last known address 11 Orton Road Peterborough and lastly Lynton Andrews 33, originally from Bristol but believed to have living at a park home near Flixham since November. The pathologist reports show that Petrov died of a gunshot wound to the head. Dumetrescu died of gunshot wounds to the body. Andrews died of stab wounds to the neck and upper body. One of the stab wounds severed his jugular artery and he died from a loss of blood. The pathologist states that death occurred between 1900 and 2200 on Tuesday evening. Ballistics show that the same gun was used to kill Petrov and Dumetrescu who were known employees of this man, Bogdan Stancvic'

She pointed to a picture on the board of a hard faced white male with thinning hair.

'Stancvic is suspected to be the major supplier of drugs in Peterborough'

'Why is he still walking the street than Ma'am?' asked DC Clarissa Marks of the Kings Lynn's team

'That's because he is a very shrewd operator Skid. He covers his tracks' replied Booth using Marks' nickname knowing that she hated it. 'He is far too clever to be caught by the likes of you' she snapped at her causing Marks to blush with embarrassment.

'Can I continue now or has anybody else got any stupid questions?' Nobody answered.

'The gun which was used to shoot Demetrescu and Petrov was found at the scene with Andrews prints all over it. The knife wounds suffered by Andrews match that of a knife found at the scene which had Dumetrescu's prints all over it. It all points to a fight involving the three dead men and that somehow they managed to kill each other. At this stage we don't know how many others were at the scene and whether the aftermath has been stage managed. The question is "Why were the drugs left at the scene?" Lynton Andrews appears to be the key to this puzzle. Andrews has been staying in Flixham for the past three months with this man Dennard Hoyte' pointing to a picture that had been taken of Hoyte the previous day at the Flixham station.

`Arthur interviewed him yesterday. He claims that he doesn't know what Andrews was doing at the picnic site. He said that he dropped Andrews off at the Three Feathers in Flixham at 330pm and arranged to meet him later in the Red Lion to watch the football on TV. Hoyte also claims that he was with a woman named Valerie Davey yesterday afternoon and that he crashed his car into a wall in Deehan Road at 1940 on Tuesday evening when on his way from her flat to meet Andrews. This has been confirmed by the officer at the scene, PC May, who said that Hoyte was at the scene of the accident until around 2030. His car is still in the garden at number 59 Deehan Road so we can assume that he wasn't present at the scene at the time of the murders'

`Unless he can run like Linford Christie' DS Mick Judge said `or more appropriately ski like Alberto Tomba'. This raised a few chuckles from the team Booth turned and ripped into him

`This is a fucking serious matter DS Judge so no more stupid jokes. I haven't ruled out Hoyte as a suspect yet. He claims that a Basil Smith from Bristol may have been involved.  Smith is suspected of being a major drugs dealer in Bristol. Andrews apparently crossed Smith and both Hoyte and Andrews were hiding from him in Flixham.  I also want to interview Ion Rodescu and Ilie Radu, two known small time Romanian's who have a history of selling small quantities of drugs. As you know Rodescu received a kicking from somebody in Flixham on October 25th and Radu was shot in Flixham on November 23rd. Both of them appear to have moved away from the Flixham area. I want this cleaned up quickly so I am giving each of you specific tasks. Report any significant findings back to me as soon as possible. DI Green, get in touch with Bristol CID straight away and find out all that you can about this Smith character. Find out where he was on Tuesday. I'm not convinced that he was involved because cocaine with a street value of half a million was left at the scene but I need to rule him out. Di Franklin, I want you to track down Ion Rodescu. DS Brown, you do the same for Radu. He isn't long out of hospital but he has moved on. DS James, who some of you know from Wisbech, I need you to find out all that you can about Stancvic's recent activity. I want to know where he was on the night of Tuesday 27th January. Liaise with Peterborough on this. I have spoken with Chief Superintendent Steve Whalley of Peterborough CID and he will give you all the help that he can. Take DC Ring with you. DS Judge, seeing that you are full of jokes you can go through the CCTV between Flixham and Peterborough to see if you can track the movements of a dark blue Mercedes 280. Its number plates are DD54STR. We have recovered  three mobile phones from the scene so DC Butler speak to the phone companies and get them to send us the phone records for these phones. We may be lucky if they are not burners. I want to find out who they have been talking to. Arthur, I want you to interview anybody who was in the Red Lion and the Three Feathers on Tuesday afternoon and evening. Check the shops as well to see if anybody saw anyone with Andrews or Hoyte. Skid you can arrange an interview with Valerie Davey to confirm that Hoyte's story seeing that Arthur hadn't already thought to do that. After you have done that check out the CCTV in Flixham to see if there is any decent coverage of the Three Feathers and The Red Lion. If Andrews was dropped into town by Hoyte how did he end up at the picnic site? Did he get a ride with someone? Or did he steal a car?'

Daley started to protest against Booth's comment

`Valerie Davey is a married woman. I didn't want to interview her with her husband present to avoid embarrassing her'

`I have a triple murder enquiry to investigate. I couldn't give a toss if her old man finds out that she has been shagging around. If she wants to play away she should suffer the consequences.' Booth shouted angrily at Daley.

Daley didn't fail to notice that Booth referred to everyone by their rank and surname except for himself and Clarissa Marks. She never called anybody by their Christian names. It was a particular trait of hers. Marks appeared to be as popular with Booth as he was. He wondered what she had done to get into Booth's bad books.

By 0900 all of the team were off to do their appointed tasks. Something was bothering Daley. It was the number plate of the dark blue Mercedes. It rang a bell and he couldn't think where he knew it from. He was thinking about it on the trip back to Flixham when it suddenly dawned on him. His wife Bev often made up silly sentences about car number plates especially if the car was doing something daft. He never paid any attention to them though but DD54STR did stick in his mind because her silly sentence was quite funny. Back in November they had popped into the butchers shop in Flixham just before it closed. When they came out a car had parked really close in front of them making it difficult to get out. Somebody come out of the newsagents, got in the car and had driven off.

`Look at that number plate Bev had laughed DD54STR - Dave Daley 54 Soon to Retire' she had said.

The dark blue Mercedes had been in Flixham on the day that Ilie Radu had been shot. Daley didn't believe in coincidences. The probability was that that the two incidents were somehow linked. He would need to report this back to

Booth but she can bloody well wait until I have made enquiries around the town he thought to himself...

Clarissa Marks hated Booth. She had transferred to Kings Lynn from Cambridge nine months ago following her promotion to Detective Constable. She went to a private school and her accent was what her colleagues called posh. She was aged 28, single, tall and thin with lank shoulder length brown hair. She was very much a Plain Jane. She had done well in her first few months as a DC and had been instrumental in the arrest of a gang of car thieves operating throughout East Anglia. Booth, it seemed resented her success and had given her a hard time ever since. She drove to Flixham and went straight to the address that was given to her as being that of Valerie Davey. It was 0952 and she doubted that anyone would be at home. She rang the bell for the flat and a man answered. Marks announced who she was, showing her badge and asked if she could come in as she wanted a word with Mrs Davey.

`She is at work and she won't be home until after five. I am Peter Davey, her husband'

`Can I come in as I need to ask you some question too'

Davey pressed the door release button and shortly afterwards Marks was knocking on his door. Davey let her in. He was a slim man about five nine with curly blond hair and blue eyes. Marks thought that he was cute. The flat was small but it was nicely decorated and appeared to be neat and tidy.

`What does this about? Is Val in trouble?'

`Somebody claims to have been with her last Tuesday afternoon and evening and we need to check his alibi. Do you know this man Dennard Hoyte? She showed him a copy of Hoyte's photo'

Davey studied the picture wondering why this man had been linked to his wife `No I have seen him around the town but I don't know him. Why would he claim to have been with my wife? She would have been at work on Tuesday afternoon. I was working away and only got home last night'

`Where does she work' Marks asked noting down the name of the firm that Davey had given to her. Feeling a little spiteful after her treatment from Booth and feeling a little sorry for Mr Davey she continued

`Is it possible that your wife is having an affair? Are things good with you at home?'

`Things are fine with us' Davey replied reacting angrily `we have rows like everyone else does but she would never have an affair and especially with a black man. She says they don't appeal to her'

`Ok. Thank you for your time. I will try to speak to your wife at work.'

Marks left him stewing. She would love to have been a fly on the wall when Val Davey got home from work. She thought that Hoyte was a good looking bloke and she would have had no hesitation of a bit of fun and games with him given the chance. She drove straight to the builder's merchants on the outskirts of Kings Lynn where Val worked and found her on the reception area Marks had showed her ID card and asked her if she could speak to Mrs Valerie Davey

`That's me' Val replied `How can I help you?'

`Is there anywhere quiet where we can talk? It's a bit busy here and I don't want anyone to overhear us as the question is a bit delicate'

Val led them to a small kitchen area which contained a Formica topped table and a few chairs. The room was empty.

`What is this about?'

`Do you know this man?' Marks asked showing the picture of Hoyte

Davey studied the picture and hesitated before answering

`I have seen him in the Red Lion a couple of times. He bought me a drink once'

`When did you see him last'

`Not for ages. It must be before Christmas'

`He claims that he was with you at your flat on Tuesday afternoon and evening.'

Davey was flustered and she could feel herself blushing

`He is talking bullshit. He has never been to my flat. I have just had a drink with him in the Red Lion and that is it.'

`He claims that he was with you between 4pm and 730pm when he left to meet up with his mate in the Red Lion. He crashed his car into a wall just around the corner from your flat. How did he know your address if he has never been to your flat'

Davey hesitated. She was worried and didn't speak for a few seconds. She started to cry before saying.

`I am sorry. He was at my flat. I don't want my husband to find out'

`I'm afraid that it is too late. I called at your flat before I came here and I told your husband that Hoyte claimed that he was with you. I'm sorry if I may have dropped you in it' said Marks with a smirk. She thought that Peter Davey was a good looking bloke and thought Val was out of order messing around with another man.

Davey started to sob loudly.

`You bitch. You are enjoying this aren't you? He is going to go mad when I see him'

Marks confirmed with Davey that she had been with Hoyte for about three hours. She left her bawling her eyes out and headed back to the small station at Flixham to begin a job that she hated, scouring through hours of CCTV footage. She had agreed to meet with Arthur there at 3pm before reporting their findings back to Surly Shirley

20

Daley made enquiries in the local shops before calling on the two pubs. Nothing of any use was gleaned from his enquiries. He interviewed the staff in the Three Feathers first arriving just after 1100. The landlord confirmed that Andrews had been in there on Tuesday afternoon. He said that Andrews had ordered food and had a few beers. He said that he sat alone and looked unhappy. The landlord told Daley that Andrews had a reputation for being aggressive so the few regulars that were in that afternoon avoided him. He said that he thinks that he left around 5pm. Daley went from the Three Feathers directly to the Red Lion

The manager at the Red Lion also confirmed that Andrews had come in before the football which started at 6pm. He was also aware of Andrews' reputation as he had been involved in a couple of brief fights in the pub in the past and that Andrews had been the instigator of the fights. He sat in one of the booths that had small TV's in them and was watching the football. He left at around 730pm. The landlord said that he thought that is was strange that he left before the end of the football match. He had watched most of the game which was a draw so why go with about 15 minutes to go. He was also carrying a holdall. Daley asked the landlord if he could describe the holdall

`Not really. It looked like one of those that you took to football training or to the gym although I doubt it as he had a couple of pints while he was here'

`Do you have cameras in here?'

`Yes we do. Do you want to see the footage? Is Andrews involved with that shoot out near Welney?"

News had leaked out about the incident. The local radio station seemed to have good information and led Daley to wonder who their source was. PC Brooks immediately sprang to mind.

` I can't comment on an active enquiry but I would like to see your footage'

The manager took Daley into an office at the back of the pub. He was the only person serving in the pub so he told the two old men in the bar that he would be away from the bar for a couple of minutes.

He put the disc in the machine. It showed that Andrews ordered a beer at the bar at 17.24 and went to a small booth. It showed him taking a phone call at 1733. He went out of the back of the bar with the phone to his ear. When he returned five minutes later it clearly showed Andrews holding a holdall that looked identical to the one containing the drugs that was found at the picnic site. At 1937pm Andrews left the bar by the back entrance carrying the holdall. He had done this several times after 7pm. Daley initially thought that Andrews had gone to the toilet again. Perhaps he had a weak bladder. He never returned to the bar. It confirmed to Daley that Andrews was probably the drugs courier. What he didn't know was where he got them from and how he got to the picnic site. It occurred to Daley that Hoyte was supposed to meet Andrews and accompany him to the picnic site. Instead he had crashed his car on the way. He was going to have another word with Hoyte. He thanked the manager for his help and left the pub. He drove straight to Hoyte's place. He knocked on the door but there was no answer. He looked through the window but there was no sign of him but the lights were on. Daley tried the front door. It was unlocked so warily he went in. He went into a bedroom at the back of the home and found Hoyte in a bad way on the floor in his bedroom. His face was swollen and there was blood on his clothes from a mouth wound. He asked Hoyte who had done this but his answer was incoherent. It looked as though he had lost several teeth and there were cuts that would need stitches. He had received a severe beating. Daley had no signal on his phone so he radioed the station and asked them to get an ambulance sent to Hoyte's place. It arrived at 1456. Daley waited for it to arrive. He tried to make Hoyte comfortable but there were no items of first aid in Hoyte's place.

DC Marks spent the best part of two hours looking through the CCTV available in Flixham. She picked up Andrews leaving the Three Feathers at 1706 .He called into the Martin Newsagent and came out eating a chocolate bar. It was snowing and he was hunched up against the cold.  She then saw him going into the Red Lion at 1721. The car park at The Three Feathers was accessed from Main Street and was empty from 4pm onwards. The car park in the Red Lion was accessed by a side street off of Main Street so it wasn't covered by the CCTV cameras. No other sightings of Andrews were seen.
Daley got back to Flixham station at 1548
`Hi Clarissa sorry I'm late. I have just found Hoyte in a bad way on the floor at his place. He has had a right kicking and has been taken to the Queen Liz. He wasn't in any fit state to answer questions so I have no idea who did it.'
Marks immediately thought of Peter Davey. Would he have gone after Hoyte? Probably not she thought. He didn't look as though he could handle himself.
`I spoke with both Peter and Valerie Davey separately. Valerie was at work when I went to her house so I spoke to Peter first. I inadvertently let it slip that Hoyte had claimed that he was with her on Tuesday evening. Peter was away on business .Do you think that he could have been responsible for beating up Hoyte? He could have gone straight round to Hoyte's place after I interviewed him. Did he already know that his wife was having an affair?'
`I doubt it but I won't rule it out as a possibility. It looked as though Hoyte had been injured for quite some time but until we speak with him we won't know

for certain. Hoyte is a big unit. I don't know Peter Davey. Do you think that he is capable of giving Hoyte a hiding?'

'He is quite slim bloke but who knows what he is capable of once he found out that his wife was shagging around. He may have already known before I let it slip but if he did he must be a bloody good actor because he looked both shocked and surprised when I asked him if he thought his wife was having an affair'

'Did CCTV throw up anything?'

'Not really. It shows Andrews leaving the Three Feathers at 1706 and going into the Red Lion at 1721 after buying some chocolate in the newsagents but that's it. Both pubs were fairly quiet with only a handful of people going in. The weather seems to have put people off'

'Was Andrews carrying a holdall at any time?'

'Not that I noticed. He scoffed a bar of chocolate but after he had his hands in his pockets, shoulders hunched.'

'I saw him on the Red Lion's surveillance camera with a holdall. He didn't appear to have one when he came in but he came back from the toilet area with one at 1742. Does the CCTV have any decent views of the Alder Street where you access the Red Lion car park?'

'Yes but it's from a distance. What are you looking for?'

'Somebody driving or on foot going in and out of Alder Street between 1735 and 1750'

Marks loaded up the relevant disc. The images were blurred as it had started to snow and it was blowing into the lens of the camera. Just two cars entered and left Alder Street in that time period but both arrived and left within two minutes of each other. One was a white or silver Range Rover and it was followed shortly after by a dark coloured car which looked like a Ford Orion. It wasn't possible to read the number plates of either car.

'I'm going back to the Red Lion. I want to check the pub's cameras again to see if anybody came or left by the back entrance at that time'.

Marks went with him. They asked the manager if they could have a look at the camera images again for the period 1735 and 1750. They showed Andrews leaving and coming back with the bag and another man wearing a dark coat leaving before Andrews returned the bar. He never came back.

'Who is that man? Daley asked pointing at the man in the dark coat

The manager looked at the image

'That is David McLean, one of our regulars. He comes in at a couple of minutes after 5pm most days and has a quick pint or two. He is usually in here for about forty minutes. His wife works as a dental receptionist. She finishes work at 530pm and she picks him up on the way home from work. They live in Dockham, a village a couple of miles out of town.'

The barman looked at his watch. It was 458pm.

'He may be in any minute now. Can I get you a drink if you want to wait?'

They both ordered a coffee.

Sure enough at 1703 McLean walked in. He was probably in his fifties, about five feet seven, overweight with a shock of white hair.

The manager said 'Pint, David?'

'Yes please Pat I could murder one'

Daley walked to the bar. He showed his ID badge.

'Can I have a quick word Mr McLean?'

McLean looked disturbed

'What is it about? I haven't done anything'

'You are not in any trouble. We just wanted to ask you about Tuesday evening to eliminate you from our enquiries'

McLean looked relieved

'What about Tuesday evening? I came in here as usual after work and had two quick pints. My wife Alice picked me up out in the car park about quarter to six. I didn't drive home' he added as an after thought

'What type of car does your wife drive?'

'It's our car. It's a dark green Ford Orion. Why?'

'It's as I said. It is so that we can eliminate it from our enquiries. Did you notice anybody else in the car park at the same time?'

'No but some black geezer came barging past as I was going out to the car park He nearly knocked me over. I nearly said something but I have heard that he is a lunatic. If I was twenty years younger though I would have had a go at him' McLean replied with bravado.

'Thanks Mr Mclean that is all we need from you. We will leave you to enjoy your beer'

Daley and Marks quickly finished their coffee and left.

'Booth wants us all in for a briefing tomorrow. Have you reported back to her yet?' Marks asked

'No I haven't. I will phone her when I get home. She seems to like you as much as she likes me. What have you done to upset her?'

'God knows but she really has it in for me. There are rumours that she is going to send me out here after you retire'

'Flixham is fine if you want a quiet life. It suits me with just a few months to go but it's no place for somebody with your obvious talent. You deserve better than a dead end like here'

`Thanks Gov. I am thinking about asking for a transfer. I am so frustrated. All she gives me are the shit jobs'

`Let's go back to the station and have a look through the CCTV footage to see if we can see any activity after 1930 pm. Andrews ended up dead in the car park of the picnic site but we don't know how he got there'

They spent the next hour looking at the footage. Only a couple of cars went into Alder Street but with the snow falling heavily it was difficult to get a reliable image. What appeared to be the same car drove into and out of Alder street at between 1946 and 1953. The car appeared to be a dark hatchback but both Daley and Marks couldn't be sure what model it was. Snow had settled on the roof and the bonnet of the car. There was no chance of reading the number plate.

`Let's call it a night' Daley eventually said

` See you tomorrow at the 'Shirley Show'. She finished her coffee and left for home

Daley went straight home too. He phoned Booth on his landline and updated her on what he and Marks had unearthed.

After consulting with Superintendant Alan Dillon her boss at Kings Lynn Booth held a press conference at 1700 on Thursday afternoon. She told the press that three bodies had been discovered at a picnic site on the A1101. She said that the police had recovered cocaine with a street value of a half million pounds. She told the journalists that the police teams at Peterborough and Wisbech were also assisting with the crimes which appeared to be gang related. She answered questions without giving anything away.

Dillon was a year away from retirement. He was a very fussy person and he could be very slow when making a decision. His nickname "Decisive" was filled with irony. Booth had her eyes on his job when he retired so she was keen to make an impression on those who would be selecting Dillon's replacement.

21

Booth started the briefing at 0830 sharp on Friday. She was in a better mood than the previous day.

`Good morning team. We have made some progress. We are now reasonably confident that Lynton Andrews took the cocaine to the crime scene. We can assume that they were intended to be handed over to Petrov and Dumetrescu. He has been picked up on CCTV in Flixham on Tuesday afternoon leaving the Three Feathers without a holdall but appears on camera at the Red Lion with a holdall at 1744. It would appear that he possibly met somebody driving a white or silver Range Rover in the car park at Red Lion. Unfortunately there are no cameras covering the car park but we have the Range Rover entering Alder Street at 1741 and leaving at 1745. There was another car entering and leaving Alder Street at the same time but this car had been eliminated from our enquiries. The images are poor due to the weather but there can't be too many white or silver Range Rovers in the area so that is something we will have to chase. We also recovered four mobile phones from the crime scene. Three were PAYG's so there are no details of the owners. The fourth appears to be Andrews' phone. It seems that Andrews' PAYG received several calls from one number. Interestingly one was received at 1733 which is when Andrews was in the Red Lion. He received several calls from this number after 2055 but they were never answered. Another number appears several times on Tuesday afternoon and evening on his other phone. A single call was made to another number at 1943 which wasn't answered but they called back at 1945. The call lasted less than 20 seconds. This was also to a PAYG phone. Calls were made at 1915, 1918 and 1921 to a number which was answered at 1941. A text message was sent to this number at 2002. The message was"PROBLEM SORTED I GOT a LIFT WILL XPLAIN LATER CU AT OUR PLACE AT 9". I would put money on this number being that of Dennard Hoyte which we are assuming is the D in his contact list. Hoyte was found at his place yesterday by Arthur. He had received a kicking. His phone wasn't there so I am assuming that whoever did this to him took his phone. All of the numbers that were found on the PAYG phones, and there wasn't many of them, were called by the police but all were switched off. One call was made by Andrews to a landline number in Bristol last week. That is his mother's home number, Mum in his contact list. Another was made to a contact entered as JQ. This is Joseph Quinlan who shared a cell with Andrews at Cardiff prison four years ago. DI Green made the contact. Perhaps you could fill us in on what Quinlan had to say?

DI Green stood up

`Quinlan says that he had only heard from Andrews once before last week's phone call since he had left Cardiff prison. He said that Andrews asked him if he and a mate could crash at Quinlan's place in Liverpool for a couple of days. Quinlan said that he had reluctantly agreed. He said that Andrews had helped him in prison and that Andrews was calling in the favour. It would appear that Andrews and Hoyte were heading for Liverpool some time on Wednesday. Could it be that they had planned to steal the drugs from the Romanians and scarper. Obviously something went wrong when Hoyte crashed his car. If this was the case how the hell did Andrews get to the picnic site.'? The DVLC have no record of a driving licence for Andrews either and no record of any cars registered in his name. It is not known if he can actually drive.'

Booth continued with the briefing

`Bogdan Stancvic was in Peterborough on Tuesday night. He was in a restaurant with his girlfriend so he was not directly involved. Chief Supt. Whalley says that Petrov and Dumetrescu are said to have been pretty low level employees of Stancvic. They are thought to have been muscle but don't have any custodial sentences on the records. They both came to the UK in 2005. Petrov is married with three children. Dumetrescu is unmarried but thought to be in a long term relationship. Both men have a history of low level violence.

Next subject is the car. Thanks to Arthur's wife tendency to make up phrases from number plates we have discovered that this car was in Flixham on November 23rd which is the day Radu was shot. Could Petrov and Dumetrescu be the people responsible for shooting him? It would make sense because Rodescu and Radu were small time dealers. The feeling at the time was that the shooting was drugs related. Unfortunately the bullets recovered from the Radu shooting are not a match for the gun that was found in Petrov's possession.

Next we turn to Basil Smith. He was picked up on CCTV leaving Bristol on Tuesday morning. He was seen getting into a black Range Rover with three other men who have been identified as Walter Burnett, Lester Shillingford and Albert Rowe. Burnett is believed to be second in command in Smith's gang. Shillingford and Rowe are both believed to be high ranking members of the gang. They were recorded on the ANPR system in Balham, South London at 1429 on Tuesday afternoon. The weather worsened on Tuesday afternoon and no further sightings were picked up until Wednesday afternoon at 1650 when they were seen heading north on the A10 outside of Ely. They could have been in the area on Tuesday night but we have no concrete evidence of this. Dennard Hoyte claims that he and Andrews were hiding from Smith's gang.

Were they seen in Flixham on Thursday? Arthur found Hoyte in a bad way in his home. He had received a severe beating. I think that based on what evidence we have Smith and his gang need to be brought in for questioning. I have issued a warrant for their arrest. They will be arrested when they return to Bristol. I will be going to Bristol to conduct the interviews in conjunction with Bristol CID. DC Butler will be coming with me. As I said yesterday it seems odd that drugs were left at the scene. Why would Smith, a known drug dealer, leave them behind?'

`Di Franklyn and DS Brown are to continue tracking down Rodescu and Radu. The rest of you need to concentrate on Smith's gang. Have they been seen in and around Flixham between Tuesday and Thursday? Check local hotels to see if they stayed anywhere on Tuesday or Wednesday night... Check the CCTV footage again to see if their car shows up anywhere. Are there any questions?' There were none. She closed the briefing.

22

Blake arrived home from work later than usual on Wednesday evening. He usually left the depot by five thirty but the weather had caused problems and several deliveries arrived late. Some of the smaller roads were difficult to drive on and had delayed the journey for some of the drivers. He put a Cottage pie and some chips in the oven and made himself a cup of tea. He counted the money from the holdall again. He had spent the day thinking about what to do with it. He decided that he wouldn't start spending it until he received the money from his mother's house. It could draw unwanted attention to him. He thought that it might be best if he were to hide the money in one of the drawer's under his bed and then move it to a safe place in a week or two's time. The question was where could he move it to? He had to think of a plan so that he could use the money. Money laundering was a hot topic at the moment. His cottage pie and chip were ready so he thought about what he could do while he ate. He had a good feeling about his job at Collins Transport. Danny more or less let him get on with organising things. The company appeared to be doing well. He thought that he would buy a house locally once the probate money came through. He could put down a large deposit but keep back £25,000 which he was going to keep in his bank account. He could take out a small mortgage for the difference. He didn't want to pay cash for his new house because it could draw attention. Initially he planned to open up several building society accounts and an ISA. Every week or so he could draw cash out of his current account and put most of it in his savings accounts. At the same time he would take a similar amount from the stolen money and use this for everyday spending. He would buy a newer car feeling sure that one of the many small car dealers in the area wouldn't ask questions if they were offered cash for a car. They would probably be pleased of the chance to record false amounts especially if he used his old Astra in part exchange. Dealers were in the habit of bumping up the value of part exchanges so that they could reduce the amount that they actually received for the car they sold. He planned to give Ellie and Wayne some money as well. He had decided that he would give them a thousand pounds each in cash and another two thousand pounds each later when they passed their upcoming exams.
After he had finished his meal and washed up the dishes he considered walking down to the Red Lion for a pint. Helen worked Tuesdays Wednesdays and Thursday. He toyed with the idea of asking her if she would like to go for a curry on Saturday evening. She still hadn't mentioned a man in her life or any children. He would try to bring children into the conversation tonight. He expected that the pub would be dead tonight but then remembered that

Manchester United were playing a champions league game so there might be a few in so he decided against it. He would have a chance to talk to her during the quiz night tomorrow. He opted for a night in front of the TV and an early night.

The next morning he drove to work early. Ray Nash was already in and was working on one of the Luton Vans.

`Have you got any plans for Saturday night?' Nash asked. `It's my 50th and I'm having a bit of a bash down at the sports pavilion. I have got a band playing. My missus has laid on lots of food. There will be a few spare women there too unless you want to bring somebody along. The word is that you have been sniffing round that barmaid in the Red Lion. You will be alright there mate. She is supposed to be a bit of a girl'

`Cheers Ray. I don't have any plans for Saturday yet. Who says that I have been sniffing around the barmaid? I only joined up with her in a quiz team'

`Flixham is a small town mate. You can't keep any secrets here. Order a takeaway and half the town will hear about it. I will need one of the low loaders in for a service next week. The driver reckons it sounds a bit ropey. The registration number is ND54 TKC'

`OK I will see what I can do'

He left Ray working and went to his office. He hadn't considered the small town gossip. If he started to spend money it would get noticed based on what Ray had just said. Perhaps he ought to consider Kings Lynn for a permanent home. It wasn't that far away from work but it was a big enough town not to attract attention if he was spending money. He was also worried about what Ray had said about Helen. Was she putting it around? She seemed very friendly with the men but he would reserve judgement until he got to know her better.

As usual Blake's day flew by. He got home by five thirty. He showered shaved and put on some of the new clothes he had bought when he left Mansfield. He splashed on some Tommy Hilfiger aftershave that Ellie had got him for Christmas the year before and went down the Red Lion. He was going to eat in there tonight. Thanks to his sudden windfall he didn't need to worry about not spending any money. When he arrived at seven thirty the place seemed a bit busier than usual. Perhaps the quiz was getting a following. There was liver and onions of the specials board so he ordered this from Helen. She was wearing a tight light blue top and jeans which showed off her shapely body

`We will have a team of four tonight. I have a couple of mates coming. They will be here shortly so after you have finished eating grab a seat at the bar'

Blake was nervous but he got Helen's attention.

`Before it gets too busy there is something I want to ask you '

Helen seemed intrigued

`What is it?'

`Can I ask you if you are doing anything on Saturday night? One of the men I work with is having a 50<sup>th</sup> birthday party down at the sports ground. He is invited me along and said to bring a friend. I don't have many here yet so I was wondering if you would like to join me'

`That's very sweet of you Bob but I have got a new boyfriend and I am going to his place next weekend. You should go though because there will be plenty of people there. I knew about the party. Ray Nash is popular. He knows everyone. His wife runs a keep fit class so there will be lots of her class there. Some of them are unattached. You will be OK. You are not bad looking and you will be seen as fresh meat' she said with a smile

Blake's knew that his hopes with Helen ended immediately after hearing her say this. Her two mates showed up about five minutes before the quiz started. They were both crude and loud and spent the whole evening dropping innuendos about their sex lives. Helen was in her element laughing and joking with them about the size or rather the lack of size, of one of Helen's ex boyfriend's manhood. It was an awkward evening for Blake and he was relieved when the quiz was over. They came second from last and he may as well have been on his own because Helen's mates were not the sharpest tools in the box. Karen, the loudest of the pair, thought that the answer to the question "what is the state capital of Pennsylvania" was Florida. He finished his pint and went home feeling foolish for thinking that Helen fancied him. He did find out that she had an ex husband but It was a long time since he was on the lookout for women and he was out of his comfort zone when it came to trying to chat them up. Perhaps he would have to try the internet dating that he had heard about.

23

Ds Marks spent the rest of Friday morning studying CCTV footage for Tuesday and Wednesday again. Visibility was hampered by the snow on Tuesday evening. By 1930 the cameras were rendered useless as the snow was so heavy. The cameras facing directly into the wind had snow on the lenses and for about two hours it was impossible to get any images from the remaining cameras. Very few cars were on the road anyway and even fewer people ventured out apart from the dark hatchback that they had spotted the day before. She saw the Range Rover several times. It went into Collins Transport on Tuesday morning and again on Wednesday. On both days it was seen coming out of the depot at around 1730. She checked some footage from other cameras and was convinced that this was the car that had gone in and out of Alder Street on Tuesday evening. There were a couple of dark coloured hatchbacks seen going into and out of the depot as well but none that she could definitely identify as being the same car that had pulled into and out of Alder street the night before. She called Daley and told him what she had found. He was busy interviewing shop owners but said that he would call into the station soon. Marks switched footage from another camera. A black range rover drove down Main Street at 1418 and left on the Swaffham road at 1527. That was the way to Hoyte's place. The number plate was barely visible as it was covered in muck from the road. She checked and found that this was possibly the same car that Basil Smith was reported to be in when it left Bristol on Tuesday. Daley arrived at the station at 1223 after a fruitless morning which threw up no new leads. Marks told him that she had seen the Range Rover going in and out of Collins Transport. She had the registration plates checked and they showed that it was owned by a Daniel Collins. She also said that she thought that Basil Smith's car was on camera in Flixham on Wednesday at 1448.

`Danny Collins. That's very interesting. I didn't know that he had changed cars. He had a break in at his depot in October and he wasn't driving a Range Rover then. I think he had a white BMW, That's good work Clarissa'

`Obviously you know him 'she replied pleased with the compliment

`Yes. He is very well known around the town. He wasn't very complimentary about the local police force when we met last. Somebody broke into his offices and nicked a couple of computers and a few other bits and pieces. He is a bit of a wide boy. He has trucks going to and from the continent so he could easily be bringing drugs in. The trouble is that he doesn't associate with anybody who could be considered to be of a criminal element and how would he know

Andrews who has only been in town for five minutes. I think that we need to have a chat to see what he was doing in Alder Street on Tuesday evening'
They drove to Collins Transport and parked in the parking area in the depot.
Ray Nash and Bob Parsons were working on a truck
He shouted across to Nash
`Good afternoon Ray. Is Danny about?'
`Probably in his office' he said and carried on working.
He went into the office building and asked June the receptionist if they could have a quick word with Danny
`He is very busy today. I will ring through to see if he can spare you five minutes'
She called through to Collins' office
Daley heard her talking to him. She put the phone down and said that he could spare them a few minutes but could they wait for a bit as he was sorting out a problem with the transport manager

Bob Blake was talking to Collins about one of the younger contract drivers who had been exceeding his tachometer hours. He was taking longer than he should do to do his drops. Blake wanted to get rid of him if he continued to do this but he wanted to get Collins' approval. He didn't want to start firing people so soon into the job without discussing it with Collins first. Collins didn't seem that interested in what the driver had been doing and was rather dismissive of the fact that he was over on the readings.
`He has probably stopped off somewhere to get his leg over. You know what these young lads are like. Give him a bollocking, dock time from his pay and warn him that we won't continue to use him if it happens again'
`OK Danny I will do that but I think that we may need to set an example of him if it happens again. We don't want the other drivers to think that they can get away with it'
Blake had the feeling that Collins mind was on other matters so he left it at that. He left Collins office.

Daley and Marks were told to go through
`Good afternoon DS Daley. Who is your friend? We haven't had the pleasure' he said looking at Marks
`This is DC Marks. We want to ask you a few questions about Tuesday evening. We have been studying CCTV footage regarding something that we are investigating which we believe happened in the Red Lion. Unfortunately the cameras only cover Main Street. Your car or a car that looks very similar to yours was seen entering into Alder Street at 1741 and leaving again at 1744.

The car park for the Red Lion is accessed off Alder Street. Can you tell us what you were doing there?'

Collins didn't reply immediately. He sat thinking to himself looking as though he was trying to remember. He wasn't. He was trying to make up an acceptable excuse

'Tuesday afternoon, Tuesday afternoon let me think. I remember now' he said after about 30 seconds.

'My wife and daughter had a car accident on Tuesday afternoon. Graham May called in at the depot to tell me what had happened. I left work in a rush. I couldn't remember if I had picked up my mobile so I pulled into Alder Street to check to see if it was in my briefcase. I needed the phone in case the hospital wanted to get in touch. It was in my briefcase so I just turned around and went back out onto Main Street and then on to the hospital.'

Daley considered his answer before asking

'Did you know Lynton Andrews?'

'He played football for Flixham Rangers who I sponsor. He was a reasonable footballer but a bit too aggressive. He got sent off a couple of weeks ago. I have spoken to him the bar after games. He seemed a bit of a moody bastard if truth be told. His mate Denny is a completely different kettle of fish. He is a bloody good footballer too. He has sorted our defence out'

'Ok Danny we won't take up too much of your time'

'No Problem. I'm always willing to help the police. You never know when you are going to need them'

Daley and Marks left the depot.

'What do you think Gov? He knew both Andrews and Hoyte. I don't buy that excuse about his phone. Why didn't he just pull into the side of the road? It wasn't busy'

'It does seem a bit lame. He gave me the expression that he was thinking on his feet. I think that I will tell Surly Shirley and let her decide if she wants to take it any further. I want to find out more about that new transport manager. I haven't seen him before. It's bloody typical that the weather was bad and we couldn't get decent images from the cameras. He looked at his watch. It was 1428. You had better head back to Kings Lynn and report what you have found back to Booth. I am going to ask a few questions about the new transport manager'

24

Bogdan Stancvic wasn't a happy man. Two of his most reliable men had been killed and he was a quarter a million out of pocket. He would have made a lot more if he had got his hands on the cocaine. Unlike Ivan Petrescu who had a massive operation he couldn't afford to lose such a large sum of money. He had contacted DS Keith Lleweln who was based in Peterborough and arranged to meet him at Ferry Meadows at eleven thirty on Friday morning. Lleweln was in Stancvic's pocket. He was bent and supplied information to Stancvic for which he was rewarded with cash payments.

Lleweln was already there when Stancvic arrived. He was wearing a heavy blue padded jacket and a cap. He was overweight and the coat he was wearing made him look even fatter.

`What have you been hearing about the incident on the A1101? What conclusions have the police come to so far?' Stancvic asked getting straight to the point

Although Lleweln wasn't directly involved in the case there was lots of chat about it at Peterborough. He knew Jackie Ring who he'd had a brief fling with when she was a PC and he had remained on good terms with her. He had phoned her just before the meeting with Stancvic so she filled him in with the gaps. In return he gave her some limited information about Stancvic's team.

`The theory is that there was a disagreement between rival gangs and the three bodies found at the scene killed each other. What has baffled them is that the cocaine was left at the scene. They believe that somebody else was in attendance because one of the deceased, Lynton Andrews, didn't drive so they think that somebody drove him to the scene. The police suspect that his mate Dennard Hoyte would have accompanied Andrews but he had a car crash on Tuesday evening so he wasn't able to go. He was still in Flixham at 0820 talking to the police about the accident. Hoyte received a hiding from an unknown person or persons on Wednesday afternoon. The only suspects are the husband of a woman that Hoyte was shagging and a gang from Bristol who Hoyte and Andrews were on the run from. The gang are known drug dealers but are not suspected of being involved at Welney because of the drugs that were left behind. Kings Lynn are aware of the relationship between you and the two Romanians but as you have a strong alibi they cannot press charges against you as there is no direct connection between you and them on the night. They could have been acting alone. They are also interested in two other Romanians Ion Rodescu and Ilie Radu who are small time dealers. Both ended up in hospital in October and November. One had a beating the other had been shot. The police are trying to find them but they have both left the town.

The blue Mercedes found at the picnic site was seen in Flixham on the same day that Rodescu was shot'

'The Romanian community in England is tight knit when it comes to their fellow countryman. Radu has returned to his family home in Bucharest. His friend, Rodescu went to Eastbourne where he had family. He had debts which he did not repay. I am reliably informed by one of my contacts in Brighton that he has met his final resting place in the English Channel'

Stancvic gave Llewelin a knowing look before asking.

' Was there any mention of money left at the scene?'

'There was no money, just the Cocaine. Why do you ask?'

'There was a trade being done at the picnic site. I was buying the cocaine and I handed over a quarter of a million pounds. This appears to have vanished'

'Bloody hell, it hasn't been mentioned at all. It wasn't there when the police first arrived so I don't think that they even know about it. I will pass this news onto DCI Booth at Kings Lynn who is heading up the investigation. I wonder if the person who took Andrews to the trade off took off with the money. This puts a different angle on matters'

'Do it. They might want to have a word with a Danny Collins. It was his couriers who were at the trade. He didn't mention to me that only one of his couriers was present at the trade. He has made a killing over the past year so its time he faced the music. It's time to throw him under the bus.'

'Who is Danny Collins? I don't recognise his name'

'He owns Collins Transport. He has been bringing goods into the country from the continent for me for a couple of years now'

Llewelin phoned Kings Lynn CID as soon as Stancvic had left and asked to be put through to DCI Booth saying he had some information for her about the Welney incident.

Booth answered in a very abrupt tone

'What do you want DS Llewelin? I am very busy investigating a triple murder. Is your information related to this case?'

' I believe that it is. There is a strong rumour circling Peterborough that a large amount of cash went missing from the picnic site on the A1101. The word is that a trade was taking place, money for drugs. From what I have heard on the grapevine about the case no mention has been made about any cash being found at the site'

'And where did this word come from?'

'This came from one of my sources who obviously I won't name. He also told me that a Danny Collins was involved. Ilie Radu has returned to Romania and is living in Bucharest. Ion Rodescu is dead and is buried somewhere in the English Channel'.

`Keep this to yourself for now DS Lleweln. I will make some enquiries this end but it would be far easier if I could speak with the informant'.

`There is absolutely no chance of that' Lleweln replied. He could just imagine the consequences if Booth found out how he had got this news.

Booth was angry with this reply.

`I will speak to your bosses about this' She snapped and ended the call.

`Miserable cow' Lleweln said out loud once the call had ended. Not even a thank you for the tip. He had heard that Booth was very unpopular bitch who never gave credit to her team. Based on his conversation with her he thought that the rumours were true. He didn't think that Whalley would give him a hard time if he refused to name his source.

Booth was seething. Why had nobody heard these rumours and reported them to her. She was going to give DS James and DC Ring a piece of her mind. She wasn't impressed with Chief Superintendant Whalley either. Why didn't she hear of these rumours from him? Booth was aware that there was a Romanian community in Peterborough and she guessed that Williams informant was a member of this community. She had no doubts that Bogdan Stancvic was involved but proving it was another matter.

25

Booth was in a foul mood when DC Marks knocked on her door.

`What do you want Skid'

`We have tracked down the white Range Rover. It belongs to Danny Collins who owns a haulage company that makes trips to and from the continent. He gave us a lame excuse for why he was in Alder Street claiming that he was checking to see if he had left his phone at work. DS Daley thinks that he is worth further investigation. I can also confirm that Basil Smith was in Flixham on Wednesday afternoon '

"I will decide on who needs further investigation. You can go back to Flixham and continue with the CCTV footage and after that you and Arthur can have another word with Peter and Val Davey.  Peter Davey has reasonable cause to beat up Hoyte '

Marks thought about arguing that Hoyte was beaten up the night before she spoke to Davey but thought that it was pointless trying to speak to Booth when she was in this type of mood.

As soon as Marks had left Booth called DC Butler and told him to meet her at Collins Transport at 1630. She was going to have a word with Danny Collins. DC Butler was showing promise and she thought that he would be a good back up for her at the interview. She didn't rate any other members of her team. DI Green was competent enough but lacked drive. Di Franklin seemed to spend more time in the pub than he did on active investigation. DS Brown was a plodder who never showed any initiative. DS Judge never seemed to take anything serious and was always cracking jokes and trying to be funny. He was the source of many of the nicknames that the team had and had no doubt been responsible for hers. DS Daley was old school and had been put out to grass in Flixham.  DC Marks irritated her. She did some good work in her early days with the team but she appeared to let it go to her head. Booth believed that Marks thought that she was better than the rest of her team because she had been to private school. Not many of the team enjoyed working with Marks.

Lesley Farmer called Val at work on Friday morning. She had heard the news about Lynton Andrews and wondered if Val had heard from Denny.

`Did you hear about Lynton?' she asked. `He only went and phoned me that evening to ask me if I would give him a lift. He said that he and Denny had some business out of town but Denny had crashed his car and couldn't make it.

I told him to fuck off. He hadn't been in touch since we all went out last week and there was a blizzard outside'

`Denny was with me on Tuesday evening. He crashed his car on the way to meet up with Lynton. He told the police that he was with me. Some bitch of a copper went to see Pete at home and told him that Denny had said that he was in my flat. Pete went mad when I got home. He called me a fucking slag and said that our marriage was over as he couldn't forgive me. We had a massive fight. I told him to fuck off because I was bored shitless with being at home by myself all of the time. I said that was why I went with Denny. I told Pete that Denny was much bigger and better than him in bed and had showed me what I had been missing for all those years while I was with him. He started to cry and fucked off back to his mother's house. I don't know what will happen. We will probably get a divorce and end up selling the flat. I won't be able to afford anything on my own. I haven't heard a word from Denny since. His phone just rings out or is switched off. I hope that he is OK'

`Shit. What a mess but you haven't been happy with Pete for ages so perhaps it's for the best. Listen I have been invited to Ray Nash's 50th birthday party on tomorrow night. Do you want to come with me? We can get pissed and forget about our troubles for the night'

`Sound like a plan' Val said. She went home in a slightly better mood. Her mood soon changed when she got home. She was having a cup of tea when DC Marks rang her intercom.

`I need to have another word with you please Mrs Davey'

`I have said all that I need to say to you. Thanks to you I have split up with my husband'

Marks nearly said that she wasn't the one who was playing away but she let it go.

`It's actually about your husband that I need to speak to you'.

Reluctantly Davey let Marks in. Davey sat with her arms crossed. She never offered Marks a seat let alone a cup of tea.

`How did your husband react when you got home and you talked about Hoyte?

`He said good for you girl. I don't mind you fucking a big black bloke behind my back. Why don't you bring him round so that I can watch' she said in a sarcastic tone. `How do you think he reacted? He went ape shit. See that big hole in the door. That's where he put his fist through. We had a massive row and he fucked off to his mum's place. I haven't seen or heard from him since last night'

`Dennard Hoyte is in hospital. Somebody beat him up. He has a fractured eye socket, a broken cheek bone as well as severe bruising to the body as well as the testicles. One of my colleagues interviewed him this morning. He says that somebody jumped him from behind on Wednesday evening and he didn't see who did it.'

The news came as a complete surprise to Val Davey and she thought that this is the reason why Denny hadn't been in touch with her.

`It wasn't Pete. He isn't a fighter. Denny is a big bloke. He would have murdered Pete if they had a fight. Pete has always avoided confrontation and besides you never told him until Thursday morning. He isn't clairvoyant'

`Perhaps your husband already knew about Hoyte and you before I spoke with him. It's a small town and I doubt if the gossip wouldn't have got back to him. How long have you been seeing Hoyte?'

`I met him in the Red Lion on the Friday before Christmas. He phoned me a couple of times at work but we didn't meet up because Pete didn't stay away for a couple of weeks. We went out for a curry in Kings Lynn last week. Denny came back to my flat and we did it for the first time that night. Last Tuesday was only the second time I had been with him'

`Where in Kings Lynn did you go?'

`We went to the Wetherspoons pub first and then for a curry at the Golden Lion. It was the first good night out I have had for ages.'

`Did anybody you know see you?'

`Just Lesley Farmer a mate of mine. She made up a foursome with Lynton Andrews the bloke who was killed on Tuesday. We deliberately went out of town so nobody would see us'.

`Do you have an address and a contact number for her? '

`Why do you need to speak to her? She has done nothing wrong'

`We are trying to find anybody who came into contact with Andrews.

Davey reluctantly gave Marks Lesley's address and phone numbers.

She left Davey's flat and immediately contacted DS Brown who was co-ordinating the information on the incident

She asked him to check Lesley Farmer's phone number with those made from Andrew's mobile on Tuesday.

It was a match.

`Do you want to tell Booth or shall I?' Brown asked.

`You can have that privilege' She replied

26

Booth met up with Butler outside of the Collins Depot
She marched in with Butler in her wake.
She showed her ID to Susan Rudd who was on reception duty
`I want to see Danny Collins' she said
`He is very busy at the moment' Susan replied
`That makes two of us then' Booth wasn't going to be deterred
`I am afraid that he told me that he doesn't want to be disturbed'
`I want to see him NOW' she bellowed `so go and tell him'
Nervously Susan went into Collins office
Collins was talking to Petrescu on his mobile. The conversation wasn't going well.
`What part of I don't want to be disturbed do you not understand?' he shouted at her. He wasn't in a good mood
`I'm sorry Danny but I have a DCI Booth in reception and she is demanding to see you'
At that moment Booth barged in.
Collins quickly told Petrescu that he had to go because the police were in his office and needed to talk to him. He said that he would phone back as soon as he could. He stood up and glared at the six foot tall detective who towered over him.
`What rights do you have barging in here? I was talking to a business associate'
Booth Ignored Collins protests
`I have information that leads us to believe that you are connected to the triple murder at the picnic site on the A1101 on Tuesday night'
`That's bollocks' Collins said somewhat apprehensively. `I have already told DS Daley that I was at Kings Lynn hospital on Tuesday evening. I left here at about 530pm and didn't get back to Flixham until after nine. I went for a couple of beers in The Star. Bill the landlord will vouch for me. I also have a receipt for the car park which I paid on my credit card. Six bloody quid for less than three hours'
Booth continued
`We have reason to believe that a known associate of yours was involved in a drugs trade off. Somebody is believed to have accompanied him to the site where he was murdered along with two other men who were involved in the trade. The drugs were left at the scene but somebody wandered off with a large sum of money'

This news threw Collins. He assumed that the police had recovered both the drugs and the money. He also wondered how Booth knew that money had been taken. Who had passed this information to her? DC Butler was also surprised as it was the first he had heard of it

Collins quickly recovered his composure.

`I told DS Daley that I only know Andrews from football so he is hardly an associate. I sponsor Flixham Rangers. He plays for them. The only times that I have spoken to him are in the bar after the game. We talked about the game but that's as far as it goes. The man is a ticking time bomb and was always looking for a fight. Other than that you have nothing to tie me with Andrews. I run a respectable business here and I resent the inference that I have been doing something shady'

Booth could see that Collins had every angle covered but she didn't believe in coincidence. Collins was in the vicinity of the Red Lion at the same time as Andrews appeared with his holdall. Collins' trucks did trips to and from the continent. She had a gut feel about Collins.

`Lynton Andrews was seen on camera going into the Red Lion early on Tuesday evening. He wasn't carrying a holdall. He made a trip to the toilet and returned with a holdall, the description of which matched the one found at the picnic site full of cocaine. The bar was almost empty and the only other person to leave by that entrance was a customer who was being picked up by his wife. We have eliminated that person from our enquiries. Your car is seen on camera turning into Alder Street. It leaves a few minutes after and at the same time Andrews appears back in the bar with the said holdall. Your company makes regular trips to and from the continent and therefore has ample opportunity to bring cocaine in hidden amongst the cargo. You gave a statement to DS Daley in which you said that you turned into Alder Street and checked your briefcase to make sure that you hadn't forgotten your phone. I think that is bullshit'

Collins smirked

`So you think that this is enough evidence to think that I was involved. I would like to point out a few things that you may have overlooked. I was on the way in a rush to the Queen Liz having been told by PC May that my wife and daughter were involved in a road traffic accident. Why would I spend time fucking about dropping bags off to somebody that I hardly know in a pub that I rarely use. Two, I could have pulled into the side of the road but if my phone wasn't in my briefcase I would have had to have done a U turn in Main Street. It's not the widest of streets and it may have been difficult with the conditions. It was far easier to turn into Alder Street and turn around in the Red Lion car park. Three, Has it occurred to you that somebody may have left the holdall in the toilets or hidden it somewhere at the back of the pub.? Are there any cameras covering the back entrance to the pub? Anyone could have walked into the car park area earlier in the day and stashed a holdall and finally, do you have any evidence on camera showing me with the holdall? You won't have as I didn't have it so unless there are any more questions I would like you to leave as I have a business to run.'

Tony Butler almost smiled at the look on Booth's face. She never had a shred of evidence tying Collins to this case and he had just pissed all over her.

'There is just one thing that you have not considered Mr Collins. Your name was put forward to us by a police informant based in Peterborough. Why would somebody from there put you in the frame?'

'Perhaps he is a business rival who wants to slur me' Collins said with some uncertainty in his voice. 'I am not prepared to discuss this matter any further without the presence of my solicitor.'

'I will need to speak to your staff and drivers to see if anyone here can help us' Collins looked at his watch.

'It will have to be on Monday then because most of them have either left for the day or are about to leave. Good afternoon Detective inspector' He picked up his phone and proceeded to dial his wife Paula who was recovering at home.

Booth didn't like the way she had been dismissed in such an embarrassing way by Collins. She realised that he had walked all over her.

'I will be back on Monday' she said slamming the door as her and Butler left

'Arrogant sod' Booth snarled as they went back to their cars. 'Mark my words he is hiding something'

'Where did you find out about the missing money and who put Collins name in the frame Ma'am?' Butler asked

'A DS from Peterborough told me early this afternoon. I haven't had chance to share this news with the team yet but I will do tomorrow morning. I am going to have somebody's guts for garters for this. How is it that a detective who is not working the case can pick up street chat yet my team didn't? DS James and DC Ring were supposed to be liaising with Peterborough but they missed it'.

Booth drove home with a headache. Graham Brown phoned her to tell her that Andrews had spoken with Lesley Farmer on Tuesday evening. He said that Skid had discovered this when she re interviewed Val Davey

'It's a pity she couldn't have discovered that earlier. I will speak to her at the briefing tomorrow morning. I want everyone in at 0800 so can you let them all know.' Booth said sourly

Marks had told Daley that Peter Davey was staying at his mother's as well as the news about Lesley Farmer. He knew Peter's mother who was an acquaintance of his wife. He called at her house and asked her if Peter was home. She said that he was and welcomed him in. She offered him a cup of tea which he accepted. He was parched.

`Have a seat' she told him pointing to an armchair in the lounge. I will call Peter for you.

Peter came down from upstairs. He was pale and thin with curly blond hair that looked unkempt. Daley noticed that he had a bruised knuckle. He got straight to the point.

`Hi Peter. Dennard Hoyte who claims to have been with your wife on Tuesday afternoon and evening was found badly beaten at his home on Thursday morning. He is being released from hospital today. I have to ask you if, under the circumstances, you had any involvement in this matter'

`I didn't but I wish that I had. I would have enjoyed hurting him. He has wrecked my marriage. I didn't find out about it until your colleague told me about it on Thursday afternoon.'

`Can I ask how you got those marks on your knuckles?'

`I punched the door in my flat during a row with Val. There is a great big hole in it if you want to check. I had nothing to do with Hoyte getting beaten up. I have seen him around the town and if I am honest he is too big for me to take on. I would have got battered if I tried to start a fight with him'

Daley studied Davey. He was about 5' 9" and probably weighed less than 140 pounds. He couldn't imagine him taking on Hoyte who was probably eight inches taller and three stone heavier in a fist fight.

`Thanks Peter. I am sorry that I had to ask you that but we needed to eliminate you from our enquiries'

He finished his tea and left. He decided that he would call at Lesley Farmer's house. It was after 1700 when he knocked on her door after getting her address from Marks.

The door was opened by a short overweight woman in her early thirties who was dressed in a worn red sweatshirt with Mickey Mouse on the front and grey track suit bottoms. Daley showed his id card and asked if he could come in and ask a few questions.

`What is it about?'

`Did you know Lynton Andrews one of the men who was found dead earlier this week. I am sure that you have heard about the incident'

Val had told Farmer that she had already told the police that they went out as a foursome with Denny and Lynton so she wasn't going to lie to the old copper stood in front of her.

She invited him into her living room which was completely the opposite of her appearance. It was neat and tidy.

'I met him in the Red Lion before Christmas. I went on a dinner date with him, his mate and my mate Val Davey. We had a curry in Kings Lynn. He came back to my house afterwards and we had sex. He left in the morning and I haven't seen him since. I didn't want to either. He wasn't a good shag and he got abusive because I wouldn't let him shag me up the arse' She said in a matter of fact way

``What do you mean by getting abusive?' Daley enquired

'He just said that he had spent a fortune on taking me out and that I should be grateful that somebody wanted to fuck a big lump like me. He said that he liked anal sex and that I should try it. I wouldn't let him so I asked him to leave but he said that it was too late. He didn't drive and he wasn't going to walk back to his place. He just turned over and went to sleep. I slept in my boy's room and I could hear him through the walls. He spent all night snoring and farting and he buggered off first thing in the morning.'

'Have you spoken with him since?'

'I spoke with him once. I was in the bog and my bum had just touched the seat when my mobile rang. By the time I had finished the call ended. I didn't recognise the number and I thought that it might be about my two boys who are at their father's this week so I phoned the number back. It was Lynton. He asked me if I could give him a lift to a business meeting that he had that evening. He said that Denny had crashed his car and it was an important meeting. I told him to fuck off. It was snowing like mad and even if I had wanted to give him a lift it would have been crazy going out in that weather'

'What time did he phone you?'

'I'm not sure. Emmerdale was on the telly and I had gone for a wee in the adverts so it would have been between half seven and eight'

'Did he say who he was meeting or where it was?'

'No he just sounded agitated and to tell the truth he must have been desperate to phone me asking for a favour especially after our night together. He must have known that I would say no'

'Thanks for this information Lesley. It has cleared up things for us. We didn't know who he had phoned because your phone is a pay as you go so it isn't registered to your address.'

'I only use it for emergencies when I am out. I was a bit pissed when I first met him otherwise I wouldn't have given him my number. I never give blokes my number unless I know them really well'

Daley left her and went home. He had a message in his voice mail from Graham Brown saying that Booth had called a briefing first thing in the morning. Another bloody Saturday down the pan he thought to himself. Bev will be unhappy.

27

Danny Collins phoned Petrescu and told him why the police wanted to see him. `Somebody from Peterborough has pointed the finger at me. I can only think of one person who would do that and that is Stancvic. I can understand that he is pissed off but to grass me up is not on'

`Believe me Stancvic would be pointing a gun at you not his finger' replied Petrescu `you have cost both of us money and we both want it repaid'

`That detective who was here told me that there was no money found at the site. Just the drugs were recovered by the police. It seems that somebody lifted the money'

`So I hear' said Petrescu `but at this moment I am only interested in recovering my money so when can I expect you to give it to me'

`I haven't got that sort of money easily to hand and I don't think that I should be considered responsible. How do you know that Stancvic's men actually took the money to the exchange? We all know that there were risks involved and we have had a good run. This time it went tits up. I'm not prepared to start paying out to you until we know who took the money if of course it was ever there to be taken in the first place as we only have Stancvic's word for this. I don't see why my couriers would suddenly start shooting his couriers. I am also drawing a line under our partnership. I am not bringing in goods with the police all over me'

`You will continue to deliver my goods until I decide not to use you' hissed Petrescu

`Tuesday's delivery will be the last for the foreseeable future. I'm taking the risks and I'm not doing it anymore so it will be better for you if you found somebody else to do your deliveries' Collins replied.

He was beginning to lose his temper

`You are making a big mistake' Petrescu said menacingly. He disconnected. Collins sat in his chair feeling very worried. Why had that idiot Andrews used somebody else to drive him to the picnic site? Who had nicked the money? Did Stancvic's men actually take the money to the trade? Did the person who did the driving take it or had some bent copper lifted it? Nobody knew for sure at the moment and he wasn't going to be bullied by Petrescu or Stancvic until answers were found.

Something that Collins had said resonated with Petrescu. Perhaps Stancvic never took the money to the trade. Petrescu couldn't understand why violence erupted at the trade. Granted he didn't know too much about Collins new couriers but they had caused no issue at the two previous trades and by all accounts had been very professional. Bogdan Stancvic had been a fairly recent business associate of Petrescu having been introduced to him by another Romanian Georghi Adescu from Hull who Petrescu had been dealing with for many years. Stancvic's quick rise to a fairly large player in the UK drugs world had been based on fear. He and his employees were not averse to violence. He had a gang of around twelve to fifteen loyal men who did most of the dirty work for him but there are stories claiming that Stancvic took part in beatings. Stancvic obviously thought that he was a big player but he was, compared to Petrescu's world, small fry. He was getting too big for his boots. Petrescu didn't like being questioned or shown a lack of respect by associates that he considered inferior to him and the way Stancvic was talking and behaving pissed him off. Despite the bravado shown by Danny Collins in the phone conversation Petrescu knew that he would never overstep the mark in his dealings with him and Stancvic. He would have seen what treatment had been dished out to his former couriers Radu and Rodescu and he was very contrite when he heard what they had been doing. Collins hadn't however mentioned that only one of his two black couriers had attended the trade. This information had come from Stancvic's tame copper. Collins, to Petrescu's mind, was at fault for using unreliable couriers. .Petrescu never held back when it was time to make a calculated risk.  He always backed his judgement and he had made his decision. He called Floran Chipciu. He gave him a name and hung up.

Danny Collins was a worried man when he arrived home. His wife Paula could tell there was something wrong from the look on his face. She knew about Danny's sideline business and that things had gone wrong on Tuesday night
`What's wrong Danny? You look as though you have got the weight of the world on your shoulders'
`I have just spent the afternoon being interviewed by the coppers. First of all DS Daley started asking questions about where I was on Tuesday night. I fobbed him off but later DCI Booth came barging into my office and started grilling me about the murders on Tuesday. I was seen on camera going into Alder Street when I dropped the cocaine off. Luckily there are no cameras at the back of the Red Lion so nobody saw me hand over the holdall to Andrews. I was wearing gloves so I haven't left my dabs on the bag. The only evidence that they have is my car in Alder Street. I have always been very careful. She is coming back on Monday to interview my staff but apart from Dimi and Mircea nobody knows about my dealings with Petrescu and Stancvic. Booth let slip that they only recovered the cocaine. There was no money at the scene. She also said that somebody from Peterborough had fingered me. That has got to

have been Stancvic. He has been on the phone wanting me to pay him for the money he lost and Petrescu wants his money too. These guys don't fuck about so I am worried what they are going to do because I haven't got the amounts of money that they want. I told Petrescu that I shouldn't be blamed. I asked him why Andrews would start a fight with two armed men. I know that he is a head case but what prompted him to pick a fight with two armed Romanians? I suggested that perhaps Stancvic never sent the money to the trade. It's funny how the police didn't mention it at their press conference. They just mentioned the drugs. I told Petrescu that I'm done with our arrangement. He wasn't a happy man. I'm going to phone Stancvic later to tell him that I haven't got his money and that I am done with dealing with him as well.'

Paula was concerned. She knew that Stancvic was violent because Danny has told her that he thought that Stancvic was responsible for shooting Radu and beating up Rodescu. Who knows what he would do to Danny. They had discussed a way out if things went wrong. Danny would just tell the police that he was unaware that the Romanians were bringing drugs in on one of his trucks. Until he had to use Hoyte and Andrews all of those involved were Romanians. Dimi was the main driver; Mircea drove on the odd occasion. Radu and Rodescu were the couriers and Stancvic was the receiver of the drugs. . Danny would give names and claim innocence.
`What are we going to do?' she asked him.
`That depends. I need to speak to Denny Hoyte. I haven't heard from him since Tuesday night. I need to know if he knows who was with Andrews at the picnic site. Hoyte wasn't. He had been shagging some tart on Tuesday evening and drove his car into a wall on Deehan Road on his way to meet Andrews in the Red Lion. If he has fucked off I may be able to shift the blame to him and Andrews by claiming that they were in league with the Romanians. I just don't know what to do at the moment'
 He opened a bottle of red wine and quickly drunk the first glass. Paula had cooked a pasta dish so they continued the conversation over dinner.
`How do you fancy a month in the Canary Islands? We could rent a nice villa with a pool and just relax in the sun. I know it will mean taking Charlotte out of school but we could just say that she is still recovering from the accident. Isn't half term at the end of February? We could come back after that'. Danny suddenly said
`What about the company. Who would run that while we are away for a month? Who would pay the drivers and do the payroll? Wouldn't we just be putting off the problem for a month? It would still be there when we got back.'

Before he had chance to reply his PAYG mobile rang. He deliberated before answering. It was Stancvic.

`When are you going to get my money?' he said getting straight to the point without any niceties.

Collins was annoyed and decided that he would give Stancvic a piece of his mind.

`I have told Petrescu that I don't think that I am to blame so I am not paying anybody until we find out what happened to the money that you claim you have lost. The police didn't mention it and as my man was killed at the scene it wasn't my team that took it. For all we know some bent copper found it and kept hold of it. I told Petrescu that there was always the chance that something could go tits up and we all knew the risk. I also told him that I am done with this venture. I have got the police all over me thanks to a tip off from somebody in Peterborough. I don't suppose you had anything to do with that? '

`My money was there for the exchange. My two men were killed at the scene together with your man but whoever accompanied him to the exchange left and they took my money' Stancvic reacted angrily

Collins lost his temper

` Have you got a fucking crystal ball then?  How do you know that somebody was with Andrews and that so called somebody cleared off with the money that you claim to have lost? You, just like me, know absolutely jack shit about what actually happened on Tuesday night. If you think I am going to give you a quarter of a million based on your speculation you have got another think coming. I don't have that sort of money. My house is mortgaged, our cars are leased and my business isn't making much profit. I don't have twenty five thousand pounds to my name let alone a quarter of a million. I haven't got it and even if I did I wouldn't give it to you. Do I make myself clear?'

He cut the connection and turned his phone off.

Collins was red in the face from anger.

`He can go fuck himself. I'm giving him fuck all until we know for sure what happened'

`What do you think he will do?' Paula asked.

 She was frightened. She had rarely seen Danny lose his temper like that before.

`What can he do? If he kills me he won't get his money back. This house is mortgaged to the hilt so there isn't much capital in it for him. Our cars are both leased through the company.  On paper, at least in the UK, we don't have anything much to our name. The company only shows a small profit after our dividends. Only you and I and our accountant know about our offshore savings.

Everything is hidden there away from Gordon Brown's grasp. Everything is in place for us to piss off to Tenerlfe in five or six year's time when Charlotte finishes school and I sell the company'

`I hope you are right. I am scared that Stancvic will hurt us or at least threaten to'

`If he does I will go to the police. I will tell them that he threatened us if I didn't use my trucks to bring his goods in. I always use Dimi or Mircea so I could say that they worked for Stancvic and if truth be told they may well be on his payroll. I might be charged with being an accomplice but if I said that I did it under duress I might get some lenience'.

He didn't sound very convincing to Paula and to himself he doubted if he was brave enough to grass on Stancvic.

28

Denny Hoyte was released from hospital on Saturday morning. He had to get a bus back to Flixham. He didn't have much money left so his only option was to stay in the park home especially as he had to go back to the hospital on Friday to have the stitches removed from his mouth. He needed to find his mobile. He had forgotten to take it with him when he went in Flixham on Wednesday. He thought that it was in his jacket pocket but realised he had left it behind when he went to phone Lynton. He needed to speak to Collins. He needed money and he decided that he would threaten Collins for it. He was in pain still from the kicking Barnett had given him. His face was a mess and his ribs hurt. His balls were bloody painful and he was pissing blood. It was difficult to walk. Eating was hard work too. His face was very badly bruised and chewing especially on the left side of his mouth was excruciating. Fortunately the bus went to Swaffham so he was able to get off close to his place. He found his phone which had fallen off the arm of the two seat sofa and was wedged deep between the arm and the cushion. He was relieved that neither the police nor Smith's gang had found it as he was certain that they had searched his place. He needed to make some calls but the battery was flat and there was fuck all chance of getting a signal in the park home. He thought that he would rest for an hour to give the phone chance to get some charge and then have a very slow walk towards town. He needed food as well as the cupboards were bare. He was hungry. After an hour there was enough power on his phone to enable him to make a couple of calls so he set off towards town. When he was about halfway his phone pinged into life. He had several missed calls. He recognised one of them. It was Val. He had no further interest in her. To him she was just a fuck, albeit a good one but with the state of his balls he wouldn't be doing any shagging for a good while yet. He didn't want her around him. He would have to stay here for another week and once he felt a bit better he would nick a car and fuck off. His phone rang and to his disappointment it was Val again. He didn't answer it. She left a voicemail message. She knew he had been in hospital and asked him how he was. She asked when she could see him again. He deleted the message and put a block on her number. He sent her a text message saying that he was leaving town as soon as he felt better and that he didn't want to see her again. He told her to stop phoning him as he had put a block on her number. He said that she meant nothing to him. She was just a convenient fuck that they both enjoyed at the time. He phoned Collins but his call went to voicemail. He left a message saying that he needed to talk to Collins about the trade. He said that he had something that may be of interest to Collins. He hadn't but he thought that this would make Collins call him back. He felt knackered so he decided not to go any further, He turned around and headed back to the park home. By the time he got back he felt really tired so he went to bed for a kip and didn't wake up until the early hours of Sunday morning.

Booth marched into the briefing room five minutes late and in a foul mood. She started by telling the team that they had let her down. The only news that anybody had given her was about one of the phone numbers that Andrews had called. No mention was made of the footage from the Red Lion and the CCTV footage throwing up the white Range Rover. She wasn't giving credit to anyone for that

`I received a phone call yesterday afternoon from a DS from Peterborough and he gave me more information than the lot of you put together and he isn't even on the bloody case. The information that he has received from his source claims that Rodescu is floating around in the English Channel, Radu is back In Romania, A large sum of money reputed to be £250,000 is missing from the trade and lastly Danny Collins who owns Collins Transport is said to be involved. I intend to concentrate on Mr Collins. His car was in the vicinity of the Red Lion at the same time that Lynton Andrews appeared carrying a holdall that he didn't have with him when he went into the Red Lion. I believe that Collins is the key to this case. He has the means to bring drugs into the country from the continent. I also want to find out what happened to the money. We need to find out who was Andrew's driver on Tuesday evening. Ds Judge interviewed Dennard Hoyte yesterday afternoon. As you know he received a hiding from one or more people. He claims that this happened on Wednesday afternoon. He says that he didn't see who it was because he was attacked from behind. I have ruled out Peter Davey for this attack after Arthur interviewed him. Basil Smith was interviewed by the police in Bristol yesterday. He claims that he was in Balham on Tuesday evening and stayed at a mates place because of the weather. He says that there is likely to be footage of him on camera in the White Swan in Balham as he spent several hours drinking with business associates. He admitted coming to Flixham on Wednesday afternoon to find Andrews and Hoyte. He did go to Hoyte's place on Wednesday with three others who had also been with him in Balham. He says that they wanted to have a word with Andrews and Hoyte but they weren't at home. There was no sign of Hoyte's car and when they knocked on his door there was no answer. Unfortunately we have no evidence at this stage that they were involved in either the events on the A1101 or the beating up of Hoyte`.

Daley raised his hand stopping Booth when she was in full stride, much to her annoyance

`Excuse me Ma'am but have you considered that an opportunist accidentally stumbled on the scene in the car park before John Beattie reported it to us. A member of the public may have stopped at the site. Could they have walked off with the money? Perhaps John Beattie found it. We were not aware of it at the time so he was never questioned about anything that went missing'

Booth glared at Daley. If looks could kill she would have needed a licence for her face.

`Yes Arthur it had occurred to me but my team of detectives cannot provide any evidence of this. You were the first at the scene. Did you see any evidence of anyone being there that morning? I doubt that you even looked. I want a word with you in my office after this meeting'

Daley's intervention seemed to provoke more anger from Booth.

`Ds James and DC Ring are no longer needed in this case seeing that you have been wandering around with your thumbs stuck up your arses and failed to pick up on the rumours in Peterborough so you can return to Wisbech immediately. Skid, I want you to check the CCV footage for Flixham again after 2000. See if you can find any footage of Collins. DC Judge, I want you to arrange for an interview with Beattie. See if there is any footage of him carrying a case or holdall which could contain money when he left the Toyota garage in Wisbech. The rest of you will be required to meet me at Collins Transport at 0900 on Monday. We will be interviewing all of Collins' staff individually to see if anybody gives us any fresh information. Arthur, after I have seen you in my office I want you to call in at Collins Transport and get a list of all their employees. I have been told that they use contract drivers so I want their names too. Email this to me today. The rest of you can find out anything useful about the company'

Booth left and went straight to her office. Daley gave her a few minutes and then went to her office. DS Judge said in a voice loud enough for those still in the briefing room to hear

`Surly Shirley is in a good mood today. It must be PMT. You really pissed her off Arthur. I reckon you are going to get a bollocking. Either that or she will have you working all weekend.'

Daley knocked on Booth's door

`Enter' she said

`You wanted to see me Ma'am? 'Daley asked

She laid into him straight away

`Of course I considered that somebody found the money and went off with it. I have also considered that perhaps a Detective Sergeant who was first on the scene and is due to retire shortly might have found the money and took it but I didn't say anything about that either. Are you trying to make me look foolish Arthur?'

Daley was livid but also shocked by this accusation

`From where I am standing you are making a pretty good job of looking foolish all by yourself. How dare you infer that I took the money? The first I heard of it was when you mentioned it this morning even though you had been told about it yesterday afternoon. Did you not think that it would have saved your team a lot of time on pointless investigations trying to track down Radu and Rodescu when you already knew where they were? Young Clarissa told you that we thought that Collins was worth further investigation and yet you bit her head off even though he had been suggested as a suspect by your DS in Peterborough. You may think that I am old school and old fashioned but I have never done and never will do anything that could be considered corrupt. If you think I have then I suggest you call in internal affairs. If you do I will be raising a complaint against you for that slur on my character'

He got up, left and slammed door. Booth was stunned by the ferocity of his response. Daley had always come across as a mild mannered man. She had him down as a plodder biding his time his time until retirement. She didn't want his likes on her team. She had obviously touched a nerve but she wasn't going to stand for his insubordination. She stormed out of her office and set off in pursuit of him. He was about to leave the CID room.

`Arthur, Get your arse back in here now 'She bellowed across the room. Daley ignored her and stormed towards the door and burst out of the room. He'd had enough of Booth. If she suspended him so be it. He left the room leaving Booth looking very angry standing by her office door. The detectives who were still in the room raised their eyebrows at each other. It was obvious that Arthur was in a temper when he came storming out of her office but is it was unlike him to act in such a way. Booth looked at them. She had a look of fury on her face

`Why are you lot still here? Get and do your jobs' she shouted at them before slamming the door on her way back into her office'

Mick Judge was the first to comment

`Oh dear somebody has got the hump. Could you hear anything that was being said in there Tony?'

Butler's desk was the closest to Booth's office but he had his back to it.

`Not really but I could hear Arthur's raised voice.  See if you can find out what went on Skid .You have been working with Arthur recently and you seem to get on well with him'
`I will give him a call later when he has cooled down'

29

Daley went straight to Collins Transport. Ray Nash and Bob Parsons were working in the garage.

`Is anybody working in the offices today?' Daley asked

`Bob Blake, the Transport Manager is still in there. Danny popped in but only for half an hour'

Daley went in and saw Blake in an office on the right. His door was open. Daley went in an introduced himself

`Good Morning. I'm DS Daley. We haven't met' he said showing his ID `Do you mind if I ask you a few questions?'

`How can I help you?' Blake replied wondering what the hell was going on. Daley was here yesterday followed by two other detectives and now he was back.

`Firstly can you tell me your name and how long you have worked here?'

'Is there any reason why you need to talk to me? Have I done something wrong?'

Blake was getting concerned. Had somebody seen him on Tuesday night

`No. Just call its Sod's Law that you are the only person in the office and I need some staff information. I hope that you can help me '

Blake sighed with relief

`I am Bob Blake. I started working here a couple of weeks back. I am renting a house in Turnberry Close. I moved here from Mansfield in Nottinghamshire.'

`Thanks. Is there a Mrs Blake?'

`There used to be but we divorced last year. That is one of the reasons I came to work for Collins Transport in Flixham. I wanted a fresh start. There were no jobs in my area hence the move here'

`Do you have the names and addresses of any of the staff who work here?'

Blake thought about it before answering.

`I don't have access to the staff's personal details but the drivers are all contract drivers. I have their contact details if that helps. It will take me a few minutes to put the list together if you don't mind waiting. You would need to speak to Danny or Paula Collins for the rest of the staff'

`Do the drivers have regular routes or are they just given random deliveries and collections?'

`As I said I have only been here for a couple of weeks. Before I joined it seemed a bit haphazard but I am trying to keep the same drivers to the same routes especially those that go to Europe'

`Can you tell me a bit about the journeys that the drivers make?'

Blake spent the next ten minutes telling Daley about the deliveries and collections for the Value Shopper group, the trips via Harwich Felixstowe and Kings Lynn. At the same time he was putting a list of names phone numbers and email addresses together. He gave the list to Daley
Daley thanked him.
`I expect some of our officers from Kings Lynn will be here to speak to the staff on Monday. You will probably be interviewed by somebody higher up the food chain than me'
`Can I ask what this is about? I saw two detectives in here on Friday talking to Danny and weren't you in here yesterday as well?'
`I'm sorry but I cannot give any details about an active enquiry. Thanks again for your help. Have a good weekend'
Daley left and went home. He emailed the details from the list that Blake had given him to Booth and said that there was nobody who had access to staff records working on Saturday morning so that would need to wait until Monday

Dc Marks spent a couple of hours looking through the footage from the CCTV cameras in Flixham. The images were slightly better once the snow had eased. Eventually she found something that looked promising. A car that looked like Danny Collins white Range Rover appeared on footage heading towards Swaffham at 2200. She played the rest of the footage and the same car appeared again in the opposite direction about thirty minutes later. It was getting late and she knew if she got in touch with Booth tonight she would be called into the station. She decided to leave copies of the discs in Booth's in tray at the station hoping that Booth wasn't in when she got there. She was in luck. She left a message on Booth's voicemail and as her shift had finished she turned her phone off. She was going to visit her parents who lived in a small village close to Bishop's Stortford

30

Peter Davey went home on Saturday morning. He had made up his mind that his marriage was over. He found Val in a confrontational mood but they managed to keep their tempers in check.

`I'm not prepared to forgive you for what you did. Any trust that I had with you has gone out of the window. I think that it would be best if we got a divorce as soon as possible' he said.

`It's pretty obvious that you don't want children and I do. I am bored with staying at home all by myself while you were away working and when you are at home we never do anything. We just sit in front of the telly every night. I wanted more in my life which is why I strayed. I just wanted some excitement. I agree that we should divorce as soon as possible. What are we going to do about the flat? It isn't going to be worth what we paid for it so we would lose money if we sold it. I can't afford the mortgage on what I get paid and you are going to struggle to pay for it on your salary.'

`I don't know what we can do about the flat. Our fixed rate finishes in two months time and unless we can get a better deal it's going to cost us even more. I didn't say that I don't want children. I just want to wait until we are a bit better off.'

`I haven't got anywhere I can go to live and I can't afford to rent a place of my own'

`You may as well stay here until I sort out the mortgage. I'm not sure if I will be able to get a better deal as the banks are being much tougher on what they are prepared to lend. We will have to put the flat up for sale eventually`

The discussion left them both full of worries. Pete left the flat and went back to his mother's house.

Val was worried sick. She hadn't considered the consequences when she started seeing other men. She regretted it now. She wanted some excitement and the sex was great but it was probably going to leave her homeless and in debt. She phoned Denny but her call went to voice mail. A couple of minutes later she received a text message from Denny. When she read the message she started to cry. He said wasn't interested in her anymore. He was leaving town as soon as he got over his injuries. He had just used her. She phoned Lesley and poured her heart out to her.

`Men are such bastards' Lesley said trying to console her. `They are only after one thing. Women keep thinking that the next one we meet will be different but they never are. All you can do is put it down to experience. Let's go out and get pissed tonight at Ray's party. I have got a small bottle of Vodka that I'm going to put in my bag so we can top up our drinks without paying for them at the bar. Ray likes whisky so I'm going to get him a bottle from us for his birthday'

When the call ended Val started to cry again. She was left with a real mess

When Bob Blake got home from work he found a letter from his solicitor enclosing a cheque for £102,985.25.  Probate had been completed and that was what he was due after expenses. He would have to bank the cheque on Monday because the HSBC branch in Flixham wasn't open on Saturdays. He hadn't decided whether he was going to Ray's party yet. He didn't know anybody other than those from work and they would probably be there with their other halves. He decided to start looking for a new car. He had picked out some of the smaller traders in Kings Lynn as a starter so after he had a sandwich a cup of tea and watched football focus on TV he took a leisurely drive to Kings Lynn. He wanted something that was a couple of years old preferably a hatchback that wouldn't attract any attention to him. By 4pm he had visited five garages. There were two cars that he had seen that had potential. One was silver VW Golf which was two years old and had low mileage. It was a 1.6L diesel engine. The other was another Astra. It was a 1.8l diesel engine 18 months old with 28000 miles on the clock. It was metallic blue and looked in very good condition. It was almost like a new model. Both cars were on sale at £8995.  He told both salesmen that he was prepared to pay cash and include his Astra as a part exchange. He was offered £250 part ex for the VW and £275 part ex for the Astra. He told both salesmen that he was interested but wanted to think about it. He left them his phone number and headed home aiming to get there in time for the football results. He had just got home when his mobile rang. It was the salesman for the VW. He told Blake that he'd had a word with his manager and seeing that it would be a cash deal he could have the car for eight thousand four hundred plus his Astra.  Blake told him that he would think about it. He needed to get quotes for insurance and wouldn't be able to get the cash until the end of the week anyway because he had a cheque which needed clearing.  The football results came through and Mansfield had lost again.  He put some sausages and a jacket potato in the oven and started to check how much the insurance would be for the two cars on Go Compare one of the website's that were always on the TV.  When his food was ready he sat down to eat.  There was nothing on TV again. An inane game show was on one side and Casualty was on the other after the lottery show. He hated both shows so he decided he may as well go to Ray's party. It was a ten minute walk to the sports club. He had to nip down to Morrisons to get a card and a bottle of malt whisky as a present for Ray. Bob Parsons had tipped him off that Ray was a malt whiskey drinker. He arrived at Morrison's five minutes before they were due to close where he bumped into Danny Collins at one of the last two checkouts that were open.

Danny looked at the bottle in Blake's hand.

`You are going to Ray's party then'. He also had a bottle of malt whisky.

`Ray will have enough whisky to last him until Christmas at this rate. Were there any problems at work after I left? '

`None at all but that detective who was in yesterday came in to see me. He wanted details of the drivers and the rest of the staff. I gave him the phone numbers for the drivers but said that he would have to come back on Monday for the staff details as I didn't have access to them. He reckons that the police will be back again on Monday'

`Why did you give them the driver's numbers? What did they need them for?' Collins asked

Blake detected a tone of annoyance in Collins voice.

`I didn't think it would matter. He said that some senior detectives would be in Monday and I thought that if I didn't give them to him I would have had to give it to them instead'

Collins shopping arrived at the checkout girl who started to ring it through

`I will see you later' he said and started chatting up the checkout girl who was young enough to be his daughter.

Blake went home had a shave and a shower. He looked through his sparse wardrobe for something to wear. He wasn't blessed with much choice when it came to casual clothes. He had been strictly a jeans and sweatshirt person. He selected the same blue chinos that he had worn to the quiz at the Red Lion on Thursday evening and an oatmeal coloured round neck sweater. He also wore one of the new stripes shirts that he had bought at BHS in Mansfield. It was white with dark blue stripes. He put a bit of gel on his hair, splashed on some aftershave and was ready to go.

31

The room that Ray had booked for his party was about half full when Blake arrived shortly after eight thirty. The only people that he recognised were Ray, Bob Parsons and the receptionist June Eason who was there with her husband. He went over to Ray and gave him his card and present.
`Thanks mate you didn't have to do that. Get yourself a beer. The first one of the night is on me but with the way my mates drink I couldn't afford to pay for it all night'
`Thanks Ray. How many have you got coming?'
`About eighty I think. My wife has done all the food which is over there' he said pointing to a long table which ran the length of one of the walls.
`She is going to take the cling film off at 9pm by which time everyone who said that they are coming should be here. Danny and Paula said they are coming and I asked a couple of the drivers who live locally as well'
`I saw Danny earlier in Morrisons. He said that he was coming'
Ray moved away to welcome more guests as they spilled into the room. Blake noticed that Dimi Szabo and Mircea Tiriac two Romanian contract drivers had turned up. He had spoken to both of them but didn't really know them so he wasn't too surprised that they avoided him. They looked away from him when his eyes strayed in their direction. Dimi was 32, about five feet seven, slim with dark hair and eyes. He almost looked like he was Italian. Mircea was a bit taller, overweight and with premature balding hair. He looked much older than the 37 years that showed on his driving licence. Blake got his beer and stood by himself feeling like a spare part. Fortunately June Eason sensed his predicament and came over to talk to him along with her husband John who she introduced. When the subject turned to football June left them to it and went to talk to a couple of women who had just arrived. John was a Cambridge United supporter. Cambridge were also in the Conference and like Mansfield had been relegated from the football league
`Why Cambridge United?' Blake asked him
`I was born in a village called Chittenham which is few miles from Cambridge so they were the local team. I had a trial with them when I was fourteen but I wasn't good enough. I still turn out though for Flixham but I'm not sure how long I can carry on. Injuries tend to take longer to heal when you get past 35. I'm 37 now and in my line off work you need to stay fit'
`What do you for work John?' Blake asked
`I'm a heating engineer. I work for Rumbeltons out in Wisbech so my job involves plenty of bending up and down and working in tight spaces'

`What position do you play?'

`I'm a right back. I have played there since I was a kid. I love getting stuck in but I'm not as quick as I was and I have struggled to keep up with some of the young nippy little buggers in our league. It's not like the old days when you could clatter them a couple of times before the referee pulled you to one side for a word. Now it is one foul and you are in the book'

`How are Flixham getting on this season?' he asked

`We didn't get off to the best start but then we signed two new players, a couple of black lads. One of them Denny is a bloody good centre half and we stopped conceding goals. The other one was Lynton Andrews the one who got killed on Tuesday. He was OK but a bit of a thug. He got booked several times and got sent off a couple of weeks back. I doubt if anybody will miss him. He wasn't the most popular of people. Denny, though is as good as gold but we hear he won't be playing for a few weeks. Somebody gave him a right kicking on Wednesday and he ended up in hospital. Rumour has it that it was the same people who were involved at Welney picnic site incident. Luckily for us our last two games have been postponed. The weather put paid to them so hopefully Denny will be back when they are re-scheduled"

Blake didn't admit that he had met Lynton Andrews. Best let nobody know that he'd had a run in with Andrews before Tuesday night

`I might come down and watch the next home game. When is it?'

`Next Saturday. If you are free come down and we can have a sneaky beer after the game. The prices are good in the clubhouse. They are about fifty pence cheaper than the pubs on average'

Blake and Eason continued talking about their teams performances in the Conference League. Cambridge was having a good season. They were going well and were close to the top of the league. Mansfield was languishing in mid table.

Val and Lesley were talking with June. June knew Lesley from the school gate and they were all discussing the spare men that were at the party. Lesley asked June who the little Italian was.

`He is Romanian. His name is Dimi. He works at Collins Transport as contract driver. His mate works there too.'

`I don't fancy yours' Lesley said to Val and howled with laughter.

`I don't fancy yours either. He is too short for me. I am at least three inches taller than him even without my heels. His mate looks old enough to be my dad' Val replied `Who is the bloke talking to your old man?'

`That's Bob Blake our new Transport Manager. He is a bit of an enigma. Nobody knows much about him.  Paula told me that he has just got divorced and is renting a place in town. He is a nice enough bloke though. He is not bad looking either'

`I would' laughed Lesley. She was already half cut having drunk the best part of a bottle of Pinot Grigio before she came out.

`Let's face it Lesley you would shag the old bald one if there was nothing else going.' Val said 'the amount you have put away tonight he will look like Brad Pitt to you by eleven'

`He couldn't have been any worse than that Lynton. He was hopeless .He must have spent hours in the gym because he was all muscle. He might have had big guns on his arms but he only had a small trigger'. Lesley said wiggling her little finger

The girls all roared with laughter

`Did you really fuck him?' June asked. `You kept that very quiet. Did you have any idea that he was messing about dealing drugs?'

`I had no idea that he was a drug dealer. He just said that he was having a break from work after a long spell of hard graft. We went out the week before last. I went out with Val him and his mate. Val was lucky. That Denny was a stud and was hung like a horse. Tell her about him Val'

`There's nothing to tell. We went out for a meal, he came back to my place and we fucked all night but he is a bastard. Doesn't want to know me now he has had his end away'

`Typical man' June said.

They spent the next half hour chatting and laughing eventually being joined by three other women.

Blake had a chat with Danny and Paula when they eventually arrived. Danny seemed a bit agitated and appeared to be looking for somebody in the room.

`I'm just going to have a word with Dimi and Mircea'.

He walked over to where the two Romanians were stood doing Meerkat impressions eyeing up the local talent.

`I have had the police asking awkward questions about the incident at the picnic site. Somebody from Peterborough fingered me. They are coming in on Monday morning to interview the staff. They don't have any evidence linking us with it so if they start asking questions just say nothing and we will be in the clear.'

`We will act all innocent' Mircea replied but Collins could see that Dimi was concerned

`Remember that they have nothing on us so just stay calm. Enjoy the evening and I will see you next week'.

He left them and went back to Paula and Blake

Blake ran into John Eason again at the bar. Eason had another two men with him and they teased Blake about Mansfield Town

'Looks like the girls are getting pissed' Eason said to the other men who were called Tom and Terry.

'Look at the state of Lesley Farmer. There is more of her hanging out of her dress than there is in it. You want to avoid that one mate. You wouldn't be doing a Captain Kirk there.' Eason said to Blake raising a laugh from the other two

'Captain Kirk'? Blake asked. 'I don't get it.'

'The Starship Enterprise and going where no man has been before'

'Who is the woman in the powder blue dress and the glasses' Blake asked. He had noticed her earlier. She was tall and slim. She was wearing a tight powder blue dress that finished just above the knee and some ankle boots. The dress showed of her trim figure.

'That is Val Davey. June heard that she is having trouble with her marriage. Her old man is back with his mum. Apparently she has been putting it about. Someone said that Denny is shagging her. I wouldn't want to be following him though. I have seen him in the showers'

Blake was looking at her when she turned and saw him. She gave a brief smile and turned back to talk to her friends. He caught her having glances in his direction throughout the night. Ray's wife Gemma was dancing with some of her friends and there were a couple of them that he thought were quite attractive. He thought about asking Ray if any of them were single but Ray was busy holding court in a group of males. Blake had spent the last hour or so talking blokes talk with John and his two mates Tom and Terry. Their wives joined them and managed to get them out onto the dance floor. The band was ideal for a birthday party. They wouldn't win any prizes for quality but they played a mixture of songs from the sixties through to the start of the 21st century. Most of their songs were old standards such as Hi ho Silver lining by Jeff Beck, Buck Rogers by Feeder and I Predict a Riot by the Kaiser Chiefs. June even got Blake out onto the dance floor. Blake was no Fred Astaire but he was comfortable dancing. He noticed that Dimi was in deep conversation with the woman they called Lesley. He had seen them dancing together and that Dimi had his hands all over her. The blond in the pale blue dress also joined the group of them as they congregated by the bar. Her mate was preoccupied with Dimi and she appeared to be at a loose end. Blake plucked up the courage to engage her in small talk.

'The band are playing some good songs' He said for a not very original opening line

`They are OK. I have seen them before as they are local. I hear that you are new in town and work at Collins Transport' she said `What makes you want to live in a deadbeat place like Flixham?'

`Work basically. I was made redundant at about this time last year and there were no jobs in the Mansfield area where I used to live. I split up with my wife so I decided on a fresh start. I'm renting a place in town but if the job goes well I will probably buy something in Kings Lynn as there is a bit more going on there. Do you live in Flixham?'

`I do for now but I want to get out of the place. I'm having a few problems with my marriage which I won't bore you with. We will probably split up for good. I work in Kings Lynn so I will probably go and live there. I can't afford my place on my own so I will end up sharing with somebody'

The band played a Billy Ocean song and all the woman including Val took off to the dance floor. When they had finished dancing Val ignored Blake and started talking with her friend Lesley who had escaped the clutches of Dimi. It was past eleven now and the bar was due to shut at eleven thirty so Blake got a round in for John and the two mates. It was Blake's sixth or seventh pint and he was feeling slightly merry. Much to his surprise he had actually enjoyed the night. He had met a few people from the area. He decided that he would come along to watch Flixham play next weekend. The band announced that their last song of the night was going to be "Unchained Melody" and most of the couple went to the dance floor. Blake looked around for Val but couldn't see her. Danny was nearby and asked him if he had enjoyed the evening.

`I have enjoyed myself. I met a few people and I'm going to watch your team next week. June's husband plays for them and said I should come and watch them'

`Yes he does. He is still a steady full back even though he has lost a yard of pace. I will see you on Monday'

The band finished the last song and the lights all came on signalling the end of the party. Blake downed the last of his beer, said goodnight to everyone and headed for the cloakroom to pick up his coat. Val was in the queue ahead of him on her own. She saw him when she collected her coat and waited until he got his.

`My mate has buggered off with a bloke. His mate has been hanging around me for the last half hour. I think he has gone for a piss. Will you walk home with me because I don't want him to follow me home?'

Blake thought about it before he agreed.

`Where do you live?' He asked her

`Rosario Road. It's off Deehan Road which is one of the roads off Main Street. Where do you live?'

`Turnberry Close.'

`That's only five minutes from mine. You can go down Barham Road which brings you out by that estate'

Blake noticed that she was slurring her words and she hung onto his arm as they started the walk home to steady herself.

`I'm Bob by the way. What's your name?' He asked

`I'm Val.' she replied. `June says you are divorced. Do you have any children?'

`I have two, a girl and a boy. They are both grown up so it wasn't too much of a problem when my wife and I divorced. My son is studying for A' levels and my daughter is a trainee accountant'

`They are brainy then?'

They walked on in silence for a few hundred yards before Val asked him about the house he was renting.

`It's just a small one bedroom end terrace house. It's big enough for me and it gives me the chance to look around before I decide where I want live'

The chilly air seemed to go to her head because her words seemed to get more slurred the further they went.

`My mate went off with one of your drivers and left me trying to fend off his mate. He looks old enough to be my dad. He works for you as well my friend said'

 Blake presumed that she was talking about Dimi and Mircea.

`Strictly speaking they don't work for me. They are self employed contract drivers so we pay them for the jobs that they do. If they don't work they don't get paid. The man you are referring to is only 37. He just looks older because he is going bald'

`You are kidding me. He looks much older than that. He is only five years older than me.'

`Perhaps he had a hard paper round' Blake replied.

 So Val is 32 he thought to himself calculating that there was an eleven year age gap between them. The attempt at a joke went right over Val's head.

They reached Val's flat after about ten minutes

`Do you want to come in for a coffee?' She asked him

`I wouldn't mind a quick one' he replied in all innocence

`Well you might be lucky.' She giggled

 They went in to a flat which was nicely furnished and decorated. Blake noticed a big hole in the kitchen door where Val went to make the coffee. He could hear her crashing about. She was well pissed.

`Do you want milk and sugar? It's only instant'

`White no sugar please' he shouted in the direction of the kitchen

Blake walked around the room looking at some of the many photos that adorned the walls. There were several photos of Val and her husband including a wedding photo. It must have been taken a long time ago because Val had much longer hair than she has now. The glasses were missing in the photos.
Val came back with two mugs
'Come and sit next to me she said putting the mugs on coasters.'
Blake sat down on the sofa leaving a space between the pair of them. They small talked while drinking their coffee. Blake finished his.
`I had better go" he said "I have got to find my way back to my place'.
He got up to leave. Val grabbed his hand and pulled him to her. They kissed but Blake pulled away. He hesitated but then pulled her to him and they kissed again
`I would ask you to stay the night but I have been let down badly recently'
`I wouldn't have stayed. It's not that I don't fancy you but we have both had lots to drink and I would hate it if you woke up in the morning and regretted it'
Val looked disappointed but before she had time to say anything Blake started to talk again.
`Let's go out for a drink or to dinner and get to know each other. What is your number? I will ring you tomorrow to see if you still want to when you have a clear head'
"I'm good with that" she replied.
She wrote down her number and gave it to him. They kissed again before Blake left and started the walk home.

32

Blake slept in later than he normally would and didn't get out of bed until nine. He wasn't feeling worse for wear which was a surprise as he had drunk plenty the night before. He thought about the events of last night. Val wasn't the type of girl that he normally went for or truer to the fact that he used to go for. He liked his woman to be curvy. Val on the other hand was tall and slim with small breasts but there was something about her that appealed to him. Perhaps it was her long shapely legs. There was also the question about the difference in their ages. He thought that he shouldn't get ahead of himself. Once Val had sobered up he doubted if she would be interested in him anyway. He decided that he would have a drive into Norwich and look at some more cars. He thought about the two cars that he had seen yesterday and the Astra was his favourite but it would do any harm to have a look around before buying. He decided to take a chance and took £550 from the stash of money under his bed.

After showering and grabbing a coffee and a bit of toast Blake set off Norwich. He had checked on the internet and found that most dealers were open on Sundays and that there were more than twenty to look at. He trawled around half of them and found several cars that he shortlisted. At the eleventh garage he found exactly what he was after. He found a one year old VW Golf 1.6 diesel Blue Motion. At 34000 miles it was high mileage for a one year old car but it was in very good condition. It was dark blue with a grey interior. The tyres looked as though they had been changed recently. Road tax was low at £30 a year. It was price at £9795. Blake went into the showroom and arranged for a test drive. It drove very well so when he and the salesman called Eddie returned to the garage he decided that he would have it if the price was right. `I am looking to part exchange my car in the deal and I would like to pay you in cash next Saturday if we can strike a deal. I like the car but I am concerned about such a high mileage for a one year old car. It is a bit more money than I had planned to spend so what is the best deal that you can offer me'
Eddie looked through his car price book

'We would be looking at £300 for yours in part exchange so that would take the price down to £9495. It comes with a six months guarantee and there is also a parts warranty still active from VW. How does that sound?'

'Too much money is how it sounds. I will get to the point. I am only prepared to offer you £9000 in cash plus mine. That offer is on the table for the next fifteen minutes. I will give you a deposit today and bring the rest in next Saturday afternoon after I finish at work'

Blake was chancing his arm.

'I don't think we can do a deal at that price. I don't think that my manager would agree'

'Ok' Blake said and got up to leave 'I have another Golf that I saw in Kings Lynn yesterday. The garage is offering a better deal. Thanks for your time'

Eddie was flustered. He hadn't expected such a direct approach from Blake and trade had been almost nonexistent for the past three weeks.

'Let me have a quick word with my manager to see if he can do a bit better'

'He will need to do a lot better if he wants a sale today' Blake replied. He had noted that there was a large stock of cars on the forecourt and that he was the only person in the showroom while he had been there.

Eddie went into his manager's office. The manager returned with him.

'Hello Mr Blake. I'm Don West. I gather you are keen on the Golf. I can let you have it for £9350 plus yours

'I have already told Eddie what I am prepared to pay and I won't budge from that number so unfortunately we can't agree on the price. Thanks for your time '. Blake repeated the get up and leave move.

'If you change your mind give me a ring' Don West said offering his card as Blake was leaving.

'I won't be giving you a ring. I told young Eddie here that my offer is on the table for fifteen minutes. The offer ends when I leave. I do like the car but I saw another car in Kings Lynn yesterday and they are offering a better deal and their car has a much lower mileage'. He opened the door and left. He lingered by the Golf before heading back to his car.

Don West was wavering. It had been a very quiet two months in which he had only sold three cars. All were cheaper cars which gave him less £4000 profit for the three and he needed some money to pay the staff as well as himself. Blake was offering cash so not all of it would need to go through the books. At the full price he was making £2500 profit plus what he could make on the part exchange but even at the price Blake wanted to pay he was still making a £1700 profit.

'Eddie, Go after him before he drives off and tell him we have a deal.

Eddie ran out of the showroom and waved his arms at Blake who was about to drive off

`Mr West will agree to the £9000 price'

Blake stopped his car and went in and did the deal leaving Don West a two hundred pound cash deposit.

`I will bring the balance with me next Saturday afternoon. I have received a cheque from my solicitors which needs to clear first otherwise I would have brought it in earlier'

`We will have the car ready for you then. See you Saturday' West said.

Blake left and went back to his car smiling. He couldn't believe what he had just done. He would never have behaved that way negotiating a price six months ago. He had also committed to using the money that he had recovered from the picnic site. He decided that he would withdraw nine thousand pounds from his current account so that he would have an audit trail if a question was asked at a future date where the cash from the car came from. He was going to open an ISA account and some building society accounts and gradually put money into them. He had passed a nice country pub on the drive to Norwich which advertised Sunday lunches at twelve quid for two courses so he stopped there on the way home where he had roast beef with all the trimmings, sticky toffee pudding washed down with a couple of pints of Adnams. He was starting to enjoy life in Norfolk. He would give Val a call when he got home.

Val Davey slept until ten thirty and woke up with a headache. She remembered most of last evening. Bob Blake seemed a bit different to some of the blokes that she knew. Denny wasted no time getting into her knickers and Colin the builder she shagged also wanted the fuck her at the first opportunity but Bob accepted her refusal to let him stay the night without any argument. He was a bit older than her but she quite fancied him and was hoping that he would phone her. Her landline rang at noon. It was Lesley.

`Thanks for buggering off and leaving me on my own last night' Val said angrily

`I'm sorry. I was pissed and I really fancied Dimi so when he offered to take me home I said yes. I thought that you were OK with June and her mates'

`No, I ended up asking Bob Blake to walk me home'

`He is a bit old isn't he?'

`Not really. He is probably about 40 but he is in good shape. I think he is good looking. He is a gentleman too. He came in for coffee but didn't try it on. I suppose Dimi stayed the night'

"Yes. He stayed all night too! I have never known a feller with so much stamina. He lasted for ages. He was like one of those Duracell bunnies. We did it again this morning too. It was the best shag I have had for ages. I am going to see him on Wednesday. Have you arranged anything with Bob?'

`He took my number and said that he would phone me today. I'm not sure if he will though because I was well pissed'

`I have already arranged to meet up with Dimi again in the week. I am going to shag his brains out'

`Let's hope he isn't using you like Denny did with me' Val said bitterly

33

Florian Chipciu arrived on the 0939 flight from Nice to Luton. He was an ex member of Romania's 1st Special Operations Force. He was 48 and had left the force at the age of 40. He had used Luton airport before for other jobs and these jobs became more lucrative as his reputation enhanced. He had flown under the name of Rene Dupree using one of the many false passports that he owned. He had a contact in nearby Dunstable who would supply him with the tools that he would need for this job.

He had worked for Ivan Petrescu before. Petrescu paid well and on each of his previous jobs for him the hit had been clean with no issues to worry about. Chipciu travelled light with just a small holdall which contained a change of underwear, a clean sweater and jeans. He was going to buy some cheap clothes from the big Asda store in Luton which would be disposed of after the job was completed. He had a burner mobile phone and five thousand Euros in his wallet. Three thousand of this money was in five hundred euro notes and most of this will be going to the illegal arms dealer that he was going to meet that afternoon. The dealer was going to supply him with a Glock 17 handgun with a suppressor and a switchblade plus a suitable amount of ammunition for the job he had in mind. He changed a thousand Euros into pounds sterling at a money exchange bureau at the airport. It was a lousy exchange rate but he considered this to be part of the expenses for the job. It was also an anonymous trade as well. His first stop was an Avis car rental where he hired a Ford Focus for three days using a credit card also in the name of Rene Dupree. He left the airport and went to the Asda store in Luton where he purchased a back pack, a cheap black padded jacket , a pair of black jeans ,a black sweatshirt ,some tee shirts as well as a couple of cheap pairs of socks and pants. This cost him less than one hundred pounds and it would all be disposed of after the job was done.  The cheap clothes would not stand out which was perfect because he didn't want to be noticed. He made his appointment with the arms dealer and by 2pm he was on the A505 heading towards East Anglia. He stopped on the outskirts of Peterborough and booked into a Travel Lodge for the night. He planned to do more research on his victim that evening. If the opportunity arose he would make the hit on Monday. If not it would have to be done on Tuesday before heading back to Luton where he had booked a room in an Isis hotel which was close enough to the airport to enable him to drop off the hire car and walk to the hotel. He was booked onto the first flight out of Luton to Nice on Wednesday on a budget airline.

Dennard Hoyte slept heavily on Saturday night. He woke up in the early hours on Sunday. His head ached and he couldn't get comfortable in bed. No matter how he laid his balls hurt. He was hungry so he got up but there wasn't much food in the cupboards. As he had managed to get a signal on his phone halfway into town yesterday he hadn't  bothered to walk the rest of the journey into town to stock up on food. He was now regretting it. He hadn't eaten since the meagre breakfast he'd had in hospital. There were a few slices of bread left in the bread bin. He opened the fridge and found that there was about a pint of milk left in a four pint container which was nearly a week old. He sniffed at it and it smelled ok. There was a half tub of butter and a small chunk of cheese. The small freezer section of the fridge freezer contained a chicken pie and there was about half a bag of chips. He took the chicken pie out of the freezer to thaw out. To cook it from frozen would take ages in the small oven at the park home. He put the four remaining slices of bread under the grill in the oven and made himself some coffee. He added the cheese to the toast and felt a bit better after eating it. Apart from a couple of tubs of pot noodles and a tin of baked beans the cupboard was bare. He would have to go into town especially as he wanted to call Collins. After eating he went back to bed and didn't wake up again until eleven. He slung on some clothes and started the slow walk into town. He got a signal in the same spot as he did yesterday and immediately phoned Danny Collins. Collin's phone was switched off.  Hoyte was getting low on money. He checked his pockets and found he had forty pounds left plus a bit of shrapnel. Lynton had left a few quid in coins in the drawer of his bedside cabinet so he had just over fifty quid. He was planning to nick a car so he would need money for fuel and no doubt the gas bottle would be empty again soon. The police had been in the place while Hoyte was in hospital looking for drugs no doubt. It couldn't have been a very thorough search otherwise they would have found his mobile and thankfully Lynton had the foresight to stash their guns in some bushes behind the bin storage area. He had said that as the site was empty nobody would go sniffing about behind the bin sheds.  Hoyte eventually reached the Value Shoppers store after about 30 minutes of painful walking. He spent £7.86 on a loaf, some sausages, a pint of milk, a frozen chicken curry and a small bag of own brand oven chips. This would have to last him for three days. Hoyte phoned Collins three times again on his walk into town and back but still got a message saying" We are unable to connect your call. Please try again later" Eventually Hoyte got fed up and decided to leave a text message before he got to the no signal area.

He wrote " *My mate is dead because of you and your drug dealing friends .I want ten thousand pounds from you or I will go to the police and tell them all.*"

Dennard Hoyte wasn't the only person trying to contact Danny Collins. Bogdan Stancvic was furious with the way Collins had spoken to him and he didn't like anybody hanging up on him. He wasn't sure that he believed Collins' tale about having no money. Collins lived in a big house and drove an expensive car. His business seemed to be solid enough but Stancvic had never seen his books so he didn't know how much money it was making. He also questioned why Collins would take the risk of transporting drugs for Petrescu and himself for such a paltry reward. Perhaps he was short of money after all. He phoned Collins several times during the day. Every time he failed to get through and after each attempt his temper rose. It was time to pay Collins a visit he decided.

Danny Collins switched on his PAYG mobile at 330pm. He saw that he had several missed calls from both Hoyte and Stancvic. He read Hoyte's message and replied by text *"You're not getting nothing from me so go fuck yourself. Go to the police if you want but don't forget the previous trades. You are an integral part of it "*
He ignored Stancvic. He wasn't going to let that arsehole further annoy him. He would wait until he heard from Ivan Petrescu before deciding what to do. He switched his phone off. Paula had gone shopping in London and had taken Charlotte with her for a bit of retail therapy as she had been down after the accident so he had the house to himself. Paula's arm was much better and as the hire car supplied by her insurance company was an automatic so driving to Kings Lynn station was not a problem. She was going to call in at their favourite Chinese takeaway on the way home. She said that they hoped that they would be home by 7pm. Everton were playing Liverpool in the Sky 4pm kick off. He was going to relax, watch the game and have a few beers while watching it. Tomorrow was going to be a challenge as he expected DCI Booth to turn up and give him a hard time again.  She would be questioning all of the staff but this caused him no concern as nobody other than Paula Dimi and Mircea knew about his deal with the Romanians.
By the time the game was over he had sunk eight bottles of Peroni and had left them strewn over the coffee table where they were joined by several empty bags of crisps. He thought that he had better clear them away before Paula got home as he didn't want her giving him a coating for leaving the place in a mess. He was feeling the effect of the beers.  It was dark outside and turning cold again with a brisk wind blowing. He carried the empty bottles of beer on the

fingers of each hand and the empty crisp bags and some old newspapers under his arm.  As he went to throw them in the re-cycling bin a gust of wind took one of the crisp bags and it blew towards the lawn of the front garden.

`Fuck it' he swore to himself and went chasing after it. He finally caught it by stamping on it. He bent to pick it up. It was the last thing he saw as a bullet hit him in the chest. The gunman walked towards his prone body and shot him again in the head.  He then went into Collins' house. After searching the house he came out with some jewellery and the keys to Collins' Range Rover... The front door was left open and Collins was left lying dead on the front lawn.

34

Paula and Charlotte arrived home just before seven pm. They were immediately concerned that Danny's car wasn't in the garage and that the front door was open. She parked the car in the garage and went in the house very cautiously followed by Charlotte. The TV was still switched on but there was no sign of Danny. She went upstairs and saw that somebody had been rummaging through the drawers in her chest and dressing table. Charlotte went out into the back garden which was lit up by a security light but there was no sign of her father in the shed at the bottom of the garden. She went back out of the front door to see if Danny with their neighbour. The security light came on which lit up part of the front garden. She saw her father lying on the grass in the far corner of the garden. They hadn't noticed him when they arrived home. She screamed loudly

'Mum, come quickly. I have found Dad.'

She walked towards the prone figure and screamed again when she saw the blood on her father's head and chest. Paula ran towards them and started sobbing when she saw what had happened. She cradled Danny's head in her arms. Steve Smith her next door neighbour came out to see what all the noise was about

'Is everything Ok Paula?' he asked before it became obvious that it was Danny in Paula's arms. 'Bloody hell' was all he could say. 'I will phone the police and call for an ambulance'.


Daley was in Norwich at Bev's sister's house when he received a phone call telling him that Danny Collins had been shot dead.

'I need to go. Somebody had been murdered in Flixham'

He and Bev made their apologies and left. He dropped Bev off at home and went straight to the scene where DCI Booth had assumed charge of the incident. She was interviewing Paula Collins in the lounge.

'Do you know of anybody who would want to harm your husband?' Booth asked

Paula hesitated before answering. Her immediate thoughts were that it could have been either of the two Romanians that Danny had been dealing with but she was too scared to give Booth their names.

`No, I can't think of anybody who would have done this to Danny. He was well liked by everyone. You can ask his staff at the transport company. They all loved him and would do anything for him because he looked after them'
`I am going to have to interview all of the staff at Collins Transport. We have been given information pointing to the company being involved in a drug smuggling racket. I am sure that your husband told you that his name was put forward as a suspect by intelligence from Peterborough. I need names and addresses for all of your employees including the drivers. I will be conducting interviews tomorrow so can you arrange for them to be made available. I believe that only you and your late husband have access to this'
`That information is rubbish. Danny wasn't involved with drug smuggling. He runs a respectable firm. I am in no fit state to come into the office tomorrow. My husband has just been murdered. How can you expect me to come to work so soon?' She started sobbing again
`The sooner you give us this information the better our chances of catching the killer. I thought that this would be uppermost in your mind. You will be doing your husband a service by helping us to find his killer'.
Daley heard the end of the conversation and shook his head. He couldn't believe how insensitive Booth could be. DS Graham Brown showed Daley a message on a mobile phone that he found on the coffee table in the lounge.
`I better hand this over to Booth ASAP' he told Daley
He gave the phone to Booth who had left Paula and had come outside. The message was still open. She read the message and the reply.
`I knew that Collins was involved with the incident at the picnic site and this proves it' she told Daley   `Calls from four different numbers were made to this phone in the past week and there is a text message which looks like it was sent by Dennard Hoyte today attempting to extort money from Collins. Collins replied telling him to fuck off. A few hours later Collins has been shot dead and his car has been stolen. Put out a warrant for Hoyte's arrest. I am going to have another word with Mrs Collins'
`Do you think that's wise Ma'am. Her husband has just been murdered and she will still be in shock. Why not give her a bit more time' Daley suggested.
`I have got a killer to catch and I don't have time to pussy foot around. She knows more than she is letting on. She should do everything to help us catch the bastard that killed her old man. You know where Hoyte lives. Go with DS Brown and pick the bastard up'
`I'm not sure that Hoyte is in any fit state to pull a stunt like this Ma'am. He's had a right beating and from what Mick Judge told me he had difficulty walking because of the kick to his testicles. His car is still in Deehan Road so he would

have had to walk here from his place and that's a good twenty five minute walk'

`What is wrong with you Arthur? Look at the bloody evidence. Hoyte's mate got killed, Hoyte attempted to extort money from Collins. Collins basically told him to fuck off.  Collins is found shot dead the same afternoon. His car has been stolen. Hoyte doesn't have a car as his has been wrecked. What more evidence do you need?  Hoyte is our man. I have a gut feeling just as I did with Collin's involvement in the case. I will send PC May and PC Fowler with DS Brown to arrest Hoyte instead. Make yourself useful and stop doubting me. Go and interview all the neighbours. You never know somebody might have a security camera. Take Skid with you'

Susan Voller the family liaison office arrived as Daley and Marks were leaving to question neighbours.

`Go easy with them Sue.  Booth has been all over Mrs Collins giving her a hard time' Daley whispered out of Booth's earshot

Daley thought that Booth was jumping to conclusions prematurely. According to the neighbours who were home nobody had seen or heard anything. There were no CCTV cameras in the small close where Collins lived. Surely Hoyte would show up on the CCTV cameras in Flixham Main Street if he had walked from his place to here and he doubted that they had been checked given the timescale

`I would have wanted some visual evidence of Hoyte being in the area before assuming that he was our man' Daley said to Booth when reporting back to her.

`That's why I'm the DCI and you are a DS. I make decisive decisions. You fart about wasting time' she said before walking off to give some unsuspecting PC a hard time

Dennard Hoyte was asleep in bed when the police led by DS Brown started banging on his front door. Hoyte crawled out of bed and opened the door.

`Get some clothes on Hoyte' Brown demanded

`What the fuck is going on?' said a confused Hoyte, still half asleep.

`Dennard Hoyte I am arresting you in connection with the murder of Daniel Collins. You do not have to say anything but anything you do say could be used as evidence against you' said Brown reading him his rights

`You are fucking kidding me. I haven't left this place since I got home after getting out of hospital apart from a walk down to Budgens at lunchtime today to get some grub. I haven't seen Collins for well over a week. This is all wrong. I haven't done anything'

Hoyte was handcuffed after putting on some jeans and a sweatshirt before being led to a police car where he was driven to Kings Lynn police station. He was put in a cell where he remained until he was taken to an interview room to be interviewed by DCI Booth

Booth opened by telling Hoyte that he was suspected of the murder of Daniel Collins

'This is a fucking joke. I told the other copper that I haven't seen Collins for over a week. When was I supposed to have killed him? I got out of hospital yesterday and went home on the bus. I haven't been out of the house since one today when I went into town to get some food. Look at the state of me. I can hardly walk because my bollocks took a kicking'

'Explain this text message then which was sent from the phone recovered at your home'

Hoyte went quiet for a moment. He realised that his only option was to tell the big copper the whole story while attempting to minimise his involvement in it.

'Collins approached me and Lynton before Christmas at the football ground and offered us a job. I wasn't keen on taking the job because it sounded a bit iffy but Lynton was dead keen. He couldn't drive so he needed me to do the driving. Lynton could be loose cannon and if I hadn't agreed who knows what he would have done to me. We met Collins in the car park at The Star in Flixham. He gave us a locked bag which we took to a picnic site out on the A1101 where we met some Eastern Europeans who exchanged our bag for another locked bag which we took back to Collins in the car park in The Star pub. He gave us an envelope containing a thousand pounds. We asked Collins what was in the bags but he told us that it was on a need to know basis. For Lynton and me it seemed like easy money so we didn't ask any further questions. We did two drops for him and were due to do another one last Tuesday. Unfortunately I crashed my car on the way to meet Lynton so he went by himself. I don't know how he got to the picnic site because he couldn't drive. You all know what happened on Tuesday night. Collins owed us money for doing the drop. I want to go back to Bristol but I don't have a car because of the crash. I don't have any money so I asked Collins for some'

'So when he told you to fuck all you decided to take matters into your own hands'

'When did he tell me to fuck off? I don't know that he had.'

Booth showed Hoyte the message on his phone.

'There is no signal at my home and as I hadn't been out since I got home from the shop I wouldn't have seen it. I swear that's the first time I've seen that message. I didn't kill Collins. I swear I didn't do it'

`That is all bullshit. Did Collins arrange for the kicking that you had? Were you after revenge for that? As far as I am concerned you had all the right motives for killing Collins and stealing his car. Where have you hidden it?'

`What fucking car? You are some crazy bitch. I don't know what you are talking about. I want a lawyer'

He crossed his arms and didn't say another word other than no comment.

`You say that you haven't seen Collins for over a week yet his car was seen heading in the direction of your home and coming back from the same direction about half hour later on Tuesday night. Are you trying to say that you never met up with him on Tuesday night?'

Hoyte hesitated wondering how the police knew that Collins had been to his place

`All right then it's nearly a week since I saw Collins. He came to my place looking for Lynton but as he wasn't there he fucked off in a mood. I haven't seen him since. I tried phoning him this morning but his phone was switched off so I sent him that message. You are trying to stitch me up. I want a lawyer'

`Take him back to his cell' Booth said to the duty officer

DS Mick Judge had sat in on the interview

`What do you think Ma'am? He sounded quite convincing to me. He looked genuinely surprised when you told him about the message he got from Collins. You know how poor reception is out in the sticks in this area. Perhaps he was telling the truth about no reception on his phone'

`Mark my words DS Judge. He is guilty. He never asked when or where Collins was murdered because he knows where it happened. My gut tells me that I am right. We are going to hit Collins' offices tomorrow to find out who is involved in this little caper with the drugs imports'

Mick Judge wasn't convinced but decided to keep his thoughts to himself. It was obvious to him that Hoyte was still having difficulty walking so he thought that it was unlikely that he would have wanted to walk to Collins' house from the park home site. If Booth wanted to make a pig's ear of it she can get on with it.

It was late afternoon by the time Blake plucked up the courage to call Val Davey. He was expecting to get rebuffed but to his surprise Val seemed quite pleased that he called

`Sorry about last night' she said `I had far too much to drink and with Lesley buggering off like that I wasn't in a fit state to get home by myself so thanks for being my knight in shining armour'

`I am always ready to help a damsel in distress' Blake replied. `Do you remember much about last night?'

`I remember that you were a perfect gentleman and didn't try to take advantage of me considering the state I was in. I remember that we had a kiss and that I gave you my number. I didn't think that I would hear from you again though if I am honest'

`Do you remember me saying that I suggested that we go out for a drink or to dinner?'

`Vaguely' she replied hesitating over the words

`I wanted to ask you when you were not under the influence of alcohol. Would you like to meet up?'

`I think that might be nice'

`I don't have anything planned all week. Would you like to go out on Friday evening? Perhaps we could go out for a meal together'

`Yes that sounds good. I'm not doing anything on Friday'. She wasn't doing anything all week as it was Lesley's week with the kids

`What types of food do you like and is there anywhere that you would recommend? I am new to the area so I don't know which pubs and restaurants are good'

`I don't mind what type of restaurant we go to as I eat most types of food. There is nowhere I would recommend in Flixham other than the Red Lion. Some of the village pubs have good reputations. There's the Fountain out on the way to Wisbech or the Cross Keys on the Kings Lynn road. I haven't been to either of them for a while but that would mean you having to drive'

`That's not a problem. Leave it to me and I will book something. I will ask Danny Collins to suggest somewhere. He eats out regularly. I will pick you up at eight'

`See you on Friday then'. She hung up

`That went better than I thought it would' Blake said aloud to himself. Danny would know where to go. He wanted to impress her on their first date and if he had to spend a few quid so what. It would come out of the stash under his bed.


DCI Booth had slept well. She was going to formally charge Dennard Hoyte with the murder of Danny Collins. She arranged for a duty solicitor to be at a 1300 interview with Hoyte at Kings Lynn Station and had arranged for a press conference at 1530 where she planned to announce that Hoyte was being charged with the murder of Danny Collins. She was also going to announce that Danny Collins was involved in a drug smuggling operation which culminated in the death of three men at the picnic site on the A1101. What she wanted now was to get details of the drug smuggling operation and the interviews with the staff at Collins Transport which were due to start at 0930

Paula Collins arrived at the depot at 0900 and immediately called for a meeting with all of the staff and drivers who were still on site. She told the shocked room that Danny had been shot dead in his front garden yesterday evening and that the police were due to arrive at nine thirty to interview them in relation to an alleged illegal activity involving the smuggling of drugs. Paula told the staff that this was a total fabrication made up by the police and that the staff should help them in any way they could. As far as she was concerned it was a break in that had gone wrong. Danny's car, jewellery and money had been taken.
`I know that this has come as a big shock to everyone but I feel that we should try to keep the company going. It was Danny's life's work building this company up from next to nothing to the successful company that it is now and I feel that we all have a duty to keep it going on his behalf'
She was fighting to hold herself together and there were tears from a lot of the staff. Paula called Blake into Danny's office
`Can you keep things going for me Bob? I will increase the hours that I do but I don't have much experience of dealing with contracts with our customers. Can you help with that?'
`I will do what I can Paula. I will get together with Ruth on the contracts matter. Where did the police get the idea that Danny was involved with drugs?'
`Somebody in Peterborough pointed the finger at him. I know that Danny would sometimes bring in some meat produce that wasn't on the books but he wouldn't get involved with drugs' she said lying through her teeth. She was going to have to speak to both Mircea Tiriac and Dimi Szabo who were the only

other people who knew about the side line. Danny had told her that he'd had a word with them on Saturday night but she was worried that Danny's death may have spooked them.

DCI Booth arrived at 0930 on the dot. She was accompanied by DS Brown, DS Judge, DC Butler and DC Marks. She totally ignored Daley. She didn't want to involve him at all. Booth was going to interview Mrs Collins and Bob Blake accompanied by DC Butler. Judge and Brown were to interview the office staff. Marks was to do likewise with the mechanics

Booth started with Paula Collins
She told Paula that the police had a written confession from somebody held in custody on the suspicion of Collin's murder that he and Lynton Andrews who was one of the men found dead at the Welney picnic site had been acting as couriers for what is suspected to have been drug trafficking
Paula didn't want to be in the office for a moment longer than she had too. She almost threw the staff details at Booth.
'I know nothing about this so called drug trafficking. Where is the proof that Danny was involved?' She said with confidence knowing that Danny had covered his tracks
Booth studied the list before saying anything.
`Which of the drivers do you use for trips to the continent?' was her opening question ignoring Paula's question
`I haven't got a clue. All that I do is the payroll and a few other admin items. I am the company secretary so I do all the Companies House crap. If you want to know about who drives where you will have to ask the Transport Manager' she snapped at Booth
`So you don't know what you are paying the drivers for when you make the payments. I find that hard to believe'
`I couldn't give a toss what you believe or don't believe. That is the way it's done. The drivers charge us by the hour. The transport manager allocates the routes. The accounts team verify the invoices that are given to us at the end of the week. I arrange for them to be paid directly into their bank accounts by BACS. Are we done because I have a funeral to arrange? '
`I'm not done yet. The quicker you answer my questions the quicker you can get away' Booth replied. `Who pays for the ferry and container costs?'
`We do. That's the accounts department's job. The transport manager arranges for the shipping and ferries. The drivers simply pick up the containers at the docks either in the UK or on the continent. We mainly use Rotterdam. The drivers charge us by the mile. The transport manager knows the routes and the

approximate mileage so nobody takes the piss with their invoices. Anybody over charging loses the contracts'

`Do any of the drivers make regular trips to Rotterdam?'

Paula was losing her temper.

`Are you deaf or just plain stupid? I told you that I don't know anything about what routes the drivers do. You need to speak to the transport manager for that. He has only been with us for a couple of weeks. Our previous Transport Manager, Keith Barnes, has just had major heart surgery so if Bob Blake can't answer your questions you will have to speak to Barnes. Good luck with that. I'm not answering any more questions'. She got up and left the office causing DC Butler to stifle a smile. Booth will have the right hump at being spoken to in that manner he thought.

Booth sent Butler to bring Blake to Danny Collins' office where she had taken residence.

`Mr Blake, I am DCI Booth. As you know Mr Collins was murdered yesterday. We have received a tip off that Collins Transport was bringing illegal substances into the country. I want to know which drivers were used for shipments from Rotterdam'.

`I only joined the company in January so I don't know about who went where previous to that. As a rule we tend to use the same drivers for the same routes for obvious reasons'

`What would they be?'

`If a driver has a regular route with regular drops he gets to know the people that he is making the drops for. If there is any traffic issues the driver will know alternative routes. It might mean changing the route and delivering to a particular drop earlier or later than he normally would. Most of the stores that we deliver to would understand this.'

`What about Rotterdam collections and deliveries. Who does these?'

`S&T Transport did the only collection that has been required from Rotterdam in my time with the company. I don't know if any other firms did any in the past'

`Why did you allocate this job to that company?'

`My predecessor Keith Barnes gave me details of which drivers having been working on which routes most recently. I have changed a few of them. We don't make too many collections or deliveries in Rotterdam. It's sporadic from what I have seen so far. It's usually only a couple of times a week at most. The drops for the Value Shoppers are daily'

`Who is the driver for S& T Transport? Did Mr Collins ever ask you to use this company?'

'He would normally leave the allocation of routes to me but funnily enough he did suggest that I give this job to Dimi Szabo of S&T Transport last week. There are two drivers that we use from this firm. They are Dimi Szabo and Mircea Tiriac. I gave DS Daley the contact numbers for all of the firms that we use on Saturday'

'Can you give me a copy of that list as well? Why would Mr Collins suggest S&T Transport?'

'I presume that this firm has been used regularly in the past so the same logic would apply as it does for UK jobs. I am new in the job so I assume that he was just letting me know that this was a regular trip for this firm. He knew that I was in the process of changing things'

Booth seemed uncertain with this answer

'Were you aware of anything suspicious about any trips to Rotterdam? Did anything raise doubts in your mind?' Booth asked

'No nothing at all. I was shocked when I heard the news this morning. From my limited time with the company everything seemed to run smoothly. I have only known Danny for a couple of weeks and nothing that he has said or done would make me think that he has done anything dodgy'

'OK Mr Blake. Let me have that list. I have no further questions for you at this stage'

All of the staff said much the same about Danny Collins that Blake had said. The only matter that Booth thought worth following up was the two Romanians from S&T Transport. She was still convinced that somebody at Collins Transport knew of Collins' involvement with the incident at the picnic site but at this stage she couldn't find anything

She returned to the station ready for the interview with Hoyte who would be accompanied by a duty solicitor. The interview didn't go as well has she had hoped. Hoyte denied killing Collins and other than the message on his phone there was nothing else to tie him to the murder. His solicitor wanted him to be released claiming that there was no valid reason to hold him. The search of Hoyte's home hadn't thrown up anything. They had found a gun hidden behind the garbage bins but this weapon hadn't been fired recently so no murder weapon was found there or any clothes with any DNA evidence on them either. Apart from the lunchtime trip that Hoyte said he had made there were no images of him on the CCTV footage from the town centre. This wasn't conclusive as there were many side roads where there were no CCTV cameras that Hoyte could easily have used to get to Collin's home. She could keep him in custody until Tuesday afternoon and planned to have another go at him on Tuesday morning after letting him sweat overnight. Worst case scenario was that she could still charge him as an accomplice to drug smuggling and possession of an illegal firearm but her gut feeling was that he was her man.

36

At the 1530 press conference Booth told the press and media that the police were holding a local man in custody and that they were expecting to charge him with the murder of Daniel Collins on the previous day. She went on to say that the police had reason to believe that Mr Collins was involved with the incident at the picnic site the previous week and that his murder was related to this incident. As was usual the media wanted as much detail as Booth was prepared to give and as usual Booth gave them as little as possible.

Booth returned to her office where she took a call a call from Chief Superintendent Whalley who congratulated her on the rapid solving of four murders in a week. He didn't mention the missing money though which she thought was odd so she brought up the matter

'Were you aware of the circulating rumours that a large sum of money had gone missing from the incident at the picnic site?' She asked

'No I hadn't heard this rumour. Where did you hear about it?'

'From a DS in Peterborough'

'It's the first that I have heard of it. Who was it that told you about it?'

'DS Llewelyn told me on Friday afternoon but he would divulge who his informant is'

'I can believe that. He is very protective of his CIs. I have been away for a couple of days. I took my wife away on a long weekend in Paris otherwise I am sure he would have told me.'

Booth was satisfied with the shape of events. No doubt she had earned more Brownie points. She had been told by Assistant Superintendant Dillon that she had impressed with the clean up rates.

When Paula Collins arrived home the press were camped on her doorstep. She contacted her solicitor who came to the house. He gave a statement to the press on behalf of Paula Collins refuting the claims that the police had made about Danny Collins being involved in the incident at Welney the previous week. He said that a burglary had taken place at the Collins home. Danny Collins car had been stolen along with money and jewellery and that Collins was probably killed when he tried to intervene. He followed this by saying that the police's suspicions about Danny Collin's involvement were based on an unnamed source in Peterborough who was suspected by Collins as being a business rival trying to discredit Collins Transport. He went on to explain that Collins Transport had picked up several new contracts recently and the unnamed source was probably a disgruntled rival company who had lost business to Collins Transport. He said that would not be answering any more questions and asked the press and media to leave the Collins family alone so that they could grieve.

37

As soon as Danny Collins' Range Rover left his house it was on its way to garage in Cambridge with a set of false plates which had been changed in his garden. The Range Rover was going to be re-sprayed in metallic green and would be shipped out to Romania within a couple of days where Stancvic had an arrangement with one of his many associates in Romania. He would be paid around thirty thousand Euros for it. This wouldn't make up for his loss on the drug deal but it was something and he would also make a bit on some of the jewellery that had been taken from Collins' house. Victor Dragnea was one of his most trusted men and he was driving the car to Cambridge. Stancvic had shot Collins but Dragnea had taken care of the number plates while Stancvic had been in Collins house looking for anything of value. There were no cameras in Collins' close and no security cameras in his house so Stancvic was confident that nobody had seen him murder Collins. On arriving home he burned the sweater and jeans that he had been wearing, showered and changed into a sweatshirt and jogging bottoms. Word would soon get around that somebody who had crossed Stancvic had met a messy end and this would only add to his reputation as a man not to be messed with. Viorica his latest girl friend had cooked dinner and he relaxed over it with a glass of red wine. He would contact Ivan Petrescu tomorrow and demand that he should be compensated for the money that he had lost. Petrescu had involved Collins in their venture so he was ultimately responsible for Stancvic's loss

After going through all the CCTV footage with Clarissa Marks Daley was certain that Hoyte wasn't directly responsible for the murder of Danny Collins. It was late in the day but he wanted to interview the Chamberlains who had been away for the weekend. They were expected back from a long weekend in London this afternoon. He wanted to ask them if they had seen any suspicious activity around Collins' home recently.
The Chamberlain's house was directly opposite Collins' home and overlooked their front garden. It was a large detached property with a double garage. As it was starting to get dark the security lights came on illuminating the immediate area. Daley rang the door bell which was answered by a tall attractive lady in her mid thirties. She was well dressed and had immaculate dark brown hair which looked as though it had been recently styled. Daley produced his badge and asked if she could spare him a few minutes to answer some questions. She invited him in and introduced him to her husband Phillip.

`We have only just heard the news about Danny' Susan Chamberlain said. `That is awful. I can't believe that somebody would want to kill Danny. He was a lovely man who was always friendly and helpful to us. We have only lived here since last summer and he made us feel very welcome. I'm shocked at the number of murders that have happened in this area over the past week'.
`Have either of you seen any suspicious activity over the last few days before you went away.'
They both looked at each other before saying that they hadn't.
Phil Chamberlain said `I have security cameras that cover the front and back of the house. I wonder if anything shows up on them over the weekend'
He left the room to retrieve the footage and came back with two discs which he put in a laptop. He fast forwarded the images which showed the Chamberlain's drive and the road outside both their house and Collins' house. There was nothing to see until a black Mercedes 500 was seen pulling up by the hedge in Collins' garden. It stayed there for twenty minutes before somebody got out of the car. The image wasn't great but it showed a thickset white man wearing dark clothing getting out of the car and going into Collins garden. He came out fifteen minutes later. Another man who was taller and heavier than the previous man also got out of the car. He went to the back of the car which wasn't fully in the camera's field of vision and returned back into view carrying what looked like a set of number plates. The image showed this man changing the number plates on Collins' Range Rover. The other man disappeared from view for about ten minutes before he returned carrying a bag of some description. The bigger man got into Range Rover and drove off. In doing so he gave a good view of his face. The Black Mercedes then reversed into Collins' drive before driving away. Once again the footage showed the face of the man driving the car. Daley had a fair idea who this man was.
`Can I have these discs Mr Chamberlain? They have given us some vital information. Nobody from the police noticed these cameras when we were here yesterday afternoon. Where are they hidden?'
"They are the latest state of the art gadgets available. My brother owns a security and alarm company in Norwich. He installed them for us when we moved into the house last summer.  He said that the alarm should be enough to put people off breaking in but if someone was determined it is too easy for somebody to disable conventional cameras just by cutting the wires to them. Mine are difficult to spot unless you know what you are looking for, I will show you.'
They went outside to the front of the house.
`Can you see the security light above the garage?  If you look at the bar holding it in place the large screw in the middle of the plate isn't actually a screw. It's a

miniature camera with 180 degrees of vision so it easily covers the front of the house'

Daley strained his neck looking for the camera before eventually spotting it.

`That's bloody clever. This place was crawling with police yesterday evening. We were all looking out for security cameras but nobody saw it. Obviously the two men in the black Mercedes didn't see it either. Thanks you so much for these discs. I am not sure when we will be able to return them to you'

`Don't worry about them. I have plenty more and they are not expensive. I'm glad that we are able to help'

Daley couldn't wait to call DCI Booth. Old fashioned police work by somebody who farted around wasting time had gained results. As soon as he got back to his car he phoned Kings Lynn station. Booth had left for the day so he called her on her mobile. The call went to voicemail. He left a message for her.

`I have just discovered security camera footage that casts doubt over Dennard Hoyte's involvement in the murder of Danny Collins. The footage shows two white men in Collins' garden late on Sunday evening. One of the men changed the number plates on Collins's car and drove it away. Good images of the faces of both men were seen on the footage. I pretty sure that one of the men involved is Bogdan Stancvic'

He phoned Bev to tell her that he had to go to Kings Lynn as he had discovered some vital evidence in regards to the murder of Danny Collins before setting off to Kings Lynn.

It was 1815 when he arrived at the station. DI Franklin was still at the station working on another investigation.

`Haven't you got a home to go to?' Daley asked. He hadn't expected any of the detectives to still be working. `Do you want to take a look at this Dave?' Daley said. `This shows that Booth has been barking up the wrong tree with regards to Hoyte murdering Danny Collins'

He placed the disc in the player and fast forwarded it to the relevant part of the footage

`Does that not look like Bogdan Stancvic?' He said when the image of the shorter of the two men appeared on the screen

Dave Franklin was a couple of years younger than Daley but they got on well hence the use of first name terms

`Fuck me, Arthur. It's him isn't it? Where did you get this from? Booth is going to looks like a right idiot after this afternoon's press conference'.

It was obvious to Daley that Franklin wasn't too disappointed at the prospect of Booth having to explain her error

` The neighbours of Danny Collins have just returned from a weekend in London. They have a really discreet security system which includes a hidden camera. You need to look really hard to find it even when it's pointed out. I called on them this afternoon to make general enquiries hoping that they would have noticed somebody dodgy in the area before they went away. They had only just got home when I called on them so they hadn't had the time to look at the camera footage. I have left a message on surly Shirley's mobile. I think that we need to have a word with Mr Stancvic don't you'

'I agree but we had better let her make that call. You know how possessive she is. I would love to be there when she sees this footage. She was so full of herself this afternoon at the press conference. I wonder where she is now'

'Her phone is switched off so I have left her a message. I bet she's not a staff motivation class at Kings Lynn College. She treats us all like shit. Did you hear what she said to me when I questioned her about Hoyte's involvement in Collins' murder?  She accused me of farting around and wasting time. Well in this instance old fashioned thorough detective work has got a result. No doubt she will still take the credit for it though'

'Of course she bloody well will. She doesn't treat any of us with any respect apart from DC Butler who seems to be her blue eyed boy. In fairness to Butler he seems to be embarrassed about it. Mick Judge has been giving him some stick about it too. He reckons Butler is giving her one and nicknamed him "teacher's pet" when he got some sandwiches for her'

They both had a chuckle about it before Daley left the station for home.

38

DCI Booth picked up Daley's message about two hours after he left it. She had been in London visiting her mother who was in hospital recovering from heart surgery. She had turned her phone off when she got to the hospital which was about five minutes before Daley had phoned her. She hadn't told anybody about her mother's condition. The doctors had put three stents in when she was in surgery that morning. Booth's brother Henry was at her bedside too. Booth didn't get on well with him. Henry felt that his sister neglected their mother and it was always him who had to take care of her. He was three years older than his sister and ran his own plumbing business

`I'm surprised that you could spare the time to come to see your mother'. Henry said in a sarcastic tone

`I have made time 'she replied tersely` but I am in the middle of two murder investigations so I am a little busy at the moment. Let's not argue now. It won't do Mum any good hearing us bitching at each other'

Their mother woke up shortly after this and Booth spent the next couple of hours chatting with her and telling her about the latest murder case. She boasted that she had the culprit in custody within hours of the crime. She also took credit for solving the Welney picnic site murders forgetting to mention that it was forensics team who had discovered that the three men had in fact killed each other. It was just after 2015 when she left the hospital and turned on her phone. She had two messages on her phone. One was from DI Franklin and the other from Daley.

She listened to Franklin's message which said that in view of the evidence discovered by DS Daley she might want to consider issuing a warrant for the arrest of Bogdan Stancvic. She presumed that Daley's message was along the same lines. So she listened to it and fumed. How could her team not have seen this camera and why didn't Daley discover it earlier. She phoned him and started by giving him a mouthful

`Why the hell didn't somebody realise that there was a camera in the house opposite and why did it take you all day to speak to the owners. I gave a press conference this afternoon based on what looked like a shut and dried case and now at this late stage you spring this on me'

Daley was at home when he took the call. He went into his study before replying to Booth.

`The Chamberlains were away for the weekend and only arrived home around 1500 afternoon. I was aware that they were not expected back until late afternoon today so I called by to speak to them to see if they had seen anybody behaving suspiciously in the days before they went away. They have a very modern security system with a very discreet camera. Even when it was pointed out to me it was hard to imagine that it was a camera. Mr Chamberlain showed me the footage that his cameras had taken over the weekend. This camera clearly shows two men in Danny Collins' garden on Sunday evening. One of the men drove off in Collins' car after changing the number plates in clear view of the camera. The other man looks very much like Bogdan Stancvic. Both men were white. It's not my fault that you jumped the gun with Dennard Hoyte. I like to be thorough before charging suspects. I don't consider my style of investigation farting around wasting time and as it has proved in this case you need to investigate all of the facts before jumping to conclusions'

`I want to see this camera footage. Get down to station in Kings Lynn now. Who the hell do you think that you are talking to? I am going to have you for this Arthur'

`It will have to wait until the morning. I have had several glasses of wine so I would be over the limit if I drive.' He lied

`First thing in the morning then' Booth fumed before cutting the connection. She accepted that she was not the most popular boss but she didn't believe that none of the officers on duty had managed to spot a hidden security camera no matter how well it was hidden. She wondered if she had been stitched up. She considered most of her team to be lazy and as for Daley the sooner he retired the better. She was going to give him a bollocking in the morning. She drove back to Kings Lynn and arrived at the station just before 2200. DI Franklin had arranged for them to be copied. He had the original discs put in the evidence room and put copies in her in tray. She loaded them into the disc player and fast forwarded the disc until the Mercedes came into view. She watched the footage for the next half an hour. It clearly showed the two white men doing exactly what Daley had said. She cursed to herself and considered what to do next. Stancvic was clearly in the garden but she had no actual footage of him shooting Collins. She decided that a warrant for his arrest was going to be issued and he would be nicked first thing in the morning.

39

Bogdan Stancvic was in a very good mood when he arrived home. He had spent Monday afternoon with another of his young girlfriends who had a body to die for and knew how to use it. He had spoken to Ivan Petrescu on Friday and given him a piece of his mind. He knew that Petrescu was a big player but he didn't mince his words when telling Petrescu that he was at fault for the loss of the money that Stancvic's team had taken to the exchange. When Petrescu questioned whether Stancvic had actually taken money to the exchange he launched into a blistering attack.

`If I say that my money was taken for the trade it was there. How dare you question my integrity? For all I know this was a set up organised by you. You could have easily left a small batch of cocaine behind knowing that the police would exaggerate what they had recovered and took off with the rest of it together with the money'

`Have you finished?' Petrescu said `Why would I want to try to con small fry like you. The value of the deals that we do is chicken shit compared to others that I deal with. You are just a small time player who thinks that he is a big time criminal. Did you have anything to do with the murder of Collins? If that was down to you I believe that you have made a grave mistake. If Collins was to blame killing him has cost us both. I will not be dealing with you again'.
He disconnected the call.

Stancvic's garage opened automatically when he arrived home at just after seven thirty. He parked the car in the garage. It started to close as he went towards the front door. He never made it. He felt a hand grab his head and something sharp cut his throat. He died in a pool of blood shortly afterwards struggling to reach his front door.

Florian Chipciu was surprised how easy the kill had been. He had sneaked into Stancvic's garden shortly after dusk and waited hidden in conifer trees that marked the boundary of Stancvic's house. He didn't know what time Stancvic was due to come home or if he was even coming home that night. He had risked a look through the kitchen window which was at the back of the property where he had seen an attractive young woman preparing a meal. Very loud was being played and the woman was swaying to the music as she was preparing the meal. The room next door to the kitchen appeared to be a dining room and he noted that a table was laid for dinner. Stancvic had no security at his house other than a security light. This was very sensitive and each time a cat came into the garden the lights came on. There were blind spots though and Chipciu had noted areas where the many cats that passed through the garden hadn't set off the lights. It seemed that the conifer trees were outside the field of detection. It was a good place to hide as it gave a great view of the entrance to the property. Stancvic obviously thought that he was untouchable.

Chipciu returned to his hire car and set off for Luton. With luck he would be able to switch his flight to a day earlier. If not he would just buy another ticket for a flight tomorrow. On the way back to Luton he stopped at a deserted dark lay by. It was one of those where you pulled off the road and it was separated from the road by some trees and bushes. He took off his sweatshirt and jeans and chucked them in a bin. He changed into the blue denims and grey pullover which were the change of clothes that he had brought with him when he flew into Luton. He headed to Dunstable where he was going to call on the arms dealer who had sold him his weapons. He hadn't needed to use the gun so the arrangement that he had with the dealer was that he would buy it back from Chipciu but at a price lower than he had paid for it. This was what he called his handling fee. The knife had been used and had been dumped in a hedge at another lay by just outside of Royston. The dealer gave him two thousand Euros for the unused gun. He drove to Luton Airport and checked into the Isis hotel where he had already had a reservation for the following night. Using his telephone for internet access he was able to switch his flight from first thing on Wednesday to a lunchtime flight on Tuesday meaning that he would be back home in Nice by early evening . He sent a text to Petrescu and attached a picture of Stancvic's dead body. It simply said "Job Completed 1935 Monday evening" He knew that Petrescu would send the agreed fee to his bank account the next day. He had arrived at the hotel at 2200.The restaurant was closed at that time of night but the hotel offered a limited room service. He ordered some sandwiches before going to sleep. He slept heavily and didn't wake until 0700. He took a shower, made some coffee in the room and went down for breakfast where he filled his plate at the buffet restaurant. His flight to Nice was with EasyJet and they only offered a limited selection of snacks so he wouldn't get chance to eat until he got home. He checked out of the hotel, returned the car to Avis and checked in at the airport in readiness for his 1218 flight. Another successful job had been completed. One hundred thousand Euros would soon arrive in his bank account and his reputation had been further enhanced. He wouldn't need to do too many more jobs before he had enough money to retire with.

40

As usual Booth called everyone into the briefing room for a briefing at 0900 on the Tuesday morning. She reluctantly told the team that it appears that Dennard Hoyte wasn't responsible for the murder of Daniel Collins as a result of some new evidence unearthed by DS Daley. She played the disc that Daley had recovered. When she reached the section where faces were seen she stopped the disc.

'I have reason to believe that this man is Bogdan Stancvic who we have all heard of. The other man has yet to be identified but a copy of this disc was sent to Peterborough this morning and we are hoping that somebody at Peterborough knows who he is. A warrant for Stancvic's arrest has been issued and it is being auctioned by Peterborough CID as we speak'.

A woman police constable interrupted the meeting.

'Excuse me Ma'am but I have Chief Superintendent Whalley on the phone for you. He needs to speak with you urgently'

'I expect that this call is to confirm his arrest. I will be back shortly' she told the team as she went to her office.

'Good morning Sir. What did you want to speak to me about? Do you have Stancvic in custody?'

'Hello Shirley. Unfortunately I have to tell you that Bogdan Stancvic was murdered last night. His throat was cut when he returned home. His girlfriend found him at 2215 last night. She was concerned that he hadn't come home for dinner as planned so she went out to throw the meal she had prepared into the bin. She telephoned him but got no answer. Apparently his car was already in the garage. She said that she never heard the car because she was playing music while preparing a meal. There are no clues to who the perpetrator might be but it looks like a hit may have been placed on him. Whoever did this knew exactly what they were doing. Stancvic's throat was cut cleanly without any sign of a struggle. It seems he was attacked after leaving his garage. Unfortunately there are no security cameras at the property. We are not aware of any fallings out with other gangs in the area. Stancvic was thought to have been building his empire. He was doing it in an indiscreet way usually resorting to violence. We suspected that he was a major player but proving it is another matter. The only consolation is that this man is no longer on the streets causing mayhem'

Booth's heart sank. Her press conference yesterday had indicated that she had a local man in custody for the murder of Daniel Collins. If Stancvic had been arrested she may have been able to rescue the situation but that was going to happen now

`Do you have a name for the other man in the security camera footage?' She asked

`We believe that he is Victor Dragnea who is muscle for Stancvic. We have just issued a warrant for his arrest but at this moment he is still at large'

`OK. Thanks for letting me know.' She ended the call and returned to the briefing room which was buzzing.


`I have just been informed that Bogdan Stancvic was murdered last night. Chief Supt. Whalley believes that it may have been a professional hit. I am annoyed that this arsehole escaped punishment because you lot failed to notice that one of the neighbours had a security camera. If we had recovered this footage earlier we could have nabbed Stancvic before he was murdered'

Daley intervened

`With respect Ma'am, as I said last night the camera was very discreet. Nobody at the scene, and that includes you, saw it and even if we had the Chamberlains, the owners of the house, were away for the weekend so we wouldn't have had access to it until late afternoon yesterday anyway'

Booth resented Daley challenging her authority again and decided to nip it in the bud before others started to copy him. She knew that she was unpopular with her team but she didn't care. Her sole priority was advancing her career. She tore into Daley in front of the rest of team

`When I have control of a murder scene I don't have time to start looking around for cameras. That is delegated to my team and in this case the team failed to do their job properly. That's the second time in less than 24 hours that you have questioned me. You are the only person to have seen this camera which you claim is difficult to see so we only have your word for it. It was you and Skid who interviewed the neighbours in the close yet neither of you thought to ask if there were any cameras that we should know about'

DI Franklin butted in lending his support to Daley

`I had a good look around to see if there were any security cameras and to be fair to Skid and Arthur I didn't see a camera.'

`Well that proves that you are just as incompetent as they are then DI Franklin'

Before Franklin could respond Clarissa Marks also spoke up.

`I did ask everyone that I spoke to if they knew of anybody who may have had security cameras in the close as there were two houses unoccupied on Sunday evening. Nobody that I spoke to knew about any hidden cameras'

`And if you had made sure that I was aware of the footage which showed that Danny Collins had been seen heading out to meet up with Hoyte I would have arrested Collins on Saturday evening and he wouldn't be dead now... Instead you just sneaked into the station, dumped the discs in my in tray, left a

message saying that you had found something in the footage in Flixham from late on Tuesday night that I might want to take a look at and then turned your bloody phone off so I couldn't ask you what it was that you had discovered.'
Booth decided it was time to change the subject before anyone else jumped on the bandwagon and had a go at her.
`The other man in the footage at Collins' house is Victor Dragnea. A warrant is out for his arrest but he is still at large".
She decided to move onto the interviews at Collins Transport
`Your reports are saying that nobody was aware of anything dodgy going on at Collins Transport. I want these two Romanians who own S&T transport put under observation. I am going to get customs to check their loads when they return from Rotterdam. I am convinced that it is these two who are bringing the drugs in. DS Judge, can you get them in for an interview. The new transport manager, Bob Blake, was of no use as he is new in the job. I want to interview his predecessor Keith Barnes. He has been working for Collins Transport for many years. He has had heart surgery recently and is due to retire. He must know something. DS Brown, Can you speak to his family to find out if he is fit enough for an interview and if he is arrange for one as soon as is possible. I am going to charge Dennard Hoyte for acting as a courier in a drug smuggling operation and for possession of an illegal firearm. He has admitted acting as a courier. He is an escape risk so I am going to arrange for him to be held on remand. I also want to find out where the money went to. Andrews didn't drive so somebody took him there. Danny Collins went somewhere after returning from the hospital on Tuesday evening. The footage shows Collins driving in the direction of Hoyte's place and returning thirty minutes later. Did Hoyte know where the money was and is that why Collins was visiting Hoyte? The key to all of this is Collins. We need to fill in the gaps so I want all of you to concentrate on filling in these gaps. Re -check everything to see if there are any more clues as to who drove Andrews to the picnic site and also to answer what happened to the money if there was actually any money involved. Stancvic killed Collins. Why? Who killed Stancvic and why? '
Booth was concerned. She had dropped a clanger when telling the media that she had somebody in custody that was going to be charged with the murder of Danny Collins. She had seen the media coverage outside the Collins home where her solicitor had refuted the police claims about Collins and the three murders at Welney and as things stood at the moment she was no closer to solving the cases.
Di Brown came into her office. He told her that Keith Barnes had received heart surgery but was still in Papworth hospital. His family didn't want him to be questioned until he had made a full recovery.

Booth took her frustration out on Di Brown.

`We are going to interview him today. We will leave straight away' she said.
`Five murders have been committed in a week and for all we know he may have information that leads us to the killers'.

They arrived at the hospital just over an hour later. The doctor treating Barnes was reluctant to let Booth speak to him.

`He has had major heart surgery and there have been some complications. He is not in any condition to be questioned'

`I have five murders to investigate and I need to speak to him urgently as he may have some vital information which will help with the investigation. I will be as quick as I can but I cannot wait'

The doctor reluctantly agreed but asked her to go easy.

Booth introduced herself to Barnes who was lying in bed with tubes all over the place. He didn't look at all well. Booth wasn't bothered by this and she went straight onto her questions

`Danny Collins was murdered on Sunday evening and we believe that he was involved with an incident at a picnic site on the A1101 where three men were killed on Tuesday night last week. What do you know about Danny Collins and S&T Transport bringing drugs into the country?'

Barnes looked shocked at this announcement and looked as though he was ready to burst into tears. He struggled to get his words out when he replied `I have worked ... with Danny for over 15 years. To my knowledge.... he has never.... been involved in anything illegal...I cannot believe ....what you are insinuating'

`What about S&T Transport? Why did they always do the Rotterdam trips?'
`Two reasons......They were the cheapest and......they...were good...at what.....they did. We .......never....had..........any ...problems with....them'
`Did you trust Szabo and Tiriac the two men who owned S&T? Did you have any reason to believe that they were in any way corrupt? Could they have been acting on their own initiative?'
`No'

The doctor intervened
`I think that is enough questions for today Inspector'
`It's Chief Inspector' Booth replied curtly. `I need to ask just one more question'

She stared at Barnes before her next question.

`Are you aware of any unofficial collections made on behalf of Collins transport in your time working for them. Is everything put through the books?'

Barnes hesitated before answering. He was aware that meat products were sometimes brought in that were not on the original collections list and that they were sold on the black market

`I cannot...be certain... that any of ...our drivers...ever made......unofficial ....collections.......but if......they did.....it was done...without the firm's........knowledge'. He started to cough and struggled to breath

`That is enough Chief Inspector...No more questions' The doctor stepped in between the Booth and Barnes. Reluctantly Booth left the room followed by DS Brown. She left without thanking the doctor for letting her speak to Barnes

` I will be back when Barnes was in a better condition because I don't believe that he was being honest with me' she told Brown

41

DC Clarissa Marks had been instructed by Booth to team up with DS Daley and concentrate on talking to all the people that Lynton Andrews and Dennard Hoyte had come into contact with in their short time in Flixham.

Daley enjoyed working with Marks. She seemed quite thorough in her work and he considered her to be an ally as they were both in Booth's bad books.

`I think that we should take a fresh look at things. It would be helpful if we could get a positive identification of that dark coloured hatchback that went in and out of Alder Street at 1930 on Tuesday last week. I believe that we should speak to the bar staff to see if they noticed anybody that appeared to be friendly with either Andrews or Hoyte. I will also speak to all of their football pals at Flixham Rangers. I think that they train on a Tuesday night'. Daley said

`Do you think that it's worth asking the manager of the Red Lion if we can have a look through his camera footage for the week previous to see if there is any sign of anybody who may have spoken with Andrews and Hoyte?' Marks asked

`That's a good thought. I think that it may be worth having another word with Val Davey and Lesley Farmer too. I think its best that I speak to them as you didn't get off on the right foot with Mrs Davey. Let's meet up at Flixham station at 1500 and share what we have found. I will interview the players at training tonight to save you hanging around and getting home late'

`Ok. Thanks Gov. I will see you at 1500'.

Daley drove to Kings Lynn to interview Val Davey at work. She wasn't pleased to see him.

`What do you want now? I have told DC Marks everything that I know'

`I just want to ask you if you noticed anybody that Andrews and Hoyte seemed to get on with. You went out on dates with them. Did they seem friendly with anyone?'

`Andrews was a moody git. He was very aggressive and just seemed to be looking for an excuse to start a fight. Denny was totally different. He is very relaxed and chatted with anybody. I don't remember him talking to many blokes but he wasn't shy in coming forwards with the ladies'

`The police are trying to discover how Andrews got to the picnic site where he was killed. He didn't drive. Hoyte didn't take him. He asked Lesley Farmer and she declined so we have no other leads.'

`Considering how bad the weather was I don't think anybody would have volunteered to drive Andrews, unless of course, he forced them to. He seemed the sort to threaten somebody into doing what he wanted' Val answered

Daley thanked Davey for her help and set off back to Flixham to interview Lesley Farmer. The interview didn't throw up any new information so he headed back to Flixham station to have another look through the CCTV for last Tuesday and the following day. This time he concentrated on activity after 1930. He found the footage showing the dark coloured hatchback but he couldn't improve the image of it. The snow was too heavy and it was impossible to work out how many people were in the car. He tried looking at other cameras for around the same time but again nothing that was useful was found. He kept checking the cameras for the rest of the evening. There were very few cars on the road as a result of the snow. At around 2110 the snow suddenly eased. It was lighter snow now rather than the blizzard type conditions for the previous three hours or so but visibility was good enough to make out images. Danny Collins car was seen at 2210 and again at 2243. A dark coloured hatchback was seen in the snow at 2054 pulling off the road into Turnberry Close. Daley pondered as to whether it was the same car from earlier on. It was bloody typical that the snow should ease up completely about 15 minutes after this car came into view. He continued checking the footage into the next day. Visibility was much better of course now that it had stopped snowing. He turned to the camera which covered the turn into Turnberry Road and watched as almost a third of the cars that came out of Turnberry Road were dark coloured hatchbacks. He noted at least three older model Astras, a couple of VW Golf's and a Honda Civic. Any of these cars could have been the one going into Alder Street. He returned to the station and met up with DC Marks

`Did you have any joy?' He asked

`I could only find them on camera on three nights. They didn't appear to be socialising with anybody. Andrews isn't the social sort but he did manage to get into a fight with somebody on a Thursday night a couple of weeks ago. Somebody hit him full on the chin but he didn't appear to feel it. He just decked the bloke with one punch.'

`Who was he fighting with?'

`I'm not sure but I think it may have been the transport manager at Collin's Transport.' She showed Daley the piece of film where the fight happened

`Let's go and have a word with him about this incident'

They took Daley's car and drove to Collins Transport. The depot seemed fairly quiet. Daley noticed that there were two older model Astras in the car park. One was dark blue, the other dark green

`Can we have a quick word with Mr Blake please?' Daley asked the young lady on reception. It wasn't the usual receptionist he noted.

`He is very busy at the moment' the young lady replied

`We won't take up too much of his time' Daley replied

The girl phoned to speak to Blake who came out of his office. He looked harassed.

`How can I help you DS Daley?'

`Can I have a quick word in private?' Daley replied

`Sure, come into my office. We will be alone as Susan is covering reception '

They followed him through

Blake closed the door behind him.

`Can I ask what this is about?'

`It's about Lynton Andrews and the fight that you had with him in the Red Lion. What was it all about?'

`To be honest I don't really know. He was arguing with Helen the barmaid accusing her of overcharging him. I had joined up with Helen for the quiz. I was stood at the bar listening to the argument. He saw that I was listening, took offence and started to shove me so I hit him as hard as I could. It was as though he never felt it. The next thing I knew I was on the floor after he felled me with one punch'

`You didn't think to mention it when you were interviewed on Monday especially as he was found dead a few days after your fight' Marks asked

`I didn't know the bloke's name. I didn't know that he was one of the men killed at the picnic site. To be frank it's not the sort of thing that you want to tell anybody. I was put on my arse with one punch and if his mate hadn't of intervened he would probably have given me a serious hiding.'

`What make of car do you drive?'Daley asked

`It's a green Vauxhall Astra. Why do you ask?'

Blake was hoping that any concern in his voice wouldn't be picked up by the two police officers who ignored his question

`What time did you get home on Tuesday evening? Did you go to the Red Lion?'

Blake hesitated before answering.

`I didn't go to the Red Lion and I'm not sure what time I got home. Susan my assistant left an email from the Value Shoppers central warehouse on my desk. The email had been sent earlier in the day but Susan forgot to give it to me so I had to reschedule a lot of the routes for the next day. She will confirm this as I had words with her about this. It would have been around 630pm before I left for the day'

`Did you go straight home?'

`No. I went to Morrisons to get some shopping. As it was quiet in there I was in and out in no time so I would have got home just after 7pm'

`Did you go out again that evening?'

`I didn't. The weather was awful and I just did a bit of housework. You know washing ironing cooking. It was an exciting evening!!'

`Ok. Thank you for your help. We will let you get on with your work'. Daley said and they both left the office

`As they left Marks asked Susan about Blake.

`How is your new boss? I hear he had a pop at you last week for forgetting about an email'

Susan blushed.

`It's early days yet. He seems Ok but he can be grumpy if things are not done the way he likes. He did have the hump about that email though'

`I have a boss who is a bit like that too' Marks replied

Susan looked nervously at Daley...

` She doesn't mean me' he said with a smile

As they left Marks had a sneaky look at Blake's Astra. It was spotless inside.

`I would say that his car has been cleaned recently. I wonder if he has tried to hide something or is he just one of those men who clean their car religiously each weekend '

`I think he is worth further investigation. I wonder if he has been a naughty boy in the past. I will check with the Nottinghamshire police force to see if he has a record. He wasn't slow when it came to sticking one on Andrews so I wouldn't be surprised if he has a history of brawling'

Blake noticed that the two coppers were checking his car out. He had been vague about his movements before he ran into Andrews on Tuesday evening. He was going to have to find somewhere to hide the money that was under his bed just in case they came sniffing around his house. Where could he hide it though?

Marks went back to Kings Lynn after the meeting with Blake. She wrote a report on the additional findings from the cameras in the Red Lion. Daley said that he would write up a report for the interviews with Blake, Davey and Farmer. He thought again about the comment that Val Davey had made about Andrews. Perhaps he had forced somebody to give him a lift but who could it have been as he wasn't seen leaving the Red Lion with anybody and no other cars were seen in the vicinity. Perhaps he had gone out the back door and kept away from the cameras. Had Collins arranged for somebody to give him a lift? There were too many questions and not enough answers. He decided to check up on Blake with Nottinghamshire Police but discovered that he had no police record. He went back to the station to write up reports and went home at 1700. Bev was surprised that he was home so early.

`I didn't expect to see you so soon' she said

`I have to go out again later to interview the lads at the football club to see if anyone knew about Lynton Andrews' social group. We don't know how he got out to the picnic site. He was seen on CCTV in the pub until just after seven thirty. He went out of the back towards to back exit and the toilets but just disappeared. There is no camera coverage at the back of the pub. The next time he is seen he is dead in the picnic car park.'

Bev made him a quick meal. She fried some eggs bacon and mushrooms for him and gave him some of the apple pie she had made earlier to wash it down.

`I think that your pension forecast arrived today. Do you want to open it now?'

`No I will have a look at it later. I need to go out again soon'


When Daley arrived at the training session Roy Gayle was putting the players through some sprint exercises. Daley apologised for interrupting the session but said that he needed to speak to all the players individually. Roy Gayle suggested that he started with the goalkeeper Steve Casey

Daley took him to one side

`I am trying to get some background information on Lynton Andrews. Do you know if there was anybody that he was particularly friendly with apart from Dennard Hoyte?'

`I don't like talking ill of the dead DS Daley but Andrews was a moody bastard. He was very aggressive and everyone in the team was wary of him because he had a temper and he was a big unit. He came to training, kicked the shit out of everybody in the practice games, had a couple of beers and hardly spoke with anybody. I think that you will find all of the players will say the same thing about him'

`Are there any of the players that you feel would have been intimidated by Andrews into helping him with a problem? Anyone that you feel could have got on the wrong side of him?'

`Not really. He did have a bit of a go at John Eason. Andrews clattered him a couple of times in a practice game so John did him in a tackle. He went over the top of the ball catching Andrews on the top of his ankle. Andrews didn't like somebody giving him some of his own treatment so he started throwing punches at John. John is pretty handy can look after himself so he threw some punches back. Everybody piled in to pull them apart and Roy had to calm them down'.

`When was this?'

`A couple of weeks back before the snow started and training got cancelled'

Daley thanked him for his help. He got the same story from the rest of the players but he left both Roy Gayle and John Eason until last.

He called Eason over and asked him about the run in with Andrews

`The bloke was an animal. All he seemed to want to do was intimidate his opponents. He clattered me a couple of times so I gave him some back. He could dish it out but couldn't take it back so he started throwing punches at me before the lads jumped in and pulled us apart. He won't be missed'

Eason was a solidly built man with big shoulders and Daley imagined that he could handle himself.

`Did you speak with him after this incident?'

`No. Why would I. I didn't like him and I doubt he liked me. He was a liability to the team and he wasn't much of a footballer either'

`He didn't call you to ask for a lift the Tuesday before last?'

`He didn't have my number so he couldn't have called me and anyway if he had I would have told him to piss off'

Daley had no more questions

Daley spoke to Roy Gayle last but got a similar story from him. Andrews wasn't popular and he said that he only kept him in the squad because he wanted to keep Dennard Hoyte interested. It was yet another dead end for Daley.

42

Blake was feeling edgy because of the money hidden in the draw under his bed. He was concerned because it was an obvious place for it to be hidden. He considered other places where he could stash the money but with his house being so small there were no suitable places. The loft would be just as obvious a place. He thought about his bed. It came apart into two halves. The bottom half of the bed contained two drawers for storage and he had put the money in one of these drawers. He took the mattress off of the bed to examine the other half of the bed. The top half of the bed was sealed underneath. There were no drawers in it. The base of the bed was covered with a black felt type covering with a shiny finish which was stapled to the edge of the frame. He pulled out some of the staples. Apart from some wooden slats which strengthened the bed this section was empty. There was plenty of room to store the money in it if he lifted the staples which was easy enough to do and knocked them in again after he moved the money into it. He decided to put the money in the side nearest to the window which was the side that he tended to sleep on. If anybody discovered this money they would only have been able to find it by lifting up the bed. They might be able to hear that there was something inside the bed moving around. To try to alleviate this he thought that he would buy some cheap pillows and stuff them inside the bed frame to cushion the money should it move around or better still a cheap duvet which would serve the same purpose. A trip to the shops was required but it would have to be after work tomorrow. He was going to have to go into Kings Lynn to open up some building society accounts and also open a cash ISA. He was allowed to invest £3600 each tax year so he could put some in this month and the full £3600 in April. The problem was that he had £240,000 to hide and it was going to take him a long time to move this amount of money. What could he do to in effect launder this money?

He thought about it while cooking himself a chicken curry. The curry sauce was out of a jar of course but he had taken a couple of chicken breasts out of the freezer that morning so that they had thawed out by the time he got home from work. He cut the breasts into small chunks fried them in a little oil poured in the Jalfreizi sauce and put some rice in a saucepan to boil. He thought about gambling at a racetrack. He didn't know too much about horse racing and rarely had a bet apart from wasting a few pounds on the Grand National each year. He had however heard stories from one of his mates in Mansfield of big punters laying sizeable bets on course and getting paid out in cash. Slowly he had some semblance of a plan. He checked on line and by chance there was a race meeting at Huntingdon on Saturday week and another meeting at Market Rasen the following Saturday. He decided that he would go to these meetings as they were not too far to travel. He would concentrate on the on course bookies and watch to see who was placing big bets. If anybody had big wins he could use this as cover for any amounts of money that he deposited with the building societies as he thought it unlikely that the bookies would remember who they paid out to. All he had to say was that he won x amounts of money with a certain bookie at the meeting and if anybody wanted to check with them the bookie should have a record of the payout. He knew who to speak to on the subject. Nev, one of his mates from the football supports club was a big gambler and went racing on a regular basis. Blake would bend his ear on the subject when they next met in Mansfield

He had a busy weekend lined up. He had already been on the internet looking for somewhere to take Val to on Friday night and had decided upon a pub called the Cross Keys which was on the outskirts of Kings Lynn. The menu looked decent with plenty of choice and the food was reasonably priced. He phoned them and booked a table for 830pm on Friday night. He was sure that this was one of the places that Val had mentioned. He had phoned his bank to advise them that he wanted to withdraw £9000 in cash to pay for a new car and that he would be coming in Friday during his lunch break to get it. As was usual the bank asked him to bring identification in the form of his driving licence and a utility bill. Fortunately a council tax bill had arrived that day. The bank also asked him about the large balance in his bank account and what he planned to do with the money once the cheque had cleared. He explained that he was in rented accommodation but he would be buying a house in the near future so the money in his current account would be used for this. The bank suggested an easy access deposit account. The interest rate was only 2.4% but at least it was earning some interest. Blake said that he thought that this was a good idea and suggested opening a deposit account and transferring £90,000 into it. He asked if he could set the account up on Friday when he came in. The bank arranged an appointment for him at 1.15pm and said that it wouldn't take too long to do the necessary paperwork.

He had planned to pick up his new car on Saturday as soon as he had finished work. He wanted to watch Flixham Rangers on Saturday afternoon so he was hopeful of getting back with time to spare to catch most of the game. He was also going to go back to Mansfield on Sunday so that he could give some money to Wayne and Ellie. If he left early on Sunday morning he could meet up with them for lunch and drive back to Flixham later that afternoon. It would also give him a chance to have a drive in the new car. He checked the time. It was half past seven. He knew that there was a Champions league on Sky that evening. Manchester United was playing against Inter in Milan so he decided to nip down to the Red Lion to watch the game.

The Red Lion was fairly quiet when he went in. Helen was working behind the bar. She greeted him with a big smile on her face.

`Hello Bob, How was Ray's party. Did you have a good time there?

`Yes it was a good night and I met a few new people as well so I'm glad that I went. How was your weekend?'

`Not great if truth be told. It ended with a row so I won't be seeing him again. I'm now regretting that I hadn't joined you at Ray's party. I would probably have had a much better time. Hindsight is a wonderful thing'

He ordered a pint and wandered off in the direction of the biggest screen to watch the match which had just started. Helen's comment threw Blake. It felt like she was sounding him out for a date. He fancied Helen. She was like a blond version of Debbie being similar in shape and build to her.  He was in no rush though as could always try again with her if things didn't work out with Val.

The match turned out to be a dull game. United had a two nil lead from the first leg and just sat back Milan didn't have the guile to break them down and it ended goalless. He had a couple of pints and went home. Helen waved goodbye to him with a big smile on her face.  He went home with a certain amount of confusion in his head. After being single for over a year he now had a date with a younger attractive woman in Val and an older woman that he definitely fancied dropping hints to him.

43

Dimi Szabo's mobile rang. He answered it with trepidation. It was Ivan Petrescu who went straight to the point without any niceties.

'Do you have any idea what happened to the money that Stancvic claims his men took to the exchange and have you spoken with Mrs Collins yet about continuing our bit of business? There are plenty of people in England who I could do business with so I am keen to resurrect our arrangement once things quieten down'

'I haven't heard anything about the money. The word on the streets is that some bent copper must have lifted it, that's of course if there was actually any money. The police have been sniffing around the depot so I haven't had chance to speak with Paula Collins yet. It seems as though the new man, Bob Blake, has been tasked with running things after Danny's demise. I don't know him well enough to raise the subject with him. I hope we can get things moving again as it was a nice earner for me'

'If you can get me any information about the missing money that leads to me recovering it there will be a reward for you. I have a contact in Stancvic's team. He tells me that he is sure that Stancvic took money to the picnic site but there was no sign of it when the bodies were discovered the next day by a passing car driver. See if you can find anything about him but be discreet. If it was a bent copper that took it I don't want to warn him that we suspect that it was lifted by the police. I am also hearing that one of the two Schwartzers that Collins used went by himself yet he didn't drive. See if you can find out how he got there'

'I will try to get some details to you but it might be difficult. It's a murder enquiry and the police have closed ranks'

'Do what you can' Petrescu said before ending the call

Szabo felt sick. He knew of Petrescu's reputation and he didn't want to be on his wrong side. He didn't have a clue how he was going to get any news that may result in Petrescu's money being recovered and he dreaded the consequences. He decided that he would seek advice from Mircea. He phoned him and told him the details of his phone conversation with Petrescu.

'Shit. You don't want to be in debt to that bastard. The word in the Romanian community is that he placed the hit on Stancvic just because he didn't show Petrescu the respect Petrescu thought he deserved.'

'He wants to resume the collections from Rotterdam as well. Fuck knows how that is going to work without Collins'.

'We could always offer to do the drops ourselves'

`It's too risky. I don't mind bringing the odd shipment into the country and taking a bag of cash out again but I don't want to get involved with meeting up with dealers to hand over the stuff. Look what happened with Radu and Rodescu. Some of those bastards would rob their own grandmothers. We would have to carry guns to protect ourselves too and I'm not cut out for that. I told Petrescu that I would try to help but if I can't help what else can I do'
`OK I will also try to find out details too. Let's put the word out to the community'

DCI Booth had an air of frustration about her when she called into the Norfolk Constabulary headquarters at Wymondham for a meeting with Tony Pasby the acting Chief Commander of the newly formed East Anglia Police Force.  She knew that she had cocked up with the press briefing and was expecting to be taken to task over it. What she hadn't expected was a severe bollocking. Word had got back to Pasby that Booth was extremely unpopular with her team. Someone and she suspected it was Whalley, had Pasby's ear.
She was told in no uncertain manner that although her rise to DCI had been a fast one her progress would halt unless her attitude changed. It was made very clear to her that she needed to be a team player and that she had to stop alienating her team.  Pasby was also unhappy with the press briefing claiming that she had jumped the gun and acted arrogant manner in front of the cameras. There had been a drug smuggling operation in her area that remained undetected until three people were murdered at the picnic site at Welney on January 27th. A local man was murdered because of his involvement in the operation and a known drug lord who had also been implicated in the operation had also been murdered. Several days had passed and she was still no closer to finding out how the operation had worked. She was dismissed with this belittling of her efforts still ringing in her ears.
On the drive back to Kings Lynn she considered who had been telling tales. Was it James and Ring who were transferred across from Cambridgeshire to help with the enquiry? Could they have been talking to her team in Kings Lynn about how unpopular she was?  Daley and Marks had suffered some ridiculing at her hands recently. Was it them who had been telling tales? She was determined to find out who had knifed her in the back and when she did she would make their lives hell. She felt badly let down by her team and despite the warning from Pasby she wasn't going to change her style. It had been effective so far and one setback wasn't going to change things
Her phone rang. It was her brother
`Shirley. I have some bad news I'm afraid. There have been some complications with Mum's operation and she has taken a turn for the worse. Her doctor says

that she has less than a 30 per cent chance of surviving. You had better come to the hospital as soon as you can. They are operating on her as we speak'
`I will come down straight away.' She told her brother. She pulled into the next lay by where she sat for twenty minutes in floods of tears.  The news from the hospital had been the last straw for her after her bollocking from Pasby.

44

Compared to recent events it was a quiet week in Flixham. No progress was made by the police in uncovering the drug trafficking which they believed to be centred on Collins Transport. Apart from Hoyte's confession there was no evidence to prove that Collins Transport had been the centre of the operation. Szabo and Tiriac had been interviewed but pleaded ignorance. They both said that they were totally unaware of any illegal substances being brought into the county and if there was it wasn't being carried by their trucks. John Beattie was seen on camera leaving the Wisbech Toyota dealership without a bag of money. He was just carrying a lightweight bag which contained trade plates. He was picked up on camera hitching a lift in a heavy good vehicle which dropped him off near Cheshunt without stopping. When interviewed he said that he hadn't seen any bags at the crime scene other than the one which the police had recovered. DCI Booth took compassionate leave to be with her mother who was fighting for her life in hospital. Sadly she passed away on Booth's fourth day of absence

DI Green was asked to take over the lead in the case while Booth was away on compassionate leave. Daley decided that he would concentrate on trying to track down the mysterious dark hatchback that was seen on the night of the deaths at the picnic site. He was going to check any security cameras that may have footage of the A1101 so he set about calling on all of the houses that were on the road from Flixham to the picnic site. The task took several days but to no avail. No meaningful footage was available. He went through the Flixham camera footage twice more. On the second of these he noticed that one of the headlights on the dark hatchback was slightly off kilter. The nearside light was pointing slightly higher than the off side light. What appeared to be the same car was seen pulling into Turnberry Close the same evening. He asked the patrol officers who covered Flixham to keep an eye out for any dark coloured hatchback whose headlights matched this description. It was a long shot but there was nothing else to go on.

Life carried on at Collins Transport with Bob Blake taking on more responsibility. He decided that he would give some training to Ray Pearce and Susan Rudd so that they could take a more active role in the logistics involved with the delivery schedules. Susan had seemed keen to take on a more active role but Ray immediately asked if he was going paid extra for this additional work and seemed reluctant.

His attitude pissed Blake off.

`This company has had a major setback with Danny's death. Danny was instrumental in the running of the company so all of us will have to do a bit more. If we don't the company may not survive. Do you think that I'm getting any more money when Paula asked me to try to step into Danny's shoes? I can tell you that the answer is no. We all have to muck in and take on a bit more work. If you aren't prepared to make a short term sacrifice I suggest that you look elsewhere for work because you are no use to this company'

`It's not fair though is it? The company has been doing well and it's not as though it couldn't afford to pay us a bit more. My salary is shit'

`It's a bloody sight more than you'll be getting on the dole though isn't it. That's where you will be heading if you don't buck your ideas up. You either muck in or you can sod off'.

Blake was really annoyed. He wasn't going to let the lazy little git get away with shirking responsibility.

Blake's response startled Pearce. He got wind of Blake's temper from the bollocking he had dished out to Susan when she failed to pass some emails to him promptly. The threat of losing his job suddenly dawned on him.

`Ok I will help' he muttered before skulking off back to his desk.

Blake was secretly pleased with the outcome of his harsh words. It would give the staff at Collins Transport the impression that he was a tough proposition. It wouldn't do any harm for the staff to be a bit wary of him. Paula came into the office every day and did a full day's work. Danny's funeral was going to take place on Monday week and he felt that Paula wanted something to do to take her mind off matters. Between them they had re-assured their customers that things would run smoothly and wouldn't be impacted by Danny's death. The Value Shoppers distribution manager raised some concerns over the suggestions in the media about drug smuggling. Paula told him that there was absolutely no truth in the accusations. The police assumed that as Collins Transport had used a haulage company for the Rotterdam trips that was run by two Romanians they had put two and two together to make five because it was a Romanian who the drug gang leader. She went on to say that the police had interviewed everyone at Collins Transport and had found no evidence of any wrong doings. She said that the matter was in the hands of her solicitor.

Friday arrived in a flash. Blake attended his appointment at the bank and opened a deposit account which gave him instant access. He also collected £9000 in used £50 notes which were placed in a plastic wallet. It seemed to take the cashier ages to count the 180 notes. He returned to work and the afternoon passed quickly without any issues. At 545pm he left and went home. On arriving at home he quickly swapped the notes that he had collected from the bank with those from under his bed. He doubted that there was any way that the stolen notes could be traced but he wasn't going to take any chances. He took another £100 in used £20 notes from the stash which he was going to use for the meal tonight. He began making a note on how much of the money that he had used on a piece of paper which he left with the remaining money. He figured that he had to keep a strict record just in case anyone questioned his spending. He would eventually have to put it on a spreadsheet. His current old laptop was dated so he would buy a new one with the latest version of Excel already on it.  He showered and shaved before pondering on what to wear. It was quite chilly out so he settled upon a pair of beige chinos a dark blue round neck sweater and another of his striped shirts. This time it was a white shirt with dark blue stripes. He slapped a bit of gel on his hair and splashed on some aftershave and was ready to go. He suddenly felt very nervous, a bit like a teenager on a first date. He selected his favourite Elbow album for the drive and set off on the short drive to Val's place arriving dead on eight.


He rang the entrance bell on her flat.
`I'll be right down' Val said on answering
He went back to the car and waited. She appeared at the door after a couple of minutes. She looked different to how he remembered her from last Saturday. She was wearing a light coloured coat and high heels which made her look taller than he had remembered. He leant across to open the passenger door for her. She got in leaned across and pecked him on the cheek
`Hi' she said. ` You are a stickler for time keeping. You arrived dead on eight. Lucky for you I got home from work on time.'
She pulled the car door to shut it but it didn't close
`You have to slam it' he said apologetically `it's a bit stiff. I'm getting a new car tomorrow. I got this one on the cheap while I was out of work. It's been reliable but it's tatty'
`What type of car are you getting?' she asked
`It's VW Golf. It's just about a year old so it's much tidier than this thing. We are going to the Cross Keys.' He said. `You mentioned it and one of the guys at work said it was good so hopefully it will be'
They small talked on the way to the Cross Keys. Inevitably Danny Collins was the topic of the conversation.

`The papers are saying that the police are claiming that Danny was involved in drug smuggling. Is that true?' she asked him

`I have only worked there for a short time but I can honestly say that I have seen no evidence of anything like that. The company seems to be doing well. We have a nice contract with Value Shoppers. We also have contracts with a lot of the fruit and vegetable farms in the area. I don't see why Danny would have jeopardized things by getting involved with drug smuggling. He appeared to have a healthy lifestyle based on what I have seen. His wife Paula has strenuously denied the accusations. I have had to work more closely with her this week as I'm taking on more responsibility so I tend to believe with her.'

`It must have been a shock for you. You take on a new job and within weeks the owner is murdered'

`It was but for purely selfish reasons it may work to my advantage. Paula doesn't know too much about running the company so I have an opportunity to take charge of matters and run things the way that I see best for the long term for the company. I have already decided to give more responsibility for two of the younger members of the team'

They continued chatting away easily to each other and soon arrived at the Cross Keys. It was the first time that Blake had been to the place. It was a typical modern chain style pub but it did have a nice bar with a log fire burning away. They were led to a table for two in the far corner of the restaurant.

`What would you like to drink? Would you like me to order a bottle of wine or would you prefer something else?' He asked

`Will you be sharing it with me as I don't think I could manage a bottle to myself?' she replied

`I will have a pint but I will have a glass of wine as well as that will be within the driving limit'

`Ok I will have some wine then. Do you prefer red or white' she asked

`I invited you out so you can choose'

`Thank you. I would like some white wine. Chardonnay would be nice if they have any'

Blake looked at the wine menu and selected a bottle of Australian Chardonnay. It was priced at £16.95, around the middle of the prices.  They decided to skip starters. He fancied a steak so he ordered a sirloin cooked medium rare which he ordered with chips and mushrooms. Val ordered a sea bass with new potatoes and some green beans.

The food arrived promptly and they continued small talk over dinner. Blake talked about his life in Mansfield, his break up with Debbie, his mother's death and the trouble that he had finding a job after his redundancy. Val talked about her problems with Pete and how she had strayed because she was bored with being left at home on her own. She said that she had wanted children but Pete didn't and how this had aggravated the problems that were growing in their marriage. They both found it very easy to talk to each other.

When they had finished their main course the waitress cleared their plates and asked if they would like to see the dessert menu. Blake was keen as he had spied homemade apple pie and custard on the specials board when they came in.

`I could do a pudding if you would like one' he asked

`Just a Cranberry sorbet for me please I'm quite full'

Blake felt guilty. Val wasn't a big eater. He had eaten steak and chips and was now going to get stuck into apple pie and custard. She had eaten her fish but had just picked at the vegetables

`Shall we have some coffee as well?'

`Yes please '

Blake had made his pint and one full glass of white wine last all evening. He would have loved another pint or two but he didn't want to get done for drinking and driving. Coffee was a substitute.

They continued chatting until they had finished their desserts and their coffee. It was approaching 1030pm. Time had flown by and both were surprised how late it was.

Blake asked for the bill. When it arrived he was pleasantly surprised that it hadn't been that expensive. He got change out of sixty quid. He left a fiver tip

They left the pub at 1045. As they went towards Blake's car Val stopped and kissed him on the lips. They continued kissing until Blake opened the car door

`Thank you for a lovely meal. I really enjoyed it. Would you like to come to my place next week? I will cook something' Val said

`I would love to' Blake replied.

They drove back to Flixham

Pc's Brooks and Perkins were driving back from Kings Lynn. It was nearing the end of their shift so Brooks, who was driving, did it at a very leisurely pace. Perkins noticed that the car that had caught them up had a dodgy headlight

`Look at the light on that car behind us Steve. One of the headlights is off kilter. Weren't we asked to watch out for dark coloured hatchback cars with dodgy headlights?'

`Yes, but do we want to land ourselves with a problem just before the end of our shift' Brooks replied

`It's only just after eleven. We have got almost an hour to go. I reckon we should at least pull it over to see who is driving. We can at least take a number'

`If we must Polly' Brooks reluctantly agreed

He slowed down and waved his arm out of the window indicating that the car following had to stop

'Shit' Blake said 'I hope that large glass of wine hasn't taken me over the limit'

Perkins and Brooks got out of their car. They asked Blake to switch off his engine and asked to see his driving license.

'Is there a problem officer?' He asked

'Are you aware that your offside headlamp is faulty sir?' Perkins asked.

Brooks was busy taking down the number plate

'No I wasn't or I wouldn't have been driving it in that condition' Blake replied nervously. Why was it that you always felt guilty when talking to the police even though you knew that you had done nothing to worry about? His headlights seemed OK to him.

Brooks heard this reply and thought that Blake was being sarcastic

'Where have you been tonight and where are you going?' He asked

'We have been for a meal at the Cross Keys and I am taking my friend home to her place in Flixham.'

Blake was starting to get annoyed but kept his temper under control. Val didn't say a word. She just stared ahead

'Have you been drinking sir?' Brooks asked

'Yes but just one pint of beer and a small glass of wine over a meal that lasted for over two hours'

'I would like you to take a breathalyzer test'.

He asked Perkins to retrieve the kit from the back of their patrol car. He returned with it two minutes later.

'Have you taken one of these tests in the past' Brooks asked him

'No.' Blake replied. 'I try to stick within the limits'

'Take a deep breath and blow into this' Brooks instructed

He had recognised Val Davey and was aware that she had recently split up from Pete who he knew from around Flixham. He was enjoying this situation. Blake was shitting himself. He thought that he would be well within the limit but he wasn't certain. The glass of wine had been a full one .He blew into the disposable tube and handed the machine back to Brooks

'Hmmm' Brooks muttered 'you are just within the legal limits. I would suggest that you don't drink at all if a pint of beer and a small glass of wine takes you that close to the limit.' He smiled knowingly. He thought that Blake had drunk more than he had said he had but he was still well within the legal limit.

'Good evening and drive carefully' he said as parting words.

'Phew' Blake said as he drove off 'Perhaps I should have had a slightly smaller glass of wine but I'm surprised that I was close to the limit. The beer was quite strong but even so'

`PC Steve Brooks is a mate of Pete's. He plays pool with him at the sports club. Did you actually see what the reading was? I think he was deliberately making you sweat just to get at me'

Val didn't say too much more for the remainder of the journey. The incident had disturbed her. Was this what life was going to like for her if she stayed in Flixham. It was late when they eventually got back to Flixham. They kissed but Blake didn't go into Val's for the coffee she had invited him in for.

`I have to be up early tomorrow. I need to go into work earlier than usual. I've got to go to Norwich in the afternoon to collect my new car so I want to get away early'

He had told her earlier that he was going to Mansfield on Saturday evening and was meeting his children for lunch on Sunday.

`I'm free all week so I can take up your offer of cooking a meal for us. Just let me know when is best for you. I will call you on Sunday evening when I get back from Mansfield.'

They kissed again before he drove off


PC Perkins had checked the number of Blake's car.

`That's the new bloke at Collins Transport. It hasn't taken him long to start pulling the local women'

`I know who he is" Brooks replied "He was with Pete Davey's wife. She has been putting it about. She split with Pete a couple of weeks back after he found out that she had been shagging that black geezer, Hoyte, the bloke that got arrested in connection with the drugs at the Welney picnic site. I always thought that Pete was punching above his weight with her but I reckon he is best out of it. She's fit but she is a bit of a slapper as well. I will report Blake's car to Daley. He may want to follow up on the car'.

Blake went into the depot early the next morning and by 1130 he had done all that he had needed to so he left and drove to Norwich to pick up his new car with £8800 in cash in an envelope in his briefcase. The car was ready when he arrived at the garage shortly before one. It was spotless after a proper valet service had been done on it. He did the paperwork and within 20 minutes he was driving back to Flixham. Fortunately the car came with seven days temporary insurance cover so he had plenty of time to sort out some new cover. He had got some quotes already but nobody could match that from his current insurer so he would probably stick with the same company. The car was nice to drive. It accelerated well and handled corners effortlessly. It didn't take him long to get back to Flixham so he was at the sports ground for kick off. Flixham were playing Docking Rangers who were a village team who had been promoted the previous season. Both teams were mid table. He saw John Eason in the warm up.

`Hi Bob. You made it then. This should be a decent game. We are one point and one place above them in the league. We drew 2-2 at their place earlier in the season. They have a couple of lively forwards so I need to be on my toes'. It was a bright cold afternoon. The pitch looked heavy after the recent snow. It was an entertaining game which Flixham edged 4-3. John had a steady game winning a couple of crunching tackles against a young fast winger. He recognised another two of the team from Ray's party the week before. The standard of football wasn't very good but lots of effort was expended during the game which was played in a good spirit. Despite the crunching tackles nobody got booked. Both goalkeepers were suspect and should have done better with three or four of the goals. All in all it wasn't a bad way to kill a couple of hours. He didn't stop for a drink. He had told John that he was going to Mansfield that evening to see his children. It was a last minute decision He had booked into a B&B in Mansfield and had arranged to meet some of his old mates from Mansfield FC supporters club in town for a curry and a few beers that evening. He took another two thousand pounds from his stash under his bed to give to Wayne and Ellie some money. He added another £400 to pay for the weekend before leaving for Mansfield.

He put the new car through its paces on the way to Mansfield and was really pleased with it. The old Astra had done a job for a couple of months but it was a bit of a crate. It took him just over ninety minutes to get to Mansfield as the roads were reasonably quiet for a Saturday evening. He quickly found a B&B where he was shown a large room with a small en-suite shower room. It was very clean and brightly furnished with cheap but modern wardrobes and chests of drawers. There was a small 20 inch screen TV on the wall. He flicked through the channels. There wasn't many to pick from but as he only planned to sleep here and have breakfast in the morning he wasn't too bothered. He had arranged to meet Tony Martin and another two of his old mates from the supporters club in the Stag pub which was close to the football ground. Mansfield had drawn away at Kettering earlier.   He wasn't sure if Tony and his mates were still going to away games on a regular basis but Tony had said that they were going to the Kettering game as it was only about a ninety minute drive so Tony had suggested meeting up at 8pm. Blake arrived a few minutes early but the lads were already in.  He hadn't seen or spoken with Barry and Neville since before he left Mansfield so they spent time over a couple of beers catching up.

`Have you got a woman yet?' Neville asked

`Funnily enough I went out on a date last night. It was the first time I had been out with anyone since I split with Debbie'

He went on to tell them about Val. He also mentioned Helen and that he was quite keen on her if things didn't work out with Val

`You have certainly changed your appearance over the last couple of months. That must be the secret of your recent success with the ladies. Sounds like you are fighting them off with a stick. How much weight have you lost?'  You are wearing trendy gear and a sharp haircut. You have a new car. Have you won the lottery?' Barry teased

`I wish. No it's just that I have got a job that pays well and I have only myself to fend for. I haven't got a mortgage, food and utility bills for a family of four, two cars to pay for so I'm lucky to have a few quid in my pocket. I needed some new clothes as I have dropped the best part of three stone so all of the clothes that I had were too big. On top of this I had money from the sale of my Mum's house'

`So, when are you coming back to Mansfield then?' Tony

`I don't think that I will. I am enjoying the new job in Flixham. Did you hear about the bloke who got murdered in Flixham?  The bloke, Danny Collins, was my boss so I am taking on more control of the company. His wife hasn't had much to do with the running of the company so she has asked me to run things for her.'

`Fucking hell' Tony Barry and Neville all said almost in unison. `What happened to him?'

`It looks as though he interrupted a break in at his house and he was shot by one of the burglars' Blake said, not wishing to mention the involvement of the drug dealers. `I'm renting a small place at the moment but I'm thinking of buying a house in Kings Lynn as there is a bit more going on there. It's only fifteen minutes drive to work from there.'

`It sounds like you have landed on your feet Bob. I'm please it has worked out for you. Tell us about the lass you took out last night. How did you meet her?' Tony asked

Blake gave them a brief version of how he had met Val.

Tony, Barry and Neville were all single. Barry and Neville shared a flat together. Blake could only remember them having girlfriends for a very short time and he had known them for over 20 years. They were all ardent Stags fans. Neville liked his horses too so his life revolved around Mansfield Town FC, the pub and betting offices. He was only five foot five and was well overweight. He spent most of his days sat in a small office on the campus at Nottingham University where he undertook various clerical duties. Barry had been married for a few years but the marriage ended badly. He and Barry had been mates since school days so they decided to rent a flat together to save costs. Barry worked for the local council in the planning office. He worked nine to five. He liked a drink but unlike Neville he didn't gamble. Barry was a couch potato and when he wasn't in the pub he spent much of his spare time watching TV

After everybody had got a round in they set off for a new Indian restaurant called Shafiq that had only opened a few weeks back.

The food was excellent. It was probably the best curry that Blake had ever had so he wasn't surprised that the place was packed.

`Hey Nev, do you ever go to race meetings?' He asked fishing for information

`Occasionally I go down to the races at Nottingham'. Neville replied. `Why do you ask? I didn't think horse racing was your thing.'

`It hasn't been but I am thinking of taking some of the staff at Collins Transport for a day out as a sort of team bonding exercise' He lied `How does the betting work?'

`You basically have three options. You can bet on the races with the high street bookmakers who have offices on course, you can bet on the tote or you can bet with the bookies on the rails on course'

`What is the Tote? How does that work? How do they know what horse you have picked?'

`The Tote is similar to a high street bookie but the payout depends on how many others have bet on the horse. You can place win bets or place bets. It's different with the on course bookies. You tell them what horse you want to bet on and how much you want to bet. Each bookie has a list of prices for each horse so you need to look around to see which one is offering the best price. Once you find the best price you place your bet. They tell you how much the bet will pay if it is a winning bet. They record it in their ledgers and give you a ticket which corresponds to the bet in their ledgers. If you win you present your ticket to the bookie and he will pay you the agreed amount for the bet. There are usually two working at each site. Let me give you an example. If you were to place a ten pound bet on a horse at 5/1 with Joe Bloggs bookmaker he would give you a ticket with the horse name on it the type of bet and how much you would get if the horse wins which in this case would be sixty quid. Fifty pound winnings plus your stake back. If it's an each way bet your stake would be higher but you get the added security of getting some money back if the horse gets placed. This is usually a quarter or a fifth of the odds depending on how many runners there are in the race.'

`Have you ever seen big bets or big payouts?'

`My biggest win was £450 on one bet. I stuck fifty quid at 8/1 on a horse that I had a tip for. I have seen thousand pound bets from professional gamblers but those types of bets are normally on short priced horses so I reckon the biggest payout I have seen is about £4000. I usually never bet more than twenty quid on a horse so most of my wins are less than a ton'

`Do the bookies know who they are paying out to? Supposing I found a ticket and tried to cash it. Would they know if I had placed the bet?'

`They might do if you were a regular punter on their site but unless you were a blonde with big tits or had a lot of banter with them I doubt if they remember who placed a bet with them. It's just a sea of faces to them'

It was late by the time they left the curry house. Blake was feeling quite pissed. He had drunk eight pints during the course of the evening. He could manage six pints but any more took its toll. He had eaten too much so he was feeling bloated too. He grabbed a taxi back to the B&B after saying goodnight to his mates. They were a good bunch and he had invited them to come and stay with him if they fancied a weekend away.

It was only a few minutes ride in the taxi. He staggered into his room and fell onto his bed fully clothed. He went to sleep straight away but woke up after an hour. He needed a piss and as he stood over the toilet he suddenly felt sick. He threw up. Fortunately he managed to hit the toilet. He drank some water, got undressed and went back to bed.

He slept heavily and woke up at 0830 with a headache. Breakfast was between 0800 and 0930 so he had time to have a shave and a shower before he trudged down for breakfast. He wasn't hungry but he decided on an English breakfast hoping it would settle his stomach a bit. It wasn't the best breakfast that he had ever had but the room was inexpensive so he couldn't complain.

He checked out at 0950. He checked his wallet. He had spent over fifty pounds the previous night plus thirty pounds on the room so he still had the best part of two hundred and fifty pounds left in his wallet on top of the money he had for Wayne and Ellie. He had planned to buy some new clothes so he headed to a retail park on the outskirts of town. There was a Next Store, BHS, C&A and a Burtons shop on the park. He spent over £300 on shirts trousers jackets and shoes which he paid for part of it in cash and the rest on his credit card. He also purchased a light grey suit from Marks and Spencer which was also on his card. He wanted a hundred pounds in cash left over to cover lunch and some fuel for the journey home. He checked his watch. It was 1115. He wasn't meeting up with Wayne and Ellie until 1pm. He decided on a coffee so he went into the cafe at Marks and Spencer. He still felt a bit ropey and he hoped the coffee would make him feel a bit better. He took his time over the coffee and after using the toilet he left the store. He decided to call Val when he got to his car. She didn't answer but called him back ten minutes later.

`I was drying my hair and didn't hear your call. It's pouring with rain here and I got soaked coming back from Morrisons. I only walked across the car park and then brought my shopping in from the car. It's been falling down here all morning. What is it like in Mansfield? Did you have a good night last night with your mates?'

`Overcast but dry. Yes. It was a good night. I had a couple of beers too many so I didn't feel too clever this morning. We went to a new curry house in town and it was probably the best curry I have ever had. Funny thing though is that Mansfield doesn't feel like home any more. I have moved on from life there. It was good to see my old mates but nothing has changed with them. They are all stuck in a rut doing the same things day in day out. None of them are married and they seem quite happy to plod along with their lives. By moving out of the area I'm making a fresh start. If things are still going well at work I will start looking for a new house'

`I will be looking for somewhere to live soon once Pete and I have decided what to do with our flat. The problem we have is that it probably won't sell for what we paid for it so we are stuck with negative equity and our mortgage deal runs out soon. What time do you expect to get back to Flixham tonight?'

`I'm not sure. I'm meeting my children for lunch at 1pm so I will probably leave here at 4pm at the latest. I reckon I could be home by 6pm. Why do you ask?'

`I was wondering if I could come round to see you. I could bring a bottle of wine'

Blake wanted a quiet night and didn't really want company. He wanted to start on the base of his bed so that he could make a better job of hiding his money

` I have got some washing and ironing to do tonight and I had a late one last night. Why don't you come over Monday or Tuesday? I could order a takeaway.'

Val sounded a bit miffed when she replied.

'I suppose so. It's just that I enjoyed Friday night and I would have liked to have seen you again'

'Unfortunately work is full on at the moment so I haven't had much time catching up with my chores I normally do everything Saturday afternoon or Sunday mornings but with coming to Mansfield I'm all behind. Look, I'd better go but please come over if you want to on Monday or Tuesday'

'What's your address? I could come over on Monday night. Is 700pm OK?' she asked.

He gave her his address said goodbye and hung up. He was concerned that she was going to be one of those women who wanted to be with him all the time. He didn't need that sort of relationship, not at this stage anyway. He decided to have a look in BHS for a cheap duvet and ended up putting another £60 on his credit card after buying some new duvet covers towels and some lamps. He wandered aimlessly around the retail park until it was time to meet up with Wayne and Ellie.

46

He had agreed to meet up with Ellie and Wayne at the Fox and Hounds again. He arrived a few minutes early. He saw Ellie's little Citroen pull into the car park as he was getting out of his car. Wayne wasn't with her

'Hi Dad' she said. 'Wayne isn't coming. He is at home with Mum. Let's go inside and I will tell you all about it'

Blake was both annoyed and intrigued as to why Wayne hadn't come. He checked in at the restaurant desk explaining that their table for three was now for two and was led to a table in the corner. He ordered a beer for himself and a J2O orange drink for Ellie

'What's the story with Wayne then Ellie?' He asked

'He got into a fight in the town centre last night and ended up in casualty. He has had some stitches to a cut above his eye and he has broken his nose. Derrick went mad when he phoned Mum at 2am this morning. He had a big row with Mum about it because Wayne is always getting into fights because he gets pissed every time he goes out. It's causing a strain with Mum and Derrick. She has been crying a lot. I don't think things are going to well with Derrick'

'How long as Wayne been acting up like this' he asked

'He has been drinking a lot since you went to Norfolk it has got worse recently. As you know it's his birthday next week and he has organised a party at the Social Club. The club has threatened to ban him if he misbehaves again so god knows what will happen at his party as he is bound to get legless again.'

'Who was he fighting with last night?' He asked

'Some gang from the Chaucer Estate. He said there were seven of them and that they had picked on Wayne and his three mates. Wayne says that he had hurt two of them and that one of them needed more stitches than he did. The police are investigating it and he could be charged with affray. If he does it could damage his chances of his apprenticeship especially as there was some damage to furniture in the Black Bull pub where it all happened. Wayne has become very aggressive lately. He is a big lad and has clashed with Derrick a couple of times when Derrick had a go at him for his drinking. Mum and I had to pull them apart once'

'I could have a word with him but I don't think it would make any difference. Where is he getting the money from to go out drinking?'

'He has started working at Asda on a Thursday evening after he has finished school and again on Saturdays. He only earns about thirty pounds but this is enough for him to go out drinking on Saturday nights. He has got a girlfriend called Sasha who is always pissed too and I think she is a bad influence on him. From what I hear she is a bit of a scrubber. She stayed over at ours when Mum and Derrick were away for the weekend and I had a bust up with her because she left a mess everywhere she went. Wayne wants her to come to Derrick's villa in Portugal when we go away but Derrick and Mum said no'

'How are you getting on with him living in the annexe? Is he studying enough for his A'levels?'

'It's hard work. He spends all day in his room playing on his Xbox. I eat over with Mum and Derrick most nights but he doesn't join us. He eats lots of pot noodles and takeaways. I don't think I can put up with him for much longer. He is a right moody sod. Anyway that is enough about Wayne. How are you getting on in Norfolk? How is the job going? I see that you have got a nice new car. I presume that the money has come through for Nan's house'

He told her about Danny's murder and how he had taken on extra responsibilities. He also told her about Val. He hoped that she told Debbie about her too. He had changed a lot appearance wise since the split with Debbie. He looked good for his age now and he was pleased that Ellie had said so too. He told her that he was thinking about buying a house in Kings Lynn which had more going on than Flixham.

'You could come down to stay when I do buy somewhere. My current house is only a one bed so it's a bit too small for guests but it serves its purpose for now. Are you still going out with Marcus? '

'No we split up a couple of weeks ago. He was cheating on me with some girl from work'

'As you know I wasn't his greatest fan. You are a good looking girl so men will be queuing up for you' he said smiling.

It was true though. Ellie reminded him a little of Debbie when he had first met her. She was about five foot eight with a full figure. She had chestnut brown hair and a pretty face.

'How is the accounting going?'

'It's going quite well. As you know I passed the foundation stage exams in December. I have got the next level exams in June. I doing an online study package and my module scores have been good so fingers crossed'.

'Good luck with them. You never hear of a poor accountant and there is always plenty of work for them'

He was proud of her

Their food arrived. They had both ordered roast beef with Yorkshire puddings which were huge. There were plenty of vegetables on their plates as well. Ellie struggled to finish hers and even he was quite full after he had eaten it. He ordered another round of drinks. His second beer was a shandy. Friday night's incident with the police had shaken him so he didn't want to take a chance especially after having a skin full last night.

'I have got something for Wayne and you.' He handed her both envelopes which both contained £1,000. I will give you some more once I have sorted out a house in Kings Lynn. I will double what's in that envelope if you pass your exams in June.'

Ellie took both envelopes. He hadn't sealed them. She peeked inside and saw the wad of £50 notes.

'Thanks Dad.' She beamed

'Tell Wayne to use it towards buying a car. He should be able to get a cheap runabout for that sort of money as long as he doesn't piss it all up the wall'

They continued chatting about Norfolk for the remainder of the meal and had finished by 230pm. He kissed Ellie goodbye and promised to phone her and Wayne during the week. He left and had a nice drive back to Flixham arriving home at 430pm. He hoped that Val didn't check up on him as he was home earlier than he told her he would be. He set about the chores that he had told Val that he wanted to do. This took him an hour. Next was the bed. He carefully levered out the staples in the top section of the bed using a small flat screwdriver. He removed the pile of money from the drawer section. He counted it and wrapped £240,000 of it in the duvet leaving the rest to one side. He was going to open up some building society accounts with this after a trip to the races at Huntingdon next Saturday afternoon. He replaced the staples and put the two parts of bed back together and quickly remade the bed with a clean duvet set and sheets. He had just finished putting the dirty bed linen into the washing machine when there was a knock on his door.

'Fuck' he said under his breath hoping it wasn't Val. It wasn't. To his surprise he found Helen on his doorstep.

'Hi 'she said. 'I saw that you were at home and I thought that you might like some company'

She had four cans of beer in her hand which she held up. It was obvious that she had been drinking. She was wearing a short leather jacket, a pair of jeans and a tight yellow tee shirt which showed off her ample bust. She looked very attractive.

Blake was tempted to invite her in but if truth be told he was feeling tired and just wanted an early night.

'Sorry Helen. I have just arrived home from a weekend in Mansfield to see my children. I went out with some of my old mates last night. I had too much to drink and I think the curry we had was a bit iffy because I have had an upset stomach all day. Can I pass and do it another day because I'm knackered?'

Helen didn't reply for a few seconds

`Suit yourself.' she said abruptly before turning around and walking off. She didn't look back. She looked angry when he turned her down.
`That's blown that' he muttered under his breath. He went back to turn on the washing machine and soon as the cycle was complete he hung the washing over the line which was in the bathroom and he did have an early night.

47

Blake arrived at work at 730am. He had plenty to do and was getting stuck into the many tasks when June Eason phoned him at 945am

`DS Daley is here and would like a word with you'

`What the bloody hell does he want now?' He said to her, not expecting an answer `you had better send him in'

Daley knocked and entered his office

`Sorry to bother you again Mr Blake. I expect that you are very busy. I just want to talk to you about your car' Daley hadn't seen it when he parked up

`What about my car? Is there a problem with it because I purchased it from a dealer in Norwich and I have all the paperwork for it?'

Daley was confused. He didn't know what Blake was talking about.

`I'm talking about your dark green Astra'

`Oh that car' Blake replied `I part exchanged it at the weekend for a VW Golf. It's in the car park. I was worried that you had come to tell me that I had purchased a stolen car. What do you want to talk about the old Astra for?'

`A dark coloured hatchback was caught on camera going into the Red Lion on Jan 27th. We noticed that one of the headlamps was faulty. It was pointing in an odd direction. A car with a similar faulty headlight was seen driving into Turnberry Close later that evening. I was told that you were pulled over by one of our patrol vehicles who had noticed that your headlamp was also pointing in an odd direction. Your car is a dark coloured hatchback and I am not a great believer in coincidence. I believe that you were asked to take a breathalyser test. You didn't mention that you were getting rid of the car the next day. Why was that?'

Blake thought about what he was going to say before he responded to Daley's questions.

`There must be loads of dark coloured hatchbacks in the area. It is a few weeks now since the 27th. How come I wasn't pulled over before Saturday night? Could it be that the fault with the headlamp was a recent occurrence because I hadn't noticed it while I was driving? Secondly it is of no concern to the police if I decide to trade my car and get a new one. I bought a new suit at the weekend. Do I have to report that as well?'

Daley wasn't impressed with Blake's outburst.

` There is no need for sarcasm. I am trying to resolve a crime and your attitude disappoints me' He left his words hanging

`Well I suggest that you get on with trying to solve it and stop badgering innocent people. I told you what I was doing on Jan 27. I had only been here a matter of days. How the hell would I have had the time to get mixed up in events like those in such a short time? Now if that is all, I have some work to be getting on with so I would like you to leave.'

'Before I go can you tell me which dealer did you use for part exchange your car? I intend to do a thorough search of the car to see if there is any evidence that it was anywhere near the Welney picnic site. You will be surprised what we can find with forensics if we put our minds to it.'

Blake gave him the name of the dealership.

' I should warn you that I put the car through a full valet service. I didn't do it to hide evidence though. I just wanted to make it very presentable when I tried to part exchange it '

Blake was concerned though. He worried that some of Andrew's DNA might show up even though it was put through a full valet service which had set him back thirty quid...

On leaving Collins depot phoned the dealership that Blake had told him of. He asked to speak to the manager and was put through to Don West.

Daley told Don West who he was and explained why he was calling

'I'm phoning about a car you part exchanged with a Bob Blake on Saturday. Do you still have his old car or have you moved it on'

'We still have it here. It will go to the auctions at the end of the week. It's a bit tatty but it runs OK. I doubt if I will get much more than £300 for it but I had plenty of margin in the car that I sold to Mr Blake. He was a bit pushy though twice threatening to walk away if I didn't agree to the price he was willing to pay for the car. He insisted on paying cash too which is unusual these days. I got the impression that he thought I wouldn't put the right numbers through the books but I'm strictly legitimate'

'Can I as how much he paid for it?'

'It was nine thousand pounds. He paid a deposit of two hundred pounds last week and brought the rest of the money in early Saturday afternoon. It was all £50 notes'

'That's very interesting. I need to take the car in for forensic examination. There is a chance that his old car may have been involved in criminal activity. Can we collect it tomorrow morning? We will return it to you within a couple of days'

West accepted Daley's proposal.

Daley felt a tinge of excitement as he hung up on the dealership. He had a gut feeling about Blake who looked concerned when he mentioned putting his old car through a forensic test. Something didn't feel right with him and he didn't believe that it was just coincidence that Blake's car was a dark coloured hatchback with a wonky headlamp like the one seen on January 27th. He decided that he would speak to Blake again but this time at his home. He phoned Bev to tell her that he wouldn't be home until 1900. After doing a few other follow ups he returned to Flixham station.

On arrival he asked Ronnie Edbrooke if he could find the address for Blake. He phoned DI Green to update him.

"Hi Roland, I have some information which could be relevant regarding the mysterious dark hatchback. When we were scanning through the camera footage of the night of January 27 we noticed that one of the headlamps on the dark coloured hatchback was faulty. The beam wasn't pointing straight. One of our patrols pulled over a Vauxhall Astra on Saturday evening. It belonged to Bob Blake, the new transport manager. Blake had a fight with Andrews in the Red Lion the week before the 27th so he was known to Andrews. Blake purchased a new car in Norwich on Saturday. He paid £9000 in cash for it. The question is where did he get £9,000 in cash from to buy a new car? He made a point of telling me that he had put his old car through a full valet service when I suggested that we would like to examine his car. He said that he was trying to make his car look more presentable when trying to get a decent part exchange price for it. He looked concerned when I mentioned the forensics. I believe that there is cause for concern with Blake. Something about him doesn't feel right. I saw him at work this morning. I plan to interview him again at home tonight. I will ask DC Marks to join me'

`That is good work Arthur. There could be something but hasn't he only just started at Collins Transport? Would he have been trusted to get involved with drug trafficking so soon after starting with the company?'

`Probably not but I was thinking more along the lines of the money that was reported missing. What looks like his car was seen on camera going into and away from the Red Lion within the timescale that we have been looking at. He had a bust up with Andrews in the Red Lion the week before. Andrews apparently put him on his arse with one punch. From what we were told Andrews would probably beaten the shit out of him if Hoyte hadn't intervened. Andrews had no known associates other than Hoyte and Danny Collins so it could be possible that he threatened Blake and forced him to drive to the Welney picnic site. It would fit with the timings on Andrews movements. Then there is the obvious solution. Collins wife was involved in an accident so did Collins ask Blake to help him out that evening? There are a lot of assumptions but I think it may be worth following up. It would be good to get a result before Booth gets back'

DI Green wasn't convinced as there were too many assumptions but agreed that it was worth following up. Booth was due back on Wednesday so it would be good to have something positive to report to her.

48

Blake called Val that afternoon.

`I will be home just after 6pm tonight so if you still want to come over please do. Give me half hour to have a shower. We can order a takeaway when you get there.'

Val was quite relieved that Blake had phoned her.

`Ok. I will come over at about 645pm. See you later'

Lesley had called her on Sunday evening to see how her date with Blake had gone and she had told her that Blake hadn't wanted to see her on Sunday evening so she wasn't sure if things were going to progress with him. She had told Lesley that she fancied Blake. She had said that he was a gentleman and wasn't just after a quick shag which was rare in her experience

Blake arrived home earlier than he had expected. As soon as he got in he jumped in the shower and put on some of the new clothes that he had purchased in Mansfield on Sunday. He had nipped into Kings Lynn during his lunch break. He grabbed a quick coffee and a sandwich in Tesco's and had bought some condoms from the machine in Tesco's toilets just in case things developed with Val. He had just got dressed when there was a knock on his door. It was twenty past six. Surely it couldn't be Val this early he thought. He went downstairs and answered the door. DS Daley and DC Marks were on his doorstep.

`What do you want now?' He asked `I thought that I had answered all of your questions earlier'

`Can we come in?' Daley asked

`If you must but be quick about it as I have company later'

He showed Daley and Marks into his sparsely furnished lounge and offered them a seat on his sofa. He stood above them

`What is this about?' he asked

`You did answer my questions earlier but after further investigation we have a few more questions for you' Daley replied `You said that you had purchased a new car and part exchanged your old car at West Autos in Norwich. I spoke to Don West after I left you. He told me that you paid £9000 in used £50 notes for that car. We are led to believe that a sum of cash went missing from the apparent drugs trade at Welney on January 27th and here you are paying £9,000 in cash  a couple of weeks afterwards. As I said to you earlier I don't believe in coincidence. First your old car looks like similar to one that appeared on CCTV by the Red Lion car park at the same time Lynton Andrews was seen leaving the bar with a holdall full of drugs and now you turn up with a bundle of cash to buy a car'

Blake started laughing and shaking his head.

'What's so funny?' Marks asked. She was annoyed with Blake's attitude

'You must really be clutching at straws if you are going on such thin evidence. If you had asked me about the £9,000 I could have told you that I had drawn £9,000 out of my bank account on Friday. My mother died in August but she didn't have a will. As I was her only child I inherited from her. There was her house which I sold but everything had to go through probate. I have a letter from my solicitor telling me that probate had been sorted. There was a cheque for £102,985 enclosed in the letter. I banked it on Monday. It had cleared by Friday. I explained all of this at the garage which is the reason I had to wait until Saturday to collect the car. Dealers often prefer cash so that they can reduce the amount of profit that they show for a car. Give me a minute and I will dig out the letter for you'.

He left the room and turned to a pile of letters on the worktop in the kitchen. He had received several letters since he had moved in including a few for previous tenants. He retrieved the letter from the solicitor and handed it to Daley. While Daley was reading it Blake opened his wallet and dug out the mini statement that he had requested from the hole in the wall at his bank on Saturday morning. He had checked to see the deposit account had been set up properly.

'I also have this mini statement showing that I banked the cheque. I opened a deposit account and withdrew £9000 in cash which I used for the new car'

He gave the mini statement to Marks.

Daley felt deflated. He was convinced that Blake had been the driver. His car and the cash had given him further hope but it seemed as though he was totally wrong.

He apologised to Blake saying that he had put two and two together and made five. Marks looked crestfallen too. She handed back the mini statement.

'I know that you have a job to do but I have had no involvement in anything irregular at Collins. I can assure you of that. I am starting over. I moved here a few weeks ago and I haven't been here long enough to make any real friends yet. If you still think that I have somehow acquired some missing money please feel free to have a look around my house. You will see that it's very small and there are few hiding places'

`I don't think that will be necessary Mr Blake. I doubt that anyone would be stupid enough to keep hold of the money and hide it in their house especially considering the size of the amount involved'

`Is it a large sum then?' Blake casually asked hoping to find out what the police actually knew about the amount.

`I'm afraid that I cannot divulge that information'

Dc Marks had noticed several carrier bags that were on the small table in the lounge. There was a C&A's bag amongst them. She didn't know if there was a store locally

`Where's the C&A store around here? There was a store where I used to live and they had some nice clothes'

`It isn't local. I was in Mansfield at the weekend visiting my children. I did a bit of shopping while I was there. I mentioned to you earlier that I had purchased new suit. I got it in Mansfield'

`Did you pay cash for that as well?' Marks said with a mischievous hint in her voice

`No. I used my credit card. Do you want to see the receipt for it' Blake snapped back at her

Daley could feel that Blake was getting agitated.

`I appreciate that you are new in the job at Collins Transport but I need to warn you that we are very interested in the company for all of the wrong reasons. We have a signed confession from a member of the public who says that he was paid by Danny Collins to act as a courier for what turned out to be a drugs deal. Would you let me know if you find or hear of anything that would be of interest to us'

`After the police visited our offices both myself and Ruth Cross, who looks after the finances, did a thorough check of our records. Everything seems squeaky clean. It does seem harsh that the finger is being pointed at Danny Collins now that he isn't around to defend himself. Have the police considered that his name has been put forward as a scapegoat. If Danny had been doing anything illegal his wife didn't know anything about it. I have been working very closely with Paula Collins recently and she insists that Danny had done nothing wrong. She says that he was killed as the result of a bungled burglary'

`Unfortunately we have evidence that points to the contrary Mr Blake. I can't go into detail but please keep your eyes and ears open. Thank you for your assistance tonight and once again apologies for the intrusion. Enjoy your evening'

As they opened the door to leave Val Davey was coming up the path to the house. She gave DC Marks a filthy look as she brushed past her almost taking Marks' eye out with her umbrella. It had started to rain heavily.

Clarissa Marks looked very surprised to see Val Davey turning up at Blake's place.' She didn't waste any time' she thought

'Hi Bob .What did they want?' Val said as she came into the house. She kissed him on the cheek

'They seem to think that my old car was used to transport Lynton Andrews out to the car park at Welney and that somehow I had nicked a load of money. It's a load of bollocks. Daley has been to see me twice today. Talk about police harassment'

'That cow DC Marks was the one that told Pete that I had been having an affair. She had a big grin on her face when she told me that she had been to see Pete before interviewing me and dropped me in it.'

As Daley and Marks got back to Mark's car Marks said

'Is it just me or is it not coincidence that Andrews mate was Dennard Hoyte who was shagging Davey who is now shagging Blake? Is there a connection between them all?'

'He seemed very confident, almost cocky with his answers. I got the impression that he was challenging us to search his property because he knew that we would find nothing. If he was involved he would surely have moved it by now. I am not eliminating him just yet'

Blake showed Val around his small house. She had brought a bottle of Chardonnay with her. It was nicely chilled so Blake poured some for them both. He had also bought a bottle of Chardonnay from Tesco's along with a six pack of beers which had only been in the fridge since he arrived home from work so they were not very cool yet.

'What do you fancy to eat'? He asked her returning from the kitchen with the two glasses in his hand. He had bought some crisps which he hastily put into a bowl. 'Those two coppers have made me all behind. They had some bloody ridiculous theory that because they had seen a dark coloured hatchback with a wonky light that it had been my car. I bet that is why I got pulled over on Friday evening'

He hoped that he sounded convincing to Val.

'I don't know what possessed them to think that I had driven Lynton Andrews out to a bloody picnic site in a snow storm especially as I had a scrap with him in the Red Lion the week before'

'Wow, you had a fight with Lynton Andrews. He was a nasty bastard who was always looking for trouble. Did you win?'

'He probably edged it on points' he lied 'we both got one good punch in before his mate stepped in and stopped us'

Denny had told Val about how Andrews had put some bloke on his arse in the Red Lion and how Andrews would have kicked the shit out of him if he hadn't stepped in. She didn't let on that she knew what had happened.

`Do you fancy a pizza? The shop in town does good pizzas. They will be quiet on a Monday evening so it shouldn't take them too long to deliver. I have their number on my mobile?'

`Pizza would be good' he replied.

Val ordered a large Hawaiian pizza. It arrived within twenty minutes. Blake had warmed some plates in the microwave and had set the small table. They small talked over the meal. The pizza was good. Blake had devoured well over half of it. He was hungry and as Val had only picked at two slices there was plenty to satisfy his appetite.

`Tell me about your weekend. How are your children?' She asked

Blake told her about Ellie and her exams, Debbie having issues with her new bloke and Wayne drinking too much and getting into fights. He told her that Wayne never showed up for lunch as he had spent the night before in casualty

`He must take after his old man then if he is fighting' she ribbed him

`From what Ellie was saying I don't think he gets on too well with my ex's bloke Derrick. He has a big house with a two bedroom annexe which his mother used to live in. My two kids live in it but they eat with Derrick and Debbie. Wayne rarely does now. Ellie says he spends all day on his Xbox, doesn't study for his A' levels and has hooked up with some girl who seems to be a bad influence on him. I will phone him tomorrow and try to have a fatherly chat with him'

They finished the first bottle of wine so Blake opened the second. They drank it as they sat on his small sofa.  The second bottle soon emptied.

`Unless you want to walk me home in the rain I guess that I will have to stay the night. I can't drive as I have had too much to drink' Val whispered to him

`I can always get you a taxi  and you can pick your car up in the morning' Blake replied half joking

`If that's what you want but I was hoping that we could get to know each other a bit better' Val replied with a slightly disappointed tone. What was wrong with this man she thought?

`I'm only teasing you.' They kissed again before Val led him upstairs. They made love twice and once again in the morning before they both left for work. The first time was a little urgent but they took their time afterwards. Blake discovered that Val was very energetic in bed and they ended up in positions that he hadn't tried with Debbie.  He was nervous at first because it had been a long time since he been with anybody other than Debbie but she seemed to enjoy it. His confidence was boosted when she invited him over to her place on Thursday night. He thought that have must have been OK.

The next day Val phoned Lesley during a quiet period at work and told her about the previous night

`Was he any good in bed?' Lesley enquired

`You are bloody sex mad Les. All you want to know about is how good they are in bed. I have no complaints .He was better than Pete. I've invited him over to my place later this week. It turns out that he had a fight with Lynton in the Red Lion. Denny told me that Lynton had put some bloke on his arse. It was Bob. I didn't let on that Denny had told me what happened because Bob said that Lynton had edged the fight on points. It just goes to show what a small place Flixham is. My new fellow had a fight with my ex's mate. How weird is that'.

`I'm still seeing Dimi. He still seems keen on me. He is good fun to be with. He wants to go out with me and the kids on Sunday. He has suggested going to the cinema and having a Big Mac afterwards. I said that I would think about it but I'm going to agree to it. He hasn't stayed over when the kids are around.'

`I reckon that Bob is well off. His mother left him some money. He bought a new car at the weekend and paid cash for it. He is also talking about buying a house once he knows that his job is secure. He may be worth latching on to for a while'

`Blimey Val, You sound as if you are smitten'

`It's very early days yet but I'll admit that he is nice. He seems different to the other men that I have known. I know that he is a bit older than me but he is quite fit. He has a strong body and there isn't a lot of fat on him'.

`Well I hope it works out for you. You need a change of luck'

49

Blake's old car was collected from West Autos on Tuesday morning. It was put through a thorough forensic test but to Daley's disappointment there was no sign of Lynton Andrews DNA in the car or any fingerprints tying him to the vehicle. The lack of fingerprints didn't surprise Daley as he remembered that Andrews had been wearing some leather gloves but the lack of any DNA annoyed him. He was hoping for a hair or something but nothing showed up. Perhaps it was too much to ask for as Andrews had a shaved head. He thought that there might be some trace of fibres from Andrews' clothes but there wasn't. The valet service that Blake had on the car had been very good as it was sparkling inside and out. It was a dead end but despite this Daley's gut told him that Blake had been involved somehow. Clarissa Marks also shared the view that Blake was involved. She was convinced that it was his car that was on the CCTV footage. Her thoughts were strengthened by the interview with Blake last night. He seemed too confident with his answers. It was as though he had anticipated the questions that the police would ask him and had prepared answers in readiness.

Tuesday night turned out to be an unpleasant evening for Blake and Val. Pete came round to the flat and had a go at her for putting it about so soon after they had split up.
`You are making a fool out of me' he moaned. `First you start shagging that black bloke and now I hear you are having it off with some old bloke who is new in town and that's all while muggings here is paying for the mortgage on the flat'
`I can guess who told you about me and my new bloke. I bet it was Steve Brooks. He pulled us over and tested my bloke for drinking and driving. You told me that it was over between us so I can do whatever I want with whoever I bloody want. He isn't that old either. There are only a few years between us. Besides he has got more stamina than you. I slept with him last night for the first time although we didn't sleep much as he fucked me all night' she shouted taunting him. `He is the third man that I have slept with since we got married and they were all better in bed than you. Do what you want with the flat but get out and leave me alone'.
Her face was red with anger and she put her face into his while shouting at him Pete Davey lost his temper and for the first time ever he hit a woman, He punched Val in the face drawing blood from her mouth. She fell onto the floor more in shock than from the force of the blow although it bloody hurt her.

'Pack your bags and get out' he screamed at her
'I'm not going anywhere' she sobbed 'What are you going to do about it, Hit me again? My name is on the deeds to this flat as well so I have as much right to live here as you do. I'm going to phone the police and have you arrested for wife beating. Let's see what Steve Brooks thinks about that!'
 Val went into the kitchen and put some kitchen towel onto her mouth which was bleeding. Pete stood motionless. The threat of her calling the police cooled his temper. He had assaulted her and he could be arrested. He went into the kitchen after her.
'I'm sorry that I hit you. I just lost my temper'. He attempted to put his arm around her to console her.
She grabbed a knife from the rack on the kitchen work top.
'If you come near me I swear I will put this knife in you. Fuck off back to your mother and don't come near me again'
He left meekly leaving Val shaking with a mixture of anger and fear. Pete had never raised a hand to her in all the time that she had known him. Perhaps she shouldn't have taunted him about her lovers. She doubted that she would have gone through with her threat to put the knife in him though. Her mouth was sore and she had the makings of a fat lip.

Blake got home just after six. He was tired. He hadn't slept much the night before. He had called into Morrisons on the way home and bought himself a chicken pasta dish and a salad for his dinner. After eating it he called Wayne
'What do you want?' Wayne said on answering his phone
'Well a thank you for the money that I gave you would be a start'
'Do you reckon so? You get all that money from Gran's house and all you give me and Ellie is a measly grand. That isn't going to buy me a decent car. You can splash out on a new car but you expect me to run around in an old banger. What about the insurance cost? That will take up most of the money that you gave me'
'Well perhaps if you started putting a few quid by from the money you earn at Asda rather than pissing it all up the wall you might be able to buy something a bit newer. I told Ellie that I would give you some more once I have sorted myself out with a house. I'm living in a tiny one bedroom house which I'm renting so I'm going to buy somewhere. Until that is sorted out you will have to make do with an old banger as you put it. I had an old car for a few months too. As long as it gets you from A to B that's all you need to worry about. Once you have a couple of years no claims your insurance will go down and then you can buy a newer model. Just get yourself a little Fiesta or Micra to run about in for now. You can pick them up for £500'

`I'm not driving around in a crappy old Fiesta or Micra. What about my street cred?'

`It's better than a bus' Blake replied with his hackles rising. `You will have to make do with the money that I have given you. Pass your A'Levels and I will give you some more. If you don't pass them you won't get as much. You are eighteen in a couple of weeks so it's about time you started acting like an adult instead of a sulky kid. And cut down on the drinking'

`Oh fuck off Dad.' Wayne shouted before ending the call

That went well, Blake contemplated after the call. They never got round to talking about the incident on Saturday night

His mobile rang again. He answered it hoping that it was going to be Wayne. It wasn't. It was Ellie

`What did you say to Wayne Dad? He stormed out of here slamming the door behind him'

`The ungrateful little sod complained that I had only given him a thousand pounds. I told him, like I told you, that I would give him some more once I had bought a house. I also told him how much he got would depend on how he got on with his A'Levels. He wasn't prepared to buy a little Fiesta or a car like yours as a starter car complaining about his street credibility'

`He has been in a right foul mood since yesterday. He is being charged with affray and will have to appear in court in a couple of week's time. Mum and Derrick went mad at him but he just went out with Sasha on Sunday night and got legless. I don't know what happened but she dumped him on Monday which made him even grumpier. He hasn't even been to school this week yet. Mum and Derrick had a massive row about him. Mum stayed here last night and slept in my bed. Everything seems to be going to shit because of Wayne's behaviour. The atmosphere is horrible here at the moment. Derrick used to be nice but he hardly speaks to me now. I would move out if I could afford to and as soon as I pass my exams I will think about getting a my own place'

Blake felt for his daughter. He didn't want a difficult situation at home to detract from her efforts to pass her exams. He knew that her salary was low while she was trying to qualify. He also knew that he had £240,000 sat under his bed. He thought that he had a duty to help his daughter. Things hadn't been great with her while he was at home. He didn't like her boyfriend and that had caused hostility between them.

`Look Ellie, I think that I can help you if you really want to get somewhere of your own. I would be prepared to pay £300 each month towards rent for you while you are studying for your exams. Think about it and perhaps have a look around at what's available. I will let Wayne calm down for a couple of days and then I will call him'

'Would you really pay my rent while I am studying? That would help me out so much. I would like to live in Mansfield rather than have to drive in every day from Clipstone. The traffic is getting worse. I have already been looking on RightMove to get some idea of the cost of rent for a one bedroom flat and there are several in the £275 to £300 price range.'

'Well arrange some viewings and if you find any that you like we can start the ball rolling. Don't mention it to Wayne or your mum. I will make it up to Wayne when he gets his head straight'

'Thank you so much'

The call ended leaving Blake feeling a lot happier. Shortly after hanging up with Ellie his mobile rang again. This time it was Val. She was sobbing

'Pete has been round and he has beaten me up' She cried exaggerating her injuries.

'What...Why?' he asked

'That copper Steve Brooks told him that I was out with you on Friday night and he came round moaning about me going out with other men so soon after we had split up. We had a row and he punched me in the face'

'Are you OK? Are you at home? Have you phoned the police?'

'I'm at home but I don't want to involve the police. The last thing I need it that skinny cow DC Marks coming round patronising me. My lip is split and my face is sore but I am all right apart from that. Will you come around and kiss it better for me'?

'I would rather go and sort Pete out. What a brave man he is hitting his wife'

'Leave him. He will go running straight to his mate in the police and you will get done for assault'

'I will come over' he said, reluctantly. He didn't need this hassle.

50

Dimi Szabo had spent the evening at Lesley Farmer's flat. As soon as the kids were in bed they fucked. Dimi liked big girls and Lesley fitted the bill. She was a couple of stone heavier than she should be but she was very curvy with massive boobs. She was good in bed too and after they had been at it for ages he lay in bed with her smoking

`What is your new boss at Collins like? As I told you earlier Val is shagging him. She seems quite keen on him so I don't want her to get hurt'

`I haven't had that many dealings with him but I hear that he can be quite tough with the staff. He gave Susan a bollocking just after he started and I was told that he threatened to sack one of his staff last week.'

`Val says that he is loaded. He splashed out for a new car last week and took her out for an expensive meal on their first date. She said the police were at his house last night claiming that he was involved with the incident over at Welney and for some reason they thought that it was his car that they had seen on CCTV. He told them that it was a load of bollocks. They also wondered where the money had come from for the car because he had paid cash for it. He told them that it was money he had inherited from his mother who had died last year. Val said that skinny cow DC Marks had been there and she gave Val a filthy look because Val arrived when they were leaving'

Dimi suddenly became interested

` Why do you reckon he paid cash rather than a bank transfer?'

`I don't know. Val never said. Perhaps he got a better deal by paying cash for it'

`Did Val say how much he had inherited from his mothers will?'

`I doubt it because it would be rude to ask especially as she has only known him for a week or so. Anyway I don't want to talk about him or Val anymore. I'm feeling horny.

She reached down for his flaccid penis which didn't take much tempting to start to harden. `Oooh he is waking up '

Szabo left Lesley's flat before midnight. He was intrigued as to why the police were linking Bob Blake with the Welney picnic site incident. He had heard nothing from any of his many Romanian contacts and subsequently had nothing to report back to Ivan Petrescu. Danny Collins hadn't gave any hint that he had confided in Bob Blake about their little sideline but he wondered how Collins had managed to convince Blake that he and Mircea were to remain on the Rotterdam run. He decided to phone Petrescu in the morning

Shirley Booth breezed back into Kings Lynn police station. Several of her colleagues passed on their condolences but Booth thought that none of the words were sincere... She called the team together for a meeting at 0900. To her disappointment she discovered that no real progress had been made on the drug trafficking question. DI Green went through everything that the team had been doing.

`We have made a thorough investigation at Collins Transport. There doesn't appear to be anything that would give any indication that Collins has been making illegal collections. Apart from the occasional extra bit of Dutch pork and bacon everything seems to go through the books. Paula Collins has of course denied everything. DI Franklin managed to have another quick word with Keith Barnes but he is adamant that everything that Collins did while he was employed by Collins Transport was done properly. Barnes lives a modest lifestyle and nothing points to him having any money that cannot be accounted for. Danny Collins appears to have been very clever at hiding his involvement. The only slip up that he seems to have made is to have used Andrews and Hoyte who were new to the area. Without Hoyte's confession we would never have known about Collins involvement. The question that we need to ask is whether this is a new venture that is still in its infancy or whether somebody else was involved before Andrews and Hoyte arrived on the scene. Were Radu and Rodescu involved?  We have been unable to track down Victor Dragnea. He appears to have gone to ground. We cannot be sure that he is still in the country'

He ended his report by talking about Daley's theory about Bob Blake which also appeared to have led to a dead end.

Booth then dropped a surprise on the team.

`I have had financial forensics team looking into Collins affairs. It would appear that Danny Collins never had a pot to piss in. His house is mortgaged to the hilt, His car and Paula's car are both leased, he is overdrawn at the bank and his credit cards are at their maximum with just the small payments being made each month.  What is difficult to comprehend is that Collins Transport has made healthy profits over the past three years. Both Danny and Paula Collins take a salary but also pay themselves a dividend as they are the only partners. The question is why two people with healthy incomes, who take three holidays abroad in private villas and regularly eat out in expensive restaurants appear to be in debt?'

`Are they hiding money in offshore accounts' DC Marks suggested

Booth glared at her for a few seconds.

`It's possible although there is no trace of any sums of money being withdrawn. Their mortgage repayments are high at almost £1800 per month.

The two cars cost over £500 each month. Then there are utility bills, car insurance and general spending. Everything that they earn is spent each month. The only thing that we cannot account for is evidence of Collin's take from drug activity if of course there was any. Don't forget that we are not just going on Hoyte's confession that Collins was involved although I am convinced that he was. I was, as you will remember, tipped off about his involvement by a DS from Peterborough from one of his contacts in the Romanian community in Peterborough. We need to keep digging. This Blake fellow is interesting. Has anyone done a background check on him?'

Daley spoke up.

`I contacted Nottingham CID. He is as clean as a whistle. I was certain that he was involved and wondered if he knew Collins before he joined the firm but unfortunately there is no evidence of that. Is it worth the finance people having a look at his finances as I am still not convinced that he wasn't part of the process?'

`I don't think that I can justify the cost based on a hunch' Booth replied dismissing the idea. Daley was still in her bad books.

The briefing closed and nobody in the room felt that the issue was any nearer to being solved.

Paula Collins drove to Ipswich on Wednesday morning to see Geoffrey Williams, the accountant who looked after the Collins family private affairs. He had no involvement with the Collins Transport. He was also happy to involve himself with non legitimate business. For a sizeable fee he laundered the money that Collins made from his sideline. The sideline had been in force for over 18 months and Collins had made over a quarter million from the deals which was now banked overseas. Williams took 10% for doing what he did which was moving money to offshore shell companies for Collins. Williams had set up a UK company with Williams as the only named director. The money from Collins' courier work was paid into this account and then moved to an offshore company in the Cayman Islands via several different bank accounts around Europe. Paula had made her mind up. It was time to cash in. She planned to sell the transport company, sell the house and move to Tenerife where she planned to buy a villa. Danny had a pension fund which could start to pay out in seven years time when Danny would have been 55. Danny also took out life insurance but she wasn't sure that this would pay out if it could be proved that he had been involved in crime which was a shame as the payout would have been a quarter of a million, more than enough for her to spend the rest of her days in the sun.

She got straight to the point with Williams

`I want to sell the company as soon as possible, buy a villa in Tenerife and have all of the money moved from the offshore accounts to a bank account in Tenerife. Will that be difficult?' She asked him.

`Potentially it could be difficult especially if the police are looking at your finances. If you hold fire for perhaps a year or eighteen months and things quieten down you may have a better chance. I am aware that Danny was very discreet with his involvement of his dealings with Mr Petrescu. How much do the police know?'

`Danny's two regular couriers were on the take from Bogdan Stancvic which resulted in one of them getting beaten up and the other getting shot so they both took off leaving Danny with nobody to act as couriers. He met a couple of black lads who were small time criminals from Bristol. Things went tits up on the last drop. One of the couriers got killed along with both of Stancvic's men. The other one Denny Hoyte stupidly sent a text message to Danny threatening to blow the whistle. This was on the day that Danny was murdered so the police found the message which Danny did not immediately delete. They also found a message from Danny on Hoyte's phone. All that the police have is a confession from this man and a tip off from Peterborough, which we suspect came from Stancvic, that Danny was involved. They have no concrete proof of his involvement. It's just hearsay.'

`The phone message would be considered pretty conclusive though. Do you have any idea what this Hoyte fellow has said to the police? Can you keep the company going for another year or 18 months?'

`I don't know how much he has told them. The two of them did two drops before things went wrong on the last drop. The new couriers had no proof of what was in the bags they delivered and collected.'

`Can you keep the company going for another year or 18 months?'

` I am not sure if I can keep the company running for any length of time. I haven't a clue how to run things. We have a new transport manager who I am relying on but he is a logistics man so I honestly don't know what will happen with the company'

`Hopefully things will blow over. My best advice would be a sale at a later date. Are you set in stone on Tenerife because there are other locations in the sun that might be better if you want to keep things out of the eye of UK authorities?'

`I had my sight set on Tenerife but I would consider some of the other islands in the Canaries. I just want to get away from all this and live in the sun for the rest of my days'.

`Good, we can talk about alternative places at a later date'

Paula handed over a large envelope to Williams. `There is Danny's last payment from his dealings with Petrescu and Stancvic. Can you do the necessary?'

`Of course' smiled Williams `were the police aware of this money?'

`No. We have a small safe at home. It was in there. The intruders didn't discover it'.

`That's good. I will move it for you quickly'

Paula drove home with her mind stewing. She wasn't sure if she could trust Williams. All of the money that they owned was in the offshore account that Danny had set up with the help of Williams. She just hoped that she could get her hands on it. Williams seemed to want to delay her plans for getting out of the country and she wondered whether Williams actually still had their money.

51

Dimi Szabo did a Rotterdam trip for Collins Transport on the Thursday after his night with Lesley. He didn't know it at the time but it would be his last trip for the company. He had phoned Ivan Petrescu and asked if he could meet with him as he had some information that might be useful to him. He said that he didn't want to discuss it over the phone as he was sure that he was under observation. He had phoned Petrescu from a phone booth at Harwich. He had never met Petrescu who said that he would meet him at a cafe that was outside the docks. Szabo said that he would wear one of his company sweatshirts so that Petrescu would recognise him. When Petrescu made himself known to Szabo he was not what Dimi was expecting. Petrescu was tall at over six feet but pencil thin with a shock of salt and pepper hair.

`What news do you have for me' Petrescu asked in an abrupt manner

`The police are showing an interest in Bob Blake who is the new transport manager at Collins Transport. He started working there in the mid January. I was told by a woman that I'm seeing that the police were looking for a dark coloured hatchback with a faulty headlight. The snow was so heavy it was hindering visibility.  It seems that a car that was very similar to the one that Blake drives was seen in the Red Lion car park on January 27. Blake apparently had a fight with Lynton Andrews in the Red Lion the week before. The police suspect that Blake drove Andrews to the picnic site and that Blake took the money. Blake purchased a new car for £9000 and paid for it in cash last weekend. He claims that he has been left an inheritance by his mother who died recently. Blake is shagging Val Davey.  She is my woman's best mate and it was her that told my woman. Val Davey was with Dennard Hoyte on the night of the exchange. It seems he crashed his car on the way to pick up Andrews en route to the picnic site. Danny Collins spoke to us at a party on the Saturday after the last drop. He said that someone else had taken Andrews to the picnic site because the other courier had crashed his car but that he didn't say who it was. He said to act normal as the police had no evidence against him or us.'

`So the only thing that the police have linking Blake with the incident is a car with a faulty headlamp and that he works for Collins Transport. What makes you think that this information is on any consequence?'

Dimi was very nervous. Petrescu had an aura about him

`He works for Danny, Danny had an emergency call which led to him going to Kings Lynn so perhaps he asked Blake to drive Andrews to the meet'

`How would Collins have known that Andrews needed a lift if he was at the hospital then? How would he have known about the second courier crashing on the way to pick up Andrews? How would he have had time to get someone else to take Andrews to the meeting place? Would Danny not have mentioned who this person was when you spoke with him?'

Dimi hadn't thought about how Collins would have known about the car crash.

`Perhaps he asked Blake to meet up with Andrews to hand over the package. Perhaps he had a plan B.'

`He told me that he had met with Andrews early before he went to the hospital. He was expecting the pair of them to do the drop'

`Collins kept everything to himself. We didn't know who the new couriers were until Andrews got killed. All we did was bring the goods into the country, hand them over to Collins who paid us in cash. We didn't know how the goods were transferred to Stancvic. We simply delivered the money to your contacts afterwards. The police arrested Hoyte in connection with Collins death which is how I found out he was involved.'

`Are you trying to tell me that you were unaware of Radu and Rodescu's part in all of this?'

Dimi fidgeted in his seat. "We had an idea that they were involved but we never asked them and they never said anything'

Petrescu got up to leave and gave Szabo a withering look.

`You have wasted my time. All you have brought to me is speculation, I expected more from you.'

He left without saying another word.


Petrescu decided that he would follow up on what Szabo had told him and that he would act quickly. A discreet trip to England was planned. He booked a flight to Stansted early on Monday morning. He would have a quiet word with Paula Collins. Danny's funeral was arranged for Monday morning so he would take the chance to speak to her then. He sensed a business opportunity was there for the taking. He was going to speak to Bob Blake as well. Collins Transport was going to continue to act as couriers for his goods. If they refused there would be consequences. He knew that Paula Collins had a daughter and it wouldn't take him too long to get details about Blake's family history. Petrescu had acted decisively after he had got rid of Stancvic. He had taken over Stancvic's small empire putting one of his own men in place to take control of it. The Romanians who had worked for Stancvic knew all about Ivan Petrescu and had meekly fallen in line.

Victor Dragnea was the exception. Dragnea was a hard bastard and acted as Stancvic's bodyguard. He admired his boss who always treated him very well.

Dragnea had come to the UK three years ago. He had been working in Hamburg for a man called Wolfgang Schuller. Schuller owned brothels in Hamburg. Most of his working girls were from Eastern Europe. Dragnea had worked in the brothels as a minder. He dealt with any customers who caused any problems .A large number of Schuller's working girls were brought to Hamburg via Petrescu's network. Schuller had a disagreement with Petrescu. Dragnea never found out what this disagreement had been about. Schuller was found murdered two days later with his throat cut in a similar fashion to Stancvic  As soon as Dragnea had heard about Stancvic's murder he took off. He was well aware that the police were looking for him in conjunction with Collins' murder so he had gone to ground in Glasgow where he knew some Albanians who were associates of Stancvic. The Albanians were no fans of Ivan Petrescu and had issues with him in the past so they were willing to shelter Dragnea. Word had got back to Dragnea that Petrescu had assumed control of Stancvic's operation which thoroughly displeased him. Petrescu had a huge operation which covered large areas of Europe.  His operation model was to start small with local businessmen and take control if they should step out of line. As much as he wished that there was he could see no way that he could get to Petrescu. He wanted to avenge his boss's death. Stancvic was only 36, just a couple of years younger than Dragnea. Dragnea had been penniless when he came to the UK. He had a contact who worked for Stancvic and the contact persuaded Stancvic that Dragnea would be useful to his team. He told Stancvic that Dragnea was a really big tough bastard. Stancvic met with Dragnea and could see by the size of the man that he would be very useful as a driver and bodyguard so he employed him. Being of a similar age they got on very well and within a short time he had gained Stancvic's confidence. He accompanied Stancvic to many business meetings including a meeting with Petrescu around two years ago.  No doubt Petrescu would want him neutralised as soon as possible. Petrescu knew that Dragnea was very loyal to Stancvic and that he was a dangerous man. He was also aware that Dragnea had a lot of contacts among the Romanian community and that he would aware of the operations similar to Stancvic's that  Petrescu was running in Hull Edinburgh Dover and Southampton. Petrescu was also aware of Dragnea's employment, albeit at a low level, in Hamburg with Schuller. Dragnea came to the conclusion that his best option would be to try to do a deal with the police to put Petrescu away for a spell in prison. He had Stancvic's confidence and often heard his telephone conversations with Petrescu so he was well aware of the set up.  He also knew of Petrescu's involvement with human trafficking, prostitution, and his drug trafficking. Stancvic had only dealt in pills and cocaine. Petrescu was responsible for around 50% of the heroin that was on the streets of Edinburgh and many cities on the north east coast. Dragnea knew that when the police caught up with him he would be an accessory to murder so he contacted the Kings Lynn police station and asked to speak to the officer in charge of the operation involving the murder of Danny Collins. He was put through to speak with DCI Shirley Booth

'My name is Victor Dragnea. I have some information about the murders of Danny Collins and Bogdan Stancvic.' He proceeded to tell Booth all he knew about the drug trafficking, Collins murder and the reason for it. He also gave the name of Ivan Petrescu as being responsible for the murder of Stancvic and as the source of the cocaine that was coming into the UK via Collins Transport. He went on to tell Booth about Petrescu's operations in the UK and how a Wolfgang Schuller a business associate who had crossed Petrescu had been murdered by the same method as Stancvic.'

Booth interrupted him

'Why would I believe anything that you are saying? Do you have any proof?"
Dragnea continued

'Stancvic was my boss but he was very good to me so I have a sense of loyalty towards him. Petrescu knows this and if he finds me he will kill me so I am worried. I have been reliably informed that he is coming to the UK in the next few days so it isn't just the police who I am hiding from. I have been present at several of the exchanges where two Romanians, Ion Rodescu and Ilie Radu acted as couriers on behalf of Danny Collins. I know that class drugs have been shipped into the UK via Edinburgh Hull Dover Southampton as well as Harwich Felixstowe and Kings Lynn. I can give you a written statement detailing the operation but I want a deal'

Booth thought about it before answering

'We know that you were present when Collins was murdered as you were seen on camera at his house. Why would we do a deal with someone involved with murder?'

'Perhaps the images that you have will show that all I did was drive for my boss. I changed the number plates on Collins' car and drove it away. Collins was dead before I entered his property. Your images must show that it wasn't someone of my size who went into the property first'

Booth pondered on Dragnea's story. What he was indicating appeared to be true.

'You will need to give yourself up before we can discuss deals'. She knew that she couldn't guarantee his safety but that didn't matter. The information that he had given could solve the case. She didn't know much about Ivan Petrescu. She had heard his name mentioned in the past but that was about it. She would start digging.  She gave Dragnea her mobile number. He wouldn't give her his number which she guessed was probably a burner phone anyway so she didn't pursue it.

`You will need to hand yourself in at Kings Lynn police station. When will you be able to do this?'

`It will have to be on Monday. I need to get in touch with my solicitor as he will need to be present when we discuss a deal. I am a long way from Peterborough and I have plans for the weekend. If I come in will you guarantee me that I won't be charged with being an accessory to the murder of Collins and that I would be put in protective custody? I need to be kept out of the clutches of Petrescu'

`I am certain that we can work something out'

As far as she was concerned Dragnea was just another scumbag and she wasn't concerned about his future. She wasn't interested in doing any deals but if it led to the solving of the case which would be a massive feather in her cap. She could see this as a big career advancement opportunity.

`I will be in on Monday'

He hung up. He wasn't convinced that he was doing the right thing but unless he could avoid a custodial sentence it was his best chance of staying alive. Once Petrescu was behind bars he planned to return home to Romania.

52

As soon as the call ended Booth started some research on Ivan Petrescu. He was suspected of being a major player throughout Europe but nothing was ever proven against him. She thought that it was highly probable that he was the source of the drugs that were being shipped into the UK by Collins Transport even though she had no real physical proof that Collins Transport was involved. Was it a coincidence that two Romanians were found dead at Welney, a haulage company ran by two Romanians did collections and deliveries for Collins in and out of Rotterdam? Stancvic was Romanian as were Radu and Rodescu who were both dealers. There was a lot that Dragnea had said that was worth considering. She felt a rush of excitement at the thought of solving this matter. She decided that it was time for another word with Paula Collins and Bob Blake. Butler was on sick leave so she asked Ds Judge to join her.

`We are off to have another little chat with Paula Collins and Bob Blake at Collins transport' she told Judge

She hoped that Collins would be on site because she wanted to speak to them together. She was in luck and asked the receptionist to let Collins and Blake know that she wanted to interview them both that afternoon.

On arrival at Collins Transport Booth and Judge were taken into Danny Collins' office where Paula and Blake were waiting for them. They were far from pleased that they were going to be questioned again

`What is the reason for this? Why are you harassing us? You have interviewed everybody who works here and they have answered all of your questions'
Paula snapped at the two coppers

Booth got straight to the point

`Does the name Ivan Petrescu mean anything to either of you?'

`Isn't he a striker who plays for West Ham United' Blake replied quickly which annoyed Booth but raised a smile from Judge. It also gave Paula a few seconds to gather her composure

`Are you taking the piss' Booth snarled at Blake angrily. `He isn't a bloody footballer. What about you Paula. Did you ever hear Danny mention his name?'

`Never heard of him' Paula lied

`Petrescu is a major crime figure in Europe. We know that he had ties with Bogdan Stancvic who we believe was responsible for the death of Danny. Stancvic was murdered on the day after Danny's death and we believe that this is as a result of the deaths at the Welney picnic site on January 27. We are also led to believe that Dimi Szabo and Mircea Tiriac are involved in the chain because of the Romanian connection. Our sources tell us that S&T transport have been bringing drugs into the country for Petrescu. We are also led to believe that two Romanians Ilie Radu and Ion Rodescu acted as couriers on behalf of Danny Collins when several large amounts of cocaine were exchanged at the Welney picnic site over the past 18 months'

Bob Blake sat there in silence. What had he got himself involved with? He was going to have to get rid of the money.

`This all sounds a bit like Jackanory to me. What proof do you have other than hearsay?' Paula asked hoping that her uncertainty didn't show in her voice `For all you know the Romanians might have been acting alone. How do you know that Danny was involved in any of this?'

`We haven't got any physical evidence...yet but we will be interviewing Szabo and Tiriac. Let's see what they have to say" Booth replied.

Paula tried to remain calm. After all she never took an active part in Danny's sideline so she could always plead ignorance but if the truth got out it would seriously ruin the business and any hope of getting a decent amount for it when she sold it. She decided to front up

`You can interview them as soon as you like for all that I care. I am not aware of Danny's involvement in drug trafficking. As I have already said how do you know that it wasn't the Romanians acting alone?'

`There is the small matter of messages sent to Danny's phone and sent from his phone in response to Dennard Hoyte's messages. How do you explain that?' Booth replied

Paula couldn't. She couldn't believe that Danny had been so stupid in not deleting the message from Hoyte and actually sending him a text message. `I don't know anything about that' she replied with a tone of defeat in her voice.

`We will speak again once we have interviewed Szabo and Tiriac'.

Booth left with a smug smile on her face. She knew from the look on Paula's face that she was very aware of Ivan Petrescu

After Booth left Blake was the first to speak

`What the hell had Danny been up to? If news of this gets out it will ruin the company. Value Shoppers will drop us like a hot potato'

`I honestly don't know' Paula lied. `I don't know what to do for the best. Perhaps we should let Value Shoppers know sooner rather than later. It might be better coming from us. Could we not spin a story that the Romanians were acting alone and that Danny was murdered because he threatened to go to the police?'

Blake was deep in thought before he replied

`But how does that explain the phone messages to Dennard Hoyte?'

`It doesn't' Paula replied `but perhaps we could claim that he was being blackmailed if the news of it ever reached Value Shoppers'

53

Danny Collins funeral took place at Flixham church at eleven thirty on a cold dull February Monday morning. The small church was packed. Blake along with all of the staff from Collins Transport had attended. He was laid to rest in the cemetery at the church. A wake was held at the Sports ground and most of the people who had attended the funeral turned up at the wake.

Blake had enjoyed a busy weekend. He went to Huntingdon races. He studied the bookies especially when payouts were made. The first race was won by a 6/4 favourite. Danny saw one punter bet £400 to win £600. He took a note of the horses name and that of the bookie that had taken the bet. The next two races were won by outsiders and he didn't see any large payouts. He had to wait for the fourth race which was a valuable handicap hurdle. Several large bets were made on Sunny Lad. The odds tumbled from 12/1 to 5/1 and it started as favourite in an open race. It romped home. He saw one punter collect £1100 for a £100 bet placed at 10/1. Again he noted the name of the bookie that had paid out to a scruffy looking man in a flat cap. He even had a couple of bets with the two bookies that he had seen make the large payouts. Both were ten pound mugs bets placed on the name alone. One lost and the other Leggy lady came in at 5/2. He saw Val on Thursday night and again on Saturday. They called into the Red Lion for a couple of beers before taking a Chinese takeaway back to Blake's place on Saturday. She stayed the night and once again he didn't get much sleep. He stayed at hers on Thursday after she had cooked a meal for him. He was enjoying her company. She was had a healthy sexual appetite as well which was a bonus after his celibate year. She helped take his mind off the issues surrounding Collins Transport.

Booth had questioned Dimi and Mircea but they stuck to their guns and denied any knowledge of the drugs. As no physical evidence could be found no action could be taken against them. Blake however had decided to cut them loose. As far as he was concerned there was no smoke without fire. He remembered Danny specifically asking him to put Dimi on future Rotterdam trips and he distinctly recalled Danny in deep conversation with Dimi when he returned from Rotterdam the morning on January 27.

Blake didn't go to the wake. He allowed all of the staff to go to the funeral but asked them to return to work after an hour at the wake because they still had a business to run. He told them all to be back by 2pm. After leaving the funeral he went into Kings Lynn and paid £1600 into one of his building society accounts before returning to work.

Later that afternoon when the staff had returned Susan called through to him to say that a potential new customer, Mr King, wanted to speak to him.

`Show him through' Blake replied excited by the prospect of new business.

Susan brought through a tall very thin man with black hair speckled with grey into his office. Blake guessed that he was in his late forties. He looked vaguely familiar but Blake couldn't place him. He was wearing a heavy grey overcoat over an expensive looking grey suit and an immaculate white shirt and a navy tie.

Blake introduced himself and offered his hand to the man. He took Blake's hand and almost crushed his fingers with a vice like handshake. Blake almost winced with pain before his hand was released

`What can I do for you Mr King?' King took off his overcoat and placed it over the back of his chair.

`It is not what you can do for me it's what you WILL do for me.' He replied with a strong eastern European accent.  There was a threat in his voice.

`You can start by reversing your decision not to use S&T Transport. They are part of a successful business that I have been operating. In future S&T will do all of your Rotterdam trips'

Blake started to protest as he stood up `Who do you think you are coming in here and telling me who I have to use on which trips. It is of no concern of yours'

`Shut the fuck up and sit down. I understand that the police have been showing an interest in you with regards to money that went missing from the Welney picnic site on Jan 27. It was my money that went missing and I want it back'

Blake had to think quickly. Was this man Ivan Petrescu? He decided to call his bluff.

`I don't know anything about any missing money. I don't know what arrangements you had with Danny Collins but I had no knowledge of it. I started work here less than two weeks before Jan 27. I presume that you represent Mr Petrescu. The police spoke with Mrs Collins and me last week and asked if we had heard of an Ivan Petrescu. I hadn't and Mrs Collins said she hadn't either. I suggest that you leave now. Any arrangements that you may have had with Danny ceased with his death. Go or I will call DCI Booth right now' he said reaching for the phone

Petrescu grabbed the phone from Blake's grasp. He ripped the cord from the socket in the wall.

`If you relay any of this conversation back to the police there will be consequences. I know that you have a woman in Flixham. I know you have a daughter Ellie who works in Mansfield and I also know that you have a son Wayne who has had a bit of trouble with the police in Mansfield. Do as I say or they will all come to harm'

Blake was seething with anger but he refrained from sticking one on the skinny bastard who was threatening his children. How did he know about Val and his family?

`You are overlooking some key factors about this company. As soon as Value Shoppers hear about Danny's involvement with drug smuggling they will cease trading with us. Without them this company won't survive. Dimi Szabo and Mircea Tiriac have been interviewed by the police and will no doubt be kept under observation for the foreseeable future'

`This company will survive with or without Value Shoppers. I had a word with Mrs Collins earlier this afternoon. I am going to take a controlling interest in the company.' Petrescu announced with a grin on his face.

That's where I have seen him Blake thought remembering that the man had attended Danny's funeral. Blake wasn't going to allow this man to dictate to him.

`If that is the case you are going to need a new transport manager because I'm not prepared to work for you.'

Blake got up and went to walk out. Petrescu grabbed him and with a strength that belied his build threw Blake back into his chair.

`You will continue to work for me for as long as I need you' he said with menace in his voice towering above Blake as he slumped in the chair.

Blake attempted to stand up again. As he did Petrescu threw a sharp punch to the bridge of Blake's nose. His eyes watered and his nose began to bleed.

`I told you to sit down' Petrescu barked at him with his face close to Blake.

Blake did as he was told

Petrescu stepped away from Blake. He interlocked his fingers and stretched his arms

`This is how things are going to work in future'

Blake gambled. He stood up quickly and as Petrescu moved towards him to throw a punch Blake ducked. He made a grab at Petrescu's balls and squeezed hard. Petrescu gasped and as his hand grabbed at Blake's hand to pull it away from his balls his guard had dropped. Blake head butted him with a really strong butt. He heard the bones in Petrescu's nose break and as he staggered backwards Blake caught him flush on the chin with a heavy right hand punch. Petrescu dropped to the ground. At that moment Susan opened the door to see what the commotion was.

`Phone the police now.' Blake shouted at her.

Petrescu tried to scramble to his feet so Blake kicked him under the chin. He fell backwards, his head hitting the office wall. He was knocked out.

Within five minutes PC's May and Fowler arrived at the depot. They arrived to see Bob Blake with blood down the front of his shirt and another man with his arms tied behind his back with a tie sat on the floor of Blake's office
` What's been going on here?' Fowler asked
`I believe that this man is Ivan Petrescu. DCI Booth mentioned his name last week in connection with a drug smuggling ring that is believed to be centred on this company. He came in and threatened my family if I didn't re-instate S&T transport. They are suspected of being responsible for bringing the drugs into the country. Perhaps you should call her now'
As he was speaking Daley and Marks arrived. Daley took charge of matters and took details of what had happened.
In their hurry to get to the scene neither of the two PCs nor Daley and Marks had noticed the grey Range Rover parked in the corner of the depot. Nor had they noticed the two men sitting in it. The two, Marian Varga and Ioan Copilu were Petrescu's minders. They were both UK based and had met Petrescu at Stansted Airport earlier that day. Both were armed. They had been instructed to stay in the car by Petrescu as he didn't expect to have any trouble with Blake. When the panda car turned up they pondered what action to take. When the panda car was followed by another car containing police officers they decided that things had gone wrong and it was time to extract Petrescu from whatever situation he had found himself. They rushed into the building with their guns in their hands. Susan Rudd saw the guns and screamed as the two men burst into the room. Clarissa Marks was the first to react by aiming a karate style kick at Varga's hand which held the gun. It flew out of his hand and landed under Blake's desk. Copilu hesitated before he fired his gun twice at Marks because Varga was between him and Marks who had followed up her first kick with another one to Varga's head putting him on the ground. The bullets hit Marks high in her chest and stomach. She went down. PC May and Daley jumped on Copilu before he could fire his gun again. The three of them fell to the ground. PC Fowler grappled with Varga in an attempt to overpower him so Blake also jumped in. Superior numbers resulted in the police taking control the situation and both men were handcuffed, as was Petrescu by this stage.
Daley rushed to Marks aid.
`Have you got any first aid equipment?' he shouted at Blake.
She was still conscious but had lost a lot of blood. By this time Ruth Cross and Ray Pearce had come to find out what was going on. Ruth was first aid trained

so she took charge of trying to stop the bleeding from Marks' wounds. Pearce phoned for an ambulance which was on its way.

Twenty minutes later the depot was crawling with police. DCI Booth was one of the last to arrive. She had been on a conference call when the incident was phoned into Kings Lynn. DI Green had assumed charge at that stage but Booth took over as soon as she arrived.

Blake gave a statement saying what had happened. He told the police that the thin man who he believed was Ivan Petrescu had ordered him to re-instate S&T transport and that he was taking over the company. When he refused the man had first threatened his family and then attacked him. Blake said that he had fought back, butted the man who had fallen over. Blake kicked him under the chin as he was scrambling to his feet and this had knocked the man out. He had told Susan Rudd to phone the police. Two constables were first to arrive followed by Daley and Marks. Two gunmen then arrived. He said that DC Marks had shown great courage when disarming one of the gunmen and that the other police officers had managed to overpower and disarm the other gunman. Fowler and Daley confirmed the latter part of Blake's story.

DC Marks was rushed to Kings Lynn hospital where she was being operated on to remove bullets from her stomach and upper chest and shoulder area. She remained in a critical but stable condition.

Ivan Petrescu was taken to Kings Lynn police station for further questioning as were Copilu and Varga. They were both arrested and charged with the attempted murder of DC Marks

54

Booth interviewed Petrescu who was accompanied by his solicitor. He had arrived very quickly after the phone call he received. DC Butler also attended the interview. Booth started the interview by telling Petrescu that she had information connecting him with the drug smuggling operation that had led to the death of five men.

'That is rubbish' Petrescu replied in a confident tone. 'I went to speak to the transport manager at Collins Transport to talk about the company that I was considering take a controlling interest. We argued and he attacked me without warning'

'Mr Blake claims that you threatened his family and that you attacked him'

'That is his word against mine and that is up to you to prove otherwise. I just went to what I considered to be an innocuous business meeting'

'Why then would you take armed men to an innocuous business meeting?'

'The men who arrived with guns were hired drivers from a business associate. They met me at Stansted airport and drove me to meet with Mrs Collins and then with Blake. I wasn't aware that they were carrying guns and at no time did I ask them to intervene.'

'Who is the business associate that you got the drivers from?'

'That is confidential. There is no reason to tell you and involve somebody else just because two of his employees have broken the law.'

She hadn't charged Petrescu with anything yet. She was in a difficult position as the only offence that she could charge him with at this stage was for assaulting Bob Blake which he had denied. He didn't seem the least bit concerned. She could see why he had remained at large for so long. His solicitor just sat taking notes. He didn't intervene and seemed happy for Petrescu to answer the questions. It was time for her to change tack.

'The problem that I have Mr Petrescu is that I have been given some information by an employee of Bogdan Stancvic that implicates you in both the importing of class A drugs into the UK via Collins Transport and the death of Mr Stancvic. This employee says that he was present at several meetings between you and Mr Stancvic. He says that you and Mr Stancvic had a disagreement during a telephone conversation the weekend before last and that he was expecting some retaliation from you. The police knew that you were due to fly to the UK today based on the information that this person gave us. This person wants to make a deal with the police because he says that he is in fear of his life. It is you that he is afraid of'

Victor Dragnea was the name that immediately came to Petrovic's mind. He didn't know how much Dragnea knew and whether he had any evidence that could put Petrescu behind bars. He had become a snitch and when Petrescu got himself out of this situation Florian Chipciu was going to get another contract.

`In that case why have you not charged my client?' The solicitor spoke for the first time

Booth had to bide her time until she had chance to speak with Szabo and Tiriac who should be able to verify what Dragnea had told her. Dragnea hadn't shown up either so she was in no mans lands until he did. She could retain Petrescu for 24 hours before she had to charge him so she still had time.

`That is because I want to get all my ducks in a row first. I don't want some clever barrister getting your client off on a technicality. I have a couple of people to speak to first and then I will charge him'

Petrescu was taken back to his cell much to the protests of his solicitor despite knowing that he could be held without charge for 24 hours.

Fortunately Dragnea phoned her that evening. He was running late because his solicitor had been retained on business and had taken longer than he had anticipated. Dragnea said that he was on his way to Kings Lynn from Scotland and was staying in a hotel overnight. He would be in Kings Lynn by late morning and would accompany his solicitor to the meeting with Booth.

Booth told him that she had Petrescu in custody. She never told him that Petrescu hadn't been charged at this stage. If thing worked out as she hoped Petrescu would be charged and she would get another big feather in her cap.

Booth eventually got hold of Szabo early the next morning for all the good that it did her. She had already caught up with Tiriac on Monday evening. It was obvious to her that both men were scared of what would happen to them if they grassed on Petrescu. Again they both pleaded ignorance to bringing anything into the country from Rotterdam that wasn't on the shipping documents. Booth also went to see Paula Collins.

`We have arrested Ivan Petrescu. It seems that he went to see Bob Blake and threatened Blake's family if he refused to continue with the business venture that he had with Danny. Are you still maintaining that you don't know Petrescu?'

Knowing that Petrescu had been arrested Paula was slightly more forthcoming `I met that bastard for the first time this afternoon. He had the nerve to turn up at Danny's funeral. He threatened me and Charlotte if I didn't sell him the transport company for a negligible price. I don't know what Danny had got involved with. I don't know enough to run the company so I reluctantly agreed to sell it to him'

That was the confirmation that Booth needed. She could now charge Petrescu with extortion as well as assault but she needed Dragnea to come forward and provide a written statement just to seal the deal. Booth wasn't sure if Paula Collins statement was enough to charge Petrescu with even if she added it to the assault charge

Victor Dragnea didn't trust DCI Booth. He had driven down from Glasgow on Monday evening stopping at a service station on the A1M near Wetherby which had a hotel. He had spoken with Stancvic's solicitor who had agreed to attend the meeting on his behalf but had advised Dragnea not to attend it himself because he couldn't be sure if Booth would honour the agreement.

He had phoned DCI Booth from his hotel room to tell her that he was en route but wouldn't get to Kings Lynn until the next morning. She seemed angry about this but she told him that Petrescu was in custody. She stressed the point that he needed to meet her before lunch on Tuesday. Something didn't seem right to Dragnea and he wanted to avoid setting himself up

He left for Kings Lynn early the next morning. He didn't go straight to Kings Lynn police station. Instead he took a detour to Fakenham. He was going to call on Mircea Tiriac. He had phoned him to say that he was calling in on him early in the morning so Tiriac was at home waiting nervously for the big man to arrive. Dragnea was dismayed to hear what Tiriac had told him

`Why didn't you tell the police that Petrescu is the supplier of the drugs that you were bringing in to the country?

`Why do you think? He would find out and that would be the end for me. I'm not going to risk it'

`You are a gutless bastard. He will get away with it again' Dragnea snarled before attacking Tiriac. Three seconds later Tiriac was out cold but Dragnea couldn't resist kicking him several times in the ribs. He decided that he was going to phone Booth again

He phoned her on her mobile

`Where are you?' She demanded impatiently

`I'm about an hour away' he lied. `Have you charged Petrescu and is he still in custody?'

`Yes we have' Booth lied back to him. Petrescu had been in custody for 20 hours. His solicitor was pushing for him to be released that afternoon so the sooner Dragnea handed himself in and gave a written statement the sooner she could charge Petrescu

`What have you charged him with?'

`Intent to supply class a drugs and extortion' she lied again
Dragnea was thinking fast.
`Did Dimi Szabo and Mircea Tiriac confirm my story to you about bringing Petrescu's drugs into the country?'
`I can't discuss that with you. All I can say is that they have helped us with our enquiries' Booth replied. She wasn't to know that Dragnea had met with Tiriac.
`I need you get to Kings Lynn as soon as possible'
Dragnea hung up without responding. "Fucking lying bitch" he swore loudly. He realised that Petrescu was going to be released without charge if Szabo and Tiriac hadn't backed up the information that he had given to Booth. It was only his word against Petrescu. Any decent brief would have a field day in these circumstances. He phoned his solicitor to tell him that the deal was off.
Booth interviewed Petrescu again at 1430. She told him what Paula Collins had said. Petrescu denied this of course.
`We had a frank discussion about the business. Mrs Collins wanted more money than I thought the company was worth. We argued over the price but at no time did I threaten to harm anyone. I will admit that the conversation did get heated but she eventually agreed to my price. I can only assume that she is having second thoughts about selling to me and is making excuses to get out of the deal'.
`Once again it is her word against my client's' the solicitor added 'so unless you are going to charge my client I suggest that you should release him immediately'
Dragnea still hadn't arrived at the station. Booth half expected that he wouldn't because of the way he abruptly ended their last telephone conversation so reluctantly she had to release Petrescu without charges. All that she could charge him with was assault and attempted extortion but as his solicitor had smugly pointed out it was just their word against his. Booth knew that with Dragnea's written statement she could charge Petrescu and she fully expected that Szabo and Mircea would change their minds and back up Dragnea's story.

55

Petrescu wasn't going to get away with killing his boss if Dragnea had anything to do about it. He decided to gamble again. He drove to Kings Lynn police station but he didn't go in. He waited in the public car park that was opposite and provided a good view of the entrance to the station. He waited for nearly three hours before his ordeal became worthwhile. Ivan Petrescu came out of the station just before 5pm accompanied by a small man carrying a briefcase. His solicitor Dragnea presumed. The two of them left and went towards the police station car park where they got into a dark coloured Jaguar. The small man was driving. Dragnea tailed them keeping his distance. He followed them along the A10. Traffic was very heavy at that time of day so it was easy enough to stay out of sight. He thought that they were heading to Peterborough but they joined the A14 just outside of the town. Dragnea thought that they must be going to Stansted Airport. He was going to have to act quickly

Ivan Petrescu had entered the country with just hand luggage which was still in the Holiday Express Inn at Stansted Airport. His passport was in the small bag that he had carried with him. The bag contained some shirts socks and underwear which was enough for the short stay. Fortunately he had booked the room for two nights when he arrived on his Monday morning flight. The room was inexpensive so he was quite prepared to leave early if he needed to. It was as well that he had because he hadn't envisaged spending 24 hours in custody. Things hadn't gone as expected thanks to Bob Blake who was going to regret his actions. Petrescu wanted to get back to Rotterdam as soon as possible. He didn't want to be in the country when Blake met the unfortunate end that he had planned for him. His solicitor dropped him at the hotel. He offered to wait and drop him off at the airport but Petrescu wanted to shower and shave to wash the stench of the custody cell from his body. There was blood on his suit jacket and down the front of the shirt that he had been wearing for two days. He looked in the mirror to discovered dark rings under his eyes from the bruising from Blake's head butt and a cut across the bridge of his nose which he was sure was broken. His face looked a mess and would draw attention to him when he went through customs at Amsterdam Airport. Petrescu was annoyed that he had fallen for Blake's manoeuvre. He was going to teach that bastard a lesson. He managed to book himself onto a flight to Amsterdam at 2210 so he had a couple hours to kill after he had showered. The hotel had a restaurant. He was hungry because he had eaten very little while in custody. The menu in the restaurant was basic but the hunters chicken with vegetables that he ordered was edible. He needed carbohydrates and it served its purpose. He washed it down with two pints of lager. He went back to his room collected his bag and checked out.

Victor Dragnea also went into the large hotel restaurant and made sure that he was sat at a table well out of Petrovic's sight. He didn't think that he would be remembered but because of his size he wasn't going to take any chances. He was very hungry and selected a mixed grill from the menu.  The meal had given him time to cook up a plan. He wasn't carrying a gun so he would have to use his hands to take care of Petrescu.  When Petrescu had finished his meal Dragnea paid for his and went to the hotel bar. He ordered a beer and took a seat which allowed him to see the hotel lobby. Dragnea had guessed that Petrescu would be heading back to Holland. He checked the flights out of Stansted that evening and early the next morning. There were two that evening and several the next day. One flight was due to leave 45 minutes after Petrescu had arrived at the hotel. The second flight was at 2210. He hoped that this was the flight that Petrescu had booked because he didn't fancy staying in his car all night. He was in luck.  At 2035 Petrescu checked out of the hotel and started the half mile walk to the airport terminal. He was unaware that Dragnea was following him. The area was well lit so Dragnea had to pick the right place. He could see an underpass ahead of them which could be that place. As Petrescu walked towards it Dragnea upped the pace of his walk. He was wearing training shoes so his footsteps didn't give him away which was an achievement as Dragnea was six feet six tall and weighed two hundred and sixty pounds. When Petrescu had reached the entrance of the underpass two women walked towards him coming from the opposite direction. The women were Oriental and were chatting away loudly in a language that Dragnea didn't understand. The sound of their voices as they passed by Petrescu muffled the sound of Dragnea sprinting towards him. He grabbed Petrescu around the neck and with one quick movement broke his neck. It was all over in a matter of seconds. Petrescu had been caught totally unaware and was unable to do anything against Dragnea's bulk and brute strength. Dragnea went back to his car. Nobody had seen him other than the two oriental ladies and he very much doubted that they had taken any notice of either him or Petrescu. He began the long drive back to Glasgow. He was going to book a flight from Glasgow Airport back to Bucharest before he headed back home to Campania a small town Romania where he was born.

The news of Petrescu's death reached DCI Booth the next morning. There were no clues as to who was responsible. Essex police considered that it was a gang execution. Booth was upset at how events had turned out. Although she knew all the details involved in moving Ivan Petrescu's drugs to Bogdan Stancvic via Collins transport she didn't have sufficient evidence to give to the Crown Prosecution Service to make them consider it a worthwhile case. She concluded that Bogdan Stancvic had tried to rip off Petrescu at the Welney picnic site trade but the question of whether any money had ever been at the exchange was impossible to prove. The main participants were all dead now anyway so there was nobody to charge. As a matter of course Bob Blake was questioned about the death of Petrescu but this was just a formality. He was in Flixham on the night in question as both Val Davey and the Pizza delivery man confirmed. The whole affair was considered to be a failure which would be a stain on her record and act against her future progress. Tony Pasby made this very clear to her.

56

The rest of February and then March dragged on as life returned to a semblance of normality in Flixham. Paula Collins and Blake did manage to convince Value Shoppers that the Romanians had been acting on their own and that Danny had been murdered when he threatened to go to the police. Even so their representative told them that there was to be a reduction in the amount of business that would be given to Collins Transport as the company felt that it was unwise to "put their eggs in one basket". They decided to split their delivery contracts between Collins Transport and three other haulage companies all of which were based in Norfolk. S&T transport never worked for Collins Transport again. Blake heard that Mircea Tiriac had returned to Romania but Dimi Szabo was still trying to scratch a living as a man with a van. He had moved in with Lesley Farmer.

The demise of Petrescu came as a relief to Blake. He was beginning to feel confident that he had got away with stealing the money from the Welney picnic site incident. Only DS Daley and DC Marks had shown any interest in him. What did concern him was how Petrescu had been alerted to him? How did he know that Blake had been questioned by the police? He had successfully moved £15000 into his building society accounts. He had told Ray Nash that he had been very lucky at the races over the past few weeks and had won several thousand pounds at Huntingdon, Market Rasen and Fakenham over the past few weeks. Blake was enjoying going to the races and even managed to pick a few winners of his own. He had found something to replace Mansfield FC on a Saturday afternoon.

'How the hell do you manage to pick out so many winners? I do the occasional Yankee but I'm lucky if I get two winners out of the four'. Ray complained

'I only bet at the racetrack. I watch the bookies to see where the money is going, especially if it is from smaller trainers. Some of them are well known for getting a horse spot on for a race. I have seen bets of over a grand being placed on a horse. When this happens I reckon that somebody is in the now so I will bet on the same horse as well. Sometimes I will only have one or two bets at a meeting. I have been lucky but my luck will change eventually'

'Let's hope it doesn't change before the Grand National on Saturday. Let me know what horse you are going to bet on so that some of your luck can run off on me. Who did you get in the office Sweepstake? I drew Knowhere and Big Fella Thanks. Do they have much of a chance?'

'They are as good as any. I drew State of Play and Mon Mone. I will have £10 on State of Play and £5 each way on Mon Mone.'

Blake headed to Mansfield after work on Saturday. He left just after ten o clock as business was slow now that Value Shoppers put less their way. Val had bent his ear all week about coming along for the weekend but he put her off much to her disappointment after telling her he was going to racing at Southwell after seeing Ellie and then meeting up with his old mates for a beer or two in the evening. Ellie had found a flat in Mansfield and as he had promised Blake was going to help her with the rent. He went straight to the lettings agent where he met up with Ellie. They went to view the flat which Ellie had her heart set on. After the viewing they went back to the agents. He gave the agent £2300 in cash to cover the deposit and the rent for the first six months of Ellie's tenancy. Ellie was so pleased and hugged him with tears in her eyes.

`Thanks Dad I am going to move in on Tuesday after work. One of Derrick's friends is going to help me. Derrick says that I can have some of his mother's old furniture that he has stored in his garage and I'm taking the stuff that I took to his place from my bedroom'

`Good luck with the move. Let me know if you need anything'. He gave her another £200. `You can buy a housewarming present with this'.

She thanked him again

`Are you sure? You have just paid my rent for six months.'

`I'm making up for not being there for a year. I must dash as I'm going to the races at Southwell'

He got there after racing had started and missed the first race but had time to see three large bets place on a 3 to 1 shot in the fifth race. He noted the name of the horse and bookie involved. He almost felt sorry for the bookie that had paid out £2000 for a £500 bet. He had two bets himself but both lost. He watched the Grand National on TV at the course. He couldn't believe his luck. Mon Mone the 100/1 shot won the race. He had £625 to collect from the betting office in Flixham on Monday plus the sweepstake at work. He decided that he would spend all of the sweepstake winnings on cakes for the staff.

After the race meeting he met up with Wayne for a quick drink before he was due to meet with Tony and Neville. Barry went to watch Mansfield play away at Woking on the supporters coach. They had lost three nil. Barry was a glutton for punishment. It was a long journey from Surrey to Mansfield which involved the M25 so Barry wasn't expected to get back in time to meet up for a curry. Blake was apprehensive about meeting Wayne. They hadn't spoken since the argument that they had after Blake had given him money for a new car. Ellie had told Blake that Wayne had been getting drunk most weekends. He bought an old Ford Orion with the money that Blake had given him but had crashed it within a couple of weeks. He was lucky to escape with just cuts and bruises. He had been drinking but had just managed to pass a breath test. He did end up in court following the fight in Mansfield a few weeks earlier. He was fined and given a suspended sentence. As a result it led to him losing his apprenticeship. Blake wasn't impressed and told him so when he turned up at the pub they had agreed to meet in.

`If you are not careful you will end up in a series of dead end jobs'
Much to Blake's surprise Wayne agreed with him
`I know that I have cocked things up. The car crash made me realise that I have been drinking too much and that I need to knuckle down. I am going to concentrate on passing my A Levels. My boss at Asda says that they have management trainee schemes so I am going to try to get onto one of them'
`If you pass your "A" Levels I will reward you financially. How are things at home with Derrick and your Mum?
`Not good. He is a total knob. They always seem to be arguing and Mum is always crying. I think that they might break up soon. He will probably kick her out so we will have nowhere to live'
`That's a concern. Has Mum said anything to you then?'
`She said that things are difficult between them at the moment. I think that she is a bit jealous of you especially as Ellie told her about your new young girlfriend '
`She isn't that young. She is nearly 33 so there is only ten years between us. I will bring her to Mansfield the next time I'm here so that you and Ellie can meet her. Anyway I must be getting a move on I'm meeting with Tony and Neville later. We are going for a curry at Shafiq later. What are your plans for the evening?'
`I'm going home. I have got a new girlfriend. She is coming over and we will get a pizza delivered. I will have the place to myself. Derrick has gone away on a golf weekend and Mum is going out with Jan and Mary. She said that she hasn't seen them for ages'
`Ok. Enjoy yourself and remember what I said about your exams' He gave Wayne £20. `Have a pizza on me'
`Thanks Dad'. Wayne hugged him and left
So Debbie is going out with Jan and Mary he thought recalling Debbie saying that she couldn't stand them. She must be bored.

Blake Tony and Neville made their way to the restaurant after a couple of beers in the Swan in the town centre. It was busy in the restaurant with only two or three tables still vacant. About ten minutes after they had taken their table three women came in and were seated at the table next to him. It was Jan Mary and Debbie. He didn't recognise her at first. Her long hair had gone and had been replaced with a new short hairstyle. She had put on weight and looked tired. He ignored her and carried on placing his order with the waiter Debbie spoke first

'Hello Bob. I didn't expect to be seeing you in here. You are looking well'

'I wish I could say to same about you. What's happened to your hair? I thought you said you didn't like short hair.'

He could tell that she hadn't appreciated his comments.

'Derrick likes it' She replied almost apologetically 'And that's what counts now'

'Yes but for how long. I hear that things are not going well'

'Well you have heard wrong' she replied in temper.

That was the last of the conversation between them for the rest of the evening. Blake tried to ignore her and she did the same but he caught her glancing in his direction a couple of times during the evening. He had been bitchy but he couldn't care less. She was no longer his wife and it had been her choice.


Blake returned to Flixham the next morning and spent the evening with Val at his place. He told her that he had seen his ex wife

'Did you speak to her' Val asked

"I did. I told her that I didn't like her new hairstyle and that she didn't look too good. She looked tired and had gained weight. She didn't like what I had to say so we didn't speak much after that. We never said goodbye when she left the restaurant. My son told me that things are not going well with her new bloke. She can be a moody cow and he is probably realising what he let himself in for. I'm well out of it and I have moved on to better things'. He smiled pulling Val towards him

'So you don't miss her at all 'Val enquired

'Not in the slightest. Do you miss Peter?' He fired back at her

'No' she said sounding convincing. 'But I have to see him next week to see what we are going to do with the flat. He wants to sell it so I could be homeless soon'

'I am told that the property market is dead so I doubt that you will sell the flat quickly. It's a buyer's market at the moment. I have been looking on RightMove. Some houses have been up for sale for a year. Nobody can get mortgages without a big deposit'

'Are you thinking about buying something then?'

'Not yet. I need to make sure that everything is OK with the job. We have lost a lot of business in the past couple of weeks.'

He hadn't told Paula Collins that Petrescu had told him that he was taking a controlling interest in the company. She hadn't mentioned it either but he assumed that she was looking to sell the company .They had a strategy meeting in the morning and he planned to broach the subject then.

The next morning Paula arrived at the depot later than usual. She looked flustered when she came into Blake's office.

`Good morning Bob. Did you have a good weekend?'

`I did but I am worried about Value Shoppers. I think that we have got much less than 25% of their business for the coming week'

`I am worried too. I have reason to believe that the police have been looking at our finances. My accountant phoned me at home this morning. That is why I am late'

`I need to ask you something and I would like an honest answer'

Paula looked concerned

`What do you want to know?'

`It's something that I have been dwelling on for a while now. Ivan Petrescu told me that he was taking a controlling interest in Collins Transport. You haven't mentioned it. Did you agree to sell to him?'

`It isn't how it seems. He threatened to hurt Charlotte if I didn't sell 51% of the company to him. I didn't have much choice. He offered me a paltry sum too'.

`Are you still considering selling the company?'

`It is probably best. I don't know enough to run the company and with the loss of business I cannot afford to pay somebody to do what Danny did. Perhaps with a new owner Value Shoppers would return some of the business to the company which would mean everyone's jobs would not be put in danger'

`Can I ask how much money you would want to sell of the company? I may know somebody who might be interested'

`I am considering moving abroad so I would only be interested in a quick sale. The company has a fleet of 14 trucks. Three of them are less than a year old, seven are less than 5 years old and the remainder are between 5 and 8 years old. They must be worth £150,000. I would be looking for at least £200,000. My accountant says that the company is doing well.'

They were not the exact words that the accountant had used. He said that it was just about keeping its head above water.

`I think that you are both being a bit optimistic with that valuation but let me speak to some people who may be prepared to invest in the company,' Blake replied. `In the mean time how are we going to take things forwards?'

`Ruth says that we have enough money to keep things going until the end of the month. We are owed money from Value Shoppers. They usually pay their invoices within six weeks. At this time of year there isn't too much coming in from the fruit and vegetable farms. Most of our business is from Value

Shoppers and bringing flowers in from the continent. We should have enough to pay the wages for our staff and the drivers this month but next month might be a struggle'.

`Should we start thinking about trimming staff at this stage?' Blake asked
`Let's review things at the end of April. I don't want a knee jerk reaction'

Blake spent the rest of the day exploring the possibility of actually buying into the company himself using the money that he still had stashed under his bed. He decided that he would speak to Ellie as she may have some clue as to what he would need to do. He wasn't seeing Val that evening so called her after he had got home and eaten.
She answered her mobile quickly `Hi Dad How is it going?'
`I'm good. I want to pick your brains on a subject that you will know much more than me about'.
He proceeded to tell her about Paula Collins plans to sell the company and that he was considering buying it. He had a copy of the latest set of accounts which were up to the end of 2008. He said that he would attach a copy to an email so that she could look at them for him to see if it was a worthwhile investment.
She phoned him back within the hour.
`I have looked at the numbers and the company seems quite profitable. It's quite lean and has performed well in these difficult times. I would recommend that you set up a limited company if you were thinking about buying into it'
`Why do you recommend that? How would I go about doing it?'
`If the company is a limited company it is the company that is liable for any debts not an individual so you would protect yourself if the company built up debts. All you need to do to set up a limited company is to buy an off the shelf limited company and just change the name or set up a new one from scratch. There are plenty of on line companies that will do this for you for around £200. You would need a company secretary and a list of shareholders. You would need to complete an annual return every year and submit an annual set of accounts. I can help you if you like'
`Based on what you have seen what do you think I should be paying for this company? What is it worth? '
`The main assets are the vehicles. The only other assets are the computers and the office furniture. The book value of the vehicles is £163,474 and the fixtures and fittings are valued at £7,203. There is finance of £85,000 outstanding on the vehicles At the end of the year there was £3917 in the bank account so at present it is probably worth around £90,000 but the assets will be devalued by 25% each year so I would suggest something around £75,000 depending on

how much is in the bank account. If you like I can prepare something for you. The other matter that you would need to investigate is the lease on the depot. How long is the lease for and how often do rent reviews kick in? The rent is affordable at present but you need to be careful. You don't need any huge hikes in the rent'

Blake was very impressed with his daughter's advice and told her so.

`I didn't realise that you knew so much. I am not sure if I can afford to make an offer of that size though'

`Why not offer to buy a controlling interest. If you offered to buy 51% of the company to start with and leave Paula with 49% with an option for you to buy the rest as the company grows it would mean that you wouldn't have to outlay so much and that she would get a dividend payment every year based on what the company earned'

`I never thought of that. Thanks for the advice. Can you send me some details of what you said so that I can get a better idea in my mind? '

`I'm glad that I can help but be careful. I presume that you will be using the money from Nan's estate and it is a lot of money to lose'

`I will be careful. I don't want to take risks and lose everything that Nan left me' he lied

He poured himself a beer and sat contemplating his next step. The irony hadn't left him. He was planning to purchase a major share in Collins Transport using money which caused the death of several men and could have led to the collapse of the company. Later that evening Ellie sent him details of what she had told him and gave him a list of websites that offered off the shelf companies for sale.

He looked up some of them and was amazed to find that for £49.99 plus Vat he could buy a readymade limited company that would be able to trade in days and for another £19.99 plus Vat he could change the name of the company to whatever he wanted to call it. Everything would be registered with Companies House. It seemed very simple.

The next day he went to see Paula who had taken over Danny's office.

`I have been thinking about our conversation yesterday. I have a proposal that may be of interest. I have had an accountant look at the last set of accounts and checked details of our lease agreement. The company was worth around £90,000 but each year the value of the vehicles reduces so now it is probably worth around £75,000'

"The lorries are worth much more than that" Paula protested

`Yes I agree but there is also outstanding finance on them which comes to about £85000'.

He showed her the copy of the company's latest accounts

'Have you thought about just selling Danny's 51% share of the company and retaining 49% as a silent partner?. I know that Petrescu made an offer along similar lines. You would still get a share of any profits in the form of dividends and as the company grows I would be prepared to buy more shares'

'How much would you be prepared to pay for Danny's 51% share of the company?'

'I would like to make the company a limited company with you and me as the two shareholders. It would be registered with Companies House. This means that if the company went bust all that we would lose is what we have invested in the company. If the company went bust now you would be responsible for any debts that arise as you and Danny were the two partners. I am surprised that Danny didn't go down the limited company route. I would be prepared to pay £45,000 for Danny's share of the company and buy more shares from you if you wished once trading improved.'

Paula was shattered by Blake's revelation about the value of the company and of the consequences of what would happen if it went tits up. Danny hadn't told her that the trucks were financed. Bob's offer was considerably more than what Petrescu had wanted to pay for his 51% of the company but it was still a lot less than the figure that she had originally thought the company was worth.

'Let me speak to my accountant about your offer. I will speak to him this afternoon'

She did this and much to her disappointment she found that Blake's valuation was if anything a bit generous. For any business matters Collins Transport used Masson and Partners who are based in Flixham. Eugene Masson, who was the senior partner, agreed that it would be better for Collins Transport to become a limited company rather than a partnership especially as there was only one surviving partner. He said that £45000 was a good offer and that she should take the offer unless she wanted to rid herself of any interest in the company. If this was the case she should aim for an offer of £95000.

On leaving Masson and Co she immediately phoned Geoff Williams. She explained what Blake had offered and what Masson had said about the offer. 'What do you suggest that I do?' She asked him

'Personally I think that it would be advisable to push him up to £50k for Danny's share of the company. You will get income from your share of any profits as well as any salary that you take until you stop working there. Let Masson and your solicitor handle the sale of your share of the company so that it avoids any suspicion. With what you have offshore you should be able to buy

a small villa in the Canary Islands and have a comfortable lifestyle for Charlotte and you. If you were to put your house up for sale today it is unlikely that you will be ready to move out to the Canary Islands until much later in the year.'
`Yes that would probably work. Charlotte has her GCSE's in July. She turns 16 in June and wants to leave school after her exams. She wants to become a hairdresser. There should be work for her in the Canary Islands. We can go away for a couple of weeks as soon as her exams are finished. I would like to live in Tenerife as it's my favourite island and I know some people out there from previous holidays. Should I open up a bank account when I go there next?'
`No, I would leave it until you have a permanent address'
Paula headed home feeling a bit happier. She wasn't going to get as much money has she had hoped by selling the company but with the small amount of equity from the sale of the house and the company plus what was in offshore accounts she should have enough money to set up a new life for her and Charlotte in Tenerife. The insurance company were still dragging their feet with Danny's insurance claim and were looking for an excuse not to pay out. She could even do some part time work to help with finances until Danny's pension kicked in. She had got some forecasts. She would be entitled to about thirty thousand as a lump sum and a monthly pension of three hundred and thirty pounds. Not much but better than a poke in the eye with a sharp stick.

By the end of the next week everything was in place. Blake had purchased an off the shelf company by the name of Albright Parts and had changed the name to Flixham Transport Ltd. Blake wouldn't budge from his £45,000 offer and transferred that amount from his deposit account to Paula's bank. The new company had two shareholders Blake owing 51% and Paula Collins owned 49%. Ellie Blake was listed as the company secretary. The assets and liabilities of Collins Transport were transferred to Flixham Transport Ltd. On Friday morning Paula and Blake held a meeting for all staff. Paula started the meeting.

`As you all know the company has suffered in the aftermath of Danny's death and was in danger of going under. I have decided that the company should become a limited company and change its name. As from Monday 24th April the new company will be called Flixham Transport Ltd. Bob Blake and I own the shares of this new company. I intend to become a silent partner in the company leaving Bob to take control of day to day affairs. This will happen once I have sold my house. Bob attended a meeting with Value Shoppers last week and I am pleased to say that they may be increasing the amount of work that they put our way but it won't be the same as the level of work that we did for them last year. We need to regain their confidence. Unfortunately we may have to make some staff changes in a few weeks time depending on how busy we become'

As soon as the meeting was over Paula left for the day leaving Blake to handle all of the questions

Ruth Cross was the first person to come into his office. She got straight to the point

`Bob, I am sixty in July and I think that it is the right time for me to go. My husband wants to retire and it would be nice if we retired at the same time. He has got a good pension from his company and I get my state pension on my 60th birthday so I would like to give you notice that I will be leaving on June 17th. I would have hoped that Raymond would have been able to do my job for me but he doesn't seem to take any interest in learning anything new'

`That is disappointing news Ruth. I will be sad to see you go. Is there any way that I could change your mind even if it was just until August? There will be some major upheaval and I was hoping that you would be around to steady the ship. I hear what you say about Raymond. Between you and me he will be leaving the company very soon'

`My husband retires on June 17 and we were hoping to retire together and go on a cruise to the Mediterranean. There are lots of deals available at the moment. I would like to finish on June 17 so I guess the answer is no'

Blake accepted the situation. He had no choice.


Ray Nash was next in to see Blake. He was obviously nervous about his job

`Is my job safe Bob?'

`Yes it is for now Ray but I was going to ask you how you felt about a change of duties. How would you feel about getting involved with the logistics side of the business? By that I mean organising the drops for the next day, managing the drivers etc. It would mean a pay rise. Could Bob Parsons handle the maintenance side of the business perhaps with some part time help?'

Ray was taken aback by this news. Blake could tell this by the look of astonishment on Ray's face that it was not something that he had considered

`That's a surprise but it is something that appeals to me.  I think that Bob would be able to manage especially if you can get him some help'

`That's good then. Keep it to yourself for now though'

Susan Rudd, June Eason and Bob Parsons all came to see Blake and all of them were concerned about their jobs. Blake reassured them all. Interestingly Ray Pearce never came to see Blake. Perhaps he knew that he had no future with the company.

Ruth Cross was going to be the main problem that he would need to solve. He needed somebody to come in and take over the billings and accounts. He knew somebody who would fit the bill perfectly.

Ellie was due to take the third year of her accountancy exams in June. He knew that she was poorly paid. He phoned her that evening

'How is the studying going?" He asked her

'It's hard work. I study for at least two hours every night. '

"How are things at work? Are they keeping you busy?

'It's a bit concerning at the moment. One of the larger firms that we do the books for have gone bankrupt so we are not too busy. My boss's son passed his year three exams in December and as he is more experienced than me he gets the more interesting work. All that I seem to be doing is VAT returns and book keeping for one man companies. How are things with you and the new company?'

'Well one of the reasons that I called you is that Ruth our accounts person is retiring and the company needs a new accounts manager. I was wondering whether you would be interested in coming to work with me in Norfolk. As you are part qualified you would be able to do our accounts for us and we wouldn't need to use an outside firm of accountants. I would be able to pay you more than you are currently earning'

Ellie sounded flustered. She started firing off questions in quick succession.

'Where would I live? What about my flat? I have only just moved in. I wouldn't get a refund of the advanced rent that you paid, what about my exams?'

'Don't worry about the advanced rent that you have paid. If you moved up here you could rent something here or even think about buying your own place. I can help you with that. You can still study and there may even be scope to let you have time off at work to study. Have a think about it and let me know if you are interested. If you are why don't you come here at the weekend? You can stay at my house. I will sleep on the sofa or stay at Val's flat for the weekend'

'Can I tell Mum? I'm having lunch with her on Friday. I get the feeling that her and Derrick are splitting up. She has hinted about sleeping on my sofa'

'Of course you can. If you decide to come and join me Mum can always stay in your flat for the rest of the tenancy so at least the rent money wouldn't be going to waste!'

'I didn't think that you would be willing to help her out. She said that you were quite rude to her when she saw you at the restaurant in Mansfield '

'I wasn't rude. I just said that I didn't like her new haircut and that she looked as though she had put on a few pounds. Anyway I have to go. Have a think about it and let me know'

Ellie called him the next evening. She said that she was very interested and asked if she could come to Flixham the weekend after next which was the May Day bank holiday weekend. They agreed that she would drive down from Mansfield on Saturday morning and go back on Monday. This would give them time to start looking at property in the area should Ellie decide to move.

58

Ds Daley was counting the days until his retirement date. May 18<sup>th</sup> couldn't come quick enough. Fortunately things had quietened down in Flixham and the surrounding area and the reported crimes were few and inconsequential. Clarissa Marks had been on sick leave recovering from the gunshot wounds. She was lucky that the bullets didn't damage any major organs but there were complications from the wound to the upper chest as it had damaged nerves which were restricting movement in her shoulder. Daley had visited her in hospital when she had recovered sufficiently to take visitors.

`I didn't know that you are a karate queen. That was a hell of a kick that put down Vargea'. He said

`I have been doing kick boxing for over four years but that was the first time I have used it in anger'

`It's as well you did because we could have all been injured or worse'

`Thanks. Surly Shirley even came to see me. It seems that I may be up for a commendation. You could see that she didn't like telling me. It was through gritted teeth' she laughed. `What has been happening in my absence? I heard about Ivan Petrescu. Have the Essex police made any progress?'

`They are working on the theory that it was a gang killing. They have some pictures on CCTV of a large man following him from a hotel near the airport but the coverage doesn't cover the area where he was found. They don't know if the man was involved because that was the only sighting of him. It has a passing resemblance to Victor Dragnea but that is mainly based on the size of the man. There are no good views of the man's face. Booth isn't best pleased. I think she had visions of taking down a major player in Europe. With him out of the picture there has been no progress on the Collins Transport angle so it's been put on the back burner. I have been keeping an eye on our friend Blake. He seems to make regular trips to building societies in Kings Lynn. It has been very quiet so I have been discreetly watching him. I was hoping that we can get the financial forensics team to fully investigate him. I pressed Booth again but she still won't sanction it. All that I can get is his bank statements. From what I can see he doesn't draw much money from his account'

`That is typical of Booth. She must be hurt by the fact that there are no cameras to perform in front of' Marks said.

Daley didn't see Marks for some time after the hospital visit. She was released from hospital three weeks after she was submitted. She rested at home for six weeks before returning to a desk job in Kings Lynn in the last week of April.

Daley saw her sat behind a computer looking bored on her first day back to work.

`Hello Clarissa. It's good to see you back at work. How is the shoulder?'

`It's slowly improving but I don't know if I will ever get full movement back. Active duty is out of the question at the moment. It seems as though my only option is a desk job if I stay in the police force. I am not sure if that is for me. You have only got a few weeks left before you retire. I suspect that you are looking forward to it?'

`I can't wait' Daley replied. `It can't come bloody quick enough. The force isn't the same as when I joined and I am best out of it. I don't fit these days'

`I think that you are a good copper and I have enjoyed working with you. I have learned a lot from you'

`Thanks Clarissa. You are young fit and will soon be healthy again so I hope that the shoulder doesn't restrict you. I hope that you manage to get a transfer away from Surly Shirley. I know that I won't miss her' he said grinning as he left her looking at her computer.

Daley's pension was reasonable. He planned to take a lump sum to fund a conservatory and a new car. His eight year old Renault Laguna had seen better days. It still drove well but he fancied something newer before things started to go wrong with it. After taxes he would have seventeen thousand a year to live on until he could draw his state pension at sixty five. Bev hadn't worked for five years. She loved cooking and pottering about in the garden and with her various groups in the town found plenty to occupy her time. They had toyed with the idea of buying a motor home so that they could travel around the country visiting areas that they had never been to before. Daley wasn't one for holidays abroad. He couldn't be bothered with hassle of airports. They had been to Majorca and Tenerife for some sun but each time they were delayed for several hours. Waiting in cramped airports was something that they decided that they could do without. Daley had a daughter, Jane, who lived in Basingstoke where she worked for a software company and a son Michael who lived and worked in Reading. He was some sort of computer programmer. He did try to explain what to his parents what he did but it was all Chinese to them. Daley only saw his children a couple of times each year. When he retired Bev had planned for more regular visits to see them. She had his future mapped out it seemed.

59

Dennard Hoyte appeared in court in Norwich at 1030 on April 28th. He was found guilty of the illegal possession of a firearm and for trafficking Class A drugs. His solicitor, a duty solicitor, pleaded for leniency on his behalf as he had co-operated with the police and that he only acted as driver under duress. His solicitor said that the guns that the police had found at the park home belonged to Lynton Andrews. He was found guilty. He was sentenced to six months in prison suspended for two years and fined £300. His time in remand had been taken into account. He asked for time to pay as he had no employment and to his relief he was released. His solicitor dropped him back in Flixham. His initial plan was to go back to Bristol now that he had been dealt with by Smith's gang. The question he had was how he was going to get there? He had little money and no idea where his car was and whether or not it could be repaired. His first port of call was the police station at Flixham where the desk sergeant told him that his car had eventually been towed away by a local garage. He was given the name and address of the garage and he set off to find it. He discovered the car sat in the corner of a small yard. It hadn't been touched and looked to be in a sorry state with the front buckled in.

`I believe that this is your car mate' a short overweight man in dark blue overalls said as he walked towards him cleaning his hand s on a dirty cloth

`You owe me £75 for towing it here plus another hundred quid for storing it'

`I don't have any money. I got nicked soon after the accident and have been on remand ever since. I was released yesterday'

`Well in that case I will have to sell the car and take what I am owed plus storage costs out of what I can get for it'

`That car cost me two and a half grand in November and I got a bargain price for it because the seller needed money. How much will it cost to get it road worthy again?'

The mechanic pondered over his answer. He sucked on his teeth and rubbed his chin with his hand

`I reckon about £700. It will need a lot of work to put it right. You will need a new wing, new bonnet, headlights and a new radiator plus a re-spray'

`Would it be worth five hundred quid to you as it is and after you have taken into account the tow cost and storage costs' Hoyte eventually replied after thinking about the garage owner's comments.

`Possibly' the garage owner said mulling over in his head how much profit he could make on the deal. The car was quite tidy if you ignored the damage caused by the crash.

`I suppose that you would want cash for it? Let me think about it. Can you come back tomorrow? '

`I can. Shall I say about ten?'

`Ok see you tomorrow then but don't be late. I like to close up early on a Saturday'

Hoyte went back to the park home. It had been unoccupied since his arrest in February. The place hadn't been touched and the little bit of food in the fridge had all gone off. The milk had gone sour and had left a horrible smell in the fridge. His bed was unmade from when he was arrested. It was a depressing sight to return to. The room which Lynton had been using reminded Hoyte how much he missed his mate. The sooner he got away from here the better but he couldn't do anything until he got some money.

Hoyte returned to the garage the next morning

`Do we have a deal? 'He asked the owner

`The best that I can offer you is £400'

`It's got to be worth more than that'

`It's a buyer's market old son. Take it or leave it otherwise I will just scrap it and take what I am owed from the scrap value. You can have what's left but it won't be anywhere near £400'

Hoyte knew that he was shafted but he had no other options and reluctantly agreed to the £400.

Overnight he had changed his plans. He had decided that he was going to Jamaica and try to start a new life there. It would cost him around £400 for a one way ticket in May. He would have to contact his father so he decided he would call on his sister in Watford to see if she could put him up for a couple of days. He would be able to phone his father from his sister's place. If he was going to Jamaica to live he needed money. The problem was that he didn't know how to get any.


Ellie Blake arrived in Flixham just after 1100 on a bright sunny Saturday morning. She went straight to Flixham Transport as it was now called to meet with her father.

`You made good time' Blake said greeting her with a hug and a peck on the cheek.

`Let me show you around. There is just me and Bob Parsons, one of the mechanics working today'

He took her around the office showing her the computers the logistics planning boards the garages and eventually introduced her to Bob Parsons. Both blushed at the introduction.

He took Ellie back to his office

`What do you think of the set up?'

`It's not what I imagined. The offices are quite modern. How is business going this month?"

He talked her through the Value Shoppers situation explaining that he was hoping to be given more work especially as he had heard rumours that some of the new haulage firms that they had been using had been having issues. He admitted that things were tough but that was a common fact with most small firms. The recession had hit hard but they were surviving.

After finishing up at work he took Ellie to his house. He had bought some nice ham and four rolls on the way in to work so they ate them with a cup of tea.

`Let me show you around Kings Lynn this afternoon. If you want to live in a town it will be better to live there rather than here in Flixham as there isn't much to do for somebody of your age. I am not going to press you for a decision as it will be a big step for you leaving all your friends behind'

`I have lost touch with a lot of my friends because I have put all of my focus on qualifying as an accountant. My mates from school are either pregnant, working in supermarkets or on the dole. I have stayed in touch with Jenny but she has a steady bloke so I don't see her that often. I must admit that I am quite tempted with a change of scenery. It all seems so clean here. It is so different to Mansfield which is becoming run down and dirty.'

`Kings Lynn isn't pristine. It has plenty of scruffy parts as well'

They set off for Kings Lynn early in the afternoon. He showed Ellie around the town centre and then they toured the estate agents so that Ellie could get some idea of both rental and sale prices. Blake then took Ellie on a drive around some of the newer housing estates. He had done this himself several times in his short time in Norfolk trying to get a picture of where he would like to live and how easy the drive to Flixham would be. Ellie was impressed with the neat houses with their small tidy gardens on the Templefield estate.

`I could buy a two bedroom house for £70000 'Ellie said with obvious excitement in her voice `The mortgage repayment would be less than I am paying for the flat in Mansfield'

`Its food for thought then' Blake replied. He looked at his watch. It was 430pm.
` Let's head home. I have booked a table for 8pm in the Red Lion in Flixham. I would like you to meet Val tonight'

`What should I wear? I didn't bring anything dressy'

`It's only a Toby place so you don't have to dress up. Jeans will be fine.'

Blake went to pick up Val leaving Ellie to get ready to go out.

`We can walk to the Red Lion from here as it is only a short journey. I am going to stay at Val's tonight so that you can have my bed. I have put clean sheets on. I will walk back here with you before going to Val's. It's only a ten minute walk from here. '

When he returned with Val Ellie was ready to go. He sensed a level of apprehension when the girls met. The evening turned out to be somewhat awkward. Ellie and Val exchanged pleasantries but didn't hit it off. There wasn't a lot of conversation going on between them. For most of the time it was Blake doing the talking and trying to get them both to join in. After they finished eating they took a table in the main bar area. The pub was quite full with a lot of youngsters, many of whom looked to be underage to Blake. Perhaps it was just him feeling old. Blake noticed a tall black guy stood at the bar chatting to two very young girls. It was Lynton Andrews mate. It was the one who had rescued him from a hiding from Andrews. He looked over in Blake's direction, smiled and raised his glass. Blake ignored him but then realised that it was Val he was looking at when she waved back to him.

`How do you know him?' He asked Val

`I went out on a double date with Lesley him and his mate, the one who got killed at Welney. We didn't hit it off so it was just a brief relationship'

`He is fit though, I would' Ellie remarked getting a frown of disapproval from Blake and a frosty response from Val

`I have since discovered that he is an arsehole. He thinks too much of himself' Val replied with a tinge of bitterness in her voice

Hoyte had decided to come down for a drink. He couldn't bear to spend the evening in the park home. Without any definite plans in his head he thought that he would try to pull. He might be lucky and find someone who had their own place and maybe somebody who even had a car. He wasn't fussy about what type of car. He just needed something to get him from Flixham to Watford. Val Davey would have fitted the bill. She was good in bed, had her own place and had a car. He may have been able to talk her into dropping him off in Watford. Unfortunately he had blown his chances with her especially as she appeared to have hooked up with somebody else. It suddenly dawned on Hoyte who the bloke she was with was. It was the guy that Lynton had chinned. He wondered who the tall busty girl with the long chestnut hair was. Could it be a friend of Val or even her bloke's daughter? Perhaps he had misread the situation. The bloke looked to be a bit older than Val. Could he just be a mate? He noticed the tall girl looking at him whenever he looked in her direction. He reckoned he was in with a chance there and wondered if she had a car.

At ten thirty Hoyte watched Val and her friends leave the bar. He finished his coke and left the pub after them. Keeping a good distance between them and himself he followed them. He shadowed them for a few minutes until they all went into a small house in Turnberry Close. There was VW Golf and a Citreon Saxo parked outside. He watched the house from a distance. The road was quiet and it seemed that everyone had settled down for the night. After a couple of minutes Val re-appeared with the older guy. They headed off in the direction of Val's flat leaving the tall girl alone in the house. The outside light was switched off. He noticed a light go on upstairs. He waited standing in a corner under some trees about 100 yards from the house. The light went off upstairs leaving the house in darkness. He felt hungry so he decided to nip back to the town centre to get some fish and chips. He would return to this house later making sure that he was out of the view of the CCTV cameras that were in the town. He hadn't noticed too many security cameras in Turnberry Close. As he walked back he studied the doors on the houses. Few of them had deadlocks so they would be easy to break into. A credit card would suffice but he had come prepared. He had a roll of tape, a small torch and a small hammer in his coat pocket. That was enough to break one of the small panes of windows on the front door of any of these houses.

He returned to Turnberry Close just after midnight having eaten his fish and chips in the company of two young girls who were well pissed. They looked underage and flirted with him in an outrageous way. He noticed that almost all the houses were in complete darkness. He thought that they must go to bed early here. He put on his gloves and went straight to number 78 and easily opened the door using a credit card. He crept in and using his torch surveyed the lounge area. He noticed a Dell laptop. He would take that with him when left. Next was the kitchen. He shone the torch around and saw a handbag on a work surface. He looked in and found a purse which contained thirty pounds. He pocketed the money. There was a driving license. The picture was of that of the young girl who was with Val earlier. Her name was Eleanor Blake and her date of birth signified that she was 21 years old. The keys to the Saxo were in the bag so he had the means of getting to his sisters even if it was in a pokey little car. There was a key rack in the kitchen. His luck was in. The keys to the VW Golf were on it. He went back into the lounge and unhooked a DVD player. The TV was small older model but it would be awkward to carry so he ignored it. He had the laptop, DVD player some money and the car keys so he had done well. He decided to take a chance and crept upstairs. One of the stairs creaked so he froze. The bedroom door was closed so he opened it quietly. Eleanor Blake was fast asleep and was snoring very lightly. Her watch was on the bedside cabinet. It looked expensive so he nicked that too. Her mobile was there too. It was an old model so he decided to leave it. It wouldn't be worth much and there was no point holding onto it allowing it to be traced. He stood looking at her shining the torch over her voluptuous body. On another day he would have enjoyed a piece of her but today wasn't that day. She stirred and he froze but she turned over without waking up. It was time for him to go. He collected the laptop and the DVD player from the lounge and left closing the front door gently behind him. He opened the doors to the golf with the key fob and put the stolen goods in the boot. He turned the ignition key but nothing happened. He cursed. It was a diesel model so he depressed the clutch and turned the key again. Bingo!! It purred into action. There was just under a half a tank of fuel in the car which should be enough to get him to Watford which he estimated was about 100 miles. His first stop was back at the park home. Lynton had brought his belongings to the park home in a large holdall which was perfect for the lap top, DVD player, Lynton's micro sound system and Lynton's 32 inch flat screen TV. He wrapped a towel around the electrical goods, collected his clothes which he put into his small holdall and locked up vowing not ever to return. He headed towards the A10. There would be traffic on it even at this time of night. He planned to follow it until it met the M25 which he would follow until he got to the Watford junction. He had slept most of the afternoon so he wasn't too tired. He would stop at South Mimms services on the M25 where he could grab a bite to eat and if necessary have a kip in the car. He doubted that the car would be missed until the morning but he was going to dump it when he got to Watford.

He hadn't seen his sister for over a year. She hadn't been too pleased when he asked if he could kip on her couch for a couple of nights. He told her that he needed to speak with their father as he was planning to fly out to Jamaica. He arrived at the service station at just before three am. Everything had gone smoothly. He grabbed a burger and coffee from Burger King and went back to the car. He did feel a little tired so it was time for a kip. He wanted to get to his sister's house by around eleven so he had plenty of time to kill.

60

Blake and Val had their first row on Sunday morning. It had started when Blake told Val that he had offered Ellie a job at Flixham Transport. He said that he needed to replace Ruth Cross who wanted to retire.

`You know that I hate working at my place so why you couldn't find a space for me? She complained.

Blake tried to explain that Ellie was a part qualified accountant and that he needed a bookkeeper to replace Ruth but this didn't pacify Val

`You could have found something else for me there though'

`It isn't possible at the moment. We are reducing staff not taking them on. The bookkeeper role is vital so I have to replace Ruth but that is it'

His mobile rang. It was Ellie

`We have had a break in 'she cried down the phone `Your car has gone. My money and my watch have been taken. I can't see your laptop either or the DVD player. Somebody must have broke in during the night'

`I will come straight home' he told her

`What's wrong with her?'  Val asked sneering. She hadn't hit it off with Ellie and resented the attention Blake was giving to his daughter.

`Someone has broken into the house and pinched my car. I need to get home' He left with the aftermath of their row still in the air


Ellie was in tears when he arrived home 'I don't know how they got in. I definitely shut the door properly' she said with tears rolling down her face.

`They must have somehow opened the front door' He called the police and an hour later PC Fowler turned up accompanied by a young PCSO

Fowler asked Blake if there were any signs of forced entry.

`I couldn't see anything'

`Are you sure all of the doors were shut properly?'

`I wasn't at home last night. My daughter is visiting so as I only have the one bedroom I stayed at my girlfriends flat last night. She closed the door when I left. That would have been around 11pm'

Fowler looked at the lock on the front door.

`You really need to get a better lock on your front door. This type of latch can be opened with a credit card. I suspect that this is how they got in. I have arranged for the SOCO team to come and dust for finger prints but this looks like somebody who knew what they were doing. What has been taken?'

`They took my car, my laptop, a DVD player my daughter's watch and some money from her purse. I left the spare keys to my car on the key hook in the kitchen. They have been taken so I guess that is how they got the car'

He could tell by the look on PC Fowler's face that the policeman thought that it was a stupid place to leave a spare set of car keys.

`Do you have receipts for the laptop and the DVD so that we can track the serial number? They will probably be sold in a pub or to a pawn shop. We might get lucky if it's the latter'

Blake fished out the receipts from a draw in the kitchen.

 `They were both new. I only purchased them a couple of weeks ago'

`Can I have these for a couple of day? I will photo copy them and return them to you as you will probably have to provide them for any insurance claim'

`Yes, no problem. Will you be able to find my car? Again it's new. I only bought it in February shortly after I moved to Flixham'

Fowler took the registration number.

 `With a bit of luck it may show up on the ANPR system' he said. The Automatic Number Plate recognition system was a fairly new tool to the police. Thousands of mages were relayed to a central computer system from all over the country every day and it enabled the police to track vehicle movements.

When the police had left Blake made coffee for Ellie. His little house seemed dirty now. He couldn't get his head around the fact that somebody had broken in and had been prowling around while Ellie lay asleep in bed. He wasn't too keen on calling the police knowing what he had hidden upstairs under his bed. The incident shook Ellie too and she decided to return home on Sunday rather than staying the extra day. Blake gave her money to make up for what she had stolen.

`Don't let this put you off moving out here' he pleaded It could have happened anywhere

`I don't know Dad. You had the murders here in February and March too. Perhaps it isn't as sleepy as it appears.'


Hoyte slept in his car for about an hour. There was a 3 hour parking limit at the service station so not wishing to draw attention to himself he continued on his journey. After leaving the M25 at Junction 20 he headed towards Watford on the A41 It was. He checked his watch. It was five o' clock. Dawn was breaking and it was just starting to get light. He pulled into a lay by. He hadn't considered that the laptop might need a password to start it up so he retrieved it from the boot of the car and booted it up. He was in luck as the machine pinged into action but there was no internet. All that was available were Word and Excel. With time to kill he opened Word to see if the owner had anything interesting to write. There were letters to banks and solicitors about limited companies, payments to Paula Collins, letters to his bank moving money from a deposit account. It seemed that Mr Blake was quite wealthy. He then opened Excel. There were just three spreadsheet files. He opened the first file which seemed to be some sort of forecast for a company called Flixham Transport Ltd. Hoyte didn't have a clue what it was about. It was all projections and cash flow forecasts so he closed it quickly. The second was just called 'cash flow'. It showed money in each month which Hoyte assumed was Blake's salary and bills such as rent electric, council tax, water rates etc. There was a credit which said 'Probate' amounting to 102,985.25 and a few days later there was a transfer to deposit account for £90000 plus a debit for £9000 which said 'car'. There was one large payment of £45,000 to Paula Collins which matched up with the payment in the word file letter that he had read earlier and on the same day a credit for the same amount which said 'from deposit account'. There was a second sheet on the cash flow file. It contained details of three building society accounts and the deposit account. The third file was just titled 'Spending'. It was showing a credit of £250,000 and lots of debits. Car £9,000, Ellie's rent £2300, Wayne and Ellie £2000. There were further small amounts for clothes, meals out, computer, DVD. There were regular small payments to ISA and Building society accounts. None of the building society credits appeared on the cash flow when Hoyte out of curiosity checked them. He wondered if there was any way he could gain access to these accounts but decided that it was too risky. None of the entries on the spending file showed up in the cash flow file apart from the £9000 for the car. Hoyte was no financial genius but even to someone of his limited education it was obvious that Blake had another source of income. Then it dawned on him. The entry of £250,000 was dated 27 January. That was the date when Lynton died. The coppers had kept harping on about missing money. Could it have been Blake who had driven Lynton to the trade? Had he killed everybody at the scene? It didn't make much sense because the bloke was a wimp. Lynton had decked him with one punch. How would he have overpowered and killed three men? His mind was racing. It must have been Blake who had been the driver. Perhaps he had more about him than it seemed. Was Blake sitting on this money? He wouldn't be able to bank it because such a large sum would raise questions. Hoyte could find no record of it in his various accounts. Hoyte had to find out and had an idea about who may be able to help him. Perhaps he would have some money to take with him to Jamaica after all.

Blake was fretting about the burglary. He needed the car but it was the laptop which concerned him more. He had kept a record of the spending from his illegal windfall in a spreadsheet on the laptop and if the laptop did turn up with the police they might realise what his records signified. When he started the spreadsheet he hadn't considered the consequences of it being stolen. It was the one entry which was causing him so much concern...Money in £250,000 dated Jan 27. He didn't sleep well that night.

61

DS Daley had arrived early at Flixham station on what was to be his penultimate Monday as a serving police officer. He had just enjoyed a rare weekend off. Ronnie Edbrooke was already in.

`Did anything of interest happen at the weekend?'

`There was a break in at an address in Turnberry Close. Somebody nicked the owner's car and a couple of electrical goods. There were a couple of scuffles outside the Red Lion last night but apart from that it was dead quiet. Tony Fowler attended the break in. His report is on your desk. It was the home of Bob Blake, the new man at Collins Transport' Edbrooke replied `let's hope it stays quiet for your last two weeks Arthur'

`I hope so too. The less I hear from surly Shirley the better' he said, leaving to go into his small office.

He had a quick look at Fowler's report which indicated that the lock on the front door had been sprung, possibly with a credit card. The report stated that Fowler had suggested better and more secure locks should be fitted to the property. Daley noticed that the car had been stolen. What also caught his attention was that the electrical goods receipts showed that Blake had paid cash for them. Daley had been able to request copies of Blake's bank statements and building society accounts records. These showed that Blake didn't draw much cash from his bank account. The building society account details had only arrived in the last couple of days and had shown several deposits ranging from £500 to £1000 being made over the past few weeks. None of these amounts had shown up on his current account. Daley considered this to be very unusual. It was time to have another word with Blake. He phoned him at the newly named Flixham Transport office. He was put through by the receptionist.

Blake answered

`I hope that you are phoning to say that you have found my car and stolen goods DS Daley'

`It's early days yet. Could I meet with you to discuss the case?'

`I'm busy at the moment. What do you want to discuss. Can we do it over the phone?'

`Not really. I could come to your house after you finish work. I expect the SOCO team will be in touch today. They will want check for fingerprints. I could come at the same time? '

`Is there any way that you can chase them up to see when they are coming?'

`I will see what I can do'

Daley phoned SOCO as soon as he got off the phone with Blake. He persuaded them to check out Blake's place at 1800 that evening. He left a message for Blake to say that SOCO would be at his at 1800. He planned to get there at 1830 so that he didn't get in their way.

Hoyte dumped Blake's car in the car park at Sainsbury's which was a ten minute walk from his sister Davina's house. He carried the electrical goods that he'd stolen from Blake in Lynton's holdall and his own bits and pieces in his own smaller holdall. Lynton's holdall was heavy so he had to stop several times to rest his arms   Davina wasn't pleased to see him. She had married her long term boyfriend, Clive, eighteen months ago. Hoyte didn't attend her wedding which upset her especially as their mother was very ill at the time of the wedding. He hadn't seen Davina since his mother's funeral the previous year and she had hardly spoken with him. It took a lot of persuasion for her to agree to let him stay at her house and it was probably Clive who talked her into it. He always got on well with Hoyte.

`What drags you here' she snapped at him when he knocked on the door of her neat little terraced home
`It's a long story'
Hoyte proceeded to tell his sister about the problems he was facing or at least the version that he thought that she would find acceptable. He told her about how he had hooked up with Lynton and how they had fallen foul of Basil Smith. He told her that they had been staying at their father's park home since November. He watered down his part in the deal with Collins saying that Lynton had set it all in motion and that they needed the money. He told her that Lynton had threatened him if he didn't act as driver for him. He claimed that he had wanted to back out after the first drop. He wrote his car off so Lynton used somebody else for the next drop and had been killed in the process. He told her that he had been arrested, charged but then released with a suspended sentence after confessing to being the driver on the first drop. He said that he wanted a fresh start and that he felt Jamaica offered him a better opportunity especially with the current state of things in the UK
`You can stay here for a couple of nights but no more. Why do you always get mixed up with the wrong people? You had a good job and you could have made it as a footballer but you threw away any chance you had'
`I wouldn't call working at Kwik Fit a good job and I wasn't good enough to have made real money as a footballer'
`You were getting paid to play football. Clive would have loved that. Do you think that my job selling perfume in Debenhams is what I had planned to do

when I left school with all of those GCSE's? Do you think that Clive doesn't get bored driving school buses? We do it to allow us to buy this house and to keep our heads above water. We would love to be able to have holidays abroad and even to start a family but we can't so we just get on with life until the time is right for us'

Davina was thirty years of old and despite being younger than him she had always acted like an older sibling. Hoyte knew that she spoke a lot of truth.

'I hope to settle down in Jamaica. I know that I have made plenty of mistakes but now is perhaps the time to start to put things right. I only want to stay for a couple of days. I want to speak to Dad to see if I can stay with him. I will also see what he wants to do with the park home. He is paying ground rent for it so at least me staying there has meant that the money hasn't gone to waste. Can I use your phone to call him? I will pay you for the call'

'We take turns to call each other every week. I phoned him last Sunday so he will be calling me this evening. You can speak to him when he calls'

'Thanks sis. Do you know if there is a pawn shop around here? I have got a couple of bits to sell. I'm not taking them to Jamaica with me'

'Are they nicked?' Clive asked

'No I have had them for ages. It's just my telly, a small sound system a laptop and a DVD player'

'There is a pawn shop near Watford town centre in the High street but I'm not sure if it's open on Sundays. What make are they' Clive asked

'The telly is a Samsung. The sound system is a Sanyo. The laptop is a Dell. I will show you.'

He took them out of the holdall. The DVD player was a Bush modelHoyte discovered. He hadn't bothered to look at the make or model when he lifted it.

'We bought a DVD player a few weeks back Clive said pointing towards the TV stand. It's a Philips with Blue Ray. The Bush is a fairly basic model. How much did you pay for it?'

'I didn't. It was Lynton's' he lied

'How did you get from Norfolk to here if you wrecked your car? Davina enquired. She didn't believe a word that her brother had said. She was sure the electrical goods were stolen.

He raised his thumb. 'I hitched a lift. One of the blokes from the football team I have been playing for dropped me off on the A10. I got a lift to the M25 yesterday evening from a brother who dropped me at the South Mimms services. I got some food and stayed there all night before hitching a lift to the Watford turn off as soon as it was light this morning. I walked from there. It's a seven mile walk which is a bloody long way lugging these bags. Could you make me a coffee? I'm gagging'

While his sister made coffee Clive helped Hoyte with his bags and led him to a small upstairs which looked like it was used to store washing. There was an ironing board and a clothes horse in the centre of the room. There wasn't a bed in the room. Clive anticipated Hoyte's question and answered before he asked it

`We have an airbed. It's quite comfortable. I have slept on it a couple times whenever Davina has got the hump with me. There is football on Sky this afternoon Portsmouth v Arsenal. Do you fancy watching it?'

Clive as well as his sister supported Arsenal. Hoyte followed Manchester United.

`I don't mind'

He couldn't be bothered to walk into town today on the off chance that the pawnshop would be open so he settled down at his sisters for the day. She cooked a nice lunch and the three of them watched Arsenal win 3-0. This was followed by a Grand Torino, a Clint Eastwood film and the Dark Knight on Sky movies. His father phoned Davina that evening and was surprised to hear that Hoyte was there too. Hoyte spoke with him and his father said that he could stay with him until her sorted himself out, much to Hoyte's relief. They all went to bed shortly after 10pm. It took Hoyte a while to get to sleep. His mind was racing thinking about Blake's £250,000. Blake had included his phone number to one of the letters to the bank. Hoyte planned to phone him and kept going over in his head what he was going to say. When he eventually got to sleep he slept soundly.

Clive and Davina left for work early on Monday morning. They gave Hoyte the spare key. Shortly after ten he left to find the pawnshop. It was open.

`Are they stolen?' The owner asked when Hoyte showed him what he wanted to pawn.

`They are not stolen. They are all mine. I am planning to go to live in Jamaica and I can't take them with me.

The owner studied the items and made sure that they were all working.

` I can offer you thirty quid for the TV, fifty quid for the mini sound system, ten quid for the DVD player and twenty five for the watch. The laptop is a good one so I can give you a hundred for it`.

`I want to hang onto the laptop for a couple of days but I will come back before I leave for Jamaica. I will accept what you have offered for the other items'

He left the pawn shop with £115 in his pocket. He got a pleasant surprise when he went to check his bank account. When he last checked there was £23.00 in it so he planned to take out £20 but the balance was £131. There was a credit from HMRC for £108. He didn't know what it was for but it had been in

his account for over a week. He wasn't going to question it so he withdrew £130. This meant that he had the best part of £580 to pay for a ticket and survive for a short time in Jamaica before he found some work out there. He hoped that he was going to have plenty of cash by the time he left but there was no guarantee that he would be able to exercise his plan in such as short period of time. His next stop was Thomas Cook to find out about the cost of flights to Kingston Jamaica. He asked for the price of the cheapest flight available in the next few days. It seems that Jamaica wasn't a popular destination at that time of year so there were flights available. The travel agent advised that flights were cheaper if he went to Montego Bay airport. He could get a flight from Heathrow for £347 leaving next Sunday afternoon with Virgin Atlantic. It had a stopover at JFK in New York. There was only one seat left. Hoyte decided to book the flight. He had brought his passport with him. It expired in 15 months time. He paid cash saying he didn't have a credit card which seemed to be a problem for the travel agents for some reason. They would have preferred a debit card but. Hoyte told them that he had emptied his bank account because he was leaving the country so there wasn't enough in his account to cover the cost of the ticket. He didn't want to have to go back to his bank just to put money in to pay for the ticket especially as there was only one seat left and it may go. They eventually accepted the cash.
He would have to act fast if he was going to get money from Blake. He decided that he would call Blake that evening

62

When Blake arrived home the SOCO team were waiting for him. They didn't take long to dust for prints and as they were leaving DS Daley arrived. Blake let him in.

'What more can I tell you' Blake complained. 'I gave all of the details to the PC who was here yesterday morning'

'I need to ask you some questions about another subject. We spoke a few weeks back about a car similar to yours being involved in the incident at Welney on January 27th. I was suspicious because you had sold your car and purchased another car paying cash for it. You gave me very plausible answers but being the sort of copper that I am I decided that it might be worth having a look at your financial records. You gave receipts for your laptop and DVD to PC Fowler and once again I noted that you paid cash for them yet I can't see any record of you drawing cash from your bank account. Nor can I see any withdrawals to match the payments that you have made into your building society accounts.'

'Who gave permission for you to look at my finances? You have no right to do that'

'That is where you are wrong. We can apply for permission when we suspect a serious crime has taken place and that the money is being laundered so let me ask you a question. Where is all of the money coming from?'

Blake was shaken but he wasn't going to let it show.

'From gambling on the horses' he answered. 'I go horse racing on a Saturday afternoon and I have had some luck over the past few months. I even won £625 on the Grand National. You can check that with Ladbrokes in town. I had a fiver each way on the winner which won at 100/1. I only backed it because I had drawn it in the works sweepstake. I keep a record of all of the wins that I have had. I am superstitious so I will use the same on course bookie if I can. I keep all of the details of the wins in my little black book which I take with me to every meeting. Would you like to see it? He took a small black notebook out of a drawer and handed it to Daley. Blake's mobile started to ring. He picked up his phone but didn't recognise the number.

'I had better take this' he said 'it might be one of the drivers from work'

He answered it. A voice that he didn't recognise was at the other end of the phone

'Mr Blake. I have your laptop and I have found something very interesting on it. Let me ask you a question. Where did the £250,000 "money in" come from? Did it by any chance come from the drug trade at Welney? Were you the driver that took Lynton Andrews there?'

Blake felt very hot under the collar but he managed to compose himself.
`Where did you get my laptop from?' He said in a loud voice so that Daley could hear him. `Was it you who broke into my house? Did you steal my car too?'
`That would be telling' the voice replied `but I am sure that we could come to some sort of deal. I want a large chunk of the £250,000. I can see that you have plenty of it left. If you won't agree I will hand the laptop to the police anonymously and let them come to the same conclusion that I have'
Blake decided to call his bluff
`If you hold on for a minute I can let you speak directly to DS Daley who is here now investigating my break in. I think that he would enjoy speaking to the culprit.'
He handed the phone to a surprised Daley
This was a turn of events that Hoyte hadn't anticipated. He panicked and ended the call straight away. "Fuck, fuck, and fuck" he cursed loudly drawing glances from a couple of old lady passer bys.
The police now had his mobile phone number and would be able to trace him through it. He quickly took the SIM card out of his phone and threw it into a hedge. His plan had badly backfired.
`Did you recognise his voice'? Daley asked `I didn't hear him speak because he ended the call when you passed him to me '
`No I didn't but his number is in my received call log. Why don't you phone it using your mobile phone?'
Daley tried but the line was dead, as he had expected
`It's dead. He was most likely using a burner phone .He will have dumped it. What exactly did he want?'
`He wanted to sell my car and my laptop back to me. What a cheeky bastard. He asked me what I would be willing to pay him for them. That's when I handed my phone to you'
`That is very unusual. A car thief will usually have a ready source to get rid of the car unless they are joy riders. I wonder if your car was stolen by somebody local. I will look into this latest development but I want to go back to my original question about you spending money that doesn't appear to come from your bank account. Looking at these entries in this book you appear to be on some sort of lucky streak. You have been to six race meetings and come out well on top each time. How do you manage to be so lucky?'
Blake wheeled out the same story that he had given to Ray Nash.
`I just watch for really big bets being placed. If somebody is betting in amounts of £500 and above I take the view that they have inside information in the form of a tip from the stables. The meetings that I have been going to are at

smaller venues so very large bets are uncommon. I don't win every time I follow a large bet but more often than not they do win. I have only had one large bet. I put £500 on a horse at Southwell and won £1500. Before you ask that was the same day that I had the Grand National winner so I knew that I was betting with money that I had already won. I was over £2000 up that day. It would have been more but I backed two losers at the Southwell meeting' Daley found this hard to believe but he couldn't prove otherwise. He felt that Blake was always ready with an answer and if he had been the driver in question for the Welney incident he was very adept at covering his tracks. The entries recorder in his little black book for wins at the races tied in with the building society deposits. Everything that Blake had said in answers to all the questions that he had been asked seemed well rehearsed.

`Thanks for your time Mr Blake. I would suggest that you replace the locks on this house with something a lot more efficient I will let you know if we hear anything about your car'.

Hoyte went back to his sister's house. He logged onto the internet using Davina's BT broadband and proceeded to look at Blake's history. Three websites appeared regularly. They were RightMove, A horse racing information site and Mansfield FC. There were also visits to sites about starting limited companies and a one off visit to a site discussing money laundering. Hoyte was due to fly to Jamaica on Sunday and managed to persuade his sister to let him stay until the weekend. It gave him five full days to get some money and he still had Blake down as the most likely source. He needed a new burner. His old phone was now in a bin in town but it was too late to get a new one until the next day. He had a few ideas of how to get to Blake. He had seen him with Val on Saturday evening. He'd had Val's mobile number on his old phone but couldn't remember her number. He knew that she had a land line. He could find it using the BT phone book on line but he was struggling to remember her surname or the builder's merchants where she worked. He lay awake that night trying to remember her surname without success but suddenly he got a chink of light. Lesley Farmer. He remembered Lynton joking about the size of her arse and saying that it was like a farmer's wife's or even more like the size of a farmer's cow. He booted up the laptop and went back to the BT phonebook page and hoped that there was only one L Farmer in Flixham. Fortunately there was just the one. He wrote down her number. He would phone her tomorrow evening and ask her for Val's phone number.

63

Blake received a call at work the next morning. It was DS Daley

`I have some good news for you. We have recovered your car. It was left in Sainsbury's car park in Watford. It was towed away and when the company entered the registration details at DVLC to find the owner it signalled an alert. The local force will be dusting it for prints but it should be ready to collect later this week. Unfortunately there was no sign of your other goods'

`That's good news. Thanks for letting me know. Can you also let me know when I can collect it?'

Hoyte noticed that Blake's car wasn't in the car park on Tuesday morning. He went into town early to get a new ten pound burner phone. He decided to call Lesley Farmer just after 1pm. Luckily she was at home.

`Hello Lesley. It's Dennie Hoyte. Could let me have Val's telephone number? I have lost my mobile so I don't have it now'

`No I will not. She won't want to speak to you after the way you treated her'

`That's why I wanted to speak with her. I want to apologise because I was an arsehole and she didn't deserve to be treated that way. I saw her in the Red Lion on Saturday. I was going to speak to her then but she was with a bloke and I didn't want to embarrass her. I left Flixham on Sunday and I am leaving for Jamaica on next Sunday. I don't know when or if I am coming back. The other reason that I want to speak to her is to warn her about her new bloke. He is not all he seems and is involved with a criminal element'

Lesley wasn't sure what to do.

`I don't think she would thank me for giving out her phone number. What has her bloke been up to?'

`I'd rather not say. I can't remember her surname otherwise I would have found her number through directory enquiries. That is how I found your number' He hoped that she didn't ask why he had remembered her surname but not Val's

`Her surname is Davey so you can bloody well look it up'. She hung up

Dimi Szabo was at Lesley's for the day. He had no work on that day.

`Who was that?'

`One of Val's ex boyfriends. He wanted to warn her about Bob Blake. Reckons he is a bit dodgy'

`Why what has he been doing?'

`He wouldn't say. He just said that he was involved with some dodgy people. I will phone Val when she gets home from work to warn her. He should know about dodgy people too. It was his mate that got killed at Welney"
She went back to bed with Dimi and forgot all about the phone call


Hoyte soon found Val's telephone number and called her that evening. He was the last person she expected to be hearing from
`What the fuck do you want?' she shouted down the phone. `I don't want to speak with you'
`Please hear me out. Don't hang up. I promise I won't bother you again after this phone call. '
`Say what you have to say and then bugger off'
`First I want to apologise for the way that I treated you. I know it's not an excuse but I had received a right kicking and was both in pain and was feeling sorry for myself especially as my best mate had been killed. You didn't deserve to be treated the way that I treated you. I really liked you but I wasn't myself that weekend. I left Flixham at the weekend and I am flying to Jamaica on Sunday. I plan to stay there. When I saw you on Saturday with your boyfriend I didn't recognise him at first otherwise I would have said something on Saturday. He is dead dodgy Val. I have it on very good authority that he was the driver who took Lynton to Welney on the night that he was killed and that he left the scene with a large amount of used notes. He still has hold of this money and is laundering it in small amounts"
`That is utter bullshit. The police have interviewed him. He was left a large sum of money when his mother died. The police were not aware of this and it explained some spending that he had been making.'
`How do you know that this money was from his mother? Have you seen any evidence of it?'
`He had a letter from a solicitor about probate which he doesn't know that I have seen. It was for over £100,000'
`I have his laptop which somebody sold to me in Flixham on Sunday. I found some interesting files on it. Ask him where the quarter of a million came from and see what he tells you. I will phone you again later in the week. Trust me Val. He isn't what he seems. I'm not going to gain anything by telling you this. I doubt that I will ever see you again. I am just looking out for you'
He discontinued the call. He wasn't being honest with Val. If he could confirm that Blake did have the money he would make another attempt to blackmail him. He decided that it would be beneficial for Val to see details of what he had discovered on the laptop. He purchased some blank CD's from Tesco and

took copies of the Word documents and spreadsheets. He kept a copy for himself and sent one to Val.

Val was dumbstruck. It didn't make sense. Where was Denny getting this from? It was strange that the police thought that Bob was involved just because his car had a dodgy light. Bob had even given her the spare key to his house so he would hardly be likely to do that if he was hiding money. His house was so bloody small it would be hard to hide it anyway. She couldn't understand why Denny would call her out of the blue like that. It wasn't as though he could gain from telling her.  She didn't know what to do. She didn't want to ask Bob outright and if she snuck into his house while he was at work to look for it how would he react if she did find anything.

64

DS Daley arrived home from work early after a very quiet day. Well it was early for him. Bev looked worried when he arrived.

`The bloody boiler has finally packed up. We haven't got any hot water. It was working this morning but it's just running cold now. The boiler man said it was on its last legs when he repaired it in March.  He said it would cost £3000 for a new one.'

`Shit. That is going to make a hole in the lump sum payment but we can afford to get it replaced. There will still be enough for the conservatory and a new car. We might have to lower our budget on a motor home though'

The lump sum from his pension was £42,000. The conservatory would cost £12,000; the new car would cost £10,000. They had decided to keep some money for emergencies in an ISA's and had a budget of £18,000 for the motor home. Bev had her heart set on buying one but it had to have a shower and toilet. They had already looked at several motor homes. The Elddis Autoquest was their preferred model and they could afford an older model, something around 8 years old. It would be big enough for the two of them. They had around twelve thousand pounds which was their rainy day savings on top of the pension lump sum but they were reluctant to bite into this money.

`We might have to buy a slightly older car if we want to get an Autoquest'.

The telephone rang. Bev answered it. It was their daughter Jane

`Hi Mum, I have some good news to share with you. Graham has proposed and we are going to get married'

`That's lovely. When is the big day planned for?'

`We are hoping for September this year. We have spoken to the local vicar and he has a spare date on September 19. The Hilton hotel in Basingstoke can also do that date. We are thinking about no more than sixty guests to try to keep the cost down. You have always said that you had money put to one side for my wedding. Will that be Ok for you? Obviously we have some money to put towards it but we cannot afford to pay for all of it. Graham's mother doesn't have a lot of money. She is a widow and lives on a small pension.'

`How much would you be looking for from us?'

`Around twenty thousand pounds but we may be able to trim that figure by a bit.'

`I would need to talk to your Dad about it'

Bev and Jane spent another twenty minutes with wedding talk before Jane ended the call

'Jane is getting married in September' Bev announced. 'She is looking to us to pay for most of it so we can forget about the bloody motor home'

'That's a bit sudden isn't it? How long as she been dating Graham?'

'Not that long. It can only be nine months at the most. I am not that keen on him'

'Me neither. He seems full of bullshit to me. He is a typical bloody estate agent'.

Daley felt deflated. He hadn't anticipated his daughter wanting to get married so suddenly and the wedding would wipe out a large chunk of his lump sum. The motor home wasn't going to happen now and he knew that it would really upset Bev.


On Thursday evening Lawrence Mortimer was attacked by three white males in Kings Lynn town centre. He died later in hospital as a result of head wounds that he sustained. The incident was similar to that of the Stephen Lawrence case and mindful of the issues that particular case had caused acting Chief Commander Tony Pasby threw all resources available to track down those responsible. It was a high profile case. DCI Booth was the lead detective on the case and saw it as an opportunity to regain some lost credibility. All of her team at Kings Lynn were put to work on the case except DS Daley. Booth made it clear to him that as far as she was concerned he was no longer required on high profile cases. He was yesterday's man. He could see out the rest of his days in Flixham solving disturbances of the peace and minor incidents. Although Daley was quite content to do that it still rankled with him. Ever since Booth had arrived at Kings Lynn she had treated him like dog shit on her shoe. She didn't like him personally or his way of working which she considered to be out dated and without any place in the modern day police force. He had one week to go so he would bide his time doing next to nothing. He would retire happy knowing that he had served his time as a member of the police force and would leave with no regrets. The more he thought about it the more he realised that there was one case that would irritate him in retirement. That was the missing money from Welney. He still had Bob Blake down as the main suspect but he couldn't prove it. His gut feel told him he was right and usually his gut feel was right. It would be good, he thought to himself if he could prove that Bob Blake had been involved somehow with the Welney picnic site incident. He would be able to stick two fingers up to Booth who hadn't backed his gut feel.

Val arrived home from work on Friday afternoon to some unexpected post. There was a letter from a solicitor telling her that Pete was starting divorce proceedings. It advised her to appoint a solicitor of her own if she hadn't already done so. There was also a CD which Denny had sent to her with a note which read "Have a close look at the cash spending and cash flow files. I will call you at 7pm on Friday evening"

She put the disc into the old Hewlett Packard PC that was in the spare room and read everything on the disc. She admitted to herself that it did look suspicious but how could she confront Bob without upsetting him. Hoyte phoned her dead on seven o'clock.
`What does your boyfriend say about the £250,000 then?' He asked her
`I haven't spoken to him yet. Your package only arrived today and I have only just finished looking at it. I will admit that it does look a bit suspicious though. I am seeing him tonight so I might raise the matter with him then'
Hoyte was agitated. He had hoped that Val would confirm the existence of the money. He didn't want to appear too pushy but at the same time he was running out of time.
`Can you let me know how he reacts?'
`Why? If you are concerned with my wellbeing what difference will it make to you if he has been a bad boy? He may have a perfectly good answer. I will decide what to do if and when I find out. She slammed the phone down ending the call'
This wasn't the outcome that Hoyte had hoped for. He would call Val again the following day and if she wasn't forthcoming with what Blake had said he would call Blake himself and threaten to send a copy to DS Daley

Blake took Val to the Red Lion on Friday evening. Things had been somewhat awkward between them after the row the previous weekend. There was a band playing in the Red Lion so Blake had suggested a bite to eat and then a few drinks while listening to the band. The band "Cinnamon Smile" had a good reputation locally so the bar was packed. They ate early and by the time they left the bar they'd had plenty to drink. They went back to Blake's house and made love before falling to a heavy alcohol filled sleep. Blake felt as though things were back on track between them.
Blake got up at 730am. He made tea and toast for himself but also took some up to the bedroom for Val who was still asleep. He woke her.
`I have to go in to work for a couple of hours to sort out some deliveries. I should be able to get away by 1030. How do you fancy going horse racing at

Huntingdon this afternoon? It's a nice day and it's the last meeting of the season there today'

`I don't mind. I have never been racing before' Val replied groggily. She had a headache and her mouth tasted like a badger had been sleeping in it.

`Get yourself ready to leave by 1030 then. It's a bit of a drive to the racecourse. We can eat at the track'

Blake left for work at 0800. Val drunk her tea and ate her toast but it only made her feel slightly better. She got up, showered and dressed. She had an hour to have a look around Blake's house to see if she could find the money which Denny Hoyte thought Blake was sitting on. She checked all of the cupboards without success. The loft was the obvious place. The hatch was on the landing upstairs. She took one of the two chairs from the lounge upstairs and stood on it to open the hatch. There was a light switch so she switched it on. The loft was lit up but the light wasn't bright. She wasn't tall enough to see into the loft though. She needed something taller to stand on. The only thing which she could see to do the job was the small round table in the lounge. If she could get it upstairs and put the chair on it she would be able to see in the loft. Fortunately the table wasn't heavy and she managed to manoeuvre it upstairs without marking the walls. She placed it under the loft hatch and stood the chair on it. She climbed up using the wall to aid her balance. She felt wary because she was still feeling rough from last night's drink but managed to peek into the loft. She was worried about falling off and breaking her neck. There was a large holdall in the loft which she could reach. Feeling apprehensive she reached for one of the straps and pulled it towards her. It felt quite light and much to her relief it was empty. Denny was talking rubbish. Gingerly she climbed off the chair and then onto the table. She took both pieces of furniture downstairs before returning upstairs to make the bed. It was while doing this that she noticed that the bed had drawers under it. They were hidden by a valance. Nervously she opened the drawer on the door side of the bed. It was filled with bedding. She went to the window side and opened the other draw. The bed was on wheels so she had to push it away from the wall to give enough space to open the drawer. It was nearly empty with just a few towels in it. As she went to pull the bed back she noticed that there were some staples on the floor under the bed. The covering on the base of the top half of the bed was loose and was hanging down at the end. The staples must have worked loose she thought and smiled when she thought about how the bed had received a hammering during their lovemaking. They must have shaken the staples out. She was about to try to push them back into place when she noticed that there was something white in the bed. Being curious she pushed her hand in and then her arm. She could feel what felt like pillows under the top half of the bed. By pushing her arm in another staple fell out leaving a gap of about foot. Blake had a torch hanging up on the coat hooks in the hall so she went downstairs to fetch it. As she was getting the torch there was a noise at the front door. She froze fearing that it was Bob but to her relief it was just somebody delivering leaflets. She checked the time. It was nine twenty. She was going to have to go home to get some fresh clothes and then get back here for ten thirty. She returned to the bedroom and shone the torch into the gap. All that she could see was what looked like a duvet and some pillows. She wondered why they would be stored in this part of the bed when there was plenty of space for them in the drawer section. She pulled on the duvet and as it moved she saw some bundles of money. She reached in and just managed to get hold of two of the bundles. The rest was just out of her reach. They were rolled up and were about two inches thick and restrained by an elastic band. One contained £50 notes and the other £20. Denny was right after all. She threw the bundles onto the bed. She was going to confront Blake when he got home. She left and deep in thought went home for a change of clothes. If the money was from the Welney picnic site Bob could hardly refuse her if she asked him for some money to help her to get a place of her own. How much should she ask for? Perhaps she could ask him for enough to buy Pete's share of the house but did she really have the nerve to blackmail him? She got back to Bob's house at ten fifteen. Bob arrived home at the same time. 'That was good timing' He said smiling but he could tell by the look on her face that something was wrong 'What's up? You don't look very happy'

'Wait until we are indoors' she snapped. They went in

'What's wrong?' he asked

'I was making the bed when I dropped an earring. It went under the bed and when I went looking for it I noticed that the base of the bed had come apart. I found piles of money under the bed. Is that the money that the police were asking about?'

Blake panicked. He rushed upstairs to the bedroom and saw that there were two bundles of money on the bed. Val followed him. He had played out this situation in his mind many times. To get at the money he had to lift the bed onto its side. He didn't think that Val had lifted up the bed to get to all of the money out. He gambled that it was still inside the bed frame.

'No it is not. That is money that my mother had stashed away at home. It was just over twenty thousand. She didn't trust banks especially after Northern Rock. I hid it because I didn't declare it when I got divorced. I didn't see why Debbie should benefit from my mother's death when she didn't make any effort to get to like her.'

`I don't believe you. Denny Hoyte phoned me. He said that he had bought your laptop in a pub on Sunday and when he opened it he found some files and spreadsheets detailing your spending. He sent me a copy. It showed £250,000 as money in on the same day that Lynton Andrews was killed at Welney. Denny reckons that you were the driver and that you took off with the money'

`So you didn't find it while looking for an earring. You were bloody snooping around because of something an ex boyfriend told you. There is nowhere near £250,000 under my bed. It was the money from my mother'

`So why are you showing £250,000 in your spreadsheet then if it's only twenty thousand that you have been hiding?'

`Have you considered that perhaps Denny changed the figures? How do you know that he just didn't make it all up to get at you? Perhaps he was jealous when he saw us together. I think that you had better go. We are finished. Get your things together and fuck off' He fumed

`I'm going to go to the police' she shouted at him.

`Go on then. I don't have anything to hide. I will show them everything. Now give me my key back and get out'

Val threw his door key at him and stormed off. He was calling her bluff but he needed to get rid of the money. He went upstairs and threw the mattress off of the bed, turned it on its side and took out the rest of the money. The two bundles that Val had found contained £15,000. There was £10,000 in £50 notes and £5,000 in £20 notes He had eleven more bundles of £50 notes and eighteen more bundles of £20 notes. Where could he hide it? He had asked one of the drivers to take him to Watford on Thursday to collect his car. That was the only place he could think of to hide the money unless he hid it in the depot but that was risky. Should he put it in a plastic bag and bury it somewhere quiet? He didn't know where though and that was also risky. Supposing somebody saw him while he was in the act of burying the money. He would need to act fast just in case Val kept her threat of going to the police. Huntingdon races were now out of the question.

Val walked home with tears in her eyes. She didn't believe Blake's story but she couldn't be certain that he wasn't telling the truth. She kept asking herself why Denny would make up a story and doctor spreadsheets to try to incriminate Blake. Was he jealous that she was seeing Blake? It seemed a far-fetched reason for such an accusation. She phoned the number that Denny had given her as soon as she arrived home. It went to voicemail so she left a message for him to phone her back. He returned the call an hour later

`Did you find anything?' He said straight away

`There was some money hidden under his bed. I could only reach two bundles of notes. One of £20 notes the other £50 notes. I don't know how much was in them as I didn't have time to count them. He said that this was money that he got from when his mother died. She had it tucked away in her house and that he hid it because he didn't want his wife to get any of it in their divorce settlement. I don't know how much more was under his bed but he says that he had twenty thousand pounds. He claims that you changed the numbers on the spreadsheet'

`Why the fuck would I do that?'

`That's exactly what I said but he reckoned it was just to get back at me'

`What are you going to do?'

`I don't know. If I went to the police he could just hide the money. What if he is telling the truth about the money and it was from his mother but he lied about the amount'

`I wouldn't go to the police straight away. Let him sweat for a bit. If he is innocent he won't do anything but if he isn't he will move the money. Keep an eye on him for the rest of the day'

`That is going to be difficult. He accused me of snooping and dumped me ' Hoyte cursed under his breath. Things were not working out the way that he had hoped

`I'm sorry to hear that but I did warn you. Perhaps we should try to blackmail him. We could tell him that we won't tell the police if he splits the money with us.'

`So that's why you contacted me. You couldn't give a toss about my well being. You were just looking to get a cut of that money. Fuck off Denny'. She ended the call abruptly, slamming the phone down.

Hoyte cursed under his breath. If she went to the police there would be no chance of him being able to blackmail Blake. He decided it was time for his last gamble. He sent a text message to Blake but hid his phone number so that Blake couldn't trace him or give his number to the police. The message read "I KNOW THAT YOU HAVE THE MONEY FROM THE TRADE AT WELNEY. LYNTON ANDREWS TOLD ME THAT YOU DROVE HIM THAT NIGHT. I WANT £100,000 FROM YOU TONIGHT OTHERWISE I WILL PASS YOUR LAPTOP TO THE POLICE AND TELL THEM WHAT I KNOW. I AM LEAVING THE COUNTRY IN THE NEXT COUPLE OF DAYS SO YOU WON'T HEAR FROM ME AGAIN. MEET ME AT THE MIMM SERVICE STATION BY BURGER KING AT 9PM TONIGHT. IF YOU FAIL TO SHOW I WILL TAKE YOUR LAPTOP STRAIGHT TO THE POLICE AND TELL THEM EVERYTHING"

Blake received the message and tried to reply but the number was blocked. He assumed that it was from the person who had called him earlier in the week and was certain that it was Denny Hoyte. He ignored the message but he was going to have to expedite his efforts to hide the money. The problem was still where to hide it all. That evening he waited for the light to fade and went outside to his car. He opened the boot. The spare wheel was in the boot under a solid cover. It was retained by a locking screw. The jack and jack handle were also held in place by the locking screw, but there was just enough room to squeeze the money in which is what he did leaving the out two bundles that Val had found plus another bundle of twenty pounds note. If she did follow up on her threat to go to the police he could show them these bundles to corroborate his story.

At 7pm Blake's mobile rang. Once again the number was withheld.

`Have you got the money ready?' The voice at the other end of the phone asked

`Fuck off Denny' Blake replied `Val told me about your little story. How are you going to prove to the police that I have the money? You said Lynton told you that I was the driver. That is bullshit. It wasn't me and if you were so certain why didn't you contact me straight away instead of leaving it for three months. There is no money so fuck off to where ever you are going and don't bother me again'

`If you haven't  got the money how will you explain what is in the spreadsheet that I found on your laptop?'

`Do you mean the one where you changed £20,000 to £250,000?'

`I didn't change a fucking thing'

`How are you going to prove it then? It's my word against yours. I will just tell the police that you were jumping to conclusions because your ex- girlfriend told you that I had been interviewed by the police. They have no further interest in me so you can go and get stuffed. Don't phone me again' He ended the call.

Hoyte realised that he was beaten. What Blake had said was true. He couldn't prove that Blake had taken the money but he just knew that he had. If he went to the police he would have to explain how he had come to be in possession of a stolen laptop. All that he could do now was to pawn it for the £100 the next morning and then go to Heathrow to catch his flight.

65

On Sunday morning Blake drove into Kings Lynn and purchased a steering lock. He didn't want his car to get nicked again especially with the money hidden in its boot. The car had an immobiliser on it so hopefully the steering wheel lock and immobiliser would deter anyone from trying to steal it.

At the same time Blake was buying the steering lock Hoyte was in the pawnshop with Blake's laptop. He collected the hundred quid and left for the airport. It was pouring with rain. Hoyte wasn't going to miss the weather in England. When he had checked in he sent a text message to Val. It read "I THINK THAT IT WOULD BE BEST IF YOU DID GO TO THE POLICE WITH THE DISC THAT I SENT TO YOU. WHY DON'T YOU GIVE IT TO DS DALEY.? HE WAS THE ONE INTERESTED IN BLAKE. I'M AT THE AIRPORT ON MY WAY TO JAMAICA OTHERWISE I WOULD HAVE GONE TO DALEY MYSELF. ALL THE BEST "

Val was angry with both Denny and Blake. She didn't believe Blake's story about the money that she had found under his bed. She was shocked by the anger Blake had shown when she confronted him. She was pissed off with Denny for involving her. She was keen on Blake and if Denny hadn't involved her she would have been none the wiser. She didn't know what to do. It was pretty obvious that DS Daley and DC Marks had suspected that Blake was involved in the Welney incident otherwise they wouldn't have kept interviewing him. She would give it a couple of days before making a decision. She was hoping that Blake would call her to apologise so she didn't want to do anything straight away. By Wednesday she still hadn't heard from Blake. She was pissed with him and thought that she would teach him a lesson so she made her mind up what to do about the disc.

DS Daley's last week was dragging. There were no incidents to investigate so he killed time by going through a couple of unsolved recent crimes. DCI Booth called him on Wednesday morning which was a miserable wet day. She ordered him to investigate a fly-tipping incident on the outskirts the village of Saddlebow which was a couple of miles from Kings Lynn. Saddlebow was on a minor road. There was little chance of anybody actually seeing the incident. It was a shit job which Booth had enjoyed giving to him especially as the weather was foul. It was wet and very cold for the time of the year. There was a strong north easterly wind blowing straight off the North Sea and the rain was coming down almost horizontally. Daley drove to Saddlebow and soon found the rubbish that had been dumped. There were dozens of boxes of food and drums of what appeared to be cooking oil. He found bags of defrosted frozen food, salad stuff, sliced vegetables. It was all dumped in the entrance to Bailey's farm. Mr Bailey, the farmer, was a very unhappy person as he was the person who would have to pay to have it cleaned up because it was on private land rather than on a highway. Daley took a statement from Bailey who was cowering under his umbrella. It seemed that the food was dumped after 10pm the previous night as Bailey and his wife had been out for a meal and the rubbish wasn't there when they had arrived home.

`I bet it was one of the Chink restaurants or takeaway places in Kings Lynn. Looks like somebody's freezer has packed up so they have just dumped it all' Bailey complained

Daley checked the boxes and bags for any sign of the owners but there were no labels.

`I will talk to your nearest neighbours in the village to see if anybody saw any vans coming down here late last night but I am not hopeful. It's pretty quiet out here so the chances of anyone seeing or hearing anything is slim'

`That's no bloody good to me is it? I'm the mug here who will have to pick up the bill for clearing it away.'

Daley noticed that Bailey had some pigs in a nearby field

`Can't you give it to the pigs? I thought that they ate anything'

`I'm not feeding that crap to my pigs. I don't know how old that stuff is. It could contain Salmonella'

He continued to complain to Daley about police disinterest and how he paid them via his council tax. Daley couldn't be bothered to argue with Bailey. It was lashing down even heavier and rainwater was running down his neck to his back.

`I will let you know if any information turns up. He got back into the car but the bloody thing wouldn't start. He tried the ignition three times but it wouldn't turnover. He cursed loudly. He was stuck in the middle of nowhere in the pouring rain with no signal on his mobile. Bailey had buggered off back to the warmth of his farmhouse. Daley had no option but to follow him to the farm house and ask if he could use his phone to phone the AA. He was like a drowned rat when he arrived at Bailey's door

Bailey reluctantly agreed but had to make a remark about even the police phones being inefficient. He didn't invite Daley in. He just brought the handset to the door so Daley had to phone the breakdown service while stood out in the rain. The AA said that they would be about an hour before they could get to Daley. They blamed the heavy rain for the delay. All Daley could do was go back to his car and sit and wait. No cars came down the road until the AA arrived almost to the hour. It was still lashing down.

The mechanic tried to start the car but like Daley he had no luck. He opened the bonnet, fiddled about for five minutes before declaring that Daley's starting motor was knackered. He didn't have anything on board that would fix it but he would be able to tow Daley to the nearest garage which was Formula One garage in Kings Lynn where they would be able to get him fixed up.

Daley spent the next three hours at Formula one waiting for the part to arrive and then have it fitted. The bill came to £257.78. He paid up and then went back out to Saddlebow to see if anybody had noticed a van in the area late the previous night. He drew a blank so he went back to Flixham arriving back at the station at just after 4pm.

Ronnie Edbrooke was on duty

`Where have you been hiding all day? Have you got a mistress tucked away somewhere?' He joked

`Don't ask. I have had a shit day' He went on to tell Edbrooke about the job that Booth had dumped on him, the stroppy farmer and his car breaking down `Never mind Arthur At 5pm on Friday you won't have to put up with Booth and her shit any longer. A young lady dropped this off for you earlier' He handed Daley a padded jiffy bag envelope addressed to him but marked private and confidential.

He went through to his small office and opened the envelope. It contained a computer disc and a letter from Val Davey. He read the letter

*Dear Sergeant Daley,*

*I have reason to believe that Mr Bob Blake was involved with the incident at Welney picnic site on January 27th. I have been seeing Bob for a few weeks but before I met him I had a very brief relationship with Dennard Hoyte. I saw him in the Red Lion the Saturday before last when I was with Bob. Denny claims that he purchased a lap top in the Red Lion. When he opened it he discovered that it belonged to Bob Blake. He found some files on the laptop. One of the files shows a record of cash transactions made by Mr Blake since January. There is an entry which simply says "Money In". It is dated January 27th which is he said was the date of the incident at Welney. My brief relationship with Denny ended badly. He phoned me on Friday to apologise about the way he had treated me and warned me about Mr Blake saying that he was not as he seemed and that he thought that Mr Blake was the driver on the night and had taken money from the site. He suggested that there might be some money hidden in the house as Mr Blake would have to launder it. I didn't believe that Mr Blake was involved as he didn't seem the type but I do remember that you and DC Marks had interviewed him. He told me that you thought his car had been seen on camera because of a faulty headlamp.*

*I stayed at Mr Blake's house on Friday night and was still there when he went to work on Saturday morning. I was curious because Denny was convinced that Blake had been the driver on the night in question. I searched the house to see if any money was hidden. I found some bundles of notes hidden in the front section of his bed. He had removed staples and stored the money amongst some pillows and a duvet which he had stuffed in the front section of the bed. I managed to reach two of the bundles. I don't know how much was in the bundles. One contained £50 notes the other £20 notes. I didn't count them because Bob was due home from work at any minute. I don't know how many more there are under the bed as I couldn't get my arm in any further. I confronted Bob when he returned home from work. He said that it was money that his mother had left laying around the house when she died and he wanted to hide it from his wife during their divorce proceedings. I told him that I didn't believe him and mentioned the file which I have enclosed. He claimed that he had found £20,000 in his mother's house. He said that Denny had changed the numbers on the spreadsheet. He accused me of snooping. We had a row and he finished with me. Denny phoned me later and suggested that we blackmail Bob for a share of this money. I don't want to be involved in anything illegal which is why I am telling you.*

*You can decide what actions, if any that you want to take.*

*Yours sincerely*

*Valerie Davey*

Daley put the disc in his PC and sure enough the spreadsheet showed various cash transactions. As Val Davey had said there was also the money in entry showing £250,000 on the same day as the Welney incident. He went through all of the entries and discovered that there were entries that appeared to tie in with the deposits in the building society accounts. Daley read the letter again. He had a gut feeling about Blake but Blake always seemed to be one step ahead with his answers to any question put to him. His explanation for paying cash for his new car had been backed up by proof that he had withdrawn money from his bank account but the wins at racetracks seemed a bit flaky. What Daley couldn't comprehend was why Blake would make the mistake of recording everything on a spreadsheet on his laptop. It made no sense. DCI Booth took the view that any money, if there ever was any as the police had no proof that there was money involved, was long gone as was any hope of tracing it. The matter was closed as far as she was concerned. He would love to see the look on her face if he was able to prove that his gut feel about Blake was correct. He read Val Davey's letter again. The last line struck a chord with him. You can decide what actions, if any you want to take. A thought entered his head but he discounted it almost immediately. He considered it again. Should he risk telling anyone about his thought? He decided that it wouldn't be a good idea and that he should act alone. He left for home at 1700 on the dot. His evening was spent at home and followed the same pattern as the majority of his evenings at home. Bev had cooked dinner for them both. He dried up after she did the dishes. They would have a cup of tea watch some rubbish on TV and then go to bed reasonably early. Daley struggled to sleep. He was going over a plan in his head. He was going to confront Blake the following evening.

66

Thursday dragged. Daley did some follow ups on the fly tipping case. He called on several Chinese restaurants and takeaway shops to see if any of them had had food stolen. Unsurprisingly he didn't get any joy. His mind was occupied by the money that Blake was hiding. He hadn't told anybody about the letter and the disc that Val Davey had sent to him. He told Ronnie Edbrooke that the letter was from somebody wishing him a happy retirement. He considered talking to Val Davey but decided against it. He was home by five that evening but he told Bev that he had to go out again to interview a local man.
`This will be the last time'. He told Bev as he left the house.

Daley had thought long and hard about what he was about to do. He weighed up the evidence that he had to suggest that Blake had been the driver on January 27. The car on camera had a dodgy headlight like Blake's car, the money he put into savings accounts which didn't come out of his bank account, His run in with Andrews, the spreadsheet on his lap top and now finally the letter from Val Davey further pointing the finger at him. He couldn't believe that this evidence was wrong. He was convinced all along that Blake was his man and now he had the chance to nail the slippery bastard. He pulled up outside Blake's house at 1900. It was a dull overcast evening with a threat of rain in the air.  There was a light on so Blake was at home. He knocked on the door. Blake opened it and seemed surprised to see Daley on his doorstep.
`What do you want now?' He asked with a raised voice
`Can I come in and have a chat with you? It will be an off the record chat'
`If you must but I am getting fed up with this continual harassment so you should make it quick'
Daley went into the lounge and sat down without being offered a seat
`What is this all about?' Blake asked `Have you traced my stolen goods? He suspected that Hoyte or perhaps Val had been in contact with Daley but he didn't want to let on that this might be the reason for Daley's visit
`Before I start I would like to tell you that tomorrow is my last day with the police service. I am retiring.  I feel satisfied that I have been a good copper and when I do go there are very few cases that I will leave unsolved. There is just one that bugs me and that is what I want to talk about. This conversation is off the record. I am not taking notes or recording anything that we discuss.'
 He went to his pocket and pulled out the disc and the letter that Val Davey sent to him.

'I received this yesterday. There is a letter from Val Davey claiming that she found money hidden under your bed and this disc. It is a copy of files taken from your stolen laptop. Dennard Hoyte claims that he purchased it in Flixham but I suspect that it was him who broke into your house. One particular file caught my attention. This file was titled "Spending". In that file there was an entry dated 27 January which simply said "Money in". It then lists several payments made out but none of them, apart from when you purchased the car, match up with entries on your bank account'

Blake interrupted him. 'How do you know somebody hasn't changed or made up the numbers?'

'I don't but I have to ask the question why somebody would do that. There are other entries that I can check on such as the payment to an estate agent for "Ellie's rent". There is also the question of the money Val Davey claims that she found under your bed.'

'I told her where that money came from. It was money that was at my mother's house. She didn't trust banks so she kept her money under her bed. I kept it quiet because I didn't want to let my ex wife know about it otherwise she would have got half of it in the divorce settlement. There wasn't a stash of money under my bed. There were just a couple bundles of cash'

'I am afraid that I don't believe you. This is what I think happened on that night. I think that you were going into the Red Lion after work to chat up the blonde barmaid who I believe that you were quite keen on. Lynton Andrews needed to get to Welney to do a drug trade. His mate had crashed his car on the way to the Red Lion. I believe that it was you who drove him to Welney possibly under duress. I know that you had a fight with him a few days earlier. A car similar to yours with a dodgy headlamp was seen going into and out of the Alder Street around 1945. Later that evening the same or a similar car was seen turning into Turnberry Avenue. It is my belief that you took off with a bag of money left at the scene and hid it under your bed. You have been laundering this money in small amounts over the past few months making up stories about winning money on the horses. You were very clever with laundering the money but you made one fatal error. You recorded all of the entries on a laptop which unfortunately somebody nicked. That somebody was Dennard Hoyte. I would be very surprised if he wasn't trying to blackmail you when he phoned last Monday evening when I was here. I would put money on finding the remainder of the money hidden somewhere close by either somewhere in the house, in your car or at Collins Transport or whatever it is now called.'

Blake was rattled but tried to appear calm.

'That is utter speculation on your part. Where is the proof in your little story? Everything that you have is circumstantial'

'There is one sure way to find out. I can make a phone call to a judge who I am on very good terms with and get a warrant to search your house, offices and car within the hour but as I said our conversation is not on the record. Other than me nobody in the police force has seen the details on the spreadsheet or heard about the money which Val Davey found under your bed so here is how this is going to be settled. I am retiring tomorrow evening after serving for 35 years. In all that time I have done everything strictly by the book. Where has that dedication to duty got me got me? I will tell you, promotion to Detective Sergeant and posted to an outpost like Flixham. I will get a modest pension which I will have to live on until I get my state pension in ten years time. The alternative is to take another job on piss poor money to tide me over until I get my state pension. I believe that you have upwards of £200,000 hidden away somewhere but the police will find it. If they search under your bed there will be forensic evidence left there.   As far as the police are concerned that money has been forgotten. Nobody other than me and DC Marks were interested in what happened to the money as they had no proof other than hearsay that it ever existed. It is only me who still retains a belief that there was money taken from the scene. I want to offer you a deal. Give me £50,000 of it tonight and I will walk away. You will have got away with taking the money from the picnic site... I am not going to be greedy and ask for more because that will be enough money to allow me to have a better retirement'

Blake was stunned by this turn of events.

'What will happen if I tell your superiors that you tried to bribe me? That is of course if I ever had the money in the first place'

'It is my word against yours. The question is do you want to risk being arrested or do you want to get away with £200,000 of drugs money that few people are interested in?'

Blake was unsure with how to respond to this demand. Was Daley bluffing? Would he get a search warrant like he had threatened? He decided to call Daley's bluff.

'I wasn't involved so you can get a search warrant'

'OK if that is your decision'. Daley decided on a counter bluff. 'I will get a warrant to search your house car and offices. I will phone a judge now.'

He phoned Malcolm Davies who had retired two years ago. Blake of course had no idea of this.

'Good evening Judge Davies. It's DS Daley here.  How are you keeping?' He said in a loud voice so that Blake could hear the conversation. Davies exchanged pleasantries with Daley for a couple of minutes before Daley continued with the matter in hand. `I have a gentleman who is being difficult and I need a warrant to enable the police to search his property and his offices. I am retiring tomorrow and this case is my only outstanding case so I need to get a warrant issued tonight if I am going to be able to solve this case before I retire.'

Davies played along. Daley had used this trick in the past. They were on first name term and whenever Daley addressed Davies as Judge Davies he knew to play along.

`What is he suspected of hiding?'

`Ill gotten gains' replied Daley. `I am sorry to bother you at this late hour but the suspect is insisting on a search warrant '

He looked at Blake again

`It's your last chance' he mouthed

Blake buckled. If Daley was true to his word he would still have £200,000 and nobody would be bothering him in future for it

`Ok we have a deal on one condition'

`The suspect has changed his mind 'Daley told Davies. `I won't need the warrant now. Sorry to have bothered you' He ended the call

`What is your condition not that you are in any position to be demanding them?' Daley asked

`You won't come back in the future looking for more money'

`Don't be daft son. I am hardly likely to. I will have taken a bribe for the only time in my life and it's a decision that I found very difficult to take. It is something that I will have live with for the rest of my days. I reckon that you are in a similar position knowing that your actions are likely to have caused the death of Danny Collins. They probably led indirectly to the deaths of Bogdan Stancvic and Ivan Petrescu but nobody will lose any sleep over them. Where have you hidden the money?'

Blake felt very light headed and had to sit down before responding to Daley's question. His throat was dry and he struggled to get his words out

`It was under my bed as Val Davey had discovered but when she found it I moved it. It's now in the boot of my car in with the spare wheel. What will you say to Val Davey if she asks you?'

`I will tell her that you were telling the truth. It was money from your mother'

`What about DC Marks?'

`I won't say anything to her. We investigated you and we accepted the answers that you gave. There was no need for any further investigations. She has been off work with the injuries that she suffered in your office in February. The case is closed as far as she is concerned. I suspect that she will be moving to another area soon. She is not a fan of DCI Booth. I need to know what actually happened on Jan 27.'

Blake told him the whole story. He started by telling Daley that Andrews had threatened him at gunpoint and how he'd forced him to drive to Welney. He confessed to Daley that he was scared shitless and had expected that Andrews would kill him. He went on to tell Daley about how Andrews had shot one of the Romanians and had fought with the other one. They had killed each other during the struggle after Andrews had shot the other Romanian who was attacking him with a knife. He told him that Andrews had taken his car keys when they arrived at the picnic site. He saw the money when he went to retrieve his keys and to check that Andrews was alive. He said that Andrews and the other Romanian were both dead as far as he could tell and how he had foolishly been tempted to take the money. He said that he had regretted taking it and had almost turned around to take it back. He should have called the police but was worried that the police would not accept his version of why he had been at the scene. He was concerned that his involvement may have caused a problem with his new job not knowing that Danny Collins had been an integral part of the matter. If he had known what would happen afterwards he wished that he had taken it back. He confessed to Daley about the plans he hatched to launder the money. He said that this was the very first time that he had done anything of this kind. He had a clean record.

`I bloody well knew that you were involved. Fortunately, for the both of us as it worked out, my boss wouldn't back me up when I asked for a full financial investigation into you'

Daley told him to retrieve the money from his car. Blake did and gave Daley five bundles of £50 notes.

`Don't leave any evidence of it on your bloody laptop in future. Put the rest in a safe place but don't let any women find it next time' he said smiling as he left.

67

Daley left and went home. He had been mulling over his decision for 24 hours but it was too late now as the deed had been done. He had taken a bribe. He was disappointed with the treatment that he had received from Booth and he wasn't going to let her get any credit for him discovering the money. As far as he was concerned the money that Blake had stolen was drugs money. Both Stancvic and Petrescu were dead so there was nobody to prove that there had been any money at the exchange and nobody knew for certain how much money had been involved. Blake would benefit of course but he would always have the burden of knowing that his actions resulted in the death of Danny Collins. He had also been through the trauma of the night of January 27th when he thought that he was going to be killed.

The police had recovered a large amount of drugs so Booth was happy enough with that success. Nobody would gain if Daley told Booth that he had recovered any money except Booth who would probably claim the credit for it. All that this would achieve was allow Daley to stick two fingers up to Booth because she had doubted him. As long as Blake was careful with how he handled the remains of the money nobody would be the wiser. Blake had already shown some competence with laundering money but had made a stupid mistake when recording it on his laptop.

Daley thought that as long as he was careful he would be able to spend the fifty thousand without drawing any attention in his direction. Hoyte had buggered off to Jamaica. He was under a suspended sentence. He had been in possession of Blake's stolen laptop. He was no doubt aware that he had been seen on ANPR driving Blake's car on the M25 so he was unlikely to return to the UK in a hurry.

Daley decided that he would call Val Davey on Friday evening and tell her that Blake was telling the truth about the money that she had found under his bed. Daley's biggest concern was what to say to Bev. He hadn't told her of his plan and wasn't planning to until he had tied up the loose ends.

When DS Daley went into Kings Lynn station for the last time on Friday afternoon he was nervous. His colleagues had a collection to buy him a retirement present. They bought him a Hayter petrol lawnmower which was better than a watch he admitted to himself. DCI Booth spoke on behalf of Norfolk Constabulary and gave a typically patronising speech. She couldn't let the speech go without mentioning that she and Daley hadn't seen eye to eye over police procedures saying that he sometimes struggled to adapt to the modern police force.

The team started yelling "Speech, Speech "after Booth had spoken.
Reluctantly Daley took to the floor and addressed his colleagues
`I have been a copper for 35 years. Some may consider me to be a dinosaur.
Some may say that I am old fashioned in the way that I operate. That could be
considered down to the way things have changed which, in my humble
opinion, are not always for the better. These days a lot of a copper's time is
spent box ticking. Some are extremely good at box ticking, others are not, but
it is the box tickers who progress'. He looked in Booth's direction as he said
this getting a scowl from her and a knowing smile from Dave Franklin 'Some
carry on doing good police work but get overlooked because they are not good
at working the system. Some of you I will miss. Others I won't but I will walk
away from here today with my head held high knowing that I have been a good
hones t copper who has served the community to the best of his ability'
He received a round of applause from most of the room.
He left with a tinge of disappointment knowing that he could have walked out
with a lot of credit and proving Booth that his style of police work still had
some merit. In the end he knew that he was just another bent copper. Like Bob
Blake he had done one thing that was uncharacteristic. He reckoned that he
could live with it though.

68

Blake felt a sense of relief when Daley left. He sat rooted to his chair for thirty minutes. He couldn't quite believe how the events of the evening had unfolded. He would never have guessed that Daley was a bent copper. He believed that he could trust the old copper not to come after him again in the future. He was confident that he had got away with it.  As the old copper had told him the police were no longer looking for any money. The Romanians were out of the picture. The only matters to concern him were Val and Hoyte. Daley had told him that Hoyte had boarded a plane to Jamaica on Sunday after a warrant for his arrest had been issued so it was unlikely that he would come back to the UK. Daley said that he would tell Val that Blake was telling the truth about the money she found under his bed.

He still had the best part of £200,000 to start enjoying life with.  He decided that he could murder a pint so he popped down to the Red Lion. Helen was in there with her two mates from the quiz and greeted him with a big smile and a wave when he came in.  She was wearing a tight fitting powder blue top and her usual snug fitting jeans. She looked good.  As he was stood at the bar she came up to get a round of drinks.
`I haven't seen you for a while' she said.  `How are things with you? Are you still seeing Val?'
`We split up last weekend' he replied
`Perhaps we can go for that drink that we never got round to' she said with a smile as she returned to her friends not giving him the chance to reply.

The following day he took three phone calls that brightened his day. The first was from DS Daley to tell him he had spoken with Val Davey. The second was from Ellie telling him that she would like to take up the job offer. The final call was from the Managing director of Value Shoppers asking him he Flixham Transport would be able to take on some additional deliveries.

Val phoned him at the weekend to apologise for accusing him about the money under his bed.  She said that DS Daley had told her that he had been telling the truth about the money that she found. He told her that it was over between them. The row had in hindsight been a blessing in disguise. She was high maintenance and had already been hinting about wanting to move in with Blake when her flat eventually sold. That was not something that Blake had ever contemplated. He had moved on from her with the promise of getting together with Helen on the horizon.

Blake spent Saturday afternoon in Kings Lynn visiting estate agents. It was time for him to buy a house. When he looked back twelve months when his prospects looked bleak things were a lot more promising.
Life was good now.

Printed in Great Britain
by Amazon